JERSEY BLUE

An Irreverent Saga
of the Making of
the New World

———— REBECCA
SINGLETON

POSEIDON PRESS
NEW YORK

A Poseidon Press Book
Published by Pocket Books, a Simon & Schuster
Division of Gulf & Western Corporation
Simon & Schuster Building
Rockefeller Center
1230 Avenue of the Americas
New York, New York 10020

Poseidon Press and colophon are trademarks of Simon & Schuster
Designed by Irving Perkins Associates
Manufactured in the United States of America
10 9 8 7 6 5 4 3 2 1

Library of Congress Cataloging in Publication Data
Singleton, Rebecca.
  Jersey Blue : an irreverent saga of the making of the New World.
  I. Title.
PS3569.I5754J4   813'.54   81-17807
ISBN 0-671-44584-7   AACR2
ISBN 0-671-44583-9 (pbk.)

To my wonderful friends,
especially Joanne Michaels and Mark McCrackin

Author's Note: Although works of historical fiction do not, as a rule, contain bibliographical acknowledgments, three authors contributed so much to my understanding of New Jersey history that they merit special recognition: John T. Cunningham, *New Jersey, America's Main Road* and *Garden State;* John McPhee, *The Pine Barrens;* and Henry C. Beck, *Forgotten Towns of Southern New Jersey, The Jersey Midlands* and other works of regional folklore. In addition, I would like to thank all of the editors and historians who assisted me. Fiction may make controversial use of facts, but I am deeply indebted to those who provided them.

CONTENTS

_____ *PROLOGUE*

JERSEY BLUE tells of history spun by passion, a story that unfolds upon one five-hundred-acre tract of American land from the days of its earliest habitation. Although this tract of land is imaginary, the story relies upon the history and physical beauty of the southern interior of the state of New Jersey, which can actually be found on a map. The people who live here are also imaginary, but like real people, they will choose many names to describe the land; they will plant their flags, draw up boundaries, and eventually issue postage stamps. But in order to understand their stories, it is important to see this land as it existed before the onset of human words and maps.

It is the year 1600. No white person has set foot into the interior of the region which will become known as New Jersey. Five hundred acres of virgin wilderness lie in the southwest curve of this interior heart, untouched by human history. The Delaware River is located twenty-eight miles to the west of this land, and the Atlantic coast lies nearly fifty miles to the east. In nine years' time, Henry Hudson will sail up the coastline on his way to New York; soon after, men who seek the treasures of the Indies will encamp along the Delaware. But this particular tract of land will remain unmolested by such remote events. Twenty-eight miles is a formidable traveling distance through densely forested wilderness.

Near the center of this tract, there is a small wooded rise; when the land is partially cleared it will be possible to see most of the surrounding acreage by standing here. Even now, the

9

rise provides a fine perspective. It is an afternoon in summer. The weather is clear, and in spite of the trees the view from the rise reveals that the surrounding terrain is a nearly unbroken expanse of green that is mostly flat and a little bit boggy. The sky above is keenly blue, and the scene appears brassy with light. There is a breeze, so slight that it seems no more than the collective flutter from wings of the chickadees who are making noise in the trees. The woods display a mesmerizing breadth of color: in the nearby foliage, one could easily detect more than forty-seven different shades of green.

From the rise, it is possible to see that the prevailing oaks and pines are broken by connecting stands of white cedar trees, which curve through the woods like the fragmented joints of a finger, marking the path of a creek. This creek lies about three hundred yards to the east of the rise and flows in a northeast direction towards a distant river which will eventually be called the Mullica. The creek water is dark, with a swiftly gliding surface. The deep, haunting color of the water is created by tannins from the cedar trees which combine with iron found in the groundwater; although it varies in shade, today the creek flows nearly black, with the dim translucence of overbrewed tea.

To the left of the creek, a large crooked stand of pine trees juts from the ground at a listing angle, as the terrain here levels towards the creek. These angled trees loom above the creek-banks, casting shadows onto swampy soil that contains clay and a sticky white sand. This boggy, shadowed area is a gathering place for frogs. Downstream from here, cranberry shrubs are thriving along the creekbank; deeper into the woods, there are high-bush blueberry, greenbrier and holly, laurel and orchids, and curly-grass ferns. There are also weeds. Many animals move through the forest, and along the northern edge of the wooded rise, a faint trail zigzags through the trees. This is the path made by Indians who travel through the land on their way between their villages on the Delaware and the Atlantic shore.

If you could stand upon that wooded rise in the year 1600, it would be possible to see that from spacious skies to fragrant pines to flowing cedar creek, there is not one sign that human civilization is needed here. Humans are *not* needed here—this land tells its own story through the passing seasons, and it hides eternal secrets. But people will come. And although they will often try to hide their stories, they will tell their secrets to the land. They will bury bodies in its soil and hide love notes in trees; they will curse the fields and pick the flowers and whisper to the stars. Some of them will seem barely aware of the land, but they often swear to die for it. Occasionally, they will.

Through the passing generations, their lives will form a pattern as reliable as the seasons, because people will always make love, and they will always change the land. Within the boundaries of *Jersey Blue*, a fragile symmetry is achieved; civilization exists; the land persists. And history lies between. A tale of dreams and schemes and new machines, it always hangs on passion.

The Rane Family

IN THE year 1677, a party of Quakers traveled from England to settle in the colony of New Jersey. As the ship *Kent* sailed up the Delaware River in late August of that year, its Quaker passengers lined the wooden railings, straining to see the lush, sandy shoreline which promised them the freedom to practice their religion. But one passenger on board the *Kent* chose not to join the crowd on deck; Miss Martha Laud was toiling below, tying fresh scarlet bows on her high-heeled shoes.

Martha was not a Quaker, and although she was very fond of freedom, she had no reason to expect that the New World would offer her more than she'd enjoyed in the world so recently left. Her traveling wardrobe consisted of a sapphire-colored silken dress with a skirt that raised in folds like a curtain, revealing underskirts of muslin dyed to match. Her bodice was revealing, and her stockings were white silk; there were bows of scarlet satin on her bonnet, waist, and toes. And her tiny trunk contained just one device to protect her against the weather: a dainty sealskin muff, with edges trimmed in leather. Aboard the *Kent,* Martha blazoned through the trail of somber Quaker fashions, where her costume marked the presence of one very worldly immigrant.

Martha Laud had sailed from her comfortable home in London, a city of three million people where one might shop for chandeliers or fountain pens or Japanese chrysanthemums. It was a city with opera houses, coffeehouses, grand salons, and water closets. When she arrived in the colony of New Jersey, Martha lived in a cave on the banks of the Delaware with other passengers from the *Kent.* During that winter, she ate dried fish and slept in piles of sacking. Her muff was carried off by wolves. And then she turned eighteen.

In the spring of 1678, the Quaker settlers laid out the beginnings of a well-planned town which they called New Beverly, then Bridlington, and finally Burlington. It was located on the Delaware River near the area of Assiscunk Creek, more than thirty miles from that five-hundred-acre tract of wilderness land in the interior of southern New Jersey. But Martha Laud was a woman of special attractions beyond the lure of her frizzy carrot-colored hair and homely face, beyond her now tattered satin. (And beneath a woolen dress dyed gray, she still wore sapphire muslin.) Martha was a heroine, but not the sort that coughs up blood or pines for love or goes to work as a governess: she brought desire to the land, and so man discovered the wilderness.

The Frog Level: Passing Through

THE JERSEY sky verged into night, slung with a moon and twinked with tiny lights. As she drooped against the splintery kegs that rattled in a pitching wagon, Martha Laud appraised this heavenly vision. Diamonds on velvet, that's what it reminded her of, with stars sparking like jewels against the pure, poshy black of the night. As for the rest of the scenery, she was glad that dusk had shrouded the boring maze of cedarwood and pine trees, blocking the sight of foliage which had flared more oppressively with every mile traveled down this wretched, boggy trail into the wilderness interior of New Jersey. Every jounce of wagon wheels against the sandy, rutted soil reminded Martha that in the last ten months she'd seen enough of nature to last a lifetime: trees had branches that tore at your skirts, bushes more likely meant brambles than fruit, and animals had sharp teeth.

Even worse, all of these things lived in dirt, which Martha had no plans to do—but then, she'd never planned to leave London, particularly with a shipload of Quakers headed for the wilderness of New Jersey. Like most of the events in her life since she turned thirteen, Martha's immigration was the result not of plan but obsession; in a single afternoon, her fate had been forever changed.

Martha eased her legs against the rattling floorboards and

17

smiled, remembering how her adventure had begun. She had been thirteen years old, wandering through the West End markets of London on her way home from an errand, when a mysterious woman had beckoned to her through the crowds. Martha had approached cautiously—the aged hag was draped in a tattered black cloak; she crouched above a filthy cloth that was laden with colored bottles. As Martha came closer, a strange, musty odor made her cringe, but the woman clutched at her with grimy twisted fingers which, incredibly, glittered with golden rings.

Martha paused. She had always been fond of pretty things. Noticing her interest, the gypsy cackled. "I guessed right, for sure. I been looking for you, dearie. Would you be the little lady whose name is Desiretta?"

"That's my middle name," said Martha, surprised. "Desiretta" had been suggested by an elderly, invalid aunt whose creativity turned out to be a substitute for the legacy which Martha's parents had anticipated. No one called her by that name.

"This be yours then, dearie. A special scent it is. For the men." From beneath the folds of her cloak, the gypsy produced a small flask that was even dirtier than her hands.

"I don't—" Martha began, but the gypsy cut her short.

"You will," she replied still cackling. She pressed the flask into Martha's hand. "Take it, dearie. You'll need it. This flask be just the thing for the girl whose name be Desiretta." Then she leaned closer to whisper a graphic description of its power.

"No!" Martha screamed, staring at the woman in horror. Wrenching herself free from the gypsy's grasp, she ran through the streets without looking back. Several blocks later, she noticed that she was still clinging to the flask. She stopped to throw it beneath the wheels of a passing carriage and watched as the pottery shattered into a pool of oily dust.

That night Martha lay awake in her little-girl's bed, listening to echoes of the gypsy's promise: a magical scent which really was no scent at all, since its odor was undetectable. But no man could escape its power. The woman who wore it could instantly arouse any man she might choose—and this was no humdrum, perfunctory arousal but DESIRE, the kind of rabid, towering passion that could ignite a man, incinerate, or cause his crops to

18

shrivel. Everywhere Martha went, she would ravage and savage at will. She could helplessly paralyze. Torture to a frenzy. Cripple with lust. *You'll want it, dearie. Oh, yes. You want it.*

The next day, Martha couldn't resist imagining what might have happened if she'd kept the perfume. She strolled through the streets of London with her eyes demurely lowered, making no attempt to attract the attention of the men who walked towards her. But as each one passed, she imagined how he might turn, startled, to look at her. His gaze would follow her as she traveled down the street; he would push through the crowd, frantic to keep her in sight; when she disappeared, he would dream of her forever: the girl named Desiretta.

Martha wondered what it would be like to make an entire roomful of men burn with desire. She decided that she would like it. And in the months that followed, more and more often she played what she'd begun to think of as her secret game. She roamed through London, taking her pick from all the men she saw and conquering at will: a pair of bearded cavaliers who doffed their plumed hats with a flourish and threw themselves into a puddle of mud so that she could cross with dry feet. A lean, stern-faced puritan who followed her for miles, pelting her with flowers. A Hindu prince who begged her to share his shimmering palace. Martha soon discovered that specific details made it all the more exciting. The curl of a grenadier's mustache. The gleam in a tinker's eye. The shape of His Majesty's royal nose. Shoulders, smiles, and size. Her favorite men looked tall and broad and rich; of course, she drove them wild. She was irresistible. Dangerous, devastating Desiretta Laud.

As Martha plunged more deeply into her fantasies, she became both connoisseur and huntress. Soon she could not quite remember whether she had broken the flask or kept it, whether the old woman had been an enchantress or a fool. That entire afternoon had become like a dream with some parts indistinct and unimportant as in all remembered dreams. But one thing she was sure of always—her encounter with the gypsy had made her unique.

It had also shortened her childhood considerably and was setting her through adolescence at breakneck pace. At age fourteen, Martha's game was sufficiently visible in her maidenly gaze to alarm an uncle, who informed the Lauds that their daughter showed signs of becoming high-strung. Three years later, they were ready to admit he'd been right, but by then it was too late. Martha had already traded fantasy's euphoria for the everyday ecstasy of sensation. It was not only clear that she was "high-strung," but also that she was enjoying it. Her respectable, merchant-class parents were thoroughly stunned, and they could think of only one solution. Prevailing upon a business acquaintance, they arranged Martha's passage on the Quaker ship *Kent*, which would carry her to the colonies.

So Martha Laud landed upon the shores of the Delaware River with the founders of the community which would eventually be called Burlington, New Jersey. But long before they'd settled on its name, Martha had decided to move on. It wasn't that her Quaker companions were unpleasant in any way—she thought of them as kind, but not very lively, when she thought of them at all. But reckless passion had gone out of her life, and she meant to get it back.

She'd heard that there was a tavern downriver at Leasy's Point and vaguely plotted to head in that direction, but opportunities for young ladies to travel in *any* direction were few and far between. After months of frustration, her means of escape presented itself. Standing in the middle of town she watched a large wagon being loaded with supplies for the Eric Mullica expedition, which was camped in the West Jersey interior on the Little Egg Harbor River. She noted the cargo with growing interest: Flour. Sugar. *Whiskey*. The driver, an awkward boy, blushed and stammered but answered her question. "No ma'am, not Quakers—mostly Swedes and such, and very few women." Surely no place for such a lady as herself.

It had taken Martha thirty minutes to say her goodbyes and even less time to persuade the boy to clear a place for her among the supplies. But in spite of her unique talents and desperate condition, she had gone for several hours without noticing that she was no longer alone in the wagon. Then the man buried beneath burlap sacks in the far corner began to snore.

Tom Donnell had been exhausted when he'd hailed the wagon just before sunset. He'd left the settlement of Old Gloucester several days before and was too tired to give the figure dozing near the whiskey kegs more than a passing glance before he dropped into the far corner, pulled a sack over his face to shut out the sun, and fell into a blank, dark sleep. Now, hours later, his subconscious was sufficiently rested to form a dream . . . it was his favorite. He was flying, swift, angular and high, like a hawk rising to the clouds. His body pressed against the wind with a fierce, almost savage, sense of purpose which filled him with pleasure. To surge into the sky with muscle and flesh pulled taut, rising toward a glorious destiny.

When he was awake, Tom often wondered if hawks were born knowing not only how but also *where* to fly, and when. He was stronger, taller and meaner-looking than most men; he even looked like a hawk—dark eyes gleamed in a face built of strong, high bones, sculpting his features with planes of ridge and shadow. Surely his looks proclaimed that he had been born to soar alone above the rest—but to soar in what direction?

His lack of an answer to that question had prompted him to follow the charismatic Dubliner Robert Zane across the sea to colonize West Jersey. But after the first few years, life in the Irish Tenth of Old Gloucester seemed less dependent on destiny than the ability to trap game and grow vegetables. Tom's frustration had grown in proportion to his neighbors' contentment. Then he'd heard of Eric Mullica—a restless, bold explorer who was pushing through the dense pine forest that stretched eastward through the Jerseys to the sea. On impulse, he'd set off to join up with the expedition. But this afternoon when he boarded the wagon, he hadn't simply been exhausted —he'd been completely and irrevocably lost. Do hawks get lost?

Hawks get lost? ran derisively through his dream, shattering his flight. He was dropping like a stone, fast and faster to—

Just before his bones were broken apart on impact, Tom awoke, bolting upright.

"You were making a dreadful noise." A tart feminine voice issued from the corner of the wagon, reminding him of the woman he'd seen this afternoon. Rather plain, with carroty hair . . . he tried to remember.

"You could have waked me," he muttered, not really caring.

"Could I?" The woman crawled across the floorboards to kneel beside him, and Tom saw that his impression had been accurate: her freckled face was homely and her hair was a disaster. Then she smiled.

Dear God! Tom stared with ravaged passion as Martha seemed to change before his eyes, suddenly turning into a temptress: her green eyes seethed with naked fire like a pair of throbbing emeralds. Her lips were blooming, moist and red, like a soft and quivering, unfolding rose. Her hair flamed to a torrent of curls that tumbled to her breasts, which were billowing towards him like huge mounds of freshly yeasted dough. As Tom stared, a holocaust was raging through his breeches. Never had he felt such desire!

Before he could move or speak, she had crushed his lips with a swift, pillaging kiss which left him breathless. Capturing his shivering body beneath her own, she invaded him with hordeish kisses, plundering his mouth with her Cossack tongue, strangling his protests, until—

"No . . . please!" He tried to escape, to reason with her, but he was held captive by her arms, which manacled his flesh like ropes and chains and leather straps. "We mustn't—," he cried out again, struggling against her. Then a blizzard of fear howled through him as he felt her merciless fingers slash like sabers at the buttons on his shirt. Cool air rained onto his exposed and naked chest.

Her ravening lips formed a white-hot circle which branded him, again and again, as she breathed torrid, torturing puffs of air against his flesh, ravaging the hairs on his chest. Stroking the taut peaks that quivered beneath her fingertips, she eased forward to kiss the pulse that flailed at the base of his throat. Her lips were sweet now, almost tender, and for an instant he thought that she'd relented. Then her kiss turned savage and she sucked at his flesh, drawing it painfully between her lips, against her wanton teeth.

Tom moaned. His entire body was clenched with lust, and the delirium which drenched his senses had robbed him of his reason. As though she sensed his surrender, Martha bent close to his ear, flogging his lobe with her lavish tongue as she blew into it. "Ravish me!" she added.

With one frantic, diving motion he pushed her flat against the wagonbed and plunged into her, but the bucking, heaving

22

floorboards quickly sent them thrusting apart, into the empty air. Maddened by their separate frenzies, they rolled and lunged and leaped towards each other, grappling wildly in the wagon until, finally, he managed to pin her between the whiskey kegs. He panted above her, waiting to synchronize his attack with the prevailing rhythm. Then he plunged into her again, and this time the wagon plunged with him, driving him into her with the force of a hammer.

Gasping, exultant, they clamped together like two halves of an imperiled clam and bucked and heaved, jolted and rattled, and lurched and swayed, faster and faster, on their way to an ecstasy that they'd never dreamt of, but were nonetheless expecting. As if on cue, an eerie, thrilling noise arose to surround them—shrill, throbbing tones which amplified into bedlam. The sound smothered their last exploding cries in a blanket of sound and then roared through the night like a huge and pounding thunder. In the sky the stars sparked like jewels.

Seneca Rane shifted his weight uneasily on the driver's seat. He was ten years old, surely too old to be scared by the sound of frogs in the night. But he'd never heard a noise like this— sounded like thousands of them croaking from the shadows. Maybe it was the way the trees sloped town towards the boggy flatlands at this turning in the old Indian trail: the croaking from the hollows seemed to ricochet against the trees before it was tossed into the night, making a sound that grew fatter and louder by feeding on its own echoes.

But it wasn't just the frogs, really, that made him feel so strange. They just added to those other strange noises from the back of the wagon, which fueled the restless, spooked-up mood that had been growing in him all day. Maybe it had started in Burlington, when he'd let Miss Laud come aboard with the supplies.

That lady sure did know how to smile.

In 1678, New Jersey existed as two separate provinces which were divided by a line drawn from Little Egg Harbor to the northwesternmost boundary of the colony. West New Jersey was controlled by William Penn and the Society of Friends, who encouraged Quakers to settle in the province. In East New Jersey, the puritan influence was dominant, as settlers from England, Scotland, and Ireland joined the earliest colonists, who were mostly Dutch. Both provinces eventually rebelled against the ruling proprietors, many of whom were London businessmen who had never set foot in the Jerseys. In 1702, the Proprietors of East New Jersey and the Proprietors of West New Jersey agreed to place control of the government in Queen Anne's hands, but they retained their lucrative real estate interests (in fact, the Board of Proprietors for East New Jersey is still doing a little business today).

Changing political fortunes meant little to those settlers who ventured beyond the New Jersey towns clustered near the edges of the colony, along the Delaware River, and on the northern plains near the Hudson. Travel between these two areas increased as Perth Amboy and Burlington became capitals of the respective provinces, but the interior of New Jersey did not encourage exploration. More than a million acres of pine forest formed a natural barrier between the Delaware River and the Atlantic Ocean. This wilderness became known as the Pine Barrens; those who explored its depths lived beyond the reach of the proprietors, but few men were strong enough to challenge the natural authority of this vast mysterious land.

Captain Eric Mullica was one of the earliest exceptions. He established the first permanent settlement in the area of the Little Egg Harbor River, which became known as Lower Bank. But the captain may have had some special help—two days after their encounter with the frogs, Seneca Rane's wagon reached the Mullica encampment with two passengers among its supplies. Although Tom Donnell soon wandered off in another direction, the dazzling, devastating Martha Laud remained at Lower Bank for the rest of her life. Despite incredible hardships, the men of Captain Mullica's expedition stayed there with her.

In 1679, Martha gave birth to a daughter. She named the child Desiretta. Ten years later, she had a son, whom she named Jupiter. In 1691, Martha Laud died of a fever. The wilderness settlement at Lower Bank was abandoned less than two years later. The Little Egg Harbor River was later renamed the Mullica to honor the explorer who made the first settlement there

24

possible, but history does not mention the woman who, possibly, made it all worthwhile.

Seneca Rane was not among those men who stayed at Lower Bank, but Martha Laud had helped to shape his fate, because he could not forget the emotions that had overwhelmed him on the night they traveled through the frogs. Seneca was the son of Finnish indentured servants who had sailed to the colony of New Jersey with their Swedish master and then settled in the area known as Raccoon. During his childhood, the land changed hands twice, as the settlement of New Sweden was claimed by Holland, and then taken from Holland by the British. The settlers remained. Swearing allegiance to a succession of flags had little effect on their lives, and no effect on their land.

Seneca's parents had died in a smallpox epidemic when he was barely two, so he grew up vaguely attached to the Swedish household they had served. He was a solemn, hardworking child who was grateful for any attention. Eric Mullica had been kind to him, which was reason enough for a boy of ten to run away from home and join Mullica's wilderness exploration. But the night of the frogs changed his life. It was the most personal experience that life had ever provided for Seneca Rane, and he seized upon it as an omen. Surely the land had touched him there, or he had touched the land.

Seneca left the Mullica settlement and moved from place to place, seeking any kind of work that paid real wages. Fifteen years later, the omen of the frogs became reality. In 1690, when he was twenty-two years old, Seneca paid $180 cash and was issued a deed from Burlington County for: "One hundred acres of land, to be measured from the farthest creek that flows into the Little Egg Harbor River, to the intersection of the Indian trail where the hill levels towards a crooked stand of trees." Armed with seed and tools and a gun, Seneca set off to claim his dream.

Arriving in early spring, he immediately set to work clearing the wooded rise above the sharply leveling ground where the frogs croaked, which he came to think of as the frog level. He managed to plant a patch of summer vegetables which along with game and fish from the creek provided an easy supply of

25

food while he tackled his main project: At the crest of the hill overlooking the frog level, he laid the foundations for a large cabin, measuring carefully to center it on the slope. The walls rose steadily throughout the summer, but it was slow work since he took so much time to carve the notches precisely in each log, insuring a perfect fit. He finished setting the roof just before the autumn rains, and worked inside throughout the winter, carving furniture and finishing the interior. By spring, he had created a work of art: his log walls marched skyward in uniform precision, creating perfectly squared corners, top and bottom; his door hung so neatly in its frame that when bolted from the inside, not a crack of sunlight was visible.

That spring he planted corn, rye, and vegetables in straightly plowed furrows, but his mind was still on the cabin: something was missing. Then he collected rocks of the same shape and size to set at regular intervals through the grass, marking the way to his cabin. Every day for one hour Seneca walked alone, back and forth between the lines of stones; in a wilderness visited only by passing seasons, he slowly created a well-traveled path to his door.

———— By European standards, land in the colonies was cheap and abundant, and those who settled in West New Jersey often bought farms of several hundred acres. In East New Jersey, the real estate situation was more complicated, as land speculators tried to profit from the tangled market created by too many proprietors. Fortunes were made or lost by investing in wilderness land, but much of it was bought by men who had no intention of actually living there. In 1695, land speculator Thomas Budd paid four cents an acre for a parcel of swampland and dunes that would later be known as Atlantic City. The interior of southern New Jersey remained largely unsettled, and the tombstone of an early traveler buried there bears this discouraging epitaph: "Died before he could get away."

1703 ————

The Frog Level: Staying

BY THE creek that sliced through the heart of his land, Seneca Rane waited for his lovers. Everywhere he looked, November gray was seeping through the radiance of autumn like an ugly, fatal stain. Death traced veins through golden leaves, it sapped the green from unsuspecting grass and lowered through an azure sky in morbid clouds that pillowed against the shimmering earth, as though to suffocate. To Seneca, this spectacle of contrasts seemed ghastly, indecent; it violated the senses, like a dirge tapped out on spangled tambourines.

The time is close. They will be coming soon. Deliberately he resisted the thought, turning away from the winter sky to stare instead at the creek. Two chunky beavers paddled through its coppery water towards their partially constructed dam, where other beavers were already at work, plastering the chinks between the piled-up logs with mud. None of them seemed disturbed by his presence; they were accustomed to his visits, just as he had grown used to the idea that his creek would regularly be revised according to their collective whim.

For thirteen years, Seneca had lived in wilderness isolation. His clothes were made from fur and animal hides. Creases at the corners of his pale blue eyes were made from squinting against the sun, and the mystical stillness in his gaze was the result of staring into a sky that would either send no rain, or send too much. A tall thick-muscled man with long blonde hair and a beard, he slowly paced the creekbank, like a gentle, graceful bear. The beavers absorbed his attention. After thirteen years, Seneca's thoughts and emotions were so intimately merged with nature that he sometimes forgot he was not part of its cycle.

Every year, nature sent winter, to set the record straight. The animals disappeared from his woods. Ice separated him from his creek and his beavers. And even when his fields weren't hidden by snow, the soil was frozen, locked against him. Huddled alone in his cabin, he had plenty of time to consider the noble advantages of man.

Instead, he made love.

Eight years before, in the middle of an endless winter, the women simply started to arrive, one by one. The first had entered wan and gasping, as though startled by her own miracle. Her eyes were violet, her skin soft as a blossom. He recognized her at once: she was Spring. They walked together for hours, kicking through glorious mounds of petals that were piled high, like leaves. She loved to hold hands. He loved to kiss her breasts. In a deep cloud of violets they made giddy, swooning love while more flowers rained onto them, tickling. He came into her bursting, like a spring torrent through ice.

Without warning, she disappeared. One morning he awoke to find a different woman lying beside him. Even before she smiled, he knew her. Summer had the most magnificent body he'd ever seen. Her casual sexuality thrilled him. As he worked in the fields, she would remove her dress and lie naked in the grass nearby. Then her strong, sun-warmed legs would stretch past his shoulders as he lifted her up, upending her against the earth so her feet were pointing to the sky as he drove his seed deep into the moist, open furrow between her thighs. He wanted her to stay forever. She did not.

Autumn was trouble, unmistakably. A flashy whore with full, bright lips, she rubbed the tips of her breasts against his sex, laughing when it stiffened: *Take me. Eat me. Fuck me. I am the party. I am forever.* She was greedy and tight, and taught him positions he never dreamed possible. Then one day, when he'd learned to crave her, she called him a fool, and left.

He had never felt so alone. But soon he was awakened in the night by an absence of sound, and he rose to discover Winter. In the dark cabin, her whiteness was overwhelming, iridescent —even her lips and the tips of her breasts gleamed white, like pearls. Her hair and eyes were the color of diamonds. She was so radiantly beautiful that Seneca didn't know whether to worship or seduce her. Then she moved to envelop him, and he drifted against the softest, lightest curves he had ever known.

He was fascinated by the exotic, diamond-bright triangle between her legs, and the gleaming lips within. Just the sight of it aroused him so deeply that he could not contain his excitement. Quickly, he penetrated her—and screamed. Her sex was cold as ice. Jerking free, he examined himself, fearing the worst. But his sex felt fuller, stiffer and more urgently alert than ever before.

Tentatively, he edged the tip of his sex into her. She wasn't slushy or damp, but rather had the slippery arid quality of a deep freeze. He probed more deeply. Her iciness produced alternating sensations of tingling and burning which were extremely pleasant, particularly if he kept moving. Soon his entire body was burning, then tingling, burning, tingling, burn, tingle, burn—a rhythm of contrasting shocks that only seemed to prolong the violence of his desire. Finally he came into her, shivering, ecstatic, relieved.

Seneca developed an extraordinary, though always cautious passion for his fourth lover, but finally she too left him, and he could summon up no more dreams. Instead, he looked outside his cabin door and discovered that it was nearly spring. Throughout the next spring and summer, as he plowed and planted and tended the fields, he brooded about his lovers. The loneliness of January seemed very far away, and it was easy to promise himself that he would never allow the women to come again. This winter, he would do some carving. Repair the harness leather. Read the Bible.

He did all of those things and still the women came to his cabin, that year and in every year which followed. And though he was frightened by his lovers, he was more frightened by the thought that he might become too sensible to believe in them. Despite their eccentricities, he loved them, and he needed them desperately—for they were the only lovers he had ever known.

The darkening sky had turned to dusk, and the beavers were now vague, splashy blurs against the tea-colored water. Seneca reluctantly headed for home. After thirteen years, the cabin looked just like he'd pictured it: the logs had weathered, but the walls still rose in firm, straight lines, and the path looked comfortably worn and welcoming. But tonight he felt no satisfaction as he approached; tonight he could only remember that the cabin was perfectly planned in every way but one—it was much too big for one person. And the path he followed to his door had been worn almost entirely by a single pair of feet.

There had been a few visitors, especially since word had spread about his magnificent carpentry. His was the first log cabin in this area. Occasionally a woodsman or wanderer would stop to praise his handiwork, and Indians passed very close to him, traveling between their villages and the seashore. But most of the settlers who crossed the interior of Jersey wilderness skirted the huge pine forest at its northern edge, while Seneca's trail to the south remained little traveled.

He'd been to Burlington twice and ventured into the settlement of Gloucester Town once every year to buy supplies. But though he was surrounded by people in those towns, he couldn't attempt to make friends; he simply attended to his errands and responded politely when spoken to. Years of solitude at the frog level had reinforced his instinctive shyness, making him nearly mute. Seneca was eloquent only through his actions. He revealed his love for the land in the patient, meticulous way he attended to his life there. But he could not speak of that love; he could only prove it.

Entering the cabin, Seneca headed for the table where he'd laid out a bowl for the stew which was bubbling above the fire. Then he hesitated, and instead slumped into the chair before the fire. He stared into it, dreading his lovers, but hoping they would come to him, soon.

Several hundred yards to the east, Mary Ross stared at the same fire, a steady flickering glow which seemed suspended above the distant trees. She was afraid to believe her eyes: cold and exhausted as she was, she felt sure that her mind had conjured up the possibility of fire just to keep her walking. Wrapping her gray woolen cloak more tightly around her shoulders, she tugged at her father's arm, changing their course to head straight for the light.

"Up ahead, father. It might be a campfire." Josiah Ross made no response, but continued babbling softly to himself. Mary was too irritated at the moment to be frightened by his condition, which had worsened since he'd awakened her at dawn three days ago in Burlington.

"We're going on a new adventure," he'd caroled in the tone she knew too well. "Fresh horizons." To Mary, these familiar phrases meant only one thing: They were on the run, again.

Mary knew it was not Josiah's fault that he had been born the third son of wealthy, titled British parents and so possessed the manners and education but not the currency of a gentleman. And it was not his fault that his attempts to seek fortune in the New World should be based on schemes, dreams and the sweat of someone else's brow, for he had been taught thoroughly: When a gentleman sits idle, he is thinking; when a worker sits idle, he is loafing.

But it was his fault that in all of his tricky dealings, most recently as a land speculator, he betrayed himself by a strange sort of innocence, born of vanity. He sincerely believed that the other men involved in his complicated deals understood them as little as he did. As a result, he was eternally discovered as a black sheep among the wolves, who fleeced him by habit before throwing him to the mercy of the already shorn. Mary believed that the Burlington ventures had been their last hope. In the years since her mother's death, there had been too many towns and too many embarrassing exits, and Josiah had slowly changed from charming rogue to a menacing fool.

Now there was only the cold and dark of a strange forest, and a pale, distant light. She pushed toward it, dragging her father through the trees.

Seneca was startled by the pounding noise at his door. Only Indians traveled this late at night, but they had never bothered him, so he threw the bolt and opened the door wide. He found himself staring down at a small, pretty woman of about twenty years, who was nearly engulfed by her cloak. She was struggling to support a white-haired man who gazed at him with burning eyes from a face that was pale as wax.

"Please—" Mary's voice was a husky rattle and she didn't have the strength to continue her speech.

Seneca said nothing. He simply pulled the old man into his arms and carried him into the cabin. Mary followed slowly, savoring every detail of this miracle: The huge blonde giant who had lifted her father like a toy and was now settling him so gently in front of the fire; the beautifully carved furniture and neat cupboard, the fragrant stew bubbling over the fire. This was a *home*. Then Seneca turned to look at her and in the growing silence, Mary was aware that she had never been looked at quite so thoroughly before.

"My father and I were traveling—our wagon, um, disappeared—stolen by Indians," she choked out the lies, each more foolish than the last. He didn't seem to notice, but guided her to the table and handed her a bowlful of stew. It was delicious. As she gobbled it down, he ladled stew into another bowl and began to feed her father, one spoonful at a time.

"Your father will be all right." His speech was slow and awkwardly melodious, but it surprised her; their silence had become so comfortable that she'd hardly noticed it. Josiah did look better. He'd stopped mumbling some time ago, and his head dropped closer to his chest; he was nearly asleep. Seneca wrapped him in blankets and carried him up to the loft. Then he quickly returned to Mary, as if drawn by a magnet. "She has violet eyes," he thought. "A summer smile. Her lips are bright and full, but without Autumn's talent for lies. And surely, this woman cannot be another one of my lonely dreams, for I would never have thought of the chaperone. This is my real lover," he concluded, "and she has come to me."

Mary watched his approach and suddenly, incredibly, she realized that he meant to seduce her. Or worse. What a fool she had been to believe that this man was different! He had seemed so strong . . . so tender . . . and so blonde. Now he would turn sly and common, coaxing her with the same glittering nonsense she'd heard so many times before. At least that would break the spell which this beast and his cabin seemed to have cast upon her. She knew that she could protect herself; every silly word he uttered would harden her heart.

33

For a time, he watched her without speaking; then slowly his hand moved to the base of her neck. He loosened the pins that held her soft brown hair in place, so that it fell to her shoulders.

Mary was shocked, not only by his action but her strange reluctance to protest it. This was some sort of trick, and she certainly wasn't going to let him . . .

He leaned forward to brush her lips with a tentative, lingering kiss, and then he lifted her into his arms and kissed her again.

But then, what could she do? Hadn't this handsome, treacherous beast deliberately lured her through the forest and tricked her with his beautifully carved cabin and his fiendish kindness and

ooh . . .

Carefully, he was undressing her, pausing to neatly fold each garment before he moved onto the next. It was a slow process, but he did it perfectly, and in time Mary felt more thoroughly naked than ever before.

. . . cabin and the kindness and the delicious—the stew! Of course he had drugged it. What else could explain why she felt so weak and tingly, why she wasn't scratching and kicking and screaming and—scream! If she screamed, her father would surely hear. She was going to

ooh . . .

Methodically, he was kissing her. Slow, thoughtful kisses that explored the contours of her lips, then a long, claiming kiss of discovery. Then he kissed her eyes, and he kissed her cheeks and the tip of her nose and the part in her hair and her neck and her chin and her breasts, and by the time he'd started to repeat the process, Mary was feeling more drugged than ever before.

It would be so selfish to disturb her father, really, besides, how could she scream when his lips were—

ooh . . . could she

scream when she was panting like this? He was so big and strong and

. . . ooh he was touching her *there*, and there was nothing, absolutely nothing she could do . . .

Cautiously, he slipped a fingertip into the delicate opening of her sex: Warm. He'd guessed as much but couldn't risk another surprise. No man could survive a shock like that, twice.

. . . ooh help . . .

He was carrying her off to his bed . . .

. . . ooh help help . . .

His body was against her and their toes were touching and their fingers and legs and things, and it was really . . . quite

. . . ooh

She was feeling so . . . help . . . could he? . . . ooh . . . he was helping . . . yes   please . . . he   was   helping . . . yes   more . . . help

oh help yes please help . . .

more please yes

oh help yes yes

ooh

yes.

With a great leap, he came gushing inside her; she trembled, and came again. Seneca was thrilled—not even Autumn had possessed such a gift. They slept, still touching fingers and legs and things, until she woke him to ask his name. He told her, and she introduced herself. Then she fell asleep.

Seneca lay awake in the darkness, feeling confused. Surely, this woman was beautiful. But Spring had never interrupted his comfortable sleep with questions. In fact, she hadn't questioned him at all. And Summer had never pulled away his covers or taken up so much room in the bed. He was sure that even reckless Autumn had never dared to snore. And worst of all, *nothing* that Winter possessed had felt so cold as Mary's dainty feet.

But as he watched her sleeping, Seneca felt a strange, tangled rush of emotions—that combination of fear and excitement which had not possessed him since the night he had first heard the frogs. None of his fantasy lovers had ever aroused those feelings, he realized—surely, this was another omen. In time, he would adjust to her feet. But what could he say to her so that she would know they were meant to be together? As he drifted towards sleep, he was struck by inspiration. Tomorrow, he would say that she reminded him of frogs. Women liked to hear such things. She would be so pleased.

In the first decade of the eighteenth century, New Jersey's political situation improved: the two provinces merged into a single colony, and the assembly (which was elected by those colonists who owned more than one hundred acres of land) was granted the right to raise and distribute money. Although the aristocratic influence of the proprietors continued and New Jersey's royal governors were often barely tolerable, colonial assemblymen could now assert a voice in their own government by refusing to appropriate money for their governor's requests, including the one for his salary. The assembly used its power to liberalize the voting laws and to demand that the crown appoint a separate governor for New Jersey, one who would not spend all of his time in New York.

This slow infusion of democratic ideals did not extend to the natives who had lived in the colony long before the white settlers arrived. The Indians living in New Jersey were Lenni-Lenape, known to other tribes in the Algonquin nation as "The Old Women," because of their peaceful ways. But like the "squalid savages" who lived in other colonies, they were feared and despised. Many colonists agreed with the Reverend Solomon Stoddard, who urged Massachusetts Bay frontiersmen to use dogs when they hunted for Indians, who "act like wolves and are to be dealt with as wolves." Being carried off by heathens was a popular theme in colonial literature, as books like John Williams's *The Redeemed Captive* became best-sellers. And so the legends of terror and violence grew, as the Lenni-Lenape tribe of New Jersey slowly ceased to exist. When the first colonists arrived, more than two thousand Indians were living in New Jersey, but only about five hundred remained by the early 1700s. By that time, about twelve thousand colonists were living in the region. One hundred years after Henry Hudson first sailed up its coast, New Jersey's total population provided an average of less than two people per square mile of land.

By these standards, the five hundred acres of New Jersey land which surrounded the frog level had nearly become a metropolis. Mary Ross chose to remain with Seneca Rane through every coming season. During their first endless winter in the cabin, Seneca confessed his other lovers to Mary. She did not scream or cry but listened with an interest that surprised him, since he'd expected her to be jealous. That April she came to him wan and gasping. In July she lay naked by his fields. In September she taught him positions she'd never known she knew. Only winter defeated her, though she developed an interest in icicles that persisted, cautiously, for a lifetime. And Seneca never saw his other lovers again.

They were married in Gloucester Town, in spring of 1704. Mary's father remained with them, and their happiness was marred only by their concern for him. Though Josiah had quickly recovered from his fever, his behavior was erratic and he seemed barely aware of his surroundings. But after Seneca and Mary Rane had lived together at the frog level for nearly a year, Josiah proved to them that for one day at least, his senses were quicker than theirs. For it was Josiah who crossed the creek to discover that they were no longer alone on the land.

Their neighbor was a Lenni-Lenape woman of thirty-four summers, a member of the Unalachtigo subtribe, whose totem was the wild turkey. During their private times, her husband had called her Keune. Her husband was dead now, leaving her alone to wonder why she always survived the diseases which had decimated her tribe—smallpox, syphilis, black measles—the diseases of civilization. She had survived to watch her people poisoned by rum, as they grew more and more dependent upon the white man to provide clothes and tools which they'd once made themselves. In exchange, the white man "bought" the land in a way that the Lenni-Lenape only understood afterwards, when they were cast out of their dwelling places by those who now claimed to possess them.

This summer, the remnants of Keune's tribe had traveled to the sea as usual, passing very close to the creek on Seneca's land, where she had picked cranberries as a child. At summer's end, the tribe met in council and voted not to return to the disputed land of their village, but instead to migrate northwest toward Kitochtanenin, the endless blue mountains famous in their legends, where other surviving Lenni-Lenape were regrouping to create a new homeland beyond the white settlements.

Keune's daughter had been too ill, and she too weak from fever to travel far, so with the infant girl she had named after the endless blue mountains, she'd slipped away from her people to return to the creek and the cranberries she remembered. Close by the berries she fashioned a hut from green saplings

37

which she covered with bark and grass mats. Now they had wood for the fire, ripe berries to eat, and water from the creek. She and her daughter could die slowly here, with dignity.

Instead, Keune had awakened from her fever to find that blankets had been tucked around her, and a dainty white hand was sponging her face with a cool cloth. In terror, she called out for her daughter, but fainted when she tried to rise. Later, she awoke to see Kitochtanenin dozing before the fire, cradled in a white woman's arms. This time she struggled upright, extending her arms wide. Speaking softly in an incomprehensible tongue, the white woman smiled as she surrendered the child. Kitochtanenin was thin and still cranky from convalescence, but Keune realized that they both would survive. This thought gave her no pleasure.

Soon Keune felt strong enough to try to communicate with the white woman, and through gestures and sign language they developed enough common phrases to learn about each other. The woman lived in a hut built on the distant hill, on the other side of the creek. From her gestures, Keune gathered that her husband was a giant and a hard worker, and from the sparkle in her eyes, she guessed that he was also a good lover. *Sen-e-ca.* The old man who always accompanied Mary to the hut was her father. He had been the one who discovered them, unconscious beside a dying fire. He had saved them. *Jo-si-ah.*

Mary had then gestured towards the child, asking for her name. *"Ki-toch-tan-en-in,"* she replied, trying to imitate Mary's careful, measured pronunciation. Mary looked bewildered and was gesturing for a repetition when Josiah suddenly whirled towards them. Pointing at the child, he began to shout in a taunting cadence: *Kit-ty, Kit-ty, Kit-ty.* Keune looked straight into his pale, glowing eyes, and to every question that followed the first, she shook her head firmly. No understand. So Kitty became her daughter's name, and when Josiah began to call Keune "Injun," then simply "Jin," she took the name as her own.

Josiah had given them a new life. He had given them new names. Now Jin waited for him to tell them what to do.

——— *Despite sporadic Indian troubles and the continuing irritation of royal governors, the colony of New Jersey had made progress from its wilderness beginnings. By 1715, iron had been discovered in the northern hills of the colony, and a forge was in operation at Hanover, on the Whippany River. Newark and Elizabethtown had become centers for the production of leather goods, and the settlement of Hoboken already boasted two operating breweries. From the port cities of Perth Amboy and Burlington, merchant ships loaded with Jersey produce and lumber sailed for Europe and the West Indies; they returned laden with British manufactured goods and West Indian sugar and rum. These ships also provided colonists with the means to send letters to friends and relatives they'd left behind. Early descriptions of colonial life were overwhelmingly enthusiastic; Mahlon Stacy, the founder of Trenton, awarded New Jersey the tourist's ultimate accolade: "This is a most brave place, whatever envy or evil spies may speak of it. I wish you all were here. . . ."*

1718 —————
The Cranberry Basin

THE WOMAN known as Indian Jin huddled behind the white-berried foliage watching as Josiah approached the girl in the distant clearing. Jin was old but clear-sighted, she thought bitterly: not only could she see, but she knew what to look for. She watched Josiah—*filthy old fool*—put his arms around the girl as if to steady her. It was a needless gesture, but outwardly innocent. However, Jin could remember all too many such gestures these past few months—always playful and teasing, as though he were still handling a child, but his hands would betray him by lingering, for the girl Kitty was in her fifteenth summer, and like other fruit in its season, she had ripened and grown lush in the heat.

Kitty. It was an ugly name, but Jin had been determined not to speak their real names aloud, for it is Lenni-Lenape tradition never to speak the names of those who are dead. She refused even to remember what her own name had been, but sometimes in the privacy of her thoughts she would assemble the lilting syllables of the girl's name: *Kitochtanenin,* for endless blue mountains that represented another time, before the rum and guns and trinkets of the white man. Mountains that the white man now called Kittatinny. When Jin had first heard the name, she wept. What could such a foolish, ugly word have to do with endless or blue?

As Jin huddled among the cranberry shrubs, her thoughts were filled with shame: Once she had been a warrior's wife; she had been daughter of the *sakima,* the chief. Now she hides behind the bushes, watching the white man who has shared her bed for fourteen years, as he fondles her daughter. "How is it that remembering what was, I can look upon what is, and survive it?"

Josiah had saved them. She must remember that. During their days of convalescence, Josiah had always accompanied Mary to the hut. While Mary cared for the invalids, he had paced in an endless circle around the fire, speaking in a rapid, private tongue. Occasionally, he would stop in his tracks and turn to face Jin, shouting a few words in the tongue she recognized as Mary's. From the first, Jin had understood more of his message than Mary ever would.

Nevertheless, she was surprised when he began to return alone at night, to share her bed. She was old (though not so old as he) and scarred from the pox that had killed her husband and so many of their tribe. She took no pleasure in the fact that he wanted her, for she could never be sure that he did. He simply took her, like a rutting buck. He was constantly hot, insatiable, all through the night his hands would restlessly travel her body. His fingers would dig at her flesh. Pinching. Stabbing into her. Pinning her beneath the blanket.

Each night she survived him. She did not see the bruises on her body because she chose not to look for them. During the day, she had Kitty. She and her daughter could fish at the creek or pick berries and there was always corn, from Seneca. Mary and Seneca had been blessed with three sons, born in successive winters. They had arrived white and perfect, like yearly tribute from the gods. Sometimes the white children came to play with Kitty; they laughed and ran together, and those were the good days.

The oldest son, Eric, was five years younger than Kitty, though he always insisted on taking charge of their games. Kitty didn't care—she was happy to adopt the role of younger brother, along with Joshan and Jeremiah, as long as she got to play too. Now there was a daughter for the Ranes, little Bethany, born last year. Kitty treated the tiny girl like a precious doll, and Jin had watched the children's endless play with growing despair, for her daughter was now fifteen, too old for dolls and games.

As always, she had not interfered. Jin was sure that their lives had been lost long before Josiah found them. This belief had enabled her to endure the surprise of survival, and everything that followed. Both she and Kitty now dressed like white women. Mary gave them patched, faded blouses and skirts made from sacking, and Jin simply accepted the clothes.

Just as simply, she had accepted the fact that Josiah moved into the hut a few months after their rescue. In truth, he hadn't altered their lives much. He took long walks in the forest, played games with the children, or paced in rapid circles around the fire at the center of the cramped, smoky hut. His white hair gathered in wisps about his baby-pink face, blending with the smoke to form a tight, drifting halo. His blue eyes were bright and bitter. But it was his laugh which frightened Jin the most: its pure, careless melody was the perfect imitation of a child's. An evil child.

Jin began spending more and more of her time working at the cranberry patch. She had always loved the sharp taste of the berry, which she remembered from tribal ceremonies as a symbol of peace. After she'd noticed how dry the vines became in winter months, she dug a shallow hole adjacent to the creek and then transplanted the bushes in the turfed-out basin. When she built up earthen banks on all sides, water from the creek filled the basin, providing moist, boggy soil for the cranberry shrubs in every season.

Soon she was growing more berries than they could possibly use. Josiah laughed at her, but that only increased her devotion. For Jin, the cranberries had become the one part of her life that she could affect. She did not care about herself, and she refused to care about Kitty. Instead, she had poured all of her love into her cranberry basin. She had taken pleasure in the abundance of berries and in Seneca's obvious admiration of her handiwork, while her daughter had grown radiant and ripe for plucking, with only Josiah to tend her.

In all these years, Josiah had never abused Kitty. She trusted him completely and surely felt more comfortable with him than with her mother, whom she must have seen as a silent, undemonstrative hag who bored her with long stories about people and ways she'd never known. Kitty did not remember that she'd ever had another name. She liked the one Josiah had given her, and she liked the games he played with her and the affectionate hugs and kisses he gave her. Now, when Jin realized that it had been madness to deny her love for her daughter, it was too late. Kitty's love and trust had been won by another. *My Kitochta-nenin.*

Jin crouched against the cool, moist earth of the cranberry basin, rocking gently in misery. She could not stop Josiah, yet she also could not resist imagining what her daughter's life might have been. At fifteen, Kitochtanenin would have prepared for courtship by making a beautiful dress from the wing and tail feathers of a turkey, weaving the feathers into an elaborate pattern, hoping to attract the suitor of her choice. When the tedious work was completed, she would put on the costume and then sit with her chaperone alongside the trail near her home.

When a potential suitor approached, love was measured at first sight; if the initial exchange of glances was sufficiently exciting, the young lovers could expect to watch over each other for a lifetime. To pledge her love, the bride would give her intended an ear of corn to indicate that she would supply the grain; he in turn presented her with a bone, which meant that he would supply the meat.

It was a tradition that lent dignity yet allowed for passion, and it had little to do with whatever Josiah had in mind, Jin knew. For Kitty, there would be no costume of woven feathers; for a young girl named Kitty, that costume would mean nothing. *That is what the white man has done for us with his trinkets and his rum—he has taken the meaning from our lives. And the curse of his diseases is that so many of us survive them.*

In summer's heat, cranberries grow dead-white among the vines; nourished in the dying time as the earth turns hard with frost, they ripen in November, bright as blood. Cranberries are the fruit of a waning season. Compared to the sweeter berries of summer, their taste is sharp and complicated.

The noon sky burned as Jin left the cranberry basin and circled through the woods behind the hut so that no one could see her approach; Josiah and Kitty would be returning soon. Pulling several saplings loose from the back wall, she created an opening several feet high and knelt there, adjusting her position to block all traces of sunlight from entering the hut. Now she had a clear view of the shadowed interior. Long ago, she had given Kitty to Josiah; today he would take her. That much was simple and certain, just as their lives had been for fifteen years. Still she waited, without knowing why.

Before she saw them, she heard their laughter. Then Kitty was running through the door with Josiah close behind. They stopped within inches of her hiding place, and Jin scarcely breathed as they looked right through her, seeing only shadows. They continued the chase until Josiah finally caught Kitty from behind and tumbled with her to the ground. She tried to be indignant but kept bursting into giggles.

Pulling a handkerchief from her skirt pocket, she began to coax Josiah to play blind man's bluff, her favorite game. He was still lying where he had fallen feigning exhaustion, but now he eased his head comfortably into her lap while she tied the cloth over his eyes. The blinded Josiah clung to her, apparently help-less, as she helped him to his feet. But when they were both standing, she pulled away from his grasp and spun him in tight, fast circles until he staggered. Then she slipped out of his range.

As Josiah fumbled noisily into a corner, Jin realized her daughter's strategy. Kitty had tiptoed into the center of the room, standing directly beneath the smokehole where the fire was laid in cool weather. Only ashes were there now, but Josiah would avoid the spot instinctively. It was a foolish game, but she was pleased that her daughter played it well.

From the smokehole above, a pillar of sunlight streamed onto Kitty, forcing Jin to recognize her beauty. Long black hair flut-tered alongside her face in fat, glossy waves like the wings of a blackbird. Her eyes were dark as ebony; they had a sassy gleam, but her dazzling smile was artless. Kitty's tall, slender figure still moved with a child's instinctive grace, as though to deny newly rounded hips and the startling fullness of her breasts. She seemed to revel in her beauty and yet be unaware of it.

As Jin watched, it seemed to her that Kitty's beauty had in-spired the light which encircled her and then flowed upward to the sky, so that the sun was created from her radiance.

It feels like that, a surging light, an excitement that has no name it rises within you, making your fingers tremble as you work the feathers, weaving a message so secret that you will understand it only when it is received by another.

Kitty covered her mouth with both hands, as though the sound of her smile could give her away. She was wholly absorbed in the game and Josiah seemed to be deliberately exaggerating his antics to please her. He made one huge, stumbling circle about the room, skirting the fireplace. Then he stopped and scratched his head, apparently stumped. Kitty closed her eyes in dread.

Your heart hammers beneath the feathers as you stand before the women; your fear is new and complicated and you cannot contain it. Their words whisper dull as rain and the thunder of your heart drowns them out and you know nothing.

Turning towards her, Josiah stretched out his arms, reaching just short of the lighted circle where Kitty stood. She gasped and cringed but didn't move. A smile creased the edges of Josiah's blindfold. Now sure of himself, he advanced slowly, crooning, "Kitty, Kitty, Kitty?"

There is a message in your dress and you have created it but you do not know its language. He is coming.

His fingers moved slowly into the light and touched her, fastening onto the fabric of her blouse. He raised his other hand to touch her breast. Kitty stiffened but didn't pull away. Josiah's hands roamed freely across her neck and breasts, and she began to look more wondering than shocked.

He is coming. Your chaperone nudges you, not knowing that you have memorized his footsteps. Do not look up. Save yourself. Do not look into his eyes.

Kitty reached up to loosen the knot in Josiah's blindfold; she pulled it from his eyes to stare at him, uncertain. Drawing her close, he embraced her, hands traveling the length of her spine as he pressed against her. Kitty moaned. She closed her eyes, curving her body upward to meet his caress. Now Kitty's face was circled by the light as he eased her onto the soft ashy dirt of the fireplace; now Josiah rolled his body onto hers, blocking out the light.

My daughter, my beloved . . . Kitty.

The force of blood rushing through Jin's heart would surely

kill her; she was blinded, deafened by the roaring pulse that forced her to rise and shaped the high keening notes of her scream. Kitty stared up at her, eyes wide with fright, but Josiah merely tightened his grip and glared at Jin. He snarled as she approached, as though to warn a rival beast from his prey.

I know that she is yours, old man. Have I not already given her to you in a thousand ways? But now we will see if you enjoy the taking. For an instant, Jin allowed her thoughts to show in her eyes and savored their effect as Josiah turned pale and wary, slackening his hold on Kitty. Then he turned once more to look at the girl, and Jin saw his eyes fix on her full, fawn-colored breasts, with tips firm as berries that pushed through the opening of Kitty's loosened blouse. He moaned softly and fell onto her, forcing his tongue into her mouth as he pressed her back into the dirt. As he ripped apart her blouse, Kitty struggled against him but he pinned her arms against the dirt and covered her with the length of his body.

As Josiah buried his face between mounds of Kitty's breasts, Jin sank her teeth into the flesh at the base of his neck. Josiah screamed and bucked, trying to shake her off, but with a grinding motion, she twisted his flesh and bit into him more deeply. His hands flailed helplessly as she clenched her jaw and with a series of backward jerks, began to drag him slowly across the floor, away from Kitty. Like a savage dog, her teeth worked at his flesh and she heard his breath grow ragged. But with a sudden heave, Josiah pulled free and whirled on her before she could react, striking her in the face with his fist. She staggered but managed to rise on her haunches before he could trap her on the ground. She circled him slowly, waiting for her strength to return.

Blood was beginning to ooze from the ugly, purplish wound at the back of Josiah's neck. His shirt had ripped open from being dragged across the rough ground, and his exposed chest was scraped raw and covered with scratches. His eyes burned with rage and excitement, and Jin watched him with growing satisfaction: *Never have you taken me without giving pain. That is what you like, isn't it old man—the pain, not the other. And I think you like to get it, too. Because old and ugly as I am, you are hot for me. Not the girl. You want me, for the pain.*

Her circles grew smaller, steadily closing around Josiah who waited at the center, watching her every move. Abruptly, she lunged at him, knocking him sideways with a vicious swipe. Fingernails snagged on his cheek, tearing pieces of flesh from the bone. She was still trying to regain her balance when he leaped from the shadows. Like a panther clinging to her back, he forced her down.

Jin's face was pressed against the ground, and she opened her mouth, welcoming the taste of ashes and dirt. Twisting her spine, he pulled her around to face him, shoving aside the shredded pieces of her blouse. One hand settled against her throat as he bent down to bite her breasts, pulling viciously at their tips. Jin cried out; the strength was draining from her, as her mind focused on the pain. If she lost consciousness, Josiah would surely kill her.

She struggled to form thoughts . . . *Blacker than any night is the darkness made of red.*

Pushing her skirt up, Josiah entered her with a quick violent thrust. She lay motionless . . . *There pain consumes, like fire.*

One hand was poised at her throat, the other roamed her body, pinching and jabbing. Still she did not move . . . *We can go there.*

He was squeezing her throat, fingers moving to choke her as he rammed harder, more deeply into her . . . *I will take you.*

With a sudden convulsive motion, she clawed the flesh on his shoulders; her fingernails slashed down the length of his spine. Josiah screamed, and his movements became frenzied. She slashed him again, and he came screaming inside her. Jin felt it as liquid fire, acid splashing the darkness of her womb . . . *and I welcome the burning.*

Josiah staggered away, muttering privately. She knew that he would sleep for hours; for this day, at least, he could cause no more trouble. Jin lay quietly, allowing that knowledge to spread sweetly through her, like rapture. Suddenly, she leaped up, remembering her daughter and calling her name in the darkness, *Kitty!* There was only silence; where her daughter had stood there was only the fireplace, luminous and empty. Jin stared into the vacant pillar of light; silvery specks of dust were drifting there, like tiny, important stars. She watched as they fell, one by one, from the brightness, and then called out again, uselessly.

There were sounds outside. Covering herself, Jin slipped through the opening at the back of the hut. There she saw Eric Rane, who stumbled through the sun-dazzled grass, coming dangerously close to Kitty. She closed her eyes in dread.

"You're peeking," Joshan accused him, from a safe distance.

"Am not!" he replied, turning to direct his attack against a favorite enemy. As Eric moved away from her, Kitty beamed at Joshan, who managed to wave despite the force of doom that lurched towards him, visibly peeking beneath his blindfold.

"You *are* peeking!" Jeremiah's voice came from another corner of the field, and Eric changed his direction again. In a nearby patch of shade, little Bethany shrieked, sensing neglect.

Kitty's favorite game. To see and hear was somehow not enough; Jin raised her arms towards the children, baring her wrists as though slashed, to drink their joy through opened veins. As she watched them play, memories flowed through her, soft and mingling, like tears. A stream of changing summers, rippled with the same laughter and games. A daughter whom time and darkness had never changed.

Jin felt a peculiar tightness in her eyes; her vision blurred, and she moved to shield her face from the glare before it occurred to her, like a faraway shock, that she was about to cry. Finally she understood and wept.

Her face still glistened as she moved to comfort Bethany, whose shrieks had steadied to a wail. "My daughter has been chosen by the sun. Always, she will live in its light," she whispered to the infant, rocking her gently. "I cannot keep Josiah away from her, but I can keep him from hurting her. And the sun . . . the sun will keep her from understanding what has been done."

In her arms Bethany whimpered, still distrustful. Jin began to rock her more slowly as she turned her attention back to the game. Eric was still staggering back and forth between Joshan and Jeremiah, while Kitty grew weak with laughter. "It is a strange but precious gift, for the daughter of a warrior," Jin crooned softly, "for a girl named Kitty, whose grandfather was chief." Slowly, Bethany sagged against her. In time, she slept.

• • •

In the years that followed, the wilderness isolation of those living by the frog level did not change. Mary Rane and her daughters continued to make all the household supplies themselves, from soap to clothing to cheese. Seneca had strong sons to help him, and they cleared new fields and made new furniture using the same simple tools and a plow. Mary and the girls each owned a single dress made of coarse linen with a laced leather bodice, and it still took nearly a year and a half to spin enough flax for one man's shirt. Theirs was a prosperous farm by colonial standards. Seneca was able to buy two hundred acres which adjoined his original homestead; the family ate supper off town-bought dishes made of burnished pewter.

In the winter, even the youngest children wore cloaks lined with fur, and Mary designed bedcoverings of brilliant woolen crewels, which she worked into homespun in curving, floral patterns. There were stories told by firelight, as the children roasted nuts, and two books, both considered so precious that only Mary and Seneca were allowed to handle them: the *Holy Bible*, which Seneca had brought to the land, and a copy of *Mother Goose's Melodies for Children,* newly printed in Boston, which he'd bought in Gloucester Town. Seneca never tired of reading the nonsense rhymes out loud, even to himself.

Like other families who lived in the wilderness, the Ranes continued a way of life that had not altered much in 150 years. This lack of change was important because in cities throughout the colonies, colonists were enjoying sophisticated comforts in their rapidly changing New World. In the New Jersey city of Perth Amboy, citizens who were willing to risk puritan displeasure could dress in extravagant fashions copied from Europe. Both men and women wore high-heeled wooden shoes and large curly wigs, and the skirts of men's jackets were stiffened with buckram. Women joyfully adopted the fad of hoop skirts which they perpetuated for almost a century; their skirts became wider and fuller, much like the girth of a tree.

A favorite style in furniture was Queen Anne; favorite wines were champagne and Spanish Madeira. More important, colonists in the cities now had access to newspapers such as the nationalistic *Boston Gazette,* and Philadelphia's *American Mercury.*

They knew what their fellow colonists were thinking. By the year 1720, a family living in Perth Amboy could argue with a Philadelphia editor but still had no reliable way to keep in touch with a son who had immigrated to the Pennsylvania frontier.

There were nearly 500 thousand people living in the colonies by the year 1720, but less than 8 percent of them were living in the cities. Colonists who lived beyond the reach of newspapers and early stagecoach lines had to rely on news from passing strangers or gossip picked up along with supplies on their yearly trip into town. The destiny of the land surrounding the frog level was changing, but its inhabitants had little knowledge of city-bred forces which would shape their fate.

In the hut by the cranberry basin, Jin survived and watched as her prophecies came true. Kitty grew from girl to woman and Jin marveled at the change. Before her daughter's beauty had been a simple fact; now it was a poem. Like an exquisite lyric, the woman Kitty was evocative, unforgettable. But her mind never altered; Kitty could only understand the simple, happy things—sunshine, laughter, and games. Josiah survived, too, although he was now nearly seventy. Jin continued to cater to his special tastes, and as she'd hoped, he never hurt Kitty, though from time to time he took her, simply because she was there to take.

In spite of Josiah, Kitty's life was touched by darkness only once. The Rane children did not share her gift for innocence, and as the boys grew older, they understood enough about the affair to tell their parents. Mary received the news with a secret source of shame. She had lied to Seneca years before, swearing that Jin had begged Josiah to move into her hut. Then she had believed her own lie, because she'd grown afraid of her father and did not want him around her children. Now she was forced to a second betrayal. In 1723, when Kitty was twenty, Mary forbid her children to make further visits to the hut.

Jin immediately understood what had happened, but she could find no way to explain to Kitty, who had lost her playmates. Weeks, then months, passed, and still she waited for them in the sunshine. She could see Eric, Joshan, and Jeremiah at work in the fields, but they did not come to her. She caught sight of Bethany near the cabin; she was teaching three-year-old Abigail and little Enos how to play a game. Kitty waved, but the children did not play with her. And there was a new tiny girl, a precious doll named Phebe tucked out of reach, one she'd never seen. While she waited, Kitty learned to play by herself.

The families lived side by side in separate isolation. Seneca and Mary's joy was a rising curve that split their sky like an abiding rainbow; beneath, lived the golden Ranes. Seneca tripled the acreage of his fields; he built a splendid barn and added a new room to the cabin, which doubled its size. His seven children grew blonde and high like the corn that ripened in his fields. His frogs roared in the night, and on his creek, the beavers built a new and better dam.

Josiah watched, and his hatred grew in proportion to their prosperity. Kitty watched, and her love never faltered. Jin watched Josiah and Kitty, and finally her worst fears came true. In 1732, Kitty gave birth to a son. She named the child Rane for her beloved playmates. Josiah laughed. He liked the name very much.

————— One of those colonists who rejoiced in the advantages of city life was Miss Desiretta Laud, who moved to Perth Amboy in *1699*, after a fascinating adolescence. Her younger brother Jupiter soon left home to wander through the colonies, but Miss Laud did not lack for company. Although thin and freckled with a mass of carroty hair, she soon became Perth Amboy's reigning adventuress. In *1719*, Desiretta became the first woman in history to pop out of a dessert. Her performance, which also featured the greatest mass of Sally Lunn ever assembled in a colonial kitchen, was witnessed by two justices for the crown and a sizable minority of the New Jersey Assembly, so it was never reported. This triumph proved to be her last: six weeks later, the irresistable Miss Laud perished in a mob. She was survived by her only child—a ten-year-old boy, to whom she had bequeathed the name Desire. But before his uncle Jupiter could be located and summoned home, young Desire Laud disappeared from Perth Amboy. Citizens there searched for days, but the boy had vanished without a trace. This double tragedy marked the official end of the Dynasty of Desire, and New Jersey forever lost its rightful reputation as "The Sweet and Savage State."

1733 ————

The Sparkling Field— and Ash

THE CORN was in, the potatoes were in, the peppers and cabbage and beans were in, each reaped more extravagantly than ever before. Only the pumpkins remained in the fields, still swelling on the vines. For many years, the land, the seasons, and the Ranes had worked in plain, sweet harmony; their music was an ongoing doxology that the harvest vindicated once each year, like a holy cymbal crash.

Except for daughter Bethany. Right now, she was running, dirt-splashed across neatly reaped furrows as she fled from freshly baked pies and scrubbed wood and a huge roast of venison, whose dripping fat crackled in the hearth of the home she was running from. There was a wildness in Bethany Rane, and the smugly splendid September afternoon merely provoked it. She felt choked by the abundance of this year's harvest and smothered by her large and loving family. At sixteen, she also felt newly beautiful, which only aggravated her sense of peril. Now she was heading for the only part of her father's land that sustained her.

It was a small field, less than half an acre, where an illogical assortment of wildflowers spread haphazardly through the grass, defying Seneca's efforts to control it, or even to correctly define it. No sooner had he decided that mallow bloomed late there, after the violets had already spread across the near bank with clover scattered throughout, than the mallow popped up early and seemed to stay forever, particularly on the near bank where no violets grew, since they ´were busily spreading throughout the field in search of the clover, which never appeared at all. Faced with such anarchy, Seneca retreated. Like Bethany, he found the flowers astonishing, but the turbulence that she reveled in made him slightly queasy.

The field was no longer blooming, but Bethany raced joyously into it, climbing onto the crest of the giant rock which saved the soil here from Seneca's plow. This added only about six feet to her perspective, but most of the surrounding land was flat and cleared of trees, so she could see farther than she wanted to. She watched her brothers as they worked in the fields. Tall and handsome, with their blonde hair gleaming like helmets in the sunlight, they marched through the furrows like a matched set of conquerors, bringing in the last of the corn.

Then she caught sight of sisters Abigail and Phebe. They were sitting by the cabin door, snapping fresh-picked beans into a wooden bowl. Bethany's mood brightened as she noticed that little Phebe was doing more eating than snapping. Her father was standing near the girls, staring at the pumpkins as he tried to guess how many hours and minutes would pass before they achieved perfect ripeness. Seneca's hair and beard had turned gray as a winter sky, and time had thickened his waist, but Bethany knew that he was still as strong and kind as the days when he'd tossed her, four years old and shrieking, nearly into the clouds. "And he hasn't lost his instincts either," she thought sorrowfully. "Those pumpkins will be bigger and better than ever before, this year. Just like everything else."

Feeling restless again, she turned towards the creek and spotted her mother, who was hurrying there to pick up the milk and butter which were submerged in cool water. Mary's soft brown hair now gleamed with silver, but her movements were girlish and quick, until she hesitated at the edge of the creek and then turned to look upstream, raising one arm, as though for protection. Bethany followed her gaze, staring into the sunken shrubs of Jin's cranberry basin to discover the old woman who crouched among them, a dark, bent shadow who was somehow darker than the shadows she moved against. Bethany shivered, unhappily. She was afraid to defy her mother's ban on visits to the hut, and she was afraid of Jin and Josiah. But she often wondered about Kitty—such a beautiful, laughing girl simply was not capable of the ugly things which Eric whispered about her. Surely, there could be no baby.

Bethany forced the thought from her mind, turning away from the scene. She closed her eyes—there, that was better. Now she could look at what she'd come to see. She breathed more deeply, concentrating on her memories of the field in June, when dense mats of tiny, glistening white flowers had appeared among the familiar daisies and violets. Phebe called the new flower "sparkle," because it seemed to shine with perpetual dew. Then, as though fearful of subtlety, the field had dizzied itself with the aroma of wild mint, which bloomed throughout the clover, strewing its scent everywhere. The total effect was riotously sensual, nearly violent; the flowered field seemed not an act of nature but an opium dream.

Instantly, Bethany became addicted. On hot summer nights, she left her bed to come here, where sparkle gleamed and a drifting vapor of mint rinsed the darkness like an ethereal tide. Pale and bare as the moon, she danced in its light. Swirling, she twirled among flowers that were beautiful as she.

It was not enough. Wild—wild—she was wild and full of magic, and only the flowers knew. The breath of night against her skin, the mint-flavored dew that clung to her bare feet, the beauty of moonlit hair and eyes and flesh, these things were not enough. Bethany felt like a glorious secret, and she longed to be revealed.

One night she was dancing near the center of the field when a distant shadow flickered, suddenly. Bethany hesitated, searching the darkness. What if someone was watching her? The thought terrified her and yet was a tiny bit thrilling, particularly if she eliminated her family from consideration, since any one of them would have come running towards her, hollering wet feet and where are your clothes. Just as savage Indians or cutthroats would have come running, ready to cut or savage.

But none of that was happening. The shadow that had flickered was still. The air was calm with summer sounds. If someone was watching, then he was a stranger who meant her no harm. Someone who'd seen her pale legs flashing against the grass, who knew that her hair was the color of starlight, everywhere. Perhaps a shy woodsman, who only wished to admire her. Or a very kind Indian, who would never dream of carrying her off. He had seen all of her and knew that she was beautiful.

Is he there? Does someone see? the questions turned in her head as she whirled in trembling circles through the grass. Her pale feet crushed at leaves, releasing a gust of mint that rushed through her, saying yes. Sparkle shimmered ... yes, while shadows flickered, and what she saw and sensed and believed on those hot summer nights was yes and yes and yes. Bethany felt that the flowers had given her a special gift; greater than the force of their beauty was the thrill of possibility that engulfed her senses. To be watched and admired like the flowers. To dazzle and astonish like they did. Now she no longer felt like a secret but part of a glorious mystery.

A cold breeze swept through the field, destroying Bethany's illusion of summer nights and flowers. Reluctantly, she opened her eyes. The sun was setting over the farm, lowering through the sky as though it intended to personally congratulate the scene below. Watching the distant figures move towards the cabin, which basked in rosy glow, Bethany groaned; she was supposed to be inside, preparing supper. She started to scramble down from the rock when she caught sight of a dark shape moving rapidly across the border of the farthest field. When it grew large, Bethany could make out a horse and rider heading towards the farm. Whoever was coming had to be coming from somewhere else. That alone was reason enough to hurry home: for once, she wouldn't feel like the only stranger at the table.

Jupiter Laud reined in his horse at the edge of the clearing. Seneca Rane's cabin by the frog level was every bit as magnificent as he'd heard. Long a woodsmen's landmark in this isolated area, it was still the most impressive settlement for many miles. To Jupiter's way of thinking, the man who had created all of this was a visionary of sorts, though he doubted if Seneca Rane would agree with that opinion.

Jupiter was a visionary, and he knew it. But while Seneca was inspired by the land, Jupiter was inspired by men like Seneca. The wonder excited by his fellow colonists was genuine—he could stare unblinkingly at their weaknesses and flaws, yet still see the worth in people too busy or tired to see it in themselves, or in each other. He had traveled through the colonies nearly all his life, as a tradesman and sailor, as a clerk for Boston lawyers and as a surveyor who had measured land from New York to Virginia. Wherever he went, he touched men's lives. In return, he touched their purses only a little; he simply accepted the hospitality and occasional generosity of the house, wherever he happened to be.

Jupiter had no home of his own, and since the death of his sister Desiretta, he'd had no family, but his life had been rich and full, and if he had not been just a few weeks short of his forty-fifth birthday, he would never have considered a change. But wandering through life was getting a bit uncomfortable, with knees that were stiff from the damp, and bones that felt the cold quicker, now. Perhaps it was time to settle down somewhere and let life seek him out for a change. These thoughts were on his mind as he approached the Rane farm, which gleamed like treasure in the final rays of sun.

The hearth fire surged, as a chimney gust roared like storm through a golden surf, raising waves of flame; just as quickly, flames retreated, spilling sparks. Heads that had snapped in unison reversed the motion and bowed once more to eat. The table lantern beamed like a steady smile; by its light, Mary Rane watched Mr. Jupiter Laud. He was the most exotic-looking creature she'd ever seen—skin dark as cedar with a foreign sheen, stained by distant weather. Not tall, but sharply lean, and viewed between the double row of her children, he looked almost dangerously nimble—like a scarecrow waving not to frighten birds but to charm the corn. Mary blinked, and the image disappeared; ashamed, she mentally carved him an extra large slice of the apple pie she'd baked for dessert.

Seated beside her mother, Bethany was dreaming differently; on first sight, she had decided that the stranger was dark as a gypsy but carried himself like a prince, despite the fact that she'd never laid eyes on either. She watched as he worked through a second plate of food, feeling considerably less aggravated by her father's glorious harvest.

Jupiter ate with a growing sense of congratulation. The roast venison was tender, dense with juice. There were pyramids of corn, soft bread with blueberry jam, creamy potatoes clotted with gravy, while string beans, onions, and squash basked in separate, runny butters. He'd been right, as usual—Mary Rane was a bit of a visionary in her own right. Jupiter turned to compliment and found himself staring not at Mary Rane, but her eldest, quite beautiful daughter. Bethany stared back at him with unmistakable interest. Quickly, Jupiter returned his attention to his plate. He felt vaguely rattled. It was obvious from the sizzle in her gaze that the child was older than he'd imagined and simply short for her age.

"What news do you hear?" At Seneca's question, Jupiter pushed aside his plate. Now he would earn his meal. "Settlers have spread into the far western reaches of Virginia and the Carolinas; land can be bought very cheap there, though the Indians are said to be fierce," he said. "And King George has granted charter to yet another colony, to be called Georgia." Eric, Joshan, and Jeremiah questioned him eagerly, as dreams spun like cartwheels. "The Mississippi Bubble has burst," he said, going on to explain about shady schemes that Mary knew too well and a huge river that she couldn't believe. "A stage line now operates between the towns of Burlington and Amboy, twice a week. Soon it will be possible to travel between Philadelphia and New York in less than three days." Seneca nodded politely and roared with laughter, inside. "In the cities, white stockings stitched with posies are the rage, for gentlemen as well as ladies, and there is a fancy sort of paper that the wealthy are buying in order to cover up their walls." Now, Seneca roared openly, setting off a flood of suppressed giggles and shrieks that encircled the table, like an embrace.

Jupiter laughed as well. Then he raised his hands, as though to warm himself in their glow. "I have a need to speak of other things," he said, more quietly.

Phebe hiccuped into the deepening silence as Seneca considered the request, staring not at Jupiter but Mary. The children turned away, watching their parents. "Yes," Seneca said at last. "We would like to hear." And heads that had snapped and bowed now clustered near, pale daffodils curving towards the sun.

Once again, more slowly, Jupiter began to speak. He told them about other families he'd met, just like them, about the thousands upon thousands of cabins like this one, scattered in the separate wilderness of distant colonies. He made them see one hundred thousand lanterns glowing through a single forest, sharing the darkness of a universal night. He asked them to appreciate the heroism of friends they'd never met, to love neighbors they'd never see. Then he was still. There was a painful need to beg for more, until the Ranes discovered that his words had lodged in minds and hearts, so they could fill the silence, too.

"I wish that you would stay," Mary said to him at the door, wondering if she meant "forever." Accepting the blanket that she offered, Jupiter swore he could only sleep beneath the stars. His knees stiffened in protest at this lie, but he ignored their warning; for several hours, another part of him had been stiffening with greater urgency and he knew that neither it nor he would be improved by sleeping so close to Bethany Rane.

Bethany waved goodbye, still dizzy from the force of his words; he had made a picture of a world and then told her that it could be her own, if she would only believe in it. And she did believe Jupiter Laud. But that is not why she danced that night in her field of flowers; she danced because she knew that he would see.

She drifted onto the grass, bare and pale as the moon she moved beneath. She could not see him but knew that he must be there, watching. For an instant she felt terror, but a reminiscence of mint rushed through her, saying yes, sparkle shimmered yes and the shadows were flickering, everywhere. Whirling, she swirled and had nearly twirled to the center of the field when suddenly, she knew that they were there: ten thousand strangers, watching from the shadows. Farmers and tradesmen and lawyers and sailors—they saw her pale legs flashing in the grass. Wives and neighbors, city-folk in white-posied stockings—they knew that her hair was the color of starlight, everywhere. All of them watching, wild for her beauty . . . but only one of them moved through the field to meet her.

The shadows went wild. "Go get him, honey," a woman cried and Bethany moved first, to hold him. "You son of a—" "BEN!"

"—gun, you're getting something pretty special!" Tucked against his chest, she heard and smiled. It was going to be beautiful.

Their shouts were growing dim now, and Bethany could barely feel the blanket that prickled her bottom, though she knew it lay beneath. Jupiter was lying alongside her and his long, dark fingers were touching her breasts, they were touching her everywhere, teasing her gently, playing with her. On and on, while the strangers and the blanket disappeared because all of her feelings were rushing to the skin beneath his fingers; he was calling up senses from the depth of her bones, and she'd never *felt* so many feelings as they swarmed to sudden places, rising where he coaxed them, with the magnet of his touch. Her mind was growing slippery—it completely disassembled, and her body felt the changing, as it changed to sudden flesh . . . she was sudden, changed and ready . . . he had changed her . . . she was ready . . . ready to be changed by his flesh . . . ready . . . ready . . . really, she was ready . . .

For an endless time Jupiter caressed her, watching her eyes grow dreamy. His swollen sex nudged against her legs, crude knight banging at the convent gate, desperate for sanctuary. Deliberately, he pushed it down, returning his hands to her breasts. Years ago, a Portuguese sailor had confided this painless way to ravage a maiden's honor: prolonged sensual pleasantries would supposedly anesthetize the lady from more bestial thrusts. Exhausted from the effort of restraint, Jupiter felt his bestiality wane and wondered if he could summon up the meekest sort of thrust. Still he persevered, wishing that the sailor's instructions had been a bit more specific regarding minutes, hours, or days.

By the time he entered her, he'd driven both of them nearly insane. It is true that she felt little, but then for one full hour she had been pounding her fists against the grass, screaming YES, with no success; her aroused senses had simply boggled. For Jupiter, who'd felt more pain than he'd dreamed possible, the episode had been more traumatic than ecstatic.

Before dawn they made love again, beautifully; by daybreak, they were gone. Shortly after, Abigail discovered that her sister's clothes were missing. Up early for milking, Eric and Joshan heard her screams. The brothers woke their parents, still arguing about who should go after Bethany. There was only one horse. Finally, Joshan won.

Joshan Rane searched through the wilderness of New Jersey, moving southwest to the settlements of Greenwich and Gloucester, until he reached the Delaware River. Then he turned north, and headed for the thriving town of Burlington. He stopped at isolated cabins and posted signs at every meetinghouse door, but the answer was always the same: no one had seen his sister Bethany or a man known as Jupiter Laud.

As time passed, Joshan grew more weary and discouraged. He bitterly recalled Jupiter's eloquent words: "We live in a single forest, which is darkened by a universal night."

"But the woods are full of strangers," Joshan decided. "And I have lost my sister to one of them, a man who whispered dreams by lantern-light."

Three weeks later, Joshan returned to the cabin by the frog level, arriving late at night. Clouds hid the moon so he followed the creek, then cut through the fields—the pumpkins were ready, looked past their peak. Why hadn't somebody?—turned at the frog level and started for the cabin on the rise, which looked strange, distorted by the shadows. He wondered why there was no light.

Suddenly, he smelled them. Dense and heavy in the air lingered the stench of charred, rotting things. Dead things. The smell spooked his horse, so Joshan tied the frightened animal to a tree and continued on foot, approaching something dark and twisted which turned out to be the tortured remnants of a precisely measured and carefully laid frame cabin. He stepped, by habit onto the worn path marked by stones and followed that path into hell.

He found Josiah and Jin first; they had fallen together near the door still clinging to each other, which surprised him; he hadn't known they had loved each other so much. They were the only things he could recognize as he stumbled through the debris, and he began to believe that some of them escaped. Ran for help? Were carried off? But there was no evidence of Indian attack. No sign of any struggle. Just burned-out wood and blackened lumpish things which could not possibly be his parents, Abigail, or little Phebe.

At the sound of footsteps, Joshan turned eagerly and then felt a shock. Kitty was standing at the edge of the rubble, watching him. He felt himself slipping through time. She looked radiantly beautiful, and barely sixteen—except for the infant Rane, whom she carried in her arms. Still, the illusion persisted and he ran towards her, with hope rising like a lark: "Kitty! The others—where are they?"

Kitty's hand slashed the air; tiny bones snapped, and hope died, screaming. She pointed to the ruins. "All gone," she told him. "All gone." It was her only reply to his questions, and he never pressed her—having gotten the answer to one question, the others no longer seemed to be worth asking. Besides, years had passed since the games of childhood. Kitty was a stranger now and a woman of thirty years, who had just lost her mother and her . . . her friend.

All night long they sat together by the ashes. Joshan tried to accumulate some sense of the disaster, but his thoughts kept flying apart, shattering to miscellany. He found himself wondering if Jeremiah had ever caught the mouse which had been sharing their sleeping loft, if Phebe had finally lost her last baby tooth, which had been so loose when he left. He suddenly realized that his father had laughed more often than he'd spoken, and he wondered why he'd never realized that before.

At dawn, he began to search the ruins, forcing himself to collect an assortment of irregular blackened shapes which were nothing really. . . . Don't think . . . *my god* . . . making a pile near what once had been the back wall of the cabin. Then he sifted methodically through the ashes, his face lighting when he plucked out a find: his mother's hairbrush, barely singed. A piece of blue ribbon Abigail always wore in her hair. The cooking pot. A single perfect leg from the supper table which had somehow survived intact.

Kitty had watched him carry these things one at a time to the growing pile. She understood that this was Joshan's game, and she did not try to help him. Instead she tickled Rane's nose with a blade of grass until he woke, and then she kissed him until he giggled.

Rane was the best friend she had ever had—he always played with her and because of him, she'd never have to feel alone or frightened. Like yesterday. It had started with a terrible crash, the smokehole had been white with light even though it was the middle of the night. Kitty had shuddered and hugged Rane under her quilt, then she heard Josiah scream with joy, and her mother called out in confusion. Jin fell when the old man struck her, but then she rose to hurry after him, out of the hut.

Kitty had followed them, taking Rane because she took him everywhere. She saw it burning, the great hut where the white family lived. She could hear their voices inside, and then Josiah was at the door. Josiah was helping—no, he was laughing. It was a game, and he was laughing and pressing against the door, bracing a log against it, the way they all used to play prisoner together before the Anger. Now the fire made it all right again. Josiah was laughing the way she hadn't heard him laugh in years, and the white children were playing, she could hear their screams. But her mother was going to spoil it, she had caught up with Josiah, and now she wanted to stop the game. She was the Anger, and she fought him. He dropped the piece of wood, and the open door was full of fire as she pushed him in. Then she leaped in after him.

Kitty sat quietly behind the bush, watching the fire burn itself out. She was feeling very sad. Then she remembered that Rane was still here. And then the one called Joshan reappeared in the middle of the fireplace, and that was nice too. She was sorry she couldn't tell him about Josiah's game, but she knew he'd approve of her silence, because telling secrets was almost as bad as cheating. She was also sorry that none of the rest of them came back, because they could have played together now that the Anger was over, but she never asked Joshan to explain his trick to her, because that was *his* secret.

Now Joshan was burying all the treasure he had gathered, a piece of quilt, something silver, and the other things. He was making a great big hole and putting all of the people and all of the things into it. Then he put more dirt into the hole, until there wasn't any more of the hole left to put dirt into. Then he was done. He called to her, and she carried Rane to stand beside him where the hole had been. Joshan held her hand and chanted. She looked at him and felt happy. It would be just like before, only now Rane could play too.

Only the cabin had burned. The barn, crammed to the rafters with more food than they could ever use, was untouched, as was Jin's hut. All winter Joshan, Kitty, and Rane huddled together in the barn, sleeping in a single comforting mound near the horse and the cow and the brilliant, rotting harvest.

In the spring, Joshan rode into Gloucester Town to sell the horse in order to buy seed, cloth, thread and a needle, cooking pots, some shot and powder for his gun. By the time he'd finished his errands, the story of his misfortune had spread through the town, and he was glad to leave the company of well-meaning people whose sympathy could not hide the fact that they were afraid of him.

Joshan carried home the tools to make life possible, and the looks he had seen on the faces of Gloucester ensured that he did not leave the farm again for many years. He planted enough crop to keep them fed, but most of the fields that his father had cleared returned to wilderness. He played endless games with Kitty and Rane but never found the time to clear away the charred remains of his family's cabin, nor did he plant any marker to indicate their grave. They lived on in the ashes of the only life they knew, and while Joshan waited and Kitty played, Rane taught himself how to walk.

This was their world when Elias Brewster wandered onto the land near the frog level, nearly eight years after the disaster. He had heard about the tragedy of the Rane family in Gloucester Town, and now the tale had grown to include conjecture about the lone surviving Rane, who was said to be a brooding recluse. Some even swore that he'd taken up with an Indian woman. However, none of the gossip had prepared Eli for the racket of the frogs.

He came to the land in the summer, with breeches pushed above his knees and shoes that hung from a cord around his neck. Eli had followed the path of the creek, and his legs were coated with boggy, white sand. He stopped at sunset, intending to wash his feet and find some shelter for the night. Suddenly, he was surrounded by a thunderous croaking, and his green eyes danced with light. He rushed towards a crooked stand of trees to listen to the frogs.

"Oh sing unto the Lord a new song," he cried, exultant. Then he remembered why they were singing and blushed.

Eli was a preacher with a mission and a message but no ministry. As the protégé of Reverend Gilbert Tennant, he'd graduated from the radical Presbyterian Log College in Pennsylvania, which advocated the new evangelical approach to religion. The Presbyterian Council back in Scotland was horrified by the new colonial style of preaching and protested by granting New World presbyteries only to those ministers who had been educated in Europe.

So the Reverend Elias Brewster, with all the courage of his convictions and the fire of his testament locked up within him, had not been granted a congregation to preach to. "I would preach in a pasture, I would preach to frogs, but they say I cannot preach without a presbytery, so my sermons are my dreams," he muttered, feeling glum.

"Please, what is a sermon?" The voice was so close that Eli jumped, then peered into the thick growth of high-bush blueberry to his right. A pair of berries blinked, and slowly the remaining parts of a small boy appeared, as Eli traced them in the foliage. The two were so closely intertwined that boy and bush might have risen from the earth as one. As Rane separated himself from the bush to walk towards him, Eli could see why he had been so well camouflaged—the child's flesh was red-brown like the branches, and this particular branch was bare of even a single well-placed leaf.

Here is a fairly convincing argument for the theory of the Indian woman, Eli was thinking when Rane interrupted, repeating his question. *"Well,"* Eli replied, feeling quite cheerful, " 'sermon' resists a speedy definition, but I would be happy to explain at length and even demonstrate, maybe once or twice. Perhaps we might converse over a bowlful of supper, if you know of one nearby."

"My mother will be pleased to have a guest for supper. She loves company, but travelers rarely come here."

"The boy said she'd be pleased but did not mention that she'd be clothed," Eli reflected as Rane took his hand to lead him from the frog level. "And I cannot think of how to ask him." Instead he said, "What's your name?" "How old are you?" and "Is it far from here?"

Then Rane said, "Rane." "Eight." And "Yes."

On the barn floor they formed a circle, cushioned by what Eli hopefully identified as clean hay; as guest, he had gratefully accepted the honor of eating farthest from the cow. Rane had not dressed for dinner and his primitive aura was enhanced by the fact that he seemed not merely to eat his meal, but to prey upon it. Hands poised above the stew like idling hawks, then plunged so fiercely down to the chunks of rabbit below that Eli half expected to hear tiny death squeals rising from the bowl.

Stop it, Eli told himself, remembering that despite his appearance, Rane was the brightest boy he'd ever met. Lacking knowledge, he seemed to have studied his primitive world as though it were a book; Eli had already discovered that his knowledge about animal mating techniques was clinically astonishing.

The Indian woman was not only clothed but beautiful, Eli thought, though she was trailed everywhere by a rowdy cluster of chicks. As she ate, they settled around her except for a lone chick which still wandered in giddy, peeping circles.

"We ate their mother," Rane announced happily. "They needed a new one." Eli nodded sympathetically, trying to remind himself that the boy had only been talking about a chicken. As if to reassure him, Kitty bent to retrieve the wandering chick, her face glowing with maternal concern.

The cow lowed darkly, and Eli turned to stare at Joshan, who hadn't spoken all evening. He was fascinated by the man's eyes —pale blue endless lights in a face that was pale as frost. Even the way his flesh draped across his bones seemed shroudlike, though his manner seemed less suggestive of death than the complete absence of life. And yet Rane had told him that Joshan was his own age, barely thirty-one!

"Impossible!" Eli thought, with a sudden burst of fire. "Never have I seen such a spectacular array of heathens!" And in that instant he decided to stay, vowing to save them all.

Throughout the winter, Eli plied them with sermons. In spring the beleaguered heathens huddled and vowed to build him a church.

They laid the foundations on the wooded rise above the frog level while Eli rode through the neighboring wilderness, spreading the news: "A church built upon cinders and ash, a new dream rising not to mark where old dreams died, but where they lived." So inspiring was his eloquence that the Cinders Church was famous before it was finished. The nearest church was almost one hundred miles away, though as Eli had pointed out to Joshan, so were most of the people. "If we build a church, people will settle here," Joshan replied. "They will walk up my father's path, just as he dreamed. That path is the only part of us which remains, but I think it is enough."

They worked through the summer in every spare moment, and for the first time since the fire, spare moments were very few. Joshan had planted a full crop this year, and Kitty sewed new clothes, while Rane adjusted to wearing them and learned to read as well. Eli always stopped work to preach to visitors curious to see if rumors about the wilderness church were true. Everyone volunteered to lend a hand, perhaps inspired by the oddly angled and distinctly precarious-looking structure that was rising from the ashes of a perfect cabin. Finally the builders admitted that they lacked Seneca's gift for carpentry and invited everyone who passed by to a roof-raising party set for August.

On the evening before, Joshan, Eli, Kitty, and Rane stood by the frog level, gazing at the church on the hill.

"It looks beautiful in the moonlight," Joshan declared and Kitty sighed, agreeing.

"It looks *better* in the moonlight," Eli said, trying for tact.

"It looks like it's going to fall down," Rane said firmly. "I think that it *is* going to fall down."

"Nonsense, boy," Eli replied. "Haven't you ever heard me preach upon the power of true faith?"

"Yes," said Rane, sounding a little frantic, "and I wouldn't want to trouble you for a repetition. Perhaps I'll go to study the Bible now, before it's time for bed." He made a rapid exit, hoping that tomorrow, a few of the truly handy would show up among the faithful. Kitty followed, turning back to wave and smile. Then they disappeared.

In the quiet, Joshan turned to Eli. "Will it last?" he said, wanting to cry, "Will *we?*"

"Yes," said Eli, watching him. "Yes." As though it is possible to know.

That night, Kitty's dreams were filled with sunlight. Rane

dreamed of carpenters. Joshan and Eli dreamed of each other; they had been lovers, for nearly six weeks.

Lacking religious affiliation, lacking even a congregation, the Cinders Church began to hold services on August 26, 1742. Despite architectural eccentricities, it survived, perhaps because its very existence was a monument to survival. In its early days, the Reverend Elijah Brewster often preached to a congregation composed of Joshan, Rane, and a beaming Kitty, but when the weather was good, settlers scattered throughout the interior of south New Jersey would make the journey, often traveling for more than a day to reach the church at the frog level. It was a time of great religious awakening in the colonies, inspired by revivalist-style preachers whose concept of Christian duty was daunting and ranged far beyond the popular colonial assumption that faith and an occasional trip to church provided exemption from the Hell that evangelists now described in vivid, ghastly detail. But many traveled to the Cinders simply because it was the first time they had been able to celebrate their faith in church.

They traveled west from isolated cabins on branches of the Mullica River; they traveled north from the cedarwood banks of Salem County, and south, some from as far away as settlements on the Toms River. Everyone who came had to maneuver through thick wilderness forests with boggy, sandy soil which trapped the wheels of their wagons. Every one of them walked up the path that Seneca Rane had made alone in the wilderness and marked with matching stones. And everyone entered a wooden-frame cabin with four walls of slightly different heights, and a roof that roamed between. On a breezy day, the east wall shimmied; even when the door was bolted shut, it let in snow and wind, and mice. But no one complained.

As the people came, Eli and Joshan added an additional room to the barn they'd converted into a cabin. Kitty took care of the younger children there, while their parents attended services. Eli continued to tutor Rane, and in 1743, he filed a petition in Pendleton County to become Rane Brewster's legal guardian. Joshan put one hundred acres of his father's land into cultivation and improved the quality of life at the frog level by purchasing Benjamin Franklin's new invention, a heat-efficient firebox which came to be known as the Franklin stove. Worshipers who traced the path of the winding, cedarwater creek in order to find their way in the Cinders began to call it Sabbath Creek, and soon that name began appearing on maps of the region. The beavers simply built another dam.

Nearly thirty-five miles northeast of the frog level, in the settlement at Cooper's Ferry, New Jersey, Jupiter Laud heard the story of the Cinders Church. Jupiter and his wife Bethany operated a ferry service between Cooper's Ferry and Philadelphia, a connection for travelers bound to New York. He also operated the tavern house on the ferry landing, where his passengers listened to him talk for hours about ideals and rights. Jupiter often repeated the story of the Cinders Church with inspiring effect, but the original names had become garbled, so though Bethany wept when she heard, she never knew that the tragedy was her own.

One year after the Cinders opened for services, a new family —one which Reverend Brewster would always refer to as his first multitude—came to live on the land surrounding the frog level. Daniel Honeyman had bought one hundred acres of land located east of Sabbath Creek. He arrived with his wife Mags and an ever-growing collection of boisterous, complicated children. Daniel's dream was to build a tavern house which would service the growing stagecoach trade. Daniel had heard that companies planned to add east-west routes across New Jersey, in addition to the ones already operating between Philadelphia and New York. According to his calculations, the old Indian trail that Seneca had traveled would provide the route, and Daniel intended to provide the hospitality.

The tavern house he built there was two stories high, of sturdy pinewood that soon weathered gray. From the outside, the building looked bleak and cheerless, and the dark, forbidding land which stagecoach drivers had to ride through in order to get there inspired its name: Dark of the Moon. Inside, there was little comfort but a lot of welcome. Travelers slept two or three to a bed on a first come, first served basis, but in the large taproom downstairs, Daniel Honeyman offered forty-two kinds of drinks made from rum, beer, and whiskey in any combination his guests could bear to swallow. In a small corner room, Mags Honeyman created a parlor tearoom, where the occasional female traveler might take refuge from the rowdy tavern house atmosphere. And Honeyman children swarmed everywhere, providing so little help that Daniel hired young Rane Brewster to work at the tavern in 1745, because business was growing.

The colony of New Jersey was still rapidly changing: the College of New Jersey (later Princeton) had started to hold classes in Newark; in southern New Jersey, Caspar Wistar built the first glass-producing factory in the colonies. But now, the land surrounding the frog level was changing, too. It had become a destination, a place where people came to share their prayers and news and gossip. Colonists began to settle in neighboring areas, drawn by the church and tavern house which stood less than nine hundred yards apart. And now Daniel Honeyman claimed his dream, as the wilderness became Frog Level.

——— *In the 1740s religion was extremely important to colonial life; so was drinking. When the Reverend George Whitefield toured the colonies in 1740, he delivered a sermon in New Brunswick which attracted a crowd of about seven thousand people. Since there were only about sixty thousand people living in New Jersey at the time, this figure represents more than ten percent of the entire population in the colony. Colonial liquor consumption was setting its own records: over two million gallons of rum were imported every year, and small towns often possessed as many as six taverns. The hospitality offered by New Jersey was already uniquely important as travelers streamed through the colony on their way to New York and Philadelphia. New Jersey's reputation has never been enhanced by its convenience as a roadway—an eighteenth-century critic described the colony as a "barrel tapped at both ends, with all the live beer running into New York and Philadelphia." New Jersey partisans might have added that, in the process of tapping, the barrel gets screwed.*

The Honeyman Family

1748 ———

Dark of the Moon

THE FEBRUARY day came to break, but its sun could not rise: that huge stone sky was an open grave, no place to see the light. Winter was howling at Dark of the Moon, baring its crystal fangs. Driven shards of ice scratched like claws at the tavern doors. From the drifted ice at Sabbath Creek, the storm came leaping, as snow battered windows which were already glazed with frost. The pinewood timbers rattled, the chimney was embattled, and the wind was breath enough to blow the house down. Outside was a beast that wanted in.

Inside was a light. On a cedarwood chest near the largest bed in the only second story that Frog Level could boast of, the candle blinked, almost sleepily. It shined upon a mammoth pile of quilts, humped in the largest bed. This mountain trembled, heaved, and bounced. There was nothing else to see.

"Whoo—whoo—" The noise was buried within but clear, as the mass became volcanic. It shuddered, rocked, and tilted towards the east—a witness might have crossed himself, or offered it a virgin. "Whoo—whoo—whoo—WHOOP—" The mountain gave a skyward leap and, presumably, erupted. One corner of the quilt became a tunnel; two noses peeked out while mouths hung open, gasping.

"Mags, darlin', that was ecstasy, thought we would have altogether smothered if we'd kept at it much longer." Daniel Honeyman kissed his wife's pink nose.

"Cold," she panted, and her nose retreated.

"My love, this winter means to kill us," Daniel replied happily. "But if the air hadn't been so icy we might never have thought to do without it. Being buried like that was a lovely change, don't you think? Warm and safe as a mother's womb, but nothing to breathe so we're feeling light and—"

"Dizzy," Mags said firmly, despite muffling layers of quilt.

"Yes, darlin'," he replied absently, reaching up to take the candle from the chest. Cupping one hand over the tiny flame, he wriggled back under the quilts. "Now Mags, just let me take a quick peek at you—there's little enough pleasure in life."

"Time to get *up*, Daniel." She warned him, but she also quickly scooted upright to face him; their heads raised two curving arches into the sagging quilts and just as quick, where the mountain had heaved, there rose a patchworked heart.

Like its visible pulse, the candle blinked; with a visible ache, Daniel gazed at his wife. After bearing nine of the healthiest, noisiest children he'd ever laid eyes on, Mags was more splendidly curvaceous, more abundantly glorious than ever. Skin like glossy cream, though it was flushed now and damp from exercise, which had also made her hair even curlier than usual—an auburn halo rippled with gold, like the heart of a flame. Though she swore she'd had freckles as a child, now he could only see dimples—in her cheeks, her knees, even her toes. Her eyes were green and sparky; if he watched closely, he could see their color deepen, like the sea. Watching now, his ache became a throb.

"Lovely Mags," he said softly, "You must be made from heaven, for your beauty is a miracle."

"Phew," she replied, blowing out the candle. "*Out,* Daniel."

His hand rustled in the darkness; then he nestled close, coaxing: "Look my darlin', a lovely big feather from the pillow your blessed auntie gave us. Just a short tickle, love, you do like it so and then maybe—" WHAM! Creamy dimpled feet connected squarely with his backbone, and Daniel whizzed beyond the quilts, beyond the bed and nearly out of the room. At five foot four, he was nearly four inches shorter and some fifty pounds less splendid than his wife.

"What a love she is," he thought as he picked himself up. "Landing me so near to my clothes. And bless her heart, my jacky's gone soft from the shock." As he pulled on his pants, she curled beneath the quilts with a cozy sigh. He turned at the door to blow a kiss. "The children will get along just fine without you in the kitchen, dear. Sleep as long as you like." He hurried away so she couldn't see his smile. If that didn't pull her out of bed fast, at least he'd wrecked her dreams. Daniel hurried along the narrow upstairs corridor, careful to tiptoe past guest rooms where stagecoach travelers were sleeping in communal clusters. "Cozy for them," he decided, shivering. Pausing near the stairs by the last pair of doors, he rapped sharply on them, as though to call out demons. Unearthly shrieks announced that he'd succeeded, but Daniel was already halfway down the stairs, out of range. Clearing the last four steps in a single bound, he leaped towards the double front doors and flung them wide, welcoming the day to Dark of the Moon.

WHAM! Wind cut, ice bit, snow drove him back—in short, the beast attacked. Daniel was knocked flat, but managed to crawl behind the doors as he struggled to close them, kicking back drifts that had already closed upon his ankles. The doors creaked and nearly buckled, but he squeezed them shut to close the bolt and leaned there, panting. A terrible, familiar noise made him whirl: sons and daughters were thundering, pouring down the stairs—Betty, Sally, Felix, Titan, Mareen?—nine Honeyman children, booming and crashing, like an incorrigible tide.

"Bless you, my darlins', for we're sure to die today!" he shouted, but it was as though winter had dragged him out by the ankles to bury his cries in white. They surged over, around, and through him—Ben, Matthew, Cedar, Micah, Mareen?—screeching and fighting and laughing, as he floundered towards Mags, who bobbed serenely in their wake.

"That blizzard's a killer," he said, clinging to her.

She smiled, and handed him a baby.

"Micah?"

"Mareen," she replied. And as they floated towards the kitchen he pinched her bottom gently, just for luck.

The guests upstairs would be stranded here, for no coach could travel in this weather. And Rane Brewster could not possibly have traveled here from the Cinders in order to tend to

the chores. As his children tormented the kitchen, their breakfast, and each other, Daniel worried about these things. Even if
he could get to the barn himself, he had only the vaguest idea
what to do once he got there. From his days as a coach driver
Daniel knew how to tend a horse, but a tavern house seemed to
require a bewildering assortment of animals in which he could
muster little interest, beyond the sincere hope that they would
not die. Instead, he counted on Rane, who simply submerged
in the churning sea of Honeymans doing what ought to be
done, and undoing those things which had been done twice, but
not correctly.

Just the thought of the boy cheered him now, for it reminded
Daniel of one of his pet theories, which he was generally fonder
of than his worries. Rane's background was a bit of a puzzle, but
given the celebrated nature of the Rane-Brewster household,
most of the folks living nearby were disinclined to press the
question. Joshan had dealt with the issue years ago by declaring,
"Rane is family. So is Kitty. So is Eli." This was not particularly
enlightening, but it was touching and memorable, and properly
touched, the congregation at Cinders Church had memorized it
to recite on cue whenever the subject was broached by an out-
sider. So, as Daniel frequently pointed out to Mags, it simply
did not matter that less than sixty people lived within a day's
ride from here; when those people have banded together to
feign indifference to a question that they are dying to know the
answer to, then they surely have become a community.

"DANIEL!"

What a lovely scream she has, he thought.

"THE DOOR!"

He turned to hear a quiet, steady thumping at the kitchen
back door, which faced the barnyard. Cautiously, he opened it.
A pair of large, startling gray eyes stared at him; the rest was
white.

"Rane. It's Rane," said Rane.

Hauling him into the kitchen, Daniel brushed uselessly at
crusted layers of snow and ice. "Good heavens, boy, how did
you—"

"I enjoy walking in the snow." In his icy white cocoon, Rane
seemed as cozy as a beaver in its pelt.

78

"Lord Almighty, I wish you'd been here when this murderous blizzard nearly ripped the very doors from our poor house. Snow indeed! None of us will survive this. You did the chores then?" he added quickly, unable to hide his relief.

"Everything," Rane replied. "And Kitty sent some extra eggs."

Daniel took them gratefully. The Honeyman chickens were prone to depression, particularly when the inn was full. Mags had joined Daniel's efforts to remove the snow, but the boy still glistened. "Stay with us until the storm passes," she pleaded.

Rane shook his head. "My books are waiting, and knowing that I can spend a full day reading will make the trip home seem short." He turned at the door. "Thank you for the invitation—I'll come again, tomorrow."

Before they could think how to stop him, he vanished into the storm. "Rane, wait!" Daniel called. "Does the Cinders still stand?"

From the distance they heard his rare, infectious laugh: "When the blizzard struck, we moved there for safekeeping— even Kitty's chickens. A church that defies gravity can surely stand a bit of bad weather."

"God bless the lot of you," Daniel cried, and heard a faint "goodbye." Shutting the door, he turned to Mags. "Well, that's done," he sighed, as though he'd actually done it.

Upstairs, sounds were unmistakable. Mags snatched up the eggs and hurried across the kitchen. "Felix—check the fires. Betsy, Sally, help me with breakfast. Benjamin— Where is Ben?" A surge of screams, as children fought for the honor of snitching first. The plop of an egg breaking. A squeal as someone slipped on the dropped egg. The steady tramp of feet on the stairs, as an inn full of hungry guests descended. Unified protests as someone opened the front door.

Humanity stirred, was squeaking; then, it began to roar. Sound came streaming through every room, turned dazzling, coalescent. Noise rose like a sun through Dark of the Moon, and the rafters perceived it, trembling. And Daniel Honeyman watched, believing: the light was Life.

By noon, the taproom was positively radiant, for the stranded travelers had so lavishly remedied themselves against the cold that they'd forgotten they weren't going anywhere. The bedlam was friendly; laughter and arguments erupted with equal ferocity. The perfect mix for a tavern house, Daniel thought proudly as he watched from behind the long wooden bar. Behind him, the kitchen door creaked open, but only whispers and giggles emerged. Betsy and Sally, he guessed at once. First-born, and twins at that, but his worry about telling them apart had diminished when he realized he'd seldom get that opportunity—they were bashful, but not quiet, he reminded himself, as the giggling increased.

Daniel pounced on the door and snatched them both into his arms. Eight years old, he thought, and already soft and pretty as their blushes. On them, his straight brown hair was satin-sleek and filled with lights. Their green eyes lacked Mags's fire, but that sweet gaze made the dimples that danced in their smiles all the more entrancing.

They snuggled against him, hiding their faces. They giggled. "We need to wash the dishes," Betsy whispered, while Sally giggled.

"Darlin', let's wait until the guests have finished their lunch," he said.

"We need to wash the *breakfast* dishes," Sally whispered, while Betsy giggled.

"But the guests are using those now, we've only got one set of —oh," Daniel stopped short, as truth dawned. He waited.

"We forgot," they whispered, pale and still; two heartbeats fluttered against his chest, like one pair of tiny wings.

"Don't worry, now," he whispered, giving them a squeeze. "Just give them an extra scrub after lunch and we'll call it fair."

Blushing and giggling, they fled, and Daniel settled in happily behind the bar, confident that the guests were in no condition to question the condition of their plates. Seeing the twins had reminded him of his favorite theory and the taproom always provided an ideal noise to theorize by, when the mix was right.

Despite their number, each Honeyman child was unique in coloring except for the two sets of twins, who looked like each other but no one else. Daniel could hardly boast of looks like Mags. His hair was sturdy, forgettable brown, and his eyes were gray-green, unless he stood against a summer sky; then they were blue. The endless number of changes rung upon these genetic bells had lent novelty to a process which might have become a lesser miracle by the time the fifth or sixth Honeyman had come along, and it also inspired Daniel's theory that each child was not only a blessing but a special souvenir of the encounter which produced it. Mags took a dim view of all this, pointing out that his chance of pinpointing the occasion seven times in a row was small. But Daniel never doubted his theory, and to him his children provided the proof.

Weren't Betsy and Sally perfect examples? Mags had been full of blushes on that occasion, although she was not much given to timidity. "In a tree?" she had asked, looking shy. And he'd hardly been able to coax her high enough to suit him, though she'd cheered up once they were nestled in a thick branch that was swaying deliciously.

"Like the birds, darlin'," he'd cried. "What a lovely time they must have on a windy day." The breeze sighed, the soft, sweet leaves were trembling and didn't a pair of doves suddenly swoop through the branches, nearly pitching them out at the moment of ecstasy? How could Mags look at Betsy and Sally and deny such stunning proof?

The kitchen door burst open and three-year-old Micah rushed him, colliding knee-high. Now look at that, Daniel thought, scooping him up, dusting him off, and wiping away streams of tears. Already the boy was beginning to laugh again. Mags said she could actually hear him laughing inside her the night before he was born. Bright curls with a thick gloss and eyes of shining, reckless blue provided the proof here, for such a laughing, shining child could only have been created with the aid of a full churn of butter. How they'd laughed that day, slipping and sliding and tasting her . . .

Another burst, and four-year-old Matthew crashed into them, knocking Micah down with him.

Wiping away fresh tears, Daniel had time to recall his only ecstatic encounter with livestock: "The cow?" Mags had said, looking grim.

"Look at Daisy's lovely wide bum. Just hop yours right up there too, darlin', while I get a stool. Whoa Daisy." The smell of the barn had turned Mags quite wild, and she wound up squirting warm milk into places he'd never thought it could go. Daisy had stepped on him twice, which probably accounted for the painfully red shade of Matthew's hair. But it was Matthew's eyes which Daniel treasured the most, for even Mags admitted that such huge, trusting brown eyes could only be found on a cow.

He looked into those trusting eyes and into eyes of buttered blue. "Scoot," he said. They scooted, and Daniel leaned back into place, less comfortably. The problem with all this theorizing was that a man began to ache from it.

By midafternoon, ballads and fistfights were breaking out in the crowded taproom, but the other children hadn't appeared, so Daniel was feeling a bit blue. Then he spotted five-year-old Cedar whisking up the stairs with a load of fresh linen. Ah that glorious dark-red hair; as always, it was wild with waves. Daniel couldn't look at her without a surge of pride, for he had plotted six months to achieve the tresses which inspired Cedar's name. Though Mags was no sailor, that color perfectly matched the dark cedarwater that flowed in Sabbath Creek, in which they had nearly drowned during the ecstasy of Cedar's making. Sort of a christening, Daniel thought with a desperate moan. At the sight of those sheets, his ache had begun to throb.

Easing from behind the bar, he headed for the front room that made Dark of the Moon unique among tavern houses. It had been Mags's idea to create a cozy parlor here, so that ladies who were forced to travel by stagecoach might have some alternative to the boisterous atmosphere of the taproom. She presided over the tea table herself, encouraging genteel, feminine conversation as she served delicate cakes and cookies and poured dark tea into real china cups. Daniel glided to the parlor door, thinking, "just a peek at her, for jacky." And looked in.

Leaning to fill an empty cup, Mags caught his look, and paused. She had been good and proper, though not technically a lady when she married Daniel. Her mother had provided no sexual information whatsoever; she knew nothing and was therefore open to any suggestion, things less innocent brides would never have permitted. By the time she'd realized that her marriage was unique, she had already produced five children and was disinclined to change the arrangement, since she loved her husband very much.

Of course, she realized that things had gotten out of hand, and she planned to set him straight soon. She had almost done so five years ago when Daniel had arranged an excursion to the settlements downstream. That day she'd spoken to him quite sharply about the general impropriety as well as the specific impossibility of what he suggested. Indeed she considered the matter well closed. But then the rain let up, the wind died down, and it seemed a shame to waste the canoe.

Remembering that day, Mags looked up to smile at Daniel, but he'd disappeared. She could hear his footsteps clearly, as he climbed to the second story. In her hands the teapot trembled, and she nearly dropped a cup. Actually, she wouldn't mind a bit of rest, with feet propped up on the huge down mattress and a sweet pillow for her head; there was little enough pleasure in life. She tiptoed up the stairs, stopping to smooth her auburn hair by the mirror near the end of the hall, then hurried to the farthest bedroom. The children would never miss them.

For several minutes the hall was quiet. Then the door of the linen closet cautiously opened, and Cedar Honeyman popped briskly from within. Shoes in hand, she creeped on tiptoes down the hall to press an ear against the bedroom door. She heard her father, talking fast.

"Now here it is darlin', you've been bound hand and foot and tied to stakes on the beach by some terrible man—I don't know, dear, he's not important—and the tide has come in but hasn't drowned you, just left a layer of sand all over your beautiful naked body—well I suppose the man took them off you, didn't he? Anyway, there you are when this handsome barbarian pirate comes across you, and he can hardly believe his eyes. This beautiful sand woman carved by the sea, but maybe it isn't, you know? So he stands over you watching and you can feel his staring eyes, but you know he's a barbarian, so—because I just *told* you he was—so you're afraid to cry out 'cause he'll chop your head off. Now this barbarian can't resist you and he's got to brush just a bit of sand away, real careful, to see if you might be real, so he pulls out his feathers— Well, of course he's got them, barbarians love feathers. But the thing is, being a pirate and having to carry a sword and all, he didn't have no place to carry them so he got himself fixed up sort of special, you know,

Instead of getting his ear pierced like the others—cause that would be a silly place to put feathers, dear, wouldn't be no good to him there—he had his jacky pierced here and there, barbarians being able to stand any kind of pain, and he's got feathers all over it, dangling from tiny rings. Now we got to cheat a bit here, so keep your eyes closed. Now here he comes towards you, and his jacky's just a fluttering—all different colors, darlin'—and he bends down to clear off one sweet corner of your titty. Now don't make a sound or he'll kill you. Here we go . . . *oh* that's nice—"

Cedar eased a crack in the door, watching intently. Mother was all tied up on the bed. She had no clothes on. Father was standing beside her. He had no clothes on. He was holding big handfuls of feathers from Aunt Hetty's pillow, and he was holding jacky, too. It looked like a dust mop and he scrunched down to clean up Mother's titty. She giggled, and wiggled. Jacky poked up out of the feathers, and they wiggled, too.

"Now darlin', you got to be quiet and hold on, 'cause this is going to be a long one. Jacky needs a bit of tickly, too . . . just a tiny *oo*—slow, now—"

Cedar carefully closed the door. It was going to be a long one. Good. She scurried to the top of the stairs and hurried down them, putting on her shoes at the bottom before she ran for the parlor. At the door, she stopped to stamp her foot as hard as she could, five times; then she hurled herself at the unguarded tea tray. From all four corners of the tavern house Honeyman children responded to her signal, thundering towards the parlor, but she still managed to polish off most of the shortcake before they hit the door.

Honeyman hospitality made Dark of the Moon a favorite tavern house among New Jersey travelers, as the stagecoach traffic through the settlement of Frog Level steadily increased throughout the 1750s. Although the French and Indian War still continued on colonial frontiers, British victories in the Ohio valley region stabilized living conditions there, and a new type of wagon began to struggle along the boggy Indian trail which had become known somewhat optimistically as the Flying Horse Pike. This new wagon was known as the Conestoga; its hemp bonnet (which stretched over curving bows to shield up to six tons of cargo) became a familiar sight, as more settlers poured into the western territories. (Not every family could afford such transportation; one family from Salem County simply packed their children into a wheelbarrow and traveled to Ohio on foot.)

At the Cinders Church, the Rane-Brewster family continued its peaceful existence, although Kitty's chickens continued to multiply, as did the Reverend Brewster's congregation. On Easter Sunday in 1755, nearly sixty people attended service at the Frog Level, some of them listening from wagons pulled alongside the church. At Dark of the Moon, the Honeymans continued an existence that had never been peaceful. Three more Honeyman children came to be. Twin sons, Payson and Job, were born late in 1748 (sandy hair and sea-green eyes, and each arrived with a single barbaric tooth). Baby Hannah was born two years later. A floral beauty with eyes of mint-green, she was credited to an indiscreet fling in Joshan Rane's wild-flower field.

There were now fifteen cabins built within five miles of Frog Level, and seven miles to the northeast, in the Pine Barrens, an ironworks known as the Audry Foundry started operations in 1750. More important, the land itself experienced another change. The first path here had been the Indian trail. Then had come the path to Seneca Rane's cabin, worn by a single pair of feet. Now a third path was visible in the earth, one started by Rane Brewster, who walked it every day, taking the shortest route from the Cinders to his job at the Honeyman tavern house. Both families began to follow his trail between their homes, and through the years a ribbon of soft dirt emerged through the densely wooded forest.

At the midpoint of this rough trail there was a large and glorious scarlet oak tree with branches that were strong and receptively angled, curving outward like fingers from the palm of an outstretched hand. It was the kind of tree that reminded people what a forest is all about. Its sprawling grandeur seemed to insist that life is a series of special occasions, and this was a message that no Honeyman could resist. In 1754, Felix, Titan, and Benjamin Honeyman met secretly beneath this tree to discuss their future. Two weeks later, the three oldest sons of Mags and Daniel Honeyman put on the glamorous uniforms of the New Jersey Regiment. In blue coats dressed with red, buckskin breeches, and gray stockings, they marched off to the barracks in Trenton. In that same year, daughter Cedar's fate was decided, amid the flaming branches of the same scarlet oak.

Shortly after her eleventh birthday, Cedar fell out of that tree, spraining her ankle. Unable to walk, she lay on the ground fighting back tears and panic. Not only was she forbidden to stray this far from the tavern alone, but she had been specifically warned against climbing trees. She had a habit of climbing straight to the top and falling out, because the branches there would not support her. Now, if she screamed for help, somebody might come, but she would be in trouble for disobeying. But if she *didn't* scream, she would be found by huge bears and eaten. These were hard choices, but they inspired the vision of her parents finding her eaten-by-bears remains. Inconsolable in their sorrow and guilt, they would carry her on a white satin bier to the Cinders where everybody would cry, and her rather extensive list of sins would be forgotten in the glorious clamor of her eulogy. The only problem was her having to be dead. She was trying to think her way around that when Rane found her.

He had been on his way home when he found her sprawled among the fallen leaves, looking furious. She started at his footsteps, then burst into tears. "I thought you were bears," she said. Rane couldn't think of any response to that, but he bent down to dry her tears, noticing as he did so that Cedar's famous hair clashed violently with the bright leaves.

He sized up her predicament at a glance, hoisted her into his arms, and carried her back to the tavern in silence. The details of her accident were forever blurred by his vague announcement, "She fell." During the subsequent rush for bandages and pillows, Cedar found that she had become not an angel perhaps, but a temporary heroine of sorts, and she knew just who had saved her. From that day forward, she was in love with Rane.

A more temperate spirit might have called it infatuation, but Cedar was quite prepared to die for love, now that she had discovered it. She knew that Rane was smart, but what alternately enticed and worried her most was that he was quiet. No one in her family could be called that—even Betsy and Sally were only shy. Rane wasn't shy at all, but he never spoke without thinking. As a result, he spoke less and thought more than anybody she knew. Cedar decided that he was deep, and loved him even more for it. But she realized that such a careful, deliberate man wasn't likely to fall in love without patient and energetic shoving.

Lovingly, she devised a series of schemes which attracted his attention, if not his adoration. One week after her rescue, she baked him a pie filled with red peppers. She tied the cows' tails together. She hid the eggs. She stole a chicken. Nothing worked. Discouraged, she slackened her efforts and was content to follow him everywhere he went. Though her somber, adoring eyes proclaimed her a martyr for love, he really didn't seem to notice her until she fell through the railings of the hog pen. As Rane carried her back to the tavern, Cedar reflected that the course of their love seemed to be progressing in a circle.

She gave up. And then slowly, she grew up. Five years after she fell in love with Rane, Cedar returned to the great scarlet oak, determined to renew her attack. That year, she won him. Cedar believed that the tree conspired in her passion. To Rane, it seemed a symbol of their love. For both of them, the difference hardly mattered. Cedar Honeyman and Rane Brewster were married on August 7, 1759. And then slowly, life at Dark of the Moon began to go wrong.

————— *In 1758, the New Jersey Assembly finally solved its Indian problem, by establishing the first reservation in the New World, in Burlington County. In return for a permanent home, the Lenni-Lenape relinquished all rights to other land in New Jersey, except for hunting and fishing privileges. The reservation was named Brotherton, in hopes that all men would be brothers. The Indians lived there for nearly fifty years, trying to make their living from the land. But rumors of starvation and illness spread. Soon they were heard in Stockbridge, New York, where the Lenni-Lenape who had migrated there invited the New Jersey Indians to come "live with us and eat out of one bowl and one spoon." In 1802, when the Indians from the Brotherton reservation accepted that invitation, there were fewer than two hundred left alive to make the move.*

1763 ———

The Tree of Hearts

ON AUGUST 7, 1763, her fourth wedding anniversary, Cedar Brewster rose before dawn. She left the cabin where her husband and son still slept and traveled through a morning dusk of indigo; in this blue darkness, her dark red hair was glowing, livid as a bruise. She walked along the back trail, towards the great scarlet oak tree. *Passion's conspirator,* she thought. *Symbol of romance.* She was carrying an axe.

At the base of the tree, she looked up suddenly, as though she expected to see herself as a child, falling from that highest branch through a tunnel of scarlet leaves down and down. Falling. Falling in love. At eleven, she had only felt the limp, reflexive terror of a child; it had not occurred to her to fear the impact, or the possibility of pain. "The sensation of falling was enough, then," she thought, remembering. Falling in love—it was as though she'd suddenly invented a religion. She'd thought of dropping to her knees, of lifting up her head, her heart, her gates; to be stoned or eaten by lions on Rane's behalf was a constant temptation. Remembering her earliest attempts to win his love, Cedar smiled. "Rane didn't even know that I was alive, but it didn't matter—*I* loved somebody. That was enough, then." But when her god had proved reluctant, she'd been wise enough to cloister herself and meditate.

Cedar put down the axe, and walked into the middle of the trail; she reached up to grasp the curving branch which hung across it. At sixteen, she had emerged from meditation; she had

89

walked to this tree, to this very branch, with an offering for her god. Then she had taken a short barnyard stroll. On that day, Rane believed that he fell in love with her at first sight, as if by magic. Cedar never corrected this impression. The details simply didn't matter—because now, they were falling in love together. Every day was a miracle. No, they were the miracle, and the days merely witnessed it. Two hearts that had been reservoirs of feeling suddenly turned into fountains, as love turned them liquid—eyes brimmed, minds floated off to sea where they surely would have drowned, except that suddenly they were unsinkable.

Tilted by love, they had showered each other with small acts of tenderness, like precious, iridescent bubbles. The tree aided this miracle; in its wide, branched crook they left love-tokens, surprises, messages. "He left flowers for me," Cedar remembered, "and poems that he'd copied from books. Finally, he left poems that he made up, himself. He wrote poems about *me*." Though she hated baking, she'd spent five hours making sugar cookies for him; despite the result, he'd eaten every one. "I remember waking up in the middle of the night, simply because I was too happy to sleep. Rane wasn't a god, anymore—he was my hero. And I was his heroine." His eyes. That was the best. Staring into his eyes was like falling into his arms. Every day she stared into his clear, gray eyes; every night, she dreamed of falling into his arms. Even more exciting was watching him secretly, as he watched her. Nothing had ever touched her the way his eyes did. As she watched his eyes, her flesh suddenly knew how it would feel to be touched by him; it was the closest she would ever come to fainting. At love's miraculous fountain, the water grew very warm and began to steam. Because in spite of his eyes, Rane would not touch her as a lover.

Then, he had written the letter. Cedar searched the crook of the tree, but there were no messages today. Four years ago, there had been his message—and hers. His had been the letter:

> My dear friend,
> How I wish I might express those sentiments which you have already carved upon my heart! But in doing so, I would assume a privilege which might not be

mine. I write, instead, to tell you of the full circumstances of my birth: My mother is of Indian blood. My father was one Josiah Ross, from Leeds, England. He was Seneca Rane's father-in-law.

I hope that you will consider very carefully the implications of these facts which I have presented, in briefest fashion. I also ask that you inform your parents so that they can best protect your interests. I would plead my case to them in person, but the friendship which has existed between our two houses might be damaged by such an encounter.

I will await a sign from you in the usual place. If I do not hear from you in two weeks, I will not embarrass you, nor torture myself, by remaining in this county.

In response, she had carved his name within a heart, upon their tree. Then, she was in his arms. The details simply didn't matter, because they were touching. They were loving. And soon, she was no longer dreaming about falling into his arms, because she knew that love was more like a rising. His hands, his mouth, the maleness of him, he would lift her with his touching. He was feeling, and she was feeling and they were rising, rising where she fully intended to go. She loved his hot, ragged breath. She loved the slippery pressure of his tongue against her breasts. She loved to watch him rise, to touch the shape that swelled beneath his trousers. Every day, she watched him rise; every night, she boiled. The fountain of her miracle was blowing steam. Time, it said to brew the tea, to boil the egg, she was a rolling boil, a whistle of steam. *Reeaaady!*

Her father had never been one to miss such things: "Now, we've set the wedding for August," Daniel told her sternly. "You won't be finished with the cabin before then." Rane was building their home at the cranberry basin, near the tree of hearts, "and with Mags in her blessed condition"—her mother was unexpectedly pregnant—"I won't worry her with this. Young lady, I'd rather see you slither down that aisle like a bitch in heat, than see you strut in like you already been at the cream. Don't shame your mother, Cedar." She nodded, piously, and passed along the news to Rane. For the next few months, a bit of religion had gone back into the miracle.

On August 7, 1763, the indigo light was draining from the sky. In the August heat, the dawn was nearly white. Cedar picked up the axe; light glinted in its blade. She stared at the scarlet oak, remembering why she had come. Turning suddenly, she threw the axe into a nearby bush, and hoisted herself onto the lowest branch of the tree. Then she began to climb.

Several hundred yards down the trail, Rane Brewster was traveling towards the great scarlet oak, on his way to Dark of the Moon. In the distance, he could barely make out the dark, curving branch that dipped over the trail. Four years ago, in spring, he had first seen Cedar Honeyman. It was not that his heart had pounded or that lightning had struck him down, but simply that, after he had seen her, he stared for such a long time at the place where she'd been—what his eyes had seen, his mind simply wouldn't believe. That night, he had passed beneath the dipping branch of the tree and a lace handkerchief fluttered over his head. Suddenly, he remembered where he had seen that dark red hair, before: scarlet leaves. Something about bears—Cedar!

Untying the handkerchief, he had headed home with senses reeling: the coincidence of seeing her that day and finding the handkerchief seemed miraculous. That night he placed it under his pillow for safekeeping, intending to return it the next day. (The handkerchief was scented with cedar oil.) By morning, having dreamed about Cedar Honeyman all night long, Rane was ready to admit that he was in love.

On his way to the tavern, he had stopped to pick daisies, which he wove into a chain. Hanging them onto the branch where her handkerchief had been, he headed for the barn to wait out the day in agony. She would find the daisies. She wouldn't find the daisies. She would be furious because he had stolen her handkerchief. She was secretly engaged. By afternoon, he was near despair. Then Cedar walked by—her glorious wavy hair was woven with daisies. His daisies. And now his heart was pounding, for the first time in his orderly, rational life.

The next morning, he'd left a copy of one of his favorite

poems. That night, she was waiting for him beneath the tree. "I could not believe it, at first," Rane thought, remembering. "I could talk to her on any subject—Greek, science, poetry—and she seemed interested. Then one day I realized, she is interested in *me*." He smiled, recalling her sugar cookies, and the terrible spelling errors in her notes. He had memorized those errors, and was always careful to repeat them in his notes, so as not to embarrass her. "To me, she was completely perfect. I was the one with the ugly secret."

Then had come the torture of the letter. He, Eli, and Joshan had all agreed that it must be written, but how they had suffered, waiting for the answer. Even Kitty's spirits had dimmed, as though suddenly eclipsed. For two nights, he had returned home to tell them, "No news." On the third day, he had approached the tree at dawn—the soft buttery light of May, but a dawn not so different from this. He had stopped to search the crook of the tree: No news. He felt a sinking in his stomach, but would have said it was his heart. Turning to leave, he saw the heart carved below. His mind racing, he stooped to read the inscription—then came a scream and something fell on him.

She said that she'd tried to write a note, but the words wouldn't come. She'd hidden in the tree so that she could watch him and then call out his name. He would look up and she would gracefully descend, but instead she had fallen on him. She told him this in less than six second's time, as they lay in a crumpled heap at the base of the tree. To Rane, who had only thought of panthers for one terrifying instant, it was enough that Cedar loved him, that she was in his arms.

Unfortunately, Cedar, who'd been falling for six years, mistook it for the perfect landing.

On August 7, 1763, Cedar Brewster was climbing the branches of the great scarlet oak tree; she heard footsteps, as her husband approached. Four years ago, those same footsteps had sounded, turning her dizzy with excitement. Now, she cringed at the sound, and turned her head away. It might have been the passing of a judgment, not a man.

On the trail below, Rane paused, as he always did, to look at the heart Cedar had carved: RAIN, it said. "At the time, it seemed a simple spelling error," he thought morosely. "I did not know that she meant it as a prophecy." He continued walking towards the tavern.

Cedar listened as the sound of his footsteps grew faint, then disappeared. "If he loved me," she thought, "he would have known that I was here." It was another test that she, or he, or love had failed—one of them had failed, and all had lost. Hiding her face against a branch she began to weep.

Four years before on August 7, 1759—their wedding day—everything in her life had started to go so wrong. At the wedding ceremony, Cedar had tried not to slither. With glassy eyes, and big, bright smiles, she and Rane had danced down the entire length of the taproom floor, they had nodded and made greetings, and Rane had even stopped long enough to help her mother, who was nearly six months pregnant, into a chair by the door. Then he grabbed Cedar, and they danced their way back up the floor, laughing and waving as they slowly, steadily made their way to the door at the back of the taproom: Hero and heroine off to a happy ending, miracle heading for the flesh. They were nearly out the door when—

"Babylon! In thy drunken revels, thou art fallen!" A stranger stood in the taproom entrance. Clothed in white, he was pale as a shroud in the shadows.

Music and laughter stopped, as a wary silence settled on the room. Mags was seated closest to the man. As she rose, she yanked the shawl angrily across her belly. "I don't know your name, sir," she said, "but this is my husband's tavern and my daughter's wedding day, and you'll not be welcome here if you mean to bring trouble."

"I bring Jehovah's wrath to godless places and preach the righteous path," the man shouted in reply.

"Be damned to you and your path," Mags cried. "God is no stranger to this house."

Suddenly, he stepped forward, pointing at her belly as though he were aiming a pistol: "I curse thee, woman! Satan will attend the birth of thy child, for a house so quick to claim the right of heaven should welcome the opportunity to taste of Hell." Then he wheeled, and ran from the tavern before anyone could stop him.

Mags screamed, and the crowd surged forward. Rane could

hear their excited voices: "Thirteenth child." "She's carrying her thirteenth child." Such foolishness, he'd thought. He was only worried by the sound of Mags screaming. Because she could not stop—she screamed and screamed. The party broke up quickly, but Cedar was too frightened by her mother's condition to leave. Afraid that Mags would lose her baby, she spent her wedding night at Dark of the Moon. Rane refused to leave her, so he spent an agonized, sleepless night in the boys' dormitory room.

After months of feverish waiting, it was hardly the celebration they had planned. Nor was the next night, or the nights which followed. For Rane, who had risen and risen and risen, could only fall. Cedar felt betrayed. For him, she was still rising. If he loved me, this could not happen, she decided. He does not think that I am beautiful. She grew rigid with shame. But she looked angry, as she spoke through clenched teeth: "Rane, for heaven's sake, can't you . . . cheer up?"

"*Please,* Cedar," he replied, although he could not think what to ask for.

Neither of them had believed this was possible. Rane's study of animals and Cedar's education at scattered doors and windows had provided no precedents. "Maybe we should try feathers," she suggested.

"I *beg* your pardon," Rane replied, as coldly as he could. To him, she seemed determined to make things worse. For example, he found her attitude of familiarity nearly contemptuous: "Jacky," she called it. Whose was it, anyhow?

Though this crisis finally passed, the problem recurred again, and again. The scars inflicted during the earliest days of their marriage blazed a trail which they could not help but follow. At love's miraculous fountains, the water turned bitter and tasted of tears.

Beyond their cabin door, the world was simply going wrong. Felix, Titan, and Benjamin Honeyman were reported missing with half of the New Jersey Regiment after a battle with French forces in New York. This news, received less than two months after the wedding, sent Mags into premature labor. And though her family didn't know it, Mags had never been able to get the intruder's curse out of her mind. After a difficult birth, she looked at the tiny, dark bundle that Betsy placed into her arms: "Too small to live," she thought with relief. Without even asking if it was a boy or a girl, she had drifted off into the most peaceful sleep she'd known in weeks.

Slowly, she understood that her son would live. She named him Jerad, and tried to forget her fears. He fought so hard to live. As Mags nursed him, Jerad lay calmly in her arms, staring with his strangely beautiful gray eyes—so light in color that she might have called them silver, if there'd been any shine. But they were completely opaque—Mags felt as though she was staring into fog. She did not regain her health after his birth. Although she knew it was foolish, she became convinced that Jerad's greedy eagerness for her milk was the cause—as though he was draining her vitality in order to survive. Although she eventually resumed work, Mags lost the bloom that had always made her so beautiful; her body sagged. She felt old, and chilled.

Her family fussed over her constantly, but they never discovered her fears. Jerad was growing into the only well-behaved Honeyman baby that anyone could remember. He did not babble; his first word was part of a sentence: "Come *now*." But it was his dreadful poise that worried Mags the most: She'd never known a baby that didn't wiggle.

Mags grew more withdrawn. She could not stop her fears, and she could not live with the thought that she did not love her child. In that sense, Jerad broke her heart. She died less than one year after his birth, and Daniel had no measure for his grief. "Mags was life itself to me," he insisted. "How can life die?" In his suffering, Jerad seemed his last link with Mags, and he cherished the boy. To all of the Honeymans, Jerad became a very special child.

Cedar and Rane tried to adjust to the changes. Betsy and Sally continued to manage the kitchen at Dark of the Moon, but neither of them could be persuaded to come face to face with a guest, so Cedar took on her mother's duties. Her brothers Micah and Matthew helped Daniel in the taproom, while sister Mareen became her unwilling assistant in the front parlor. The youngest children tried to help, and Rane worked from dawn to midnight every day, quietly saving them all. At home, their problems continued. Cedar's temper grew worse; she was furious, frantic. Rane grew silent. And as days, months, then years took them lower and lower, Cedar began to believe that she was falling once more. Falling apart. "It must be so," she decided. "Because there is no single impact, just a constant sense of crumbling."

On August 7, 1763, Cedar Honeyman Brewster sat in the great scarlet oak. She had come here to chop down the tree. Instead, she had climbed, as though to search its branches for what she had lost. Now, she was simply afraid to get down. But her son Daniel would be waking up soon, and there was work to do at the tavern; these thoughts forced her slowly to the ground. Resting at the trunk, she noticed the other heart that was carved there: MAGS, it said. One month before her death, Daniel had lured his wife to the tree: "A tree of hearts, for lovers, darlin'. You'll always be my sweetheart."

Mother was everybody's sweetheart, Cedar thought bleakly. When she was alive, I was never afraid, for long—"Mother, there's a huge spider under my bed and it's going to eat me—Mother, there are *bears*." Then she would take me in her arms, and the bad things would disappear.

Now, Cedar reached out to stroke her mother's name, carved upon the tree. "Oh Mother," she said, "I'm so frightened. The bears and the spider—are they *me?*"

A shaft of sunlight struck the blade of her axe and made the foliage dazzle.

On the afternoon of his fourth wedding anniversary, Rane asked the four youngest Honeyman children to clean out a shed behind the barn. Then he left the barnyard; he went to the wildflower field and picked some daisies to weave into a chain. When he returned, the shed was fully ablaze. Although Jerad had miraculously escaped, Payson, Job, and Hannah were trapped inside. Rane rushed into the flames, but he was too late to save the children.

As he carried their bodies into the yard, Cedar came running. She stared at the bodies. She stared at Rane, who was still clutching a handful of daisies. Then, she began to scream.

II. Micah and Celia

In 1764, two more Honeyman hearts were carved upon the great scarlet oak tree. The first was made for Mareen Honeyman, shortly after brother Matthew left Dark of the Moon to take an ironworker's job at Audry furnace. Matthew returned for a visit, bringing along a clerk from the ironworks, Miles Early. Mareen instantly developed an interest in the process of making bog iron, and the entire family was treated to Mr. Early's lectures: "Such a hammering rings through the forest as ore is pounded at the forge. Charcoal from the pines doth light the furnace fire and shells from the coast provide flux. All of nature combines in our blessed New Jersey, with a mighty pounding and a great, fiery blast that can be heard for miles. Towns will spring up everywhere in the pines, and fortunes will be made a-plenty. Mr. Audry plans to build a church and school and houses enough for all—a model community will rise near the furnace."

Mareen found Mr. Early's peculiar blend of poetry and pedantry irresistible, and soon he carved her name upon the tree of hearts. And this heart sealed the fate of Micah Honeyman, for Mareen's wedding was attended by workmen from Audry, led by their foreman, with his wife and seventeen-year-old daughter. And that daughter was none other than Celia Hartshorne. The Hartshornes were one of the few families living in a real house at Audry, where most of the workers were still crowded into barracks. This distinction, plus her father's exalted position, had enabled young Celia to develop the notion that she was princess of a small but admiring kingdom. Her parents encouraged this sense of supremacy, and she arrived at the Cinders less a celebrant than a reason for celebration.

Watching Celia settle her layers of ruffles and lace onto a bench, Cedar Brewster wiped the dirt from her son Daniel's face, and steamed. There was simply no reason, she decided, for anyone to come here looking all flouncey and ribboned, when no one for miles could afford such foolishness. Celia reminded her of a fancy china doll, and Cedar longed to bash that pretty head against a wall.

Standing at the front of the church with the wedding party,

Micah took in a very different impression. Huge brown eyes adorned the porcelain perfection of her face. Pale blonde ringlets bounced and shivered. Curves nearly burst her ruffles. Cedar later blamed his infatuation on a sweet tooth, and she may have been right, because Micah instantly perceived Miss Hartshorne as some luscious confection. His mouth watered and his hands twitched. He was blinded by hunger, if not by love.

Micah tried to pay some attention to the ceremony, but his thoughts kept drifting back to Celia. Never had he seen a woman in something so frivolous as a pale pink dress, particularly one edged with ribbons and lace. (Actually Mrs. Hartshorne had been a seamstress's apprentice before her husband had taken the job at Audry, and she had hoarded a supply of finery for her daughter's dresses.) At the wedding party in the taproom, Micah watched Celia acknowledge the advances of several workmen from Audry who were bold enough to ask her to dance. She gravely refused each one. Micah approached to introduce himself, claiming the temporary privilege of host in order to justify his impudence.

Miss Hartshorne nodded gravely, then turned to her parents: "Mother, Father, this is Mister Micah Honeyman, whose hospitality we are enjoying today." They nodded gravely.

Micah broke the silence by asking her to dance.

"I do not dance," Celia replied, offering no further explanation.

After several moments of awkward silence, Micah excused himself. That afternoon, he made a fatal error in judgment: not only was Miss Hartshorne beautiful, but she was different, and Micah assumed that anything different had to be interesting. Unfortunately, the only interesting thing about Miss Hartshorne was that she *was* different. But Micah never stopped to consider whether or not he really might want her; he simply set out to get her. His pursuit was not easily accomplished because Audry was several hours' ride from the tavern. But he visited Matthew and Mareen several times during the summer, sweating hot nights in the men's barracks and developing a hatred for the ironworks which would last for his lifetime.

With each visit, he learned new things about his love: "I do

99

not run," Celia told him, gravely. "I do not go out into the sun."
"I do not eat cheese," she informed him one day, without warning. However, there was one thing that she *did* do, and Micah was thrilled to discover it. Miss Celia Hartshorne received his lusty advances with a passive congeniality that astounded him. He had been given nearly full access to her mouth, neck, and ears. And one night, he had even managed to get one hand on her breast. Micah dared not push her further when she was only a short scream from her parents' ears, but these brief samples intensified his craving. Though Celia's mind held no inner depths for exploration, her body promised an endless variety of shallow pleasures.

Micah returned to Dark of the Moon in August, and searched out his father, who was in the taproom. Jerad was with him, as usual. "Look at this, Micah," Daniel cried. "Why, the boy's only four, and already he can tap a keg perfectly. You're nineteen years old, and you still make a mess of it."

Micah smiled, uneasily. "You'll be taking my job if I don't watch out, Jerad." Jerad looked at him calmly without speaking, and reached up to hold his father's hand. "Father," Micah continued quickly, "I would like to invite a guest, Miss Celia Hartshorne, to spend some time here, with your permission, of course."

In the darkened taproom, Daniel strained to see Micah's face. "Am I going to lose you too, son?" he said softly. "Only Cedar, and Betsy and Sally will be left . . . and my Jerad, of course."

"I'll never leave Dark of the Moon," Micah said. "I love this taproom as much as you do."

Daniel smiled. "Then by all means, invite your young lady for a visit. I don't know much about this sort of thing—you'd better check with Betsy and Sally." Daniel rose to leave, then stumbled against a chair.

"*This* way, Father," Jerad said firmly. "I won't let you fall down."

Daniel looked at Micah, embarrassed. "Guess my eyes aren't what they used to be," he muttered. He leaned against Jerad's arm, and they walked slowly from the room.

Watching them, Micah felt shaken. "I've been gone so much, lately," he realized. "I wonder how long he's been hiding this?"

But as he walked towards the kitchen, his mind turned once more to Celia's breasts. Betsy and Sally were preparing lunch. "Father has urged me to invite Miss Hartshorne for a visit," he told them.

They whispered and giggled. "Of course, we'll write her parents a note, right away," said Betsy. Sally immediately sat down at the table and produced a pen. As she began to write, Betsy said, "Oh Micah, are you in love with Miss Hartshorne?"

"Well," Micah said uneasily, "I'm quite desperate about her."

Sally looked up from her work. "How many *c*s should I put into 'occasion'?"

"Two, dear," Betsy replied. "Micah," she continued, "we must think of some ways to entertain your guest. Perhaps Cedar—"

"Let's not tell Cedar, just yet," Micah said hastily. "Celia is easily amused."

Sally looked up, again. "How many *p*s should I put into 'company'?" she asked.

"Two, dear," Betsy replied.

As Sally added the letters, Micah looked over her shoulder, pondering the result. "Are you sure?" he asked.

"Of course," Betsy said, smiling at Sally. "Two together, always—just like us."

"How sweet," said Sally, quickly sealing the letter. Micah handed it to the stagecoach driver that very afternoon.

The Hartshornes answered Micah's invitation promptly, for they had not been blind to the obvious prosperity of the Honeyman tavern: They dreamed of finer things for their daughter than they could provide, and Celia dreamed of that, too. She soon arrived at Dark of the Moon with a large assortment of finery and a cool grave nod for everyone.

After a leisurely toilette, Celia appeared each morning in the parlor, where she accepted the compliments of the ladies and attracted an unusually large crowd of men to the tea table. She did not offer to help in the kitchen. "I don't think she cooks," Micah explained to Betsy and Sally, who whispered and giggled and didn't care a bit. She didn't help with the guest rooms, upstairs. "I don't think she cleans," Micah pleaded to an icy Cedar. "I don't think she *helps*," Cedar hissed, and Micah retreated.

After Celia had limply accepted a week's worth of furtive pawings, Micah pantingly suggested an excursion beyond the tavern house walls. Miss Hartshorne did not stroll too far as a rule, but Micah tempted her with the tree of hearts, which by now had become a local tradition. All summer long, young men who lived near Frog Level had carved their lovers' names upon that tree, and Celia was not about to pass up such an honor.

Micah took the wagon, for though Rane and Cedar made what they considered to be a short walk every day, he knew Celia would tire easily, and he had no intention of exhausting her. Micah hitched the wagon to a tree, at the edge of the frog level. The frogs were in full voice this afternoon, and Celia seemed to actually appreciate the effect. "Ooooh," she exclaimed, clinging to his arm. Flexing his bicep, he felt her breasts jiggle against it, as they climbed the back trail towards the tree of hearts.

Although most couples attended this ceremony together, a few of the hearts upon the tree had been carved in secret, apparently by victims of unrequited love. One such heart belonged to Peavie Voohris, whose father's farm was a few miles south. Peavie had no known suitors, at least not until her name was carved upon the tree, when she became the subject of much discussion. As a result, the dumpy, rabbit-faced girl became something of a romantic legend, instantly desired by several suitors who were sure they wanted what another man was pining for. Since Peavie was the oldest of five dumpy, rabbit-faced daughters, her original admirer—who was apparently too shy to reveal his identity—was considered something of a Samaritan.

As they stood before the great scarlet oak, Micah pointed out Peavie's heart. "There was a terrible fight about who was going to marry her, in the taproom last week. She'd better make up her mind, soon." He took Celia's pale, perfect hand into his own, and moved around the tree. "There's the first heart ever carved—Cedar made it for Rane. She misspelled his name," he added, unnecessarily. Celia was a perfect speller. "There's the one that Miles Early carved for Mareen, and there's—" Micah stopped suddenly, as he stared at the heart carved with MAGS. For a moment, he hated Celia almost as much as he hated himself. What was he doing with this vacant beauty whom his mother would have found ridiculous?

As if in reply, the sun moved quickly from behind a cloud and Celia turned radiant, shimmering before his eyes like a fabulous dessert.

Her skin gleamed like fresh-pulled taffy; he thought of squeezing and twisting, of burying his hands in chewy and soft taffy breasts. He saw chocolate eyes and cherry lips and thought of sucking her flesh, letting her sweetness dissolve slowly onto his tongue. Her plump, golden body looked like pastry fresh from the oven. Inside, the filling would be juicy and warm, sticky and sweet. He thought of his sex as a long, stiff tongue sliding into her, to feast—his stomach growled, his mouth watered and his sex turned hard as a bone.

Micah stepped up to the tree. "May I?" he asked, holding out the knife. Celia nodded happily. As he slashed the bark, she watched with a growing sense of victory. This would make it official. He was announcing to the world that she would be the mistress of Dark of the Moon. He truly loved her. Admiring his good judgment, Celia believed that she almost loved him, too.

Micah finished carving the heart and stepped back to inspect his work. Impulsively, she kissed him and was surprised to find that his arms were closing around her with considerable force. He bent to kiss her neck, and she shivered. Gently, he led her through the dense foliage behind the tree, where after a few yards, there was a patchy clearing large enough for two. He covered the ground with a blanket and spread Celia upon it, removing her wrappings of ribbon and lace. Soon she lay before him, wholly bare. Her creamy surface quivered like fresh custard.

Licking his lips, Micah proceeded to devour her. He squeezed and licked and nibbled her breasts. He nibbled her toes. He nibbled her neck. Then he chewed and slurped and pummeled her breasts. Grabbing two handfuls of firmly round bottom, he flipped her over to sample the rest. He gobbled her up and he gobbled her down. He rolled her around. He buried his face in her neck, her breasts. He buried his face in the hair of her sex. He was gasping, moaning, calling her name . . . but though

Celia was as tasty as he'd dreamed, her lack of passion reminded him that dessert is almost always served up dead.

"Celia, my love . . . are you there?" he said hopefully, jiggling her breast.

"Mmmmmhh?" she replied, sounding drowsy.

Encouraged by this, he entered her with a passionate cry. He pounded away, and pumped, but it was like thrusting into a mound of divinity fudge—painless, but a desolate form of exercise. After a lonely interval he came, almost dutifully. Afterwards, as she cuddled placidly in his arms, he was already regretting his impulse.

The evening sky was dark when they emerged from the glade, moving cautiously onto the back trail, although there was little chance of their being seen. Celia raised her face for a final kiss at the tree of hearts, and Micah realized how little he really wanted to kiss her. As he brushed her lips, a branch snapped noisily, in the bushes nearby.

"Micah, dear—"

"Shhh," he hissed. They stood together in the darkness, listening to a quiet that did not seem peaceful.

An animal, Micah decided, or perhaps just his overworked brain. He guided Celia down the trail towards Rane's and Cedar's cabin. As they passed it, Micah could see the hearth fire through a window, and he heard the sound of Daniel's laughter. His fears seemed silly now, and he tried to shake them. Celia chattered incessantly, and Micah realized that he was in terrible trouble. She was busily planning her wedding costume, and the apparently extensive trousseau which a bride needed to take up residence at a tavern in the wilderness of New Jersey.

"Cedar will help me," Micah thought desperately. "She might kill me, but even that would be a help. If only I hadn't—" he stopped suddenly. This time he was sure there was rustling in the foliage behind them. Celia still babbled. "Hush!" he commanded her. They huddled in the center of the path, staring into the vast gloomy banks of the frog level which lay ahead. The frogs were roaring, and oddly angled trees cast jagged shadows through the mist that arose from the bogs.

Listening to the frogs, Celia stepped backwards, with a shudder. "Micah—" she whined.

"Be *quiet,* Celia." He shook her roughly. There was no more rustling. Maybe it was just a joke, Micah decided. "Rane? Cedar?" *The frogs!* He whirled, and stared into the mist, where the croaking had suddenly ceased. The hush was deadly; it was as though the night had caught its breath.

"*Run!*" He screamed at Celia, who was clawing at his arm. He pulled her along, heading straight for the frog level.

"No-no-no-no," Celia wailed, dragging her feet.

As they entered the mist, the frogs suddenly began to croak again. The noise seemed to surround them, and Micah could barely hear himself think—Celia! He grabbed her arm just in time to keep her from slipping into a bog. Terrified by the noise of the frogs, she began to fight him, trying to escape. Micah picked her up and tossed her across his shoulder as he tried to run.

Bouncing there helplessly, Celia looked around them: BEAST! giant, flaming red monster with wings like a bat and burning eyes and a huge thick glowing thing sticking up, *ugh,* huge red thing pointing out of his belly—he was coming straight at her. Yes, he wanted to stick that big hot thing in her—"Aaiiieeee," Celia screamed, grabbing Micah by the throat.

"Aaaaiiiiiiieeeee."

"Celia, *stop* it," he gasped, but she slapped at him wildly.

Cram it—stick it—ram it—he was coming, and that thing was so *huge* the tip of it was glowing with fire so thick, so thick, and he was going to cram it in, he was *laughing* and holding it up, he wanted to jam that big hot poker right between her legs— "*AAAAAiiiiiiiiieeeee.*"

Her fingernails gouged Micah's cheek, as he stumbled into a tree. But he managed to struggle blindly out of the frog level, dragging Celia with him. They ran to the wagon, where the horse had nearly unhitched itself with fright. Celia was still screaming, but Micah threw her onto the seat and leaped up after; he bolted for home, without looking back.

When the wagon was safely within the barnyard, Micah tried to comfort her. "It wasn't anything," he said, although he wasn't so sure of that himself. But Celia clung to him, trembling and sobbing so helplessly that he found himself talking about marriage and wedding gowns and everything he had sworn not to, in order to calm her down. Soon, her tears began to subside.

Betsy and Sally helped Celia to bed, and stayed by her side

through the night. Betsy left only once, to check on Jerad. Although the child was sleeping soundly, his bedroom window was wide open, filling the room with the chilly night air. Betsy closed it and then tucked Jerad's quilt more securely around him. As she did so, she noticed that his night clothes were slightly damp. In the darkened room, she smiled and stroked his hair, convinced that the dear little boy had once more wet his bed.

Celia Hartshorne never told anyone what she had seen that night, but she swore that she would never go near the frog level again. She was so distraught that Micah agreed to a quiet, early wedding, after which he joined her at Audry village, living in a small cabin near her parents while he worked at the forge. Celia would get over her fears, the Hartshornes assured him. Soon, Micah would be able to return to Dark of the Moon.

Andrew Voohris was not so lucky. The loving father of five dumpy, rabbit-faced daughters had been found lying dead at the base of the tree of hearts. His knife was still clutched in his hand, and the freshly carved heart bearing the name of his second eldest daughter solved the mystery of Peavie's secret admirer. Some who saw Andrew's body thought he'd been mauled by a cat, but others believed it was a bear. None of them liked what they saw. Even when enraged, animals rarely mauled only the face and heart, leaving the rest of the body untouched. This beast hadn't killed for hunger, they decided. It had killed for pleasure.

The fears of the woodsmen did not interest the daughters of Andrew Voohris; when their father was buried, they wept uncontrollably by his grave, convinced that he would still be alive if they had only been a little less plain.

Micah Honeyman never returned to the Dark of the Moon. Less than two years after their marriage, he and Celia Honeyman were killed in a road accident. Their horse stampeded on a lonely country road, crushing their wagon against the trees. Their infant son Micah, Jr., was sent home to Frog Level to be raised by Betsy and Sally. His aunts adored him and marveled as he grew, for the child looked exactly like his father, in youth —except that little Micah had been born with a severely crippled leg. Rane Brewster made a crutch for the boy, and soon little Micah was speeding through the grounds and falling into the creek. He looked so much like his father, with glossy chestnut curls and blue eyes, that Cedar could not look at him without feeling furious at the tears which formed in her eyes.

Cedar and Rane Brewster continued to supervise operations at Dark of the Moon. Cedar's hair was still violently red. Although Rane was over forty, his looks hadn't changed except for the expression in his eyes, which was much older than his years. Betsy and Sally worked on, giggling in the kitchen, one pair of dimpled, blushing spinsters who wore matching gray dresses and white pinafores. They sewed all of Jerad's and little Micah's clothes—breeches and short frock jackets—and marveled at how little work they had to do for Jerad. The boy was uncommonly neat. Since the age of twelve, however, he had hardly grown at all. Jerad was only six years older than little Micah, but the boys were never playmates. Jerad stayed with his father Daniel, who had gone completely blind by 1765; and the following year, his hearing had begun to fail. He was completely dependent upon Jerad, who devoted his life to taking care of the old man who grew weaker with each passing day.

In spite of Daniel's illness, the taproom at Dark of the Moon became the center for Frog Level's patriot activities. In 1774, a group of patriots from the river town of Greenwich, in nearby Cumberland County, burned an arriving shipment of British tea. In the taproom, there was general celebration: though most men were reluctant to support the idea of total independence, hoping instead for some compromise in power, anti-British sentiment was running high. In time, however, many took that final step that Thomas Paine demanded: "Ye that dare oppose not only tyranny but the tyrant, stand forth!"

There were a few exceptions. In a series of careful, lucid discussions, Rane Brewster expressed grave doubts about the legality of the patriot activities and pointed out concessions in the new taxes imposed by the British. He had not intended to champion the crown, but this was not a time for reasonable men. As the patriot cause became popular, he was branded a Tory, and Cedar was finally forced to warn him away from the taproom for his own safety.

The crowds there much preferred to hear the speeches made by Rane and Cedar's son, Daniel Brewster. Though only sixteen, he dominated the room with his angry, stirring words. Just listening to him made a man feel braver and more important. His grandfather Daniel Honeyman had asked the colonists to search their hearts and won their sympathy for the patriots' cause. His father had appealed to the colonists' minds and won their resentment. Now Daniel Brewster appealed to their pride and won both their hearts and their minds. When area residents gathered to form a militia, they asked Daniel Brewster to be their captain, and he proudly accepted their command.

Although Jerad Honeyman sent his regrets, due to his father's failing health, the rest of the young men from Frog Level marched off to war in early 1777, under Captain Brewster's command. They did not have far to march. Both armies had converged on New Jersey, turning it into a battleground. There were battles at Springfield, Princeton, and Freehold; there were battles at Red Bank and Trenton. And everywhere, there were armies—advancing, or retreating. In between, they encamped, and hungry soldiers from both sides searched the New Jersey countryside, desperate for food. By 1778, the war had moved dangerously close to Frog Level.

———— *On July 18, 1776, the colony renamed itself the state of New Jersey, by self-proclamation. That same month, a British fleet of more than one hundred ships dropped anchor off Sandy Hook, and New Jersey braced for invasion. By December, the advancing British army had chased the New Jersey Assembly from Princeton to Trenton to Burlington, where it was hastily adjourned. The state became the site of more than a dozen major engagements and whether loyalist or Tory, New Jerseyans suffered from the constant presence of the enemy. On March 21, 1778, the British staged a surprise attack on Hancocks Bridge, in Salem County. In retaliation for local support of General Washington's troops, three hundred British soldiers stormed the house of William Hancock, where a home guard of thirty volunteers, mostly old men and boys, were sleeping. There were no shots fired to awaken the guard. The British bayoneted everyone within the house, killing all thirty men. This type of deliberate massacre was uncommon but throughout the hamlets of southern New Jersey, the British had succeeded in making their point: Anyone could be next.*

1778 —————

The Woods Around

ON OCTOBER 11, 1778, Captain Daniel Brewster and most of the south Pendleton County regiment marched towards Frog Level. At midday, the autumn air was crackling; in earth and sky, the colors flourished, bright as flags. On a day like this, it was easy to think of men as heroes. In a world made for cheering, soldiers seemed to ride, as though upon prancing stallions; their uniforms were dashing, and their buttons were brass. Silvered bridles seemed to jingle as chargers beat a proud noise on the land. A virile breeze was stirring, scents of horse and leather mingled with exploding metal. On such a day, a man did not have to fight in order to sense his victory.

Therefore, it did not matter that Captain Brewster and his soldiers more or less strolled into the area wearing an assortment of ragged uniform pieces, that they disbanded (or really, wandered off) into different directions to visit wives and friends. At least, it did not matter to Captain Brewster. He was Frog Level's Revolutionary hero, chosen by friends and neighbors at the tender age of eighteen, to be the leader they would follow into battle. On a day that made its own parade, he was returning home—young, handsome, and an undisputed hero. Daniel Brewster simply did not need a horse.

Enemy activity in the Frog Level area had increased lately. British patrols foraging for livestock had become common, and now, there were rumors of enemy forces moving up the Mullica River, to attack the ironworks of Batsto and Audry. Daniel and his men had been sent home to muster volunteers, in order to protect the area if the British attacked. The massacre of patriot forces at Hancock's Bridge, in nearby Salem County, was still fresh in everyone's memory.

"Nothing like that could happen here," Daniel thought proudly, as he followed the winding path of Sabbath Creek. He believed in himself as fervently as he had once believed in Saint Nicholas; the men under his command simply copied his own attitude, and Captain Brewster became the brilliant leader he'd always known he was. As he neared Dark of the Moon, he decided to pay a visit to his ailing grandfather, whose blindness hadn't prevented him from organizing the patriot movement in Frog Level. He loved to show off for his grandfather Daniel, who didn't need eyes to see that his namesake was a hero. "And I really should have a talk with little Micah, so he doesn't get it into his head to try some soldiering tonight, with the men," he decided. "He's much too young—besides, a crippled soldier would be absolutely useless to me."

He bounded into the darkened taproom, stamping his captain's boots and shouting his grandfather's name. In his mind, a white charger pawed the air. But his grandfather wasn't there; even little Micah wasn't around. Only Jerad was there. With his flat, pewter gaze that could knock a hero off his horse. With his hard sharp-edged voice that aimed like a blade at a hero's favorite parts: "Your grandmother Kitty was a full-blooded savage, a whore. Her mother was the same. Your father's father didn't have a drop of the precious Rane blood in him—he was Seneca's father-in-law, and he was insane. He laid the Indian slut until her daughter—your grandmother Kitty—was old enough to service him. Then he laid Kitty. That's how your father was born. Rane Brewster is a bastard and a half-breed savage. A whore's son, and you—" Jerad got no further, for Daniel's hand was on his windpipe and he began to squeeze.

"Liar," he screamed. "I swear, I'll kill you—" Daniel stopped suddenly, amazed to see a grin twist the corners of Jerad's gasping mouth.

"Kill me. Go on, kill me, Captain." Jerad's voice was choked and rasping—but he means it, thought Daniel. And I'll be damned if I'm going to please him about anything. Instead he slammed Jerad's head against the wall, smiling as he sagged lifelessly onto the floor. "He'll be out cold for an hour," Daniel thought as he ran through the back taproom door. But as he hurried out of the kitchen, the darkened taproom echoed with the sound of Jerad's laughter.

Daniel ran through the barnyard and onto the back trail that led to his parents' cabin, but he realized that he was traveling too fast to think clearly, so he slowed, trying to calm himself. "I never asked questions," he remembered. "No one in the family talked much about the past, but I wasn't curious." He remembered that his friend Tabor Stread had come to him when the regiment was forming, to tell him that the men had selected him as their leader.

"Can I be your captain, Tabor?" he'd asked. "How can the men trust me, knowing about my father?"

"The past is past, Daniel," Tabor had replied. "Our struggle is today."

Daniel had been mystified by this response, since he'd been referring to Rane's Tory sympathies, and not the past. "But I never asked Tabor what he'd meant," he remembered. "Maybe I'd decided that I didn't want to know." He'd never even considered the idea of Indian blood—neither he nor his father looked like savages. Filthy beggars. Heathens. Drunken fools. The thought that he might be one of these people horrified him. He hadn't even thought of them as being people.

"How can I live with it," he thought, then. "If it is true?"

Rane Brewster was hardly a warrior, he thought with contempt. Only Daniel's popularity and prominence had protected the Brewster family against suffering for Rane's views. Daniel had personally beaten up one Tory, a lawyer from Gloucester Town, but his grandfather had broken up the taproom brawl before he'd been able to inflict serious damage. "I've already suffered enough for my father's strange ways," he thought bitterly. "And now *this*. Jerad must be lying." His feet cut more sharply into the dirt, as he sped past the tree of hearts and turned for home.

"What does it matter who said it? I want to know if it is true." Daniel confronted his father without compassion.

"There are other ways to say . . . what has been said," Rane replied, edging towards his son. "If I must call this truth or lie, then I would call it the cruelest form of truth. But truth is not often found simply by reciting a list of circumstances."

"Damn your philosophy!" Daniel ignored his father's anguished gaze. "Only one circumstance hangs over my life right now, and I want the truth of it. Am I a filthy savage?"

Rane flinched. "You are of Indian blood," he said carefully. Daniel's jaw tensed, but he did not speak as Rane continued. "Your mother thought that you should be told, but I insisted that you be spared the anxiety. So few of our neighbors were living here during those years. It seemed like a secret that could safely be buried. I did not want to see you suffer, please believe me."

Daniel stared at him, enraged. "*You* insisted—*you* wanted—if it isn't in a book, you cannot face it. You didn't want me to know because *you* were too weak to live with the knowlege."

Rane looked at his son with sorrow. "I know now what I did not know when I was young, as you are now. It is the circumstances of your life, and not of your blood which shape your destiny. Joshan, Eli, and your grandfather Daniel gave me—"

"Kept you," Daniel interrupted. "Amused themselves by teaching you to look and act and talk like them. Just as a mockingbird takes on the song of other birds in his part of the forest."

"I am like them," Rane insisted. "But that knowledge is a gift of one's middle years. In the fears of my youth, I said, 'I am different—am I better or worse than my neighbors?' Now I say, 'I am different—and therefore just the same as my neighbors, who are all different from me.' " He reached out to his son, but Daniel pulled away.

"You have spent a lifetime looking in books, to find the words you use to justify your life; then you call it wisdom. I spit on your words." Daniel's tone turned mocking, "And what have you done to *my* life? Shall I go to the reservation at Brotherton to join my tribe? How shall I explain myself to them, a fierce brave with gray eyes and a fondness for fair-haired ladies not scarred by the pox? A warrior whose Indian father speaks Greek, but no Delaware?"

"You do not belong there, my son."

"Where does *your son* belong? I know only one life, and that one has been a lie. How many of our neighbors—my *God,* how many of my *men* know about this?"

"I don't know," Rane said miserably.

Daniel felt as though he'd been suddenly mutilated. When he finally spoke, his voice was strained, and slow: "I tell you that I will never lead those men into battle again. But I will find my war, Father, and I promise you that I will spend the rest of my life fighting it."

"Daniel, I *beg* you. Your mother and I—"

"Damn both of you." Daniel watched, as his father turned pale and still. Then he pushed Rane aside, moving towards the door. "If we meet again, it will be as strangers. Explain my disappearance as best as you can. You are so *wise,* Father. I'm sure you'll think of something."

Daniel left the room, running. Rane's hand jerked outwards, a convulsive gesture, but his son was already gone. "Cedar and I have lost our son," he thought, unable to believe it. "No, *I* have lost him for both of us. I must remember that." He sagged into a chair by the fire. "Such distinctions have become invaluable to us. Through a lifetime of marriage, we have always managed to turn our losses into arguments." As he watched the flames, tears slid down his cheeks, turning shiny and golden in the reflected light.

By dusk, a noisy crowd thronged the taproom at Dark of the Moon, as soldiers regrouped and local residents came to volunteer. Men were worried; excited. Men were drinking. As the rumors spread, their voices grew louder, as though to hide the fear.

"I tell you, the British attacked Chestnut Neck last night— wiped out the whole settlement. They're headed up the Mullica River, all right."

"They'll be coming for the ironworks at Batsto and Audry."

"They'll be coming for us!"

This final remark was greeted with laughter, but it sounded uneasy, and faded quickly. Frog Level seemed impossibly far away from the British encampments, but they had heard of too many New Jersey settlements flamed by British torches.

114

Tabor Stread spoke up calmly. "They'll never get as far as Audry. Batsto is bigger and closer to their forces. The British will head for Batsto, and they'll be stopped there."

"And who among us will be left alive to dispute you if they do make it here?" a listener cried. "I say we go to Audry and fight for it. If the British make it past Audry, they'll make it here."

Shouts of agreement rippled through the crowd. Behind the bar, Cedar and little Micah exchanged worried glances; there was too much liquor and too much panic in the talk.

Jerad Honeyman moved through the crowd, speaking in a low, cajoling tone: "You know these woods. In this part of the forest, you could be as one thousand men against them."

Tabor Stread watched him coolly. "Captain Brewster will be here soon," he replied. "We'll wait for him. He'll tell us what to do." There was murmured assent, amidst a general clamor for another round of drinks.

At Stread's remark, annoyance had flashed across the pudgy face of Lieutenant Francis Penrod, who loathed his subservient position to the popular captain. Noticing this, Jerad sidled closer to the petulant figure. "More rum, Lieutenant?" he asked.

Penrod's bitter gaze brightened. "Si'down. Si'down. I could use a bit of rum and a bit of brave talk from a man who ain't too muddled to be a man."

Jerad arranged himself comfortably and dosed Penrod's cup with rum. "Who can say, Lieutenant," he asked quietly, "whether it is cowardice or something more sinister that makes these men hesitate?"

"Wot!" Penrod said groggily. "Do you suggest that the lot of them be Tory fiends?"

"No, Lieutenant, I would never make such a claim. They are for the most part, I assume, simple loyal lads who are allowing their fears to be preyed upon. But can we really say that none in this room urge caution because they have been told to weaken our fighting spirit?"

"Spies!" hissed Penrod. *"Traitors!"*

"Shall you let them get away with it?"

Shifting his gaze towards his now empty cup, Penrod muttered into it. "Well, I suppose I couldn't take the men without our brave *Captain*."

Refilling Penrod's cup, Jerad hovered close. "Lieutenant," he whispered. "Have you considered the possibility that the Captain may already be in the hands of the enemy? Who's to say that local Tories—maybe even his own *father*—have not already captured him? Or killed him."

Penrod stared in horror. *"Migod!"* he screamed. "They won't get away with this."

He leaped to his feet, raising his arms to quiet the crowd. *"The hour is late!* The enemy may be upon us within minutes, and our brave captain—*if* he has escaped the enemy's attempt to capture him"—cries of shock rippled the crowd—"may not be here to lead our fight. In war, soldiers must always fear the worst and fight their best. I say that we must proceed to Audry at once. New Jersey has provided the cannon shot to aid our glorious cause; shall we now be rendered helpless against the British bullets?"

His speech was drowned in a roar of noise. Men were already hurrying out the door. Cups were quickly drained, and as quickly guns and jugs were grabbed to take along. Even Tabor Stread was running, as Lieutenant Francis Penrod led the general stampede. "To the woods, boys," he shouted. "We must save the Captain."

Cedar, Jerad, and little Micah were left alone in the taproom. Jerad looked at the other two, unhappily. "I tried to reason with them, but I couldn't stop that fool Penrod. I'm sure that no harm has come to Daniel, Cedar."

"I'm sure of that, too," Cedar replied coldly. "Were you *really* trying to stop them?"

Jerad turned to little Micah. "Couldn't you hear my conversation with Penrod from where you stood?" he asked.

Micah hesitated. He tended to cover his instinctive dislike for Jerad by being as friendly as he could. "I couldn't quite hear what you were saying," he said reluctantly, "but you certainly *looked* sincere."

Jerad showed his teeth. "Thank you, little Micah," he replied.

Cedar knew that she could not prove otherwise. "But I still don't like him," she thought. Watching as they left the room together, she was startled to realize that over the years, she had come to like very few people. Along with swollen fingers and an aching back, she seemed to have developed a formidable personal code which very few were able to meet in order to gain her affection. She was not even sure that her husband was one of those few. Cedar leaned against the taproom wall exhausted. She heard Betsy and Sally scurrying about in the kitchen and wondered idly what they were doing in there at this late hour. Then she sighed. She really felt too tired to go home tonight, but she hoped that Daniel might be there; certainly she was not persuaded by Penrod's theory that he was in British hands. Daniel was far more likely, she knew, to be in the hands of a lady. Her proud, impetuous son courted with all the confidence that Rane had never possessed. Cedar sighed again, and this time heaved herself up and left the tavern house through the kitchen.

"Do you think that Cedar saw us?" Sally asked timidly.

"She *waved* at us. Of *course* she saw us," answered Betsy with some exasperation. Seated together at a table in one corner of the darkened kitchen, their pale sweet faces were illuminated by a single small lantern. A traveling trunk rested on the floor beside their feet. Betsy and Sally were waiting. They had planned carefully, given their short notice, for it was only this morning that the reason for action had become clear.

Jerad's laughter had startled them. "So, my sweet *dear* sisters," he had said in an ugly voice, "I have finally caught you."

Sally had pulled away from her sister's embrace, looking confused. "What are you talking about?" she asked. She and Betsy had always held each other and cared for each other.

"Do you think that I haven't guessed, living here all these years, what foul, unspeakable acts the two of you have committed? This filthy blasphemy that no decent person would condone?" he said with disgust.

Betsy and Sally stared at each other, disbelieving. "Is it a crime to love one's sister?" Betsy finally replied in a quavering voice.

"Do not try to convince me that the vile acts you practice are love." He sneered.

Jerad had continued to taunt them, using such insulting, lewd phrases that Betsy and Sally finally fled to their bedroom, bolting the door against him. "I don't understand," Sally wailed miserably.

"I don't either," Betsy replied, stroking her sister's breast. "But Jerad made me feel . . . *unclean*. He made me feel despicable. And he threatened to tell little Micah about us. That is what we must remember. Whether or not we understand Jerad, just through his telling he will make us sound despicable to Micah. We must do something."

All afternoon Betsy and Sally made their plans, lying side by side on the bed which they had shared since childhood, just as they shared everything. As children, they had shared thoughts and feelings and indulged their trivial differences. They shared dreams and fears, and by the time they grew old enough for courtship, it was little wonder that no man could win their hearts. For all of their lives, they had comforted and cherished each other. Alone, each was too shy to face the world; together, they simply transcended it.

They had never felt a need to hide their love from the outside world. Whenever they were in public, their arms were linked about the other's waist; they held hands or hovered attentively side by side. Their devotion to each other was widely admired in Frog Level. Their passion was never suspected. And when little Micah had been sent to Dark of the Moon to be raised by Betsy and Sally, their joy became complete. If Jerad turned Micah from them—"I would rather die than see Micah hurt," Sally had sobbed. "I would rather go away, and never come back."

Betsy nodded without speaking; she agreed. And the plans were made. Now they waited, side by side at the kitchen table, holding hands in the lantern-light. Soon the tavern would be nearly empty.

As they waited, Daniel Brewster was slowly jogging through the dense woods behind the tavern. He believed that his men were inside, but there was no way he could face them. "Their leader," he spoke aloud, bitterly. "What a fool I was. How many of them, I wonder, were laughing behind my back?" His torment was agonizing—if there was one thing which Daniel Brewster had loved in life, it was his career as captain of his men. He loved the uniform, the drilling, the shouted commands, and most of all, he loved to see every head turn to stare when he walked into a room. Now, he realized, his men would be left to follow the weak but crafty Francis Penrod, who would simply take over before they knew it. He would take Daniel's rank and Daniel's soldiers.

That thought made Daniel wild, but suddenly he thought of one way to turn the theft into an exchange. Francis Penrod's cabin was very close by. For at least five years, his wife Molly had been staring at Daniel with a bluntness that would be considered unthinkable for a single woman. Molly was at least ten years older than he and too thin for his taste, but while Daniel had not particularly desired her, he had felt a certain compassion for her condition, just as he would have pitied a child who didn't have enough to eat. Now his hatred and envy of Francis Penrod engulfed him with a desire for vengeance, which could easily be channeled into lust.

Running to the edge of the clearing by the Penrod cabin, Daniel stopped and considered. A lantern was flickering through the opened window in the front room. Molly would be inside alone. Still he hesitated, trying to remember whether the household had a dog. Then it came to him that once he entered that house, he could never undo the damage done today; he could never return to his family and home. In the shadows, his face grew hard. He had been their leader. And men had laughed behind his back.

Daniel slipped from the shadows and began to run, gaining speed as he neared the cabin. He remembered clearly now. The Penrods' dog had died last year.

The door was unbolted. He opened it quietly and entered the cabin, straining to catch sight of his intended victim in a room dim with firelight. "Molly?" he called out softly. He would have to move slowly, ease her fears, think of an excuse for being here, tell her—a pair of arms swooped from the shadows and locked around his chest, squeezing the breath from his lungs. Molly rubbed her chin against his back, making a pleased, throaty noise that sounded ominously like a growl. Things were not going exactly as he'd planned, Daniel realized. Perhaps she did not understand—Molly aimed a kick at the back of his legs, dropping him neatly onto the rag rug that was laid before the fire. In the firelight, her sharp-boned body looked lean and greedy as she stared down at him with glittering green eyes.

"Molly?" he said again, uneasily. "Your husband asked me to meet him here—" She leaped upon him, howling and scratching as she ripped apart his shirt and bit his chest.

Daniel was too stunned to move, but he was hardly upset. Lifting her face, he kissed her hard on the lips, trying to regain control of the situation, but Molly would have none of it. Her frail, feminine fingers were already speeding down his body, ripping off every button that he possessed. Daniel realized that his assault was going to be successful, but he wasn't sure that he could lie back and enjoy it.

Bitch! Pinned between her thighs, he was leaping and twisting and burning to spurt, but Molly rode him slowly, barely moving. In desperation, he reached up to caress her breasts. She groaned but twisted away from him, refusing to change her speed. As though to warn him, she lifted her hips until only the tip of his penis remained inside her; then she made a wide, grinding circle that nearly disconnected him before she eased back down, inch by inch she continued her rhythm, moving even more slowly than before. Daniel gritted his teeth and pounded his fists, while he grew so stiff and huge inside her that he thought he would burst open from the pain. He wondered if he would ever make love again. He wondered if she would kill him, before he came.

But Molly was a kindly soul who'd never meant to harm. After she'd pleased herself seventeen times, she was careful to please him too. By the time that Daniel completed his assault, he could barely remember his name.

Daniel sagged against the rag rug, pondering through a haze of exhaustion. He was not exactly sure what had taken place, but he knew that his performance had been sensational. Molly Penrod had been a revelation, and he wanted to hold her gallantly in his arms to comfort her while she slowly realized the enormity of her sins. But it seemed that passion was already receding before the wounds of reality, for Molly had cheerfully chucked him under the chin and said, "Get going now. Don't spoil things." For the second time in one day, Daniel felt an unbearable sense of humiliation. Of course, he decided, she probably knew about his Indian blood all along. Maybe she and fat Francis had even sat before this very fire, laughing about him.

Hatred boiled through him as he leaped up and raced from the cabin without a parting word. As she bolted the door behind him, Molly gave a sorrowful shrug. Such a nice boy, she thought. But so moody.

At Dark of the Moon, Jerad entered the darkened kitchen. Sally knew that he could see her at the table beside the lantern, but he lingered out of reach, seeming to make no shadow as he blended with the white-washed walls. Jerad had always been able to do that, she remembered—a pale, dark-haired boy who could merge with trees or rocks or sky, so that he couldn't be found. Whose round gray eyes had never gleamed—not in sun or candlelight and not with tears, even when his brothers and sisters had died; even when his father had gone blind. She shifted nervously in her chair, wondering why these little eccentricities had always seemed so precious.

When she moved, Jerad smiled—she could see the gleam of his teeth in the darkness. Now he walked toward her, looking tenderly concerned.

"Dearest Sally, why are you sitting all alone in this cold, dark kitchen?"

Sally did not speak but turned away from his friendly smile to stare intently at the floor.

Jerad followed the direction of her gaze and spotted the traveling trunk. "Don't tell me you're going away?" he cried. "With dear Betsy? Perhaps I shall tell little Micah that the two of you have eloped—together!"

Jerad's laughter stopped abruptly as his severed head dropped neatly into the opened trunk at Sally's feet. Betsy stepped into the lantern-light, still holding her cleaver. She handed it to her sister: "Here, my dear. I think that this will be easier for you to handle than the axe."

. . . It was taking longer than expected. Sally chopped a thigh bone with a cleaver while Betsy hacked at the torso, but although they had carefully rolled up their skirts and spread cloths upon the floor, Jerad was still making an awful mess.

"This is rather . . . unpleasant," Sally said in a quavering voice. Her cleaver made a dull whacking noise that was really distasteful.

"Grit your teeth," said Betsy, gritting her own. "Think of the alternative."

"Maybe we could have talked it over with him," Sally persisted, looking rather pale.

"Sally, he was *evil*. He liked to touch things and make them ugly." Getting no response, Betsy looked her sister straight in the eye. "Do it for me," she pleaded.

Sally smiled tenderly and smashed her cleaver into Jerad's rib cage.

The trunk was brimming with Jerad. Betsy tucked the blood-stained cloths around him and tightly secured the lid. As she did so, the contents of the trunk made a squelching sound, and Sally shuddered. Betsy took her firmly by the arm and they dragged the trunk out the back door, with the blood-stained kitchen floor covered by darkness and their blood-stained petticoats covered by their skirts. They headed for the woods behind the barn, where a small, neat hole had already been dug in the ground.

Suddenly, there was a burst of light, and the wooden trunk split apart from the force of an explosion that rattled through the trees, knocking Betsy and Sally to the ground. They looked up trembling, as a tremendous, eerie noise—the sound of howling laughter—reverberated through the sky. And as they looked, they couldn't believe their eyes.

BEAST! Suspended in the air above them was a glowing, monstrous creature with wings like a bat and the head of a horse with lips spread wide, forming a cunning grin. The monstrous batlike horse—the BEAST! was laughing as it stared down at them. Then it tossed its head and began to dance closer, glowing as it lowered through the sky. Some sort of huge, glowing thing was hanging from its belly, something that began to grow larger and brighter as it danced.

"What is that?" Sally whispered to Betsy, clinging to her hand. "Do you think it could be *Jerad*?"

"I don't know, dear," Betsy said, in a strained voice. She looked at the remains of the trunk. "Jerad does not seem to be where we put him, so it is possible—"

The beast screamed, whirling so close to their heads that they jumped into the waiting grave, clinging together for protection. There was a rush of wings and a final howl of laughter as the ghastly creature climbed through the sky, making a glowing trail that lingered after it vanished, as quickly as it had come.

Betsy and Sally climbed out of the grave, still clinging together.

"That thing that was hanging from his—" Sally paused, feeling dazed. "Do you suppose that was a *jacky?*"

"Perhaps, dear," Betsy replied. "Let's not think about it."

They hurried through the woods into the kitchen, where they washed the blood-soaked floor and then moved the table back into its usual place—it completely hid the dark stains which remained. Studying the effect, Sally beamed. "No one will ever know," she said proudly (this detail had been her contribution to the plan). Then she looked at Betsy. "But what will we tell the others?"

Betsy considered the question. "I think we shall tell them that Jerad decided to join the other soldiers in the forest tonight— that he ran off and we couldn't stop him," she replied. "Father will be very proud and he'll never have to worry about silly details that might have broken his heart. Our poor brave boy may be in terrible danger from the British. We may never see him again. But his grandfather Daniel and those of us who love him will know that Jerad died a *good* boy, a patriot. He will live forever in our hearts."

Sally embraced her sister, caressing her soft, blushing cheek. "What a beautiful story," she whispered. "Is it true?"

Betsy kissed her and smiled. "Yes, dear."

Then they snuffed out the lantern and climbed the stairs to their bedroom with their arms twined together and their eyes softly glowing. Just as they had always been, together for thirty-eight years.

On the morning of October 12, 1778, the soldiers who had marched off into the woods towards Audry returned home, bearing wretched, incoherent tales. None of them seemed to have been in the same skirmish, although they all agreed that they had been the victims of a surprise attack. They disagreed about the direction from which the firing came. They disagreed about their own position when it started. But they all swore that the woods that night had been darker than ever before. Those who listened to the stories wondered quietly. The soldiers might have stumbled upon a British scouting party, but the forest had been crowded with militia and volunteers from neighboring settlements, so they might have engaged in action with another patriot unit. Or, as their confused, panicky accounts seemed to suggest, they might have been shooting at each other.

More than one-third of the men who marched off into the woods that night didn't march back. For several weeks, the settlement of Frog Level was segmented by personal grief, and in their separate circles each family nursed the ugly suspicion that those who died had been accidentally slaughtered by those who so tenderly carried their carcasses back home. Wounded by neighbors, friends, or kin. Killed in panic on a night when the woods seemed so very dark. However, they soon began to ease towards a communal healing ground, each family bringing along a few precious scraps for the intricate, comforting patchwork of lies which, working together, they fashioned. Through gentle, careful stitching, the massacre slowly became a regular engagement, and the redcoats became clearly visible through the trees. Many had died, but they'd fought bravely, though clearly outnumbered. Soldiers who had survived began to remember moments of individual heroism which they shared with the widows and orphans of the brave dead men. Before too many months had passed, the incident became known as the Battle of Frog Level; by the time Lord Cornwallis was ready to surrender, its survivors were proud to call themselves veterans.

Lieutenant Francis Penrod not only survived but was immediately promoted to captain; eight months after the battle, his wife Molly gave birth to a son whom the Captain named John Francis. Molly did not survive the difficult premature labor.

Beyond Frog Level, the battles continued. The inhabitants of Wyoming Valley, Pennsylvania, were massacred by a force of Indians and Tories led by British officers—some two hundred were scalped, and many were burned alive when the fort at Kingston was set aflame. In 1781, New London, Connecticut, was seized and burned by General Benedict Arnold, now working with the British. But American victories accumulated, at Stony Point, King's Mountain, and in the waters of Chesapeake Bay. On October 9, 1781, General Cornwallis surrendered at Yorktown, Virginia, virtually ending the war. On September 3, 1783, the British officially recognized American independence.

While the new country struggled to shape its constitution, its citizens gratefully turned their attention to pressing peace-time matters: Noah Webster's speller became popular in schools, supplanting *The New England Primer,* and popular reading among adults was *Plocacosmos, or the Whole Art of Hairdressing.* A Massachusetts town meeting voted down a tax on liquor as "contrary to the genius of a free people," pointing out that liquor was "absolutely necessary" for morale. The use of the scarlet letter for adulterers was discontinued in New England, and the Carolinas made nocturnal deer hunting illegal, due to the widespread slaughter of their cows. In 1784, the *Empress of China* sailed from Sandy Hook, New Jersey, toward Cape Horn on its way to Canton, China, with a load of ginseng root. This voyage established the route which American merchantmen would make famous in promoting the China trade.

Death was changing Frog Level. Daniel Brewster was never seen there again, and it was presumed that he had been killed while trying to rejoin his unit in the woods. Rane Brewster was not able to correct this impression. On October 11, 1778, the night his son was presumed killed, Rane left his cabin after a violent argument with his wife and walked into the forest. His body was discovered the next morning, mauled by the same animal that had killed Andrew Voohris and was still terrorizing area livestock.

As New Jersey became part of an independent nation, young Micah Honeyman watched from Dark of the Moon and marveled at the cost. Frog Level was reeling. Too many men had died in battle, and soil depletion in Pendleton and Salem counties caused many of the survivors to head west. Those who remained cared for the dead as best they could. In 1780, Joshan Rane, Reverend Eli Brewster, and Kitty died peacefully within three weeks of each other. Joshan finally traced the whereabouts of his sister Bethany several years after her death. His will assigned the Rane property to her son, except for a half acre of land containing the Cinders Church and its adjoining cabin, which he donated to the Presbyterian Church. Micah dug the three adjacent graves and carved a common stone with the epitaph Eli had requested: "Psalms 68:6—God setteth the solitary in families." At first Micah found the inscription puzzling, but as the years passed he began to think that the words made sense—not as an epitaph, but a curse.

———— *By 1790, New Jersey's population had risen to nearly 185,000 people, but like the rest of the newly created states, it suffered enormous hardship from a new enemy assault. Cornwallis had scarcely surrendered before England began to flood American cities with goods priced far lower than similar domestic products. The British dumped a variety of merchandise from textiles to small factory machines, causing the economic woes described in this letter from "A Plain Farmer" which appeared in the* New Jersey Gazette: *"What had become of our money? It is gone to New York to buy goods, and goods of those kind which are not only useless, but ruinous. . . . Powder and ball, muskets and bayonets cannot conquer us, but we are to be subdued with British geegaws . . . like worms, they are eating through the bottom of the vessel, and we go down without seeing our destruction."*

1793 ———————

Ghosts and the Beavers

MIST CLUNG like an aura to the lowlands. Sabbath Creek rose, the rain fell, and fog swarmed between, blotting out beavers with a predator's poise. Seated beneath dripping cedar trees on the creekbank, Micah Honeyman inhaled more of nature's spreading gray perfection, and he began to wheeze.

Micah paid daily visits to the beavers because they were accomplishing what he could not. Young beavers were altering the dams built by their ancestors, building a future that sustained the past. Rane Brewster had once told Micah that beavers mated for life and stayed near the same waters for many generations. "Each generation leaves its special mark upon the creek, while the water goes on and on. Like my life," he thought bleakly.

Dark of the Moon tavern house was failing, and Micah blamed himself. As the lone remaining Honeyman in Frog Level, he was supposedly its proprietor, but in fact he was more like the caretaker of a ghastly, empty shrine. No stagecoach had stopped by in six months, and there had been no more than a dozen guests in the past two years. Even the settlers who still remained in the area had drifted off to Death of the Fox Tavern, near Audry, or the Five Daughters Inn on Brightwater Road, where Ben Putnam's five pretty daughters kept the taproom lively. Accommodations at the new establishments were more modern, but more important, the atmosphere was more convivial. Micah simply didn't have Daniel Honeyman's gift for turning strangers into friends. Jerad or cousin Daniel Brewster could have beaten the competition, Micah was sure, but they had both presumably been killed in the bewildering, tragic battle of Frog Level.

Micah could never think of that night without blaming himself for his dislike of Jerad, although he hadn't known that Jerad had joined the soldiers until Betsy awakened him in the night with the news. By then Jerad had been miles away in another part of the forest, perhaps already dead. "And now," he thought, "little Micah has grown up—to tend their graves, and visit beavers."

The cemetery at the Cinders seemed huge. After sixty years, the crosses far outnumbered those left alive to mourn. Micah paid daily visits to the cemetery, too, passing down the line of the Honeyman dead. Although their bodies were never recovered, crosses had been made for Daniel and Jerad. Grandfather Daniel Honeyman had finally completed his torturous disintegration into dust and was buried beside his wife. There were crosses for Micah's parents, too.

Next came the grave of Rane Brewster, mauled by animals on the same night of his son Daniel's death. Micah had tried to comfort Cedar but she was tough as brass, unapproachable. Four years later, when she lay dying from a fever, she had sent for Micah and smiled at his tears: "Rane is all I ever wanted, Micah. Pray for me, but do not pray that I will live. Pray instead that I will have another chance to love." Now she lay beside Rane, near the two most recent Honeyman graves—Micah's beloved aunts Betsy and Sally had died one year ago, providing the final blow from which neither he nor the tavern could recover.

That morning Micah had not heard them stirring, so he finally knocked at their bedroom door. There was no answer, so he opened it, and peeked in. Betsy and Sally lay side by side against their pillows, looking like a pair of delicate, elderly fashion dolls in their embroidered bonnets. When Micah approached, Sally turned to him, smiling as though to reassure him. "Good morning, Micah," she said. "Don't be afraid." Betsy was still asleep in her sister's arms. Micah reached over to awaken her. His fingers touched flesh that was cool and already growing rigid.

In a panic, Micah stumbled clumsily from the room, heading

downstairs to search for blankets or broth or whatever might be needed. It took him a few minutes to realize that nothing was needed, and several minutes more to limp shakily back upstairs to the bedroom. There he discovered that Sally had drifted into death alongside her sister, who still lay clasped in her arms.

Micah stared in shock, then felt an instant, childish terror: "Don't leave me—*please!*" He fell against the bed, shaking with sobs as he tugged violently at the quilts. "I am *alone* here," he moaned. "Don't leave me alone." Then his mind went blank.

Sometime later, he awoke in a huge, gathering stillness. Alone, he thought. Alone in this huge tavern.

The whisper kissed him like a breeze: "Not alone, Micah . . . not alone."

"What?" he'd said groggily, shaking his head to clear it. The sound came again—Aunt Betsy! No, it was Aunt Cedar's voice. He heard it near the door, now *there,* beyond the far dresser; whispers were swirling:

"Not alone, Micah."   "I'm here, Micah."
                "We're here."

Somehow he'd managed to back out of the room and ride to his nearest neighbors, where the Widow Stread and her daughter Salome had ordered him to bed. He was delirious from fever for nearly a week, and when he was finally up and about, he discovered that the Streads had already taken care of the burials. Micah would have blamed himself for that, too, but he soon realized that he would have plenty of opportunity to pay his last respects.

"Not gone."   "We're here."   "I'm here, little Micah."
        "Miiiii-cah?"   "Don't be afraid."

Urgent voices, tender voices. The voices of men and women and sweet childish voices. They came to him at night. They lingered in the taproom and drifted through the barn as he tended the few remaining animals. He lived with them every day in the shabby hulk of what had once been the first tavern, and *always* the best tavern, for eighty miles in any direction.

Micah had felt quite intimidated by his energetic popular family while they were alive; to be haunted by them after death seemed doubly discouraging. "Compared to five pretty daughters, what can Dark of the Moon offer? Just a cripple and some ghosts," he concluded dismally. And now those ghosts provided his final reason for officially closing the tavern. Since their appearance, Micah had gone out of his way to discourage prospective guests, for he was afraid that the ghosts might try to get acquainted with the customers—they'd been a very outgoing family, the Honeymans.

Slap. Whack. Splash. Cloaked in fog, the beavers were completely invisible, but Micah could still hear them, hard at work. *Slap. Whack. Splash.*

Listening, he felt a familiar tightness, as his sex swelled, and began to climb against his belly. Micah groaned, despairing. For more than fifteen years, he had been plagued by nearly constant sexual arousal. Even as a boy, his tavern chores had been filled with peril. Making up the beds could bring on agony, particularly if he examined the sags in the mattress and imagined how they got there. The barnyard was worse—collecting eggs from the hens seemed like an obscene, thrilling violation. And when he'd recently been forced to sell the barnyard mare, it was not old Nellie he missed so much as the sight of her sassy sprung rump. His excitement was often inexplicable, but consistent— the sound of bees humming made him wild or the shape of a certain chair.

Of course, when the tavern was flourishing, there had always been women with their smiles and their smells and their skirts. They had always stooped, their breasts curved near as they kissed him, calling him little Micah. When he was sixteen, women had still petted his hair and called him by that name, though in fact they no longer had to stoop. Such was the effect of the crutches. And so little Micah had awkwardly lurched through perpetual boyhood, limping through this exotic wake of smells and skirts that only women made, with one leg dangling lifelessly, and his sex swollen stiff as a board. "And now I am maddened by beavers. Or perhaps by the fog—the reason hardly matters," he decided.

Micah stumbled to his feet and limped to the edge of the creek. At least with all this fog he would not be seen. With a guilty sigh, he freed his swollen penis and began to thump away, joylessly.

Slap. Whack. Splash.

"I'm going to hate myself for doing this," he thought, picking up speed. "I hate myself already why can't I do anything unh stupid ridiculous disgusting unh *ugh.*" He came in a rush, spurting straight into the fog—and waited, listening for a splash, as the guilty proof entered the creek. But only the beavers were splashing.

Micah strained to see into the fog, envisioning the nightmare of his thick, creamy glob bobbing safely above the water, firmly stuck in fur upon a head of beaver brown. "If I wait until the fog lifts, I'll probably catch pneumonia," he realized, slipping his limp penis back into his trousers. "Besides, it serves them right. Smug little bastards." He turned to leave and then suddenly turned back, staring once more into the fog. "Dark of the Moon is closed, as of this minute," he said in a loud voice. "I wanted you to be the first to know."

Slap. Whack. Splash.

. . . Wheeze. It was time to head for home.

Micah brooded most of the way back to the tavern, but as he limped through the gate, he was startled to see a set of traveling trunks stacked beside the front door. And then he was startled again, as a small, lively woman wearing a wide gray skirt nearly knocked him to the ground. Micah clutched a handful of soft woolen blue and realized that he was clinging to the sleeve of her jacket. As she picked up his crutch, he watched her face, for once too startled to apologize. Small nose, small mouth, brown hair and the eloquent green eyes of a cat. Right now those eyes were—*laughing,* because he was staring into her face and still hanging on to her like an idiot. What could he say? What on earth was he going to do?

"Mr. Honeyman, I presume?" she said, not waiting for a reply. "My name is India Laud, and my grandmother was Bethany Rane Laud, and I've come to inspect land inherited from the estate of my great uncle Joshan Rane—though of course we never met and he actually willed it to my dear father, who died recently. God bless him. Of course my lawyer told me about the stipulations and I heartily agree—oh, I am sorry. Won't you come in?"

"Thank you," Micah replied.

As they moved into the hall, she resumed on pitch, "Of course,

I'll need a room, although I know it's considered a bit daring, but I assumed that the presbytery would have been assigned—"

"Miss Laud. *Excuse* me, Miss Laud. Thank you. Surely you do not wish to stay here?" Micah looked stricken.

"But of course," she said calmly. "As I've explained."

Micah was dazed by the thought that anything had been explained, but he tried to answer firmly. "I'm sorry, Miss Laud, but this inn is closed. I'm afraid I've already announced it in the community," he added, remembering the beavers.

"Closed! Well, you see, I would merely have called it empty, but then I have always been an optimist. Are you an optimist, Mr. Honeyman?"

"I do not believe so," Micah said heavily.

"Good. That means that I shall surely win any argument that we have, because you will lose hope before I do," she said cheerfully.

"Are we going to have an argument?"

"There's no need to. As I've explained." India smiled gratefully at her host. "Will you show me to my room or should I simply select my favorite? I do not eat shellfish, but I shouldn't imagine that would be a problem here. And I never take less than two eggs with breakfast."

"Thank you," said Micah, as his guest disappeared up the stairs.

Many hours later, Micah lay awake in his darkened bedroom, marveling at how trifling a life full of failure and a houseful of ghosts become when compared to the full-blown catastrophe of Miss India Laud. Not only was she a guest at a tavern, but she was traveling unescorted, which was simply unheard of. Micah's remedy for the impropriety of their dining together was to make the meal as uncomfortable as possible, so they had eaten a cold supper at the kitchen table, though Miss Laud had spoiled his plans by remaining in high spirits throughout. And she had spoken of her life with a frankness that was appalling. Her every word confirmed his worst fears.

India Laud had spent her life in the town of Cooper's Ferry, New Jersey, where her grandfather Jupiter Laud had established a ferry service to Philadelphia. It was generally considered to be the *worst* ferry service in the area, but passengers flocked there because Jupiter built a small tavern on the pier, where a man might fortify himself against the weather and listen to Jupiter Laud. Passengers would sit for hours as Jupiter spoke about their rights and their needs, and no one would feel the time slip by until Jupiter suddenly shouted to his boys to get the boat out before dark.

Bethany Rane Laud had worked beside her husband, watching him with shining eyes. After Jupiter's death, India's father had operated the service until he capsized trying to navigate around Windmill Island, which lay directly between Cooper's Ferry and Philadelphia. Then to protect India's interests, her father's executor had sold the business. And two of her married cousins had offered to make room for her in their homes—to protect her virtue.

"My grandfather was known as the first patriot in Gloucester County. He was a patriot before the word was coined. I tell you this because I want you to understand my dilemma. I come from a long line of patriots and prophets, and only I have survived to see our prophecies realized. Surely in a country that has just been born there is a better role for an intelligent, unmarried woman than that of spinster aunt."

"Yes, indeed, surely—" Micah said vaguely.

"Then you *do* understand." India smiled. "I am on an adventure, a giddy impulsive quest which forces me to lie fairly often. I'm sorry to say that my relatives think I am visiting a friend in Tuckerton at this very moment, and I confess that my father's executor has no idea I'm down here looking over my inheritance. What luck then that I have found a friend like you!"

"Thank you," said Micah, sounding dazed.

Then she turned on him abruptly. "Now, Mr. Honeyman, I should like to hear your story, for your circumstances certainly suggest that you have one. Never have I seen such an air of forbidding gloom, particularly in a public tavern."

"I would like to show you around the tavern house," Micah replied. "It will be much easier to tell things, that way." He was surprised to realize how much he did want to tell this troublesome woman. Miss India Laud had ruined his reputation and possibly jeopardized his health, if her relatives were prone to violence. But she was invigorating, and he suspected that if she could be tricked into silence, she might be a good listener.

After dinner, he showed her into the front parlor, repeating tales he'd heard about how Mags Honeyman had presided over a cozy tea table in the middle of a wilderness. As Micah talked, India could see the teapot steam soothingly in the drafty room, as china cups clattered above the soft, spiraling sounds of lady-like conversation. Then they walked to the taproom, and Micah told her about his grandfather Daniel, about an exuberant youth, and a brave old man who had turned the act of dying into an argument for life. When Daniel became completely blind, he still reveled in the noise of the taproom; when he became deaf as well, he loved to sit for hours in the sunshine. He would touch the grass, or the splintery wood of his bench, or the hand of a friend. Or, he would simply stretch his face towards the sun to feel its light upon his dark, soundless world.

As Micah talked, India could see Daniel so clearly in the middle of the taproom that she nearly called out his name. He smiled, and winked at her.

Finally, Micah took her upstairs to the boys and girls dormitory bedrooms, where he tried to explain the Honeyman children's genetic scramble of brown-red-curly-straight hair and blue-brown-green-gray eyes. Suddenly, India was caught up in a violent pillow fight as Honeyman children of different sizes and hues battered each other with impartial relish. The air grew thick with down and tickled her throat.

As they left the dormitories, India sneezed softly, then moved down the hall towards her door. "Mr. Honeyman, you have quite a way with words when one succeeds in forcing you into speech. I have never heard tales more beautifully rendered. Thank you."

Micah blushed and shook his head to deny the compliment even as he thanked her for it. But as they parted, he turned suddenly and called after her, "Miss Laud?" She hesitated at her door, as he spoke in an awkward rush. "Do you believe in ghosts?"

She stared at him, baffled. But when she spoke, her words were supremely confident. "Sir. Only two groups of people believe in ghosts. The elderly believe, because they are hoping for an afterlife with options, and young children believe, because they know it is true. I am twenty years old, neither old nor young. No, I do not believe in ghosts. Now, good *night*, Mr.

Honeyman." She disappeared into her room, shutting the door firmly behind her.

"Thank you," Micah had muttered in the empty hall. But now, as he lay in his bed reviewing the evening, he realized that he hadn't heard from a single ghost all evening. "Perhaps they think I've been badgered enough for one day," he decided as he drifted into sleep . . . "Two eggs, indeed."

During the next few days, they were thrown together quite often, for Micah could not think of any reason to refuse India's requests for company, and she refused to consider her impropriety. She made no pretense of interest in the Rane property, but Micah now believed her behavior to be charmingly frank rather than shocking. He was also delighted by her casual acceptance of his crippled leg. Although family and friends had always gone out of their way to help him, he was sure that India wouldn't help him up if he collapsed right in front of her. "She doesn't feel sorry for me," he decided happily. She could not have pleased him more.

Actually, India did *not* feel sorry for Micah—she was far too busy working out plans for his future. She had left Cooper's Ferry knowing that she could not face her life there, but she'd had no idea how to get the kind of life she wanted. Now, Micah Honeyman was her last hope, and true optimist that she was, she had no intention of losing him. All week she had studied his words, looking for clues to her progress.

"Mr. Honeyman, would you like to know why I have never married?" she had asked. His look had not been encouraging, but she plunged on. "According to my cousin, I chased suitors away by being too bold and too blunt." Pause. "Well, do you agree with his diagnosis?"

"Well, there is a certain piquance to your conversation, not displeasing of course."

Obviously, he was devoted to her. They would be the best of friends and the most loyal helpmates, and together they would work side by side for a lifetime. What more could she ask from marriage? The second problem had been more puzzling. Micah's inability to conceive of a life apart from Dark of the Moon was inconvenient, since of course they would have to live in Trenton. No other town would do. Finally, he had revealed his peculiar fascination with the beavers.

"For generations, the beavers remain on the same creek, and each generation improves upon the work done by its parents, year after year they make it work, going on and on," he had told her in doom-ridden tones.

India was amazed. "We have much to learn from nature," she began kindly, "but I think we must stop short of outright imitation. Furthermore, didn't a friend tell you about the habits of beavers? What if he was mistaken? A lifetime is a severe penalty to pay for a clerical error."

As he stared at her blankly, India realized the scope of her problem. Micah Honeyman would never propose to her. He would never propose to any woman because he was convinced that no woman could find him lovable, despite his curly chestnut hair and eyes of shining, haunted blue. She was sure of that. So she resisted her impulse, when he asked her for advice, to tell him to sell the inn and move with her to Trenton, where they could start a newspaper (using his name and her genius for opinions) and they could work together and like each other very much. And get married, of course. She sensed that he was much too melancholic to consider such an intelligent, commonsensical proposal. He might even think it was bold and bossy. She would simply have to seduce him.

Well.

She added up his virtues: (1) She liked him; (2) She respected him; (3) She found his bemused, sensitive manner extremely attractive; (4) He certainly needed her. It was true she had no clear idea how to go about seducing him, but she knew that she was pretty enough, though she could smile more often. More important, she was not only an optimist but a desperate one at that. If necessary, she was willing to wrestle him to the floor. She knew that she could expect little help from Micah, for he would try to protect her honor, which wouldn't do at all. Also, she was concerned about clothing, for surely it must come off, but how much? and when? She brooded and waited for inspiration, watching him with slitted eyes.

It was the middle of the night. At Dark of the Moon, deep shadows were flowing, one into the next, flooding the upstairs corridor with the fathomless black of a deep still pond. At one end of the corridor, a light appeared. It fluttered through the darkness like a tiny glowing fish. A ghostly apparition drifted in its wake—no more than a muddled haze of white. In this deep still pond, it floated uncertainly, looking lost—like a fallen cloud that never meant to swim. This apparition and the light that moved before it traveled steadily closer to Micah Honeyman's door. There it stopped, and the tiny light ceased to flutter. Suddenly, both vanished from sight.

As she stood beside Micah's bed, India held a candle which softened and grew streamy with wax. It thickened, turning warm in her hands, but still she waited, watching him sleep. She took a deep breath and then another. She swallowed hard. Then, she blew the candle out.

"Micah." The soft voice kissed him like a breeze. As he opened his eyes, the pale, flowing shadow bent close to him. The spidery lace of her gown drifted, as India laid her hand upon his chest. In moonlight, her eyes were large and brilliant.

Reaching out, he touched her cheek, tracing the line of her jaw so that his fingers brushed against her lips.

At his touch, India leaned closer staring at Micah's lips as he touched her own; staring at his mouth until the rest of his face seemed to disappear. In its angled curves, she could sense an endless number of small, important changes. All his feeling could be seen here, just by watching his beautiful mouth. Lips covered by skin that looked dangerously thin; it was excessively pink, as though to flaunt life . . . or to blush for it. Scarred at one corner, by worry or pain. His beautiful mouth. Leaning this close, she could feel his breath upon her lips. It seemed to her, suddenly, that mouths existed only to prove how badly humans need to be touched. And so she kissed him—lips touched with a quick, stunning contact that made her draw back awkwardly.

With one motion, Micah raised up, seized her in his arms and dragged her down among the pillows. Lace flapped gently, as though to protest the speed of descent. Moments later, lace was whooshing, as a ghostly apparition arched over the bed, and then puddled onto the floor.

Cushioned in down, muffled by pillows, there were only the sounds that bodies made: the soft bumping of bones, liquid noise from mouths and tongues, the pulse that knocks in neck and arms and belly. Teeth clinked together, briefly, and there was a constant rush of breathing as it gathered, mingled, and began to race, rising from the sheets, like audible heat. And finally, the indescribable slipping sounds, as two parts of radiant human flesh adjust—to meet.

Deep within the pillows, India and Micah rocked, as the mattress rocked with them. Sounds were swirling through India's mind; she heard them as music. Gradually, she became aware of one more noise—exquisite, overpowering. Within the mattress, down feathers were whirring so softly as they rose and fell like the trembling rush of a thousand barnyard feathers that never meant to fly. As the movement came faster and faster, she felt enveloped in the sound of whirring. It rose above all other sound to soar through her bones, turning them into wings. She felt the gasp of flight before she heard it, in her cry. . . .

. . . His hands covered her breasts. He *owned* them now. She felt shivers and trembles, points of flesh turned sharp with needing him, she could not control her breasts. And now he was raising her, turning her—she had never known that knees could bend like this. Or that they would want to . . .

. . . There was radiance leaking into her bones. Thick and golden, it was seeping, making a golden pool. Then it was spreading into her blood, making a golden stream. Then radiance was pouring through her flesh faster than her hammering heart could beat—until she wondered if it were possible to die, from the shining . . .

. . . These were not her hands that clung to his shoulders, that reached out so quickly to feel his sex. This was not her mouth that parted for his tongue, that swallowed him with such greed. This was some strange woman come to her lover, in the secret of darkness. This was an accident of flesh. She must remember to explain that . . . later . . .

At daybreak, Micah slept, still holding her. India rested in his arms, staring at the ceiling. She was attempting to review her situation, but it was not easy. Though she distinctly remembered blowing out the candle, her thoughts had quickly become . . . disheveled. Clearly she had seduced him, for there was no other excuse for their behavior. As for the rest of it, only one question remained. What on earth had he done to *her*? Two questions, really. Could she get him to do it again? As she watched him sleep, she smiled, optimistically. In the dawning light, her eyes burned bright as stars.

Two weeks later, India Laud and Micah Honeyman left Dark of the Moon together, heading for Trenton. Captain Francis Penrod had been delighted to purchase the Honeyman tavern and the old Rane property as well. Furniture had been included in the sale, and Micah had given away the remaining livestock. So it was a small load that they packed into the wagon on the morning of their departure.

While India waited impatiently in the wagon, Micah stood alone in the taproom at Dark of the Moon. He was listening:

"Not alone, Micah."　　　　　　"We're here."

"I'm here."

"Well, I am not going to be here anymore," he shouted, suddenly. "I'm leaving today, and I'm never coming back."

The taproom was absolutely silent. Micah listened with a sense of loss that was nearly frantic. "I'm sorry," he said. Then he turned and walked out.

As he climbed into the wagon, India said, "What were you doing in there?"

"I was saying goodbye to the ghosts," he replied.

She stared him down. "Micah, there *are* no ghosts. You were haunted by beavers."

Micah shrugged and smiled. He snapped the reins—a creak of wheels, and the wagon began to travel.

Micah and India Honeyman settled in Trenton, New Jersey. In 1794, their weekly newspaper called the *New Jersey Post* issued its first edition, condemning the Federalist policies of Governor William Howell in such scathing terms as editor Micah Honeyman never would have used to describe anybody but himself. The *Post* took the side of the Republican party, newly formed to oppose the Federalist views exemplified by Alexander Hamilton, who believed that the country should be ruled by its aristocrats, not its majority.

In spite of the popularity of Federalist policies, Americans were turning out in large numbers to celebrate yearly anniversaries of the storming of the Bastille, and they identified strongly with the French Revolution. In 1794, a Philadelphia tavern entertained the public with a reenactment of the execution of Louis XVI, advertising a spectacular climax in which the king's severed head "falls into a basket and the lips, which are first red, turn blue." The issue of women's rights was also claiming some attention, as Mary Wollstonecraft's *A Vindication of the Rights of Women* was widely discussed in America's intellectual circles.

On the land at Frog Level, such radical enthusiasms were not apparent. In fact, Captain Francis Penrod was busily wreaking aristocratic havoc on his newly acquired tavern house, The Penrod Inn. India Laud Honeyman might have been right about Micah's ghosts, for there was no supernatural interference with his redecoration efforts or even his renaming the tavern. In fact the ghosts were never heard from again, after Micah Honeyman left Frog Level and Dark of the Moon. Perhaps that was exactly what they'd wanted all along.

Although he was clever enough to leave the dark taproom with its long oaken bar untouched, Captain (as he preferred to be called) uplifted the rest of the interior of the Dark of the Moon, turning Mags's tea parlor into a billiards room that was just the thing for the gentleman traveler and transforming the beautiful faded pinewood walls with paint of modern brown. It was the outside of the building, however, which particularly attracted his attention. The large double doors were painted royal red, and the shutters added to every window were painted a matching hue. The building itself was painted gray, providing contrast to the huge white wooden sign above the doors announcing in lavish script: The Penrod Inn. This same proclamation was stenciled in large letters above the bar and above the doors of the barnyard stables. It was also repeated on large white signs which Captain erected on Flying Horse Pike, one mile from the inn in either direction: The Penrod Inn . . . The Penrod Inn. (Stagecoach drivers took particular delight in continuing to call the place Dark of the Moon.)

Captain Francis Penrod had taken command of the land which surrounded the frog level. He owned nearly all of the three hundred acres that Seneca Rane had bought and the one hundred acres that had belonged to Daniel Honeyman. His purchase of the assorted acres which separated these two kingdoms brought his total acreage to 499 and ¾ (minus the Cinders Church). He spared no expense in turning Dark of the Moon into The Penrod Inn, for he was planning to have a glorious future. He had originally planned to have a glorious career, based on his military exploits. The district surrounding Frog Level had dutifully elected him to serve in both the Constitutional Congress and the New Jersey State Assembly. Unfortunately Captain discovered that opinions were issued at far greater risk than commands, and soon he longed for a dignified retreat. When Micah and India Honeyman put their property up for sale, he grabbed at the chance for an early but stylish retirement. He still meant to have that glorious future, but now the career he planned would belong to his only son, John Francis.

At first, Captain worked slowly. In spite of the fact that he owned both the Rane property and the tavern he purposely continued to live on his humble farm with his widowed daughter Patience, relying on his hired man Jacob Hosey to run The Penrod Inn. Hosey was a wily extrovert who knew how to attract the stagecoach trade, and the tavern soon regained much of its popularity. Penrod's principal interest was maintaining it as the community center. He automatically took over Daniel Honeyman's established roles as justice of the peace and dispenser of mail, and although his hands never actually touched a letter, he did enjoy presiding at court from time to time. In the taproom, he rose to dominate the political discussions, without fear of an organized rebuttal.

As for the Rane property, even after Captain generously donated the Cinders Church and its cabin to the Pendleton County presbytery (and the fact that Joshan Rane had already done so in his will never prevented him from confessing to this particular act of charity), there was still an abundance of land, far more than he needed to fulfill his ultimate dream. There would be room for a fine manor house (and sufficient acreage to cultivate) for an absentee gentleman farmer, a brilliant politician who served his people first in Trenton and then perhaps in Philadelphia, too; Representative John Francis Penrod . . . Senator J. Francis Penrod . . . President Penrod. John Francis would be the rising star in the house of Penrod, and his family's constellation would hurtle spendidly through the heavens in his wake. And Captain Francis Penrod would pass his days in glorious comfort at the manor house, greeting distinguished guests on the vast columned porch which would overlook the bustling, cedar-lined streets of Penrod, New Jersey.

It was all within reach, Captain believed. The community of Frog Level lacked vigor. The war and subsequent hard times had depleted spirits as well as numbers. Many of the young people had headed west, and the families which remained had no leader like those produced by the Ranes, the Brewsters, or the Honeymans. Instead, they had Captain Francis Penrod, who shared a jackal's fondness for the company of weaker sheep.

————— *The most brilliant, charismatic spokesman for the Federalist cause was Alexander Hamilton, and New Jersey was closely linked with his political vision as well as his fate. In 1791, Hamilton proposed that America begin its own system of manufactures in order to compete with other nations, suggesting the development of an industrial town. The New Jersey legislature approved his favored location on the Great Falls of the Passaic River, and Paterson was started as America's first planned industrial city, equipped with fifty people and a cotton mill which was powered by a bull on a treadmill. Alexander Hamilton had inspired a New Jersey city which would realize its strength long after the date of July 11, 1804—when Aaron Burr, who was born in Newark, killed Alexander Hamilton in a duel fought on New Jersey soil. On that day, Burr ended two great political careers (his own and that of his victim) and dealt a terrible blow to the Federalist government, although the theory of aristocratic government would be kept alive by a dedicated minority for many years to come.*

The Penrod Family

The Empty Cabin

MASTER JOHN Francis Penrod would have been the apple of any father's eye. The fact that widower Penrod's only son had barely survived the tragic, perilous circumstances of his birth merely gilded the fruit, producing a golden apple to hang upon the silvered family tree. If his mother had survived his birth, she might have appraised this treasure with a shrewder eye, for Molly had been a uniquely sensible woman. But young John Francis faced a jury composed of three much older sisters and a porky, pompous ex-captain who could hardly wait to bask in the reflected glory of his son's career. His sister Patience had so often recited the gripping details of his struggle to survive infancy that well before he'd mastered addition, the boy was persuaded to believe in his own miracle. Sister Hester marveled so incessantly over his gift for spelling "geography" exactly the same way five times in a row that he easily believed he was a genius. And Anne enthused over his tendency to grow older and larger until he learned to take credit for that too.

In light of this beginning, it was only natural that everyone expected John Francis to grow up tall, dark, and more spectacularly handsome than any young man ever seen in Frog Level. And he did just that. Not so tall as six feet, perhaps, but his dark eyes gleamed, and dark hair fell across his radiantly handsome face with the careless grace of a blackbird's glossy wing. Kitty's extraordinary beauty had been translated into masculine form, with stunning results. More than one female lost her

147

heart simply by watching his hands—beautifully shaped, with long slender fingers, they moved with forcefulness and grace, turning the simplest gesture into theater. When he smiled, the broad white flash of teeth against glowing copper skin was breathtaking. He was the crown prince of Captain Penrod's realm, a local bachelor whose eligibility approached succulence. So his family praised his existence, young females worshiped his beauty, and the rest of the community admired the rosiness of his future. Not a single person in Frog Level could find fault with him . . . except for John Francis, himself.

He was frustrated by the passion inspired by a single twitch of his hands or smile, for he felt that a heart won so briskly might not withstand the test of another man's twitches. He was depressed by the adulation of the community, because he wished they would wait until he'd done something to deserve it. Finally, he feared that he was not the paragon his family insisted that he was, because he had already discovered one flaw—he was weak. He knew this because, in spite of his doubts and frustrations, John Francis did nothing to discourage his own popularity. The communal adoration was nearly predatory, but it was also very, very pleasant.

At twenty, Master Penrod was sent off to the College of New Jersey; at twenty-three, he was sent off to travel, while his father consolidated the Penrod position in Pendleton County, adding detail and color to his glorious plans. However, one day Captain looked up from his blueprints to discover that his son had been gone for nearly five years. Nervously, he scanned recent correspondence, searching for signs of depravity—or worse, rebellion.

Paris—Florence—Vienna—the boy had been in Vienna for the past three years! Symphony—Opera—Franz Joseph Haydn —Wolfgang Amadeus—he's been writing about *music,* Captain realized, with relief. Well, that was easily taken care of—if it's music he wants, he can have it right here. His sisters shall sing to him, and I know a few ditties myself. Immediately he issued a commanding letter and then resketched the future manor's front parlor, allowing room for a pianoforte and maybe a harp or two.

Reading that letter in Vienna, John Francis sensed a dimming of lights; a curtain lowered heavily onto his shoulders; it was the mantle of his destiny. He was a true musician, a gifted listener who neither played nor sang but perceived art as an artist. But he was also a son, long accustomed to obeying orders. He returned docilely in February.

After a tearful reunion in which his sisters inexplicably burst into song, Captain drew his son into the study. "Here's the plan, John Francis. The election's not 'til the autumn, and we can make good use of the time. You can read a little law with Winslow Tyler—he's one of the most prominent Federalists in Gloucester County, and you'll be needing their votes, someday. You'll be needing everybody's vote, someday," he added, with a presidential leer.

John Francis's heart sank, but he agreed without comment. He felt no interest in the law, but was anxious to study it, for he had no doubt that he would soon be a legislator.

Less than a week later, he was knocking upon the Tyler front door.

"Welcome, son. Welcome. Howd'ye. Howd'ye. Welcome to our happy home, John Francis. Call me Win, son—we don't stand on ceremony around here and we've just been on pins and needles—here's my wife, Su Annie" (Howd'ye. Howd'ye. Just call me Su Annie. We don't stand on—) "pins and needles looking forward to this—here's my daughter Lizzie" (Howd'ye. Howd'ye. Don't be shy, John Francis. Call me Lizzie.) "I never knew a finer man than Captain Penrod, like a brother to me. Closer than a brother, like a wife—now don't you get mad, Su Annie. You'll be the son I never had, John Francis. Just one of the family. Howd'ye . . ."

That night, John Francis stared uneasily at the unfamiliar ceiling above the receptively downy Tyler bed. Mr. and Mrs. Tyler were undoubtedly kind souls, and pretty Lizzie was a pleasant surprise. But the warmth of their welcome had been appalling; it appeared that he had fallen into the clutches of a family nearly as devoted to him as his own.

By the end of the following week, he'd relaxed somewhat, after hearing Winslow Tyler bestow that same fervent welcome upon his neighbor, his neighbor's cat, an undercooked roast, the month of March, sunset (twice), a light hailstorm, and the death of his favorite brother: "Death was a blessing for dear Joseph," Win said happily.

"Had he been ill, then?" asked John Francis.

"Never sick a day in his life—I'm happy to say that he died in perfect health."

"Was he perhaps . . . unhappy?"

"Everything to live for, never known a happier man. Joseph and I were as close as . . . *closer* than brothers."

At that point, John Francis gave up, realizing that condolences would seem morbid. He decided that for Winslow Tyler exuberance was merely a form of exhalation. He tweeted upon life like a child who blows mindlessly and endlessly upon a tin whistle. It was not his purpose to make music, or mesmerize rats. In fact, he was not concerned with effect at all, except for that of his mouth upon the whistle.

As a result, John Francis learned very little about the law, although Winslow emitted constant glee about the brilliance of his young clerk and the progress of their labors. Most of their time together was spent in local taverns, where John Francis listened to baffling political discussions, while dreaming of Vienna. This was not a taxing schedule, but it was during this time that he lost weight, and his eyes took on a tense, hunted look.

Finally, he began to believe that he might not survive the study of law, and though many students have probably felt a similar discouragement, it is unlikely that the reason was the same. The trouble began when other members of the lawyer's household began to express their exuberance in a more direct fashion. "To be precise," John Francis decided, "the Mistresses Tyler have their own ideas about what makes a good whistle."

Although John Francis had enjoyed several lovers, he had never encountered this particular experience, and his initiation could hardly have been more shocking. One night he was studying alone in his room, working by the light of a small candle, with only a dressing gown to cover him. As he struggled with incomprehensible advice about torts, he was suddenly grasped in a way that he'd only dreamed of (after an evening spent listening to a *castrato,* and the hand had belonged to the Vatican). Never before had he felt so overwhelmingly trapped or so exposed.

Lizzie's pretty blonde head emerged from beneath his desk, and raised between his knees. She beamed at him; her grip didn't falter. "I've been hiding in the closet, watching you. You were studying so hard that you didn't even notice me." As she spoke, she fondled his sex so carelessly, it might have been a pet.

John Francis had retreated to the back of his chair, but really, he could not go far. He tried tugging, very cautiously, but then felt an unmistakable surge, and realized that he was beginning to enjoy captivity. Embarrassed, he clutched the folds of his dressing gown and gasped out, "Lizzie, *please*." (Later he realized that his choice of words could hardly have been less fortunate.)

The act itself, he remembered only dimly; when her mouth had closed upon him the extraordinary proximity of her teeth had driven all other thoughts from his mind. But he remembered the aftermath clearly, and this had been confusing. Lizzie had not even permitted him to kiss her, or to caress her breasts. "Hush now, John Francis. I'm a lady."

He did not have long to wonder just how little Lizzie had acquired this habit. The next evening, he pleaded ill-health to avoid a family supper, and was seated at the same desk (fully-clothed, as a precaution) when there was a friendly knocking at his door. Mrs. Tyler entered, bearing a plate of cold meats, cheese, and a pitcher of beer. John Francis gave her a dazzling smile. He was starving.

"A big, strong man like you mustn't miss supper," she said sweetly. Then she dropped the tray onto the desk and plopped into his lap. "What a lovely smile you have," she said, though in fact it had completely disappeared. "Shall we visit a bit?" She heaved her ample chest, and her breasts bobbed gently against his chin, like moored balloons in a breeze.

He needed little encouragement. Su Annie's breasts were the type that might be described as projectilian—their bulk and trajectory seemed less suggestive of flesh, than of some miraculous machines. Men have always needed to tinker with breasts like these, and John Francis was no exception. No sooner had she adjusted a few buttons than his hands surged upon them. After a few minutes, his lap was bulging. Su Annie wriggled her bottom. "Oh-oh, we've got company," she said, diving into his trousers to greet it. In no time at all, John Francis was in a position remarkably similar to that of the previous night, though he accepted it much more cheerfully.

Weeks passed, and the Tyler women grasped him in every room of the house at every time of day. John Francis felt terribly guilty, for obviously he was seducing these poor females with astonishing regularity, although he couldn't think quite how. And he constantly worried that Winslow would discover the truth and shoot him. But despite these guilts and fears, John Francis did nothing to discourage the Tyler women, for though their assault upon him was surely felonious, it was also very, very pleasant.

His health suffered; his nerves grew worse. And perhaps it was this sensitized condition which enabled him to enlarge upon the theory of the tin whistle, for he became convinced that Su Annie and Lizzie each performed upon him with a style uniquely her own. Both women had a recognizable theme. Young Lizzie reminded him of the soft, pretty tones of a serenade. Her tendency to repeat the same phrase over and over and over again could be a bit monotonous, but she always ended with a neatly thrilling flourish. Her mother's theme was a bit heavier-footed, more like a mazurka—one thought of stamping boots and vigorous crescendos, occasionally in a minor key.

One night, the worst occurred. John Francis was seated at the family supper table, eating some fine roast beef, when a rustling at his trousers made him freeze. Not daring to look down, he scanned the table—Winslow and Su Annie were happily conversing at the far end, but opposite, beyond the range of candlelight, dear Lizzie's chair was empty. He stared disbelieving and felt himself seized by a soft eager hand; with the tip of her tongue, she tapped gently—performance ready to begin. Then, she began to play. Looking down, John Francis caught sight of her glossy blonde head between his legs and quickly covered it with a napkin; that seemed the least a gentleman could do.

A series of soft, slow tones. Dear, sweet Lizzie. He closed his eyes. De— *da*——de. . . . De— *da*——de.

At the head of the table, the Tylers rattled on.

"Now, Su Annie you know how fond I've always been of old Ben Wheeler. Why, just the other day I saw him and I said—"

De—*da*— de-de. . . . De—*da*— de-de-de. Lizzie was picking up the tempo a bit; obviously, all that practice was paying off. John Francis leaned against the table and began to sweat.

" 'Old Ben Wheeler, you're a friend of mine,' I told him, just like that. 'I'm mighty fond of you and if you don't believe me you can ask my wife'—"

Daaaaaaaa de ti-ti-ti.

What on earth was she doing; she was—

Scherzo! Da-*ti*-da-*ti* . . . *doooooooooooooooo*-oo.

—She was driving him nnnh—

"—John Francis was there when I said it, he heard me, didn't I tell old Ben Wheeler . . . Son?"

Doooooo . . . whee-whee ti.

"Nnnnh. Nnnnnh," he replied, nodding wildly, careful to give a friendly smile. His hand jerked, spilling a wine glass.

Da-deee-*tiiiiiiiiiiiiiiiii*-ti.

Oh Lizzie your sweet warm mouth do it to me— "NNNNNNH," he blurted helplessly, then turned white as both Tylers turned to stare.

"What's that, son?"

"NNNNNH. NNNNNH."

Tiiii *da da da.*

Oh yes suck it, you are so . . . God—

"Well, pass your plate. There's plenty more."

Do it, suck it, yes good—you are so—uhh uhhh uhhhh "NNNNNNNN-NNNN—" lurching forward, he crammed his mouth with a hunk of bread—"NNNNNNNNNHHHH HHUNH."

Beneath the table, there was delicate noise. It might have been a mouse gargling. In a rare Tyler silence, John Francis chomped his way through a huge mouthful of bread and slowly regained his breath. Then he passed his plate.

Over dessert, Su Annie turned to him cheerfully: "Mother will be joining us next week for a nice long visit. She can't wait to meet you."

"You'll love dear Dolly," Winslow caroled. "We all do."

"She'll love you, too," added Lizzie, who looked a bit glutted. She had declined her slice of pie.

John Francis received this news with panic. Since he had never previously encountered fellatio, he could hardly be blamed for assuming that it was an inherited female trait, like a knack for fine pie crust. "I will not survive a trio," he thought desperately. That night he wrote to his father, begging for a summons home on the grounds of ill-health. Captain responded promptly, and John Francis endured an exuberant Tyler farewell and escaped just three days before dear Dolly's arrival.

Home at Frog Level, there was little reason for him to campaign in the coming election, for every man eligible to vote had long ago been laid to rest in the Penrod pocket. But John Francis insisted on meeting the voters, for politeness sake, and thereby prompted the event which his father would always refer to as the Great Defeat. Although Captain had perfected his son's future he had not yet specifically designed the wife who would adorn that awesomely columned Penrod porch. In a general way, he knew that she would be pretty, manageable, and a sturdy regular breeder, from a politically useful and prominent family. But he could never have predicted that his son would meet Miss Caroline Shandy, from the rudest recesses of the county, whose father worked in Silar Harmony's slitting mill and whose mother was so inconsequential that no one (who counted) knew of her existence.

Caroline was an only daughter. Her hair was pale gold, and her skin was sheerest ivory, beneath which dark-blue veins were faintly traceable. At seventeen, she was frail, less than average height; her eyes were huge, and helplessly blue. In short, she looked abused, which is perhaps what John Francis found so attractive. He had been canvassing the district for several hours before discovering the decrepit Shandy cabin. As he approached it, Caroline was turned away from him, tending the fire which smoked beneath a huge kettle in the yard. Her wrists looked as though they might snap under pressure, like fragile twigs. At the sound of his wagon, she turned to look at him, and to John Francis, the expression in those doleful, luminous eyes begged, *Save me.*

He fell in love at once.

The rest of his visit was a blur. Caroline's father was recovering from one of his many sprains and concussions, and was propped in the only chair that seemed sturdy enough to take a chance on, in the dark, untidy room. Joseph Shandy was flattered by the candidate's visit, though he was fairly sure that he wasn't eligible to vote. John Francis had a vague impression of shuffles and clatters in the shadows and assumed that other children were about, but he carried away no impression of them. Nor did he remember meeting Mrs. Shandy. But of Caroline, he carried away an ethereal impression that was vivid as a dream come true.

He cut short his conversation with Mr. Shandy to return to the yard, where he helped Caroline and her mother carry the kettle of molten wax from the fire. He watched those incredibly fragile wrists dip the candle molds and felt that he would cry out if she spilled a drop of boiling wax onto her pale skin. She did not, but a certain languor in her movements suggested an exhaustion which John Francis had never known, and so he felt all the more tender towards her. The pale gold braid hanging down her back seemed to emphasize the coarse, cheaply dyed indigo work dress. Occasionally she paused to wipe her brow, but always she willed herself to go on. "What a saint she is," thought John Francis.

He drove the wagon slowly back home, dreaming. Caroline was an enchanted creature, he decided, like the poor princesses cast into misery by evil fairies; like the medieval maidens who had languished in need of rescue. And like a knight, he would rescue her, he would woo and win her and take her off into his enchanted future, where they would live happily ever after. There would be opposition and danger—good. For her, he would defy his family. He was also sure that her eyes would not blind themselves with love the first time that he smiled at her— good. He would have to win her. Caroline Shandy provided something that he had dreamed of all his life: she was a challenge. He said nothing about her at home, guarding his love from his father's ambition. John Francis was too weak to alter the comfortable circumstances of his life for his own good, but he was more than willing to fight for his beloved.

As for Caroline, she was hardly aware of the hold she had over the famous Master Penrod. Only when he had visited the cabin five days in a row did she begin to consider his interest. If her mother had not been so lost in drudgery, she might have been able to advise the girl. But Betty Gandy had long ago forgotten that she had ever been young—she saw nothing beyond the jobs at hand. With five sons under the age of eight, an invalid husband, and only one daughter to help, there was always too much work.

Caroline had no notions of romance or love; she had never seen evidence of them in her own family. Whenever she dreamed of a happier life, she wished only for one thing: she wanted to be somebody's little girl. She had never been a little girl, but always a big sister, her mother's helper, and her father's nurse. She dreamed of being cradled on someone's lap, rocked in blessed, cozy silence while her world faded, faded. No one that she could remember had ever held her tight. She never dreamed of a cabin of her own, of a husband and family of her own, because she saw no reason to want these things.

Caroline was not a flirt; she knew nothing about how a courtship should be conducted, but that only pleased her suitor, who had not fully recovered from the Tyler women. Her lack of response to him furthered his illusion that she was a prisoner, incapable, and certainly too pure to stoop to coquetry. He did not expect her to make conversation, although she always greeted him politely and answered any question he asked her with a sweet simplicity that pleased him.

More important to her, however, than his good looks and fine clothes and eloquent speeches was the kindness with which John Francis treated her. When he took her arm to guide her over uneven ground and steadied her when she almost fell, Caroline's eyes blurred with tears. It was the first time that anybody had been kind to her. From that time on, she looked forward to his visits. Finally, he kissed her as they walked from the creek into a shady glade. She did not mind the kiss, but afterward, when he stroked her pale gold hair, she wept for joy, turning her face against his shoulder so that he could not see.

Captain had not bothered to check his son's progress with the voters, for indeed no progress was necessary. But when his son told him how he'd been spending his time, he was aghast: "Joseph Shandy is not even a Federalist." Then, the full horror registered: "He is not even eligible to vote!"

"Father, I was not attempting to win the vote of the father but the heart of the daughter. I want to marry Caroline."

"Impossible!" roared his father.

"Then I will refuse my seat, leave Frog Level, and never return. I mean that," he added sternly. Then, calculating the degree of panic he had inflicted, John Francis continued in a placating tone: "Father, if you get to know her, you'll see how lovely and gentle she truly is. It will do me no harm to have a wife. And she will not be one of those spoiled, idle wives of wealthy tradesmen, but the purest and most virtuous of mistresses. Caroline is an angel, and I would give the world for your blessing."

"I will meet her," Captain said, bitterly. "But I do not believe it will be pleasant."

Captain fully expected to be presented with a buxom, flirtatious lass or a downright wench. He had even considered that this Miss Shandy was with child or at least could pretend to be so. What he had *not* expected was this pale wraith who looked no more than twelve. He was mystified and unable to mount any defense against this creature. John Francis's sisters, who considered the match unthinkable, found Caroline impossible to reject because she asked for nothing—not affection or even courtesy. She sat in their parlor quietly and answered every question politely. They could make pointed remarks (and did), but she took no offense. They could ignore her, and she took no offense. She was only there because John Francis had asked her to come. Caroline was not a stray cat begging to be let in; she was a cat carried home by the heir of the house, and the best pillow in the parlor could not be denied her.

Captain Penrod considered her virtues: (1) She was not only manageable but managed to show no signs of life whatsoever; (2) once John Francis was safely in Trenton, he would forget her; and (3) he believed his son's threat. So with the stipulation that no marriage could take place for at least a year, Captain generously gave his blessing to the courtship, hoping that the Shandy family would continue to remember that they were of no consequence and never would be.

Captain believed that his son was now safe from more eligible young ladies in the area, but no one in Frog Level really took this romance seriously . . . except for John Francis. He took Caroline to the tree of hearts and carved her initials in a beautiful heart. On the journey home, he carried her across the churning waters of Sabbath Creek. She was so happy that she hugged him and kissed his cheek. This spontaneous affection thrilled John Francis. He had courted her patiently, as he knew a knight must, but at last she seemed to be responding to his passion.

Despite Captain's fears, Caroline's parents were too beaten down to sense advantage in *any* circumstance of life; this romance was simply another thudding shock in their lives, like rats in the grain or rainbows, after rain. As for Caroline, her life was nicer for every minute of every day that she did not have to spend at home. She never forgot her thrilling trip across Sabbath Creek, and in November she suggested returning there to harvest the cranberries in the basin, which had just ripened. This was the perfect suggestion, for John Francis was genuinely interested in the irrigation works. Though it had not been tended since Joshan Rane's death, the berries still flourished. The idea that his beloved shared his interest in the berries seemed filled with significance. It was one more proof that they were meant to spend their lives together.

On a cold, bright afternoon, he rode to fetch her. She ran out to greet him, wearing the patched indigo dress which she always wore, with only a thin shawl to protect her against the weather. At the sight of her, John Francis nearly wept. Winter would soon savage Caroline in her drafty, scantily built cabin. In fact, she might already have caught a chill. He was glad that he'd packed lunch and some blankets; he could feed her and build a fire at the deserted cabin near the cranberry basin. With his heightened awareness of her danger, he reviewed his promise to his father. Caroline's plight was so immediately wretched—facing winter without proper clothes or shelter—that she might not survive a year. How could he force an early happy ending to their romance? No knight would settle for less, he was sure.

He smiled at Caroline, seated beside him; her mouth curled sweetly in response. She never smiled, except at him; he was the sole reason for her happiness. In winning her love, he had become master of her fate. Since he only meant to do her good, surely there could be no evil in the fact that this power over her excited him sexually. He took her hand and felt it curl helplessly within his strong grasp. He wished that the horse would bolt, so he could rescue her right now, but it trotted sedately to the clearing where the back trail neared the creek.

They walked towards the creek, and Caroline was afraid that the load he was carrying would prevent him from repeating his earlier kindness, forcing her to slosh through the icy water as she'd done all her life, without even a hand to help her. But he gathered everything into a bundle and quickly crossed to stow it safely on the other side of the creek. Then he returned, and she lifted her arms, eager to be held again. She curved her head against his shoulder as he carried her across the rough waters.

The delicate scent of her pale gold hair against his cheek was driving him wild, and she was so soft within his arms, he didn't want to put her down, but the blanket and the basket were a hindrance. Suddenly, she shivered, and he remembered how poorly she was dressed for the cold. He set her down to wrap her in the blanket, folding the layers as though he was shielding something precious in gauze. Then he picked her up, handing her the basket to carry so that he could hold her in both arms. Even the coarseness of the blanket excited him, because he knew that it pressed against her soft white flesh.

As for Caroline, it was as though her lifelong dream, which had only been measured out in blissful seconds, was now continuing for minutes. He had wrapped her tenderly in the blanket, to take care of her. She was warm and protected as he carried her through the woods, clinging to his broad, strong shoulders. She felt an indescribably pleasant glow. She wanted it to go on forever.

They walked right past the cranberry basin; John Francis felt that it was much too cold for berry-picking, so they headed straight for the old Brewster cabin, which hadn't been occupied since Cedar Brewster's death. The chimney still worked, so they cleared some space and John Francis made a fire while Caroline set out the lunch. She was disappointed that he was no longer holding her; the fire was nice, but she was not much interested in the food. She really wanted to be in his arms again.

She shook her head sorrowfully, refusing the food he offered until half-playfully, he tore a bit of meat from its bone and held it to her lips; she kissed his fingers, then parted her lips, to

159

swallow it. Slowly, in small bites, she began to take nourishment, but only from his hands. With her huge, trusting eyes fixed on him, John Francis was sure that she would starve without him. He was shaking with desire, afraid to touch her. When the food was gone, her pale hand fluttered through the shadows to capture his own; she lifted it, to stroke her hair; she stared at him, with eyes that begged for . . . what?

An ember hissed into the air and popped. Caroline screamed and leaped into his arms. He held her close to comfort her. She wanted him to hold her, to touch her. He kissed her and she responded to his kiss, wanting to feel his love. He caressed her breasts in a gentle soothing way that filled her with a pleasant glow. When he pulled away from her, breathing harshly, she pulled him back; she pulled him down, to love her.

He was holding her so tight now, it was just the way she'd dreamed. He had taken such care of her and the fire was warm and the food had been so nice; now he was holding her and she never wanted him to stop. He was stroking her hair and kissing all the places on her face that no one had ever kissed before. He was whispering to her, soft soothing sounds. She could not make out the words but she was sure that he was comforting her; everything was fine. His hands moved lower on her skirt and she moved against them. He would touch her and hold her and everything would be all right. She was surprised when he raised her skirt, but he touched her so gently. And he was kissing her mouth and her cheeks; he was over her now. She would have been frightened but then he pulled her up into his arms as he pushed into her below—he hurt her and she stiffened. But then he stroked her and held her quietly for a moment before he moved against her again, and it didn't hurt so much, so it was all right because his arms were still around her. He was still holding her. And he held her for a long time after he'd stopped hurting her, and he carried her back down the hill and stroked her hair on the way home. No one had ever held her tight before. She was going to be his little girl forever, if she could.

In late November, John Francis was elected representative to the New Jersey State Assembly from Pendleton County. Two months later, just before he left for Trenton to assume his office, he married Miss Caroline Shandy, also of Frog Level. The bride was two months pregnant. The groom's father attended the ceremony, audibly grinding his teeth. When Caroline failed to carry the child to term, Captain suspected, but could never prove, some dastardly feminine trick. And his temper was not improved by the inauguration of James Madison as the nation's fourth president on March 4, 1809.

Madison continued the Republican trend started by his predecessor, Thomas Jefferson. But the politics of expansion cut across party lines, and even Captain could rejoice as West Florida was annexed by President Madison, as Louisiana, Indiana, and Illinois became states, and a fur-trading colony was established in the Pacific Northwest. During these years, the first steamboat sailed down the Mississippi River, and even Europeans were impressed with Washington Irving's mischievous classic, *A History of New York;* Pittsburgh, Pennsylvania, developed a large network of libraries which included a frontier "coonskin library" on the Ohio River, where settlers could trade furs for books; and Harvard College began to offer scholarships to students who could not afford its tuition costs of nearly three hundred dollars per year.

Although even liberal newspapers such as India Honeyman's *New Jersey Post* regularly carried advertisements for runaway slaves, editorials now frequently questioned the morality of slavery, and Quakers and businessmen banded together to plead for peace, as the nation moved towards a second war. (The Quakers were traditional pacifists; the businessmen felt that war with Great Britain would bring commercial disaster.) As a Federalist, Captain Penrod was against the war, and he made it clear in taproom discussions that Frog Level was against it too. A few young Frog Levelers were called up by the state militia, but the militia refused to fight outside the state and the British did not choose to fight within it, so the War of 1812 was remembered in Frog Level mainly for Captain's rousing victory celebration in 1814 . . . and for the change it made in their map.

New Jersey Federalists riding to power on a peace platform in 1812 took advantage of their short-lived power to create several new pro-Federalist counties. The region surrounding Frog Level was merged with districts from several other counties to form Sand County, which dutifully re-elected Representative John Francis Penrod and later elected him as their senator. However, being part of a new county did not lessen Frog Level's problems: their livestock was still being preyed upon by wild animals—cats, some thought, or perhaps a bear. In addition, the Pine Barrens to the north had become a sanctuary for gangs of ruthless bandits who swooped down upon the area settlements, robbing and killing, and then raced back into the pines to safety. At Penrod Inn, Captain made long impassioned speeches about cats—or bears, and bandits, and the need for brave posses to ride off in pursuit of these things. But it must be noted that his rump never grazed a saddle.

Although neighboring communities had suffered bandit raids, Frog Level had so far been spared. But local citizens would not have been comforted by the reason. The bandit leader most feared by the Pineys themselves was a man named Daniel Brewster, who had quickly recruited a gang when he'd fled to the wilderness of the Pine Barrens in 1778. His targets were thirty small settlements to the east and south of the Pines. But although spies kept him fully informed about the community of Frog Level, Brewster never returned to his home and he issued orders that no Piney raids were to be staged there. This was not sentiment, but design—like Captain Penrod, Daniel planned for a glorious future. (He was killed in a robbery attempt at a tavern in Sweetwater in 1815.)

In 1810, the same year in which New York began to build the Erie Canal, Captain Francis Penrod began construction of his family mansion on the land formerly belonging to Seneca Rane. One year later, the house was complete. Frog Level had never seen anything like it—the House of Penrod, they called it. Built in the Greek Revival style, it had thirteen rooms in all, with a full basement that served as the kitchen. Two full stories high, the house was surrounded by a huge columned porch on all four sides. The columns were made of iron, as were the elaborate roof carvings. Forged at Audry, they were hauled to the house by wagon, at Captain's request. Supplies arrived from Philadelphia, too—yards of satin, lace, and velvet; thick brocades and finest crystal.

The rooms were densely furnished, but there was hardly

space enough to display the Penrod taste: both parlors were crammed with Sheraton sofas and Directoire settees, those Queen Anne chairs which looked like thrones (but not one chair in the Hitchcock style, which Captain suspected as Republican). In the family parlor, the papered walls displayed roses and grapes which grew in lurid stripes from floor to ceiling, mingling on the same trellis, for no apparent reason. In the formal front parlor, Captain was content with plain blue walls which he hung with portraits of wealthy men, who might be taken for relatives. The ceiling was his pride and joy: a fresco limned in tempera and gilt, entitled *The Cupids Cavort* (of course, they were decently clothed). These cupids looked down on a pianoforte and two harps which Captain had purchased in a haze of parental tenderness.

Captain was fond of mirrors and brass, velvet draperies and satin sashes, umbrella stands and tassels; he put these items everywhere, and his spinster daughter Patience followed behind, filling in blank spots with lace. And then they moved in, the happy family of Penrod—Captain, Patience, Caroline, and the absent John Francis. Of course, Captain was careful to point out that John Francis was the master of this house; with that public pronouncement, he then felt free to supervise its considerable hospitality. Every night he presided over his son's table with flagrant relish (wearing his pea-green satin coat with elbow sleeves decorated with golden cord, to match his epaulets). At the House of Penrod, the Captain's future suddenly was at hand, and it was glorious—particularly since John Francis so rarely got home from his political duties, and his wife so rarely came down to dinner.

———— *Although there were no battles fought in New Jersey during the War of 1812, coastline communities were harrassed by patrols from British vessels who landed to search for cattle and fresh water. For several months, the Quaker community at Reed's Beach suffered these raids in silence, but when the situation grew critical, they met to discuss the attacks. On the morning after this meeting, the British spotted a full battery of cannons bristling from the shoreline at Reed's Beach, and they discontinued their raids. These "Quaker guns" were actually logs painted and shaped to look like cannon, but they enabled the Quakers to repel the British without resorting to firearms (which was forbidden by their religion). There was great admiration for the Quaker's ingenuity, but little enthusiasm for their views on firearms. Most American citizens believed that freedom from oppression depended upon their right to own a gun.*

The House of Penrod

THE APRIL day was full of tricks: a crocus seen at ten o'clock had disappeared by two; the breeze turned cool, then warm, then cooler than before. And then, in the final hour of light, the House of Penrod briefly turned to gold. This was an illusion—the setting sun sent molten rays against walls of painted alabaster, nothing more. But the difference was so real!

In ordinary light, this house looked expensive, but slightly preposterous. (This was partially due to the alabaster paint, which Captain had ordered from Philadelphia, trying to create the effect of a marble palace—the farmers of Frog Level instantly recognized this shade of white, which perfectly created the effect of a two-story egg.) But now, as it gleamed with gold, this house looked exquisite. Its columned porch shimmered. Overly elaborate roof carvings took on the dignity of filigree, and suddenly the highest windows seemed as glamorous as turrets. Seen like this, the House of Penrod might have been a castle. It might have been a dream.

One fading ray of gold slipped into a vastly tassled bedroom to glare in the full-length, gilt-edged mirror belonging to Captain Francis Penrod. He squinted, cursed, and quickly blocked the light with velvet drapes of bright maroon. He stared and then smiled at his politely shadowed reflection. At sixty, he had clearly reached his prime. Things were working out quite nicely, he mused, slapping at his cheeks to drive the liverish tinge from his complexion. His son had risen from delegate to state senator from the district of Sand County without showing a trace of the irksome caprice which had surfaced in his early career. John Francis voted exactly as his father and other Federalists told him to, accepting every detail of the Captain's plan without complaint. His wife had been a mistake, of course, but even that had worked out pleasantly, since he was completely dependent upon his family's help with Caroline.

Thinking of his daughter-in-law, Captain paused in his toilette. No one could say that she wasn't beautiful, he thought, remembering his original requirements. Caroline Penrod had a fey, mystical beauty that seemed carved from gold and ice. After three children, she was still slender as a girl, although no longer painfully thin. She dressed only in white, in thin, frilly dresses that drifted like gossamer and shimmered in her wake. Her gold hair hung straight to her waist, held in place by a strand of ribbon. Wispy gold tendrils framed her face and those unforgettable eyes. "She reminds me of an opal," he thought uneasily. "Pale and glowing, but there's a shifting quality to her, like secret fire. I don't know that gal at all."

No one in the family understood her, but they were able to control her behavior, to some extent. When their first daughter, Delilah, was born, Caroline had shown no interest whatsoever in her child, but she was such an adorable, enthusiastic invalid that Patience couldn't scold her. The trouble hadn't really started until Delilah was old enough to toddle about. John Francis adored his daughter. He loved to pick her up and toss her into the air—*No!* Caroline screamed. *Don't touch her.* Taking this for maternal concern, he tried to play more gently, but soon it became clear that Caroline did not want him to touch Delilah at all.

During this time, she began to appear exclusively in the one white dress that she owned, which represented one of Patience's more romantic misconceptions about Frog Level society. An empire costume of embroidered gauze, it looked like the night-gown of a fairy princess, but the style suited Caroline in a strange way and she refused to wear anything else—so Patience gamely ordered it repeated in a variety of fabrics, while Captain fumed. It simply wasn't fashionable in Frog Level for a grown woman to wear her hair loose, to wear dresses which had no gathered waist.

In fact, it was appalling. But Caroline's behavior had become more appalling than her dress, though she rarely appeared before company. On family evenings, she might sit quietly while the Penrods chattered around her. But more often, she burst into tantrums or tears, refusing to do the simplest tasks by herself and demanding that John Francis spend all of his time at home with her.

When Deborah was born two years after Delilah, and Deirdre four years after that, the situation became scarcely tolerable. John Francis was forced to sneak into the nursery to visit with his daughters, and Caroline now constantly tracked his movements, warning, "Don't you go to see those other little girls. You be with *me*."

Their daughters were rosy-cheeked and raven-curled, a trio of little dark stars who had inherited their father's beauty, but Caroline refused to go near them. And she was given less opportunity since her last visit to the nursery six months ago. Then, Patience had found her rocking in a chair by the window, with two-year-old Deirdre seated on her lap: *Snap. Click.* Something silver was flashing near Deirdre's face; Caroline was slashing at her with a pair of scissors. Patience screamed and rushed towards them, kicking through a mass of butchered black curls and shredded lace—the child's beautifully embroidered gown had been hacked to ribbons. Deirdre had remained completely still throughout the attack, but when Patience snatched her up, her body felt rigid and trembled violently. "Dee-dee, Dee-dee," Patience whispered, holding her close, but she had stared remotely, with huge glazed eyes. It had been three days before Deirdre had uttered a sound. And she hadn't cried since.

Patience swore that Caroline had cut away as though she fully intended to shear the flesh from the bone, but just hadn't gotten that far yet. Captain always felt it was lucky that Hester's husband had died just then, so the widow could join their household as unofficial governess. The good times could go on; everything could be coped with. The Penrods had always looked after each other, and if Captain felt guilty about hiding the worst about Caroline from his son, then he bore that guilt very well. The shy child bride of Senator Penrod was indistinctly remembered, and it was not difficult to convince guests that she still felt unequal to their exalted company and so was protected in the Penrod familial embrace.

The dinner gong sounded—early tonight, because Captain Penrod would be joining members of his old regiment and admiring hangers-on at The Penrod Inn, to celebrate the thirtieth anniversary of the Battle of Frog Level. As he laid the final touches to his dress, Patience and Hester met at the dining room door.

"Where is she?" Hester whispered.

"I'm not sure. I took a tray to her bedroom, but she wasn't there. Are the children safe?" Patience replied.

"They're asleep. I've locked the nursery door. But—"

"Ladies." Captain bowed, handsomely. "You can whisper and gossip all evening long, as I'm sure you'll do in my absence, but let us attend to our meal promptly. Small courtesies make the servants loyal and cheery, and it don't cost a thing." He extended an arm to each of his daughters, and they strolled in to dinner.

As her chair was eased into place, Patience signaled to her sister. Hester nodded, comprehending. The key. She must find some way to explain it to John Francis, who was due home tonight to join his father's celebration. Sleepwalking, perhaps. Punishment for some misconduct. There were surely a dozen reasons for locking children into a room, but as the first course —a clear, bright consommé—was laid before her, Hester was still trying to think of more than one reason for locking a mother out.

Captain stood at the head of the table, raising a goblet of fluted crystal: "To that night thirty years ago, to the valiant battle which changed our destiny. To this blessed Penrod family and our humble, happy home."

Smiling, Patience and Hester offered their glasses, and crystal goblets gently struck *ting-ting-ting*, like music from priceless chimes.

One final note about April in Frog Level—and eggs. Velvet swags can sometimes be a hindrance. In simpler homes nearby, undraped windows were being stared from, and crude plank doors were being bolted, quick. Because the April day was done, and there was nothing of spring in this cold, black dusk—without heat and light, hope disappeared.

Something awful was surrounding the House of Penrod. This was serious darkness—it came early, and clung like a web. In this gloom, four walls of painted alabaster had taken on an alarming pallor, and the columned porch was quite suddenly ghastly. A clammy dampness was seeping there, seeping out of the earth, as though to prove that all of earth was but a grave. A single, *leaking* grave. Above the highest windows a ghost moon stared, no more than a bony imprint in the dull crepe sky that swaddled Captain Francis Penrod's magnificent creation. To-night, those stars looked sharp as glass. They seemed very far away.

This ghastly night was not simply one more April trick. This night was a warning: The earth is a grave. The moon is a bone. The web implies a spider. So do not make a wish tonight. Do not close your eyes to sleep. These stars are not for wishing. This darkness is for nightmares, not for dreams.

Ten miles north of Frog Level, two riders sped through this darkness, anticipating the night ahead. They were nearing the same turn, although they approached from different directions, and were mounted upon nearly identical chestnut geldings. And their horses passed so closely that dirt kicked up by one set of flying hoofs showered the other, so that one horse reared in fright. But the most remarkable coincidence in this near-accident was that of the riders, themselves: from their graceful, beautiful hands to the sheer white flash of their smiles, these men might have been twins.

The faster rider turned deeper into the forest, heading for the cabin that belonged to a woman, Annie Lofts. The other man gradually calmed his mount and discovered that it had lamed itself while thrashing about. He would have to stop for the night in the forest and continue his journey tomorrow. Senator John Francis Penrod was going to be very late coming home.

"If it weren't for my little girls, there would be little reason for returning home at all." John Francis stopped, embarrassed: the night was so still that for a moment, he was sure he'd spoken aloud. Then he looped the reins over the gelding's neck, to lead it slowly along the narrow rutted road. Sensing the terrible darkness, he shivered uneasily, hoping that he would find some shelter nearby. "Would she care, if I didn't come?" he wondered bitterly. He was still wildly attracted to Caroline but was baffled and angered by her behavior. He remembered how joyfully he'd received the news of her pregnancy, since even the Captain had agreed that it was political suicide to impregnate and then abandon a white female in one's voting district. But how their relationship had changed.

After Deirdre's birth, Caroline had raged hysterically, insisting that she would never let him make love to her again. But she continued to seek out his affection more aggressively than ever before. "Carry me," she pleaded at the bottom of the stairs. Whenever he sat down, she settled happily upon his lap, reaching for a hug. But when he tried to embrace her with passion, she screamed, and slapped him. As a result, his emotions were in constant torment. During his last trip home, he had become so frustrated that he'd spanked her twice, furiously. And lately, he had grown even more wretched, because his life in Trenton had taken an unexpected turn.

He had fallen in love with a bossy, misguided and infuriating woman who was fifteen years older than he, married to someone else, and a staunch Republican, to boot. India Honeyman's tempestuous editorials had become famous throughout the state, although those who read the *New Jersey Post* assumed that editor Micah Honeyman had written them. John Francis suspected differently, but his only proof was that Micah seemed to be the one person in Trenton who understood even less about politics than he did.

John Francis had sought their company because he knew that the Honeymans had once owned The Penrod Inn and would remember enough about Frog Level to comfort a junior senator who longed for home. Through long happy evenings, they had formed an unlikely friendship—Micah, the sleepy, sensitive writer of verse and short stories which sometimes appeared in the *Post,* but more often lay unnoticed in a dusty corner of his office; India, his impassioned, intimidating wife who seemed to talk more, sleep less, and move about with greater clatter than anyone else on earth—one night John Francis had gotten so cross that he'd shared this opinion with her, and was astonished to discover that she considered it a compliment—and Senator John Francis Penrod, whose life had always been planned behind closed doors. Whose function was to roll towards glory down a path that had been perfectly sloped by his loving family.

"And that is exactly what I will do," he realized suddenly, jerking the reins so that his horse nearly stumbled. He knew that his love for India was a foolish illusion, that he would never have the strength to rebel against his destiny. For despite his frustrations, despite the fact that Caroline enraged him, there was something in his anger that was very, very pleasant.

Believing this, Senator John Francis continued walking through the night.

At Annie Lofts's cabin, the other rider awoke, and turned to watch the woman who slept by his side. Annie had been beautiful, once; the dim light softened her features, making him remember. For a moment, he wished that he might mean something to her or she to him. Then he smiled. Tonight, he would keep a promise made years ago to his father, whose blood had been leaking onto a taproom floor. His father, who bragged of killing thirty-seven men, who bragged of rape, had died trying to steal a purse which had contained eighty-two cents— and a pocketwatch that turned out to be tin. But Joe would keep his promise. Tonight, he would ride from the forest with his men, doing what he loved best, and he knew how foolish thoughts of love would seem to him, then.

There were women for men like him. And for that kind of woman, Annie was as good as any. Through the open window, he could hear a rising murmur of hushed, excited voices. His men were gathering outside. They were waiting for him, in the darkness. Listening, he stroked Annie's cheeks, almost tenderly. Then he rose, dressed quickly, and hurried into the night.

At Penrod's Inn the free whiskey was flowing as the crowd celebrated the memory of fallen heroes by getting as drunk as they possibly could. At the height of the festivity, Captain Penrod rose majestically from his seat in the middle of the taproom. He always started his speeches with the same sentence, so that those closest to him would be clever enough to shout for silence. Now his voice rumbled through the room, swelling with emotion as he remembered "that terrifying night we gathered in this very taproom, knowing that our brave leader Daniel Brewster had already fallen into British hands, knowing that the lives of wives and children depended upon the wisdom and courage of the strategy we laid. Outside, *we knew not where,* the enemy waited."

At the House of Penrod, five-year-old Deborah stood on tip-toe to watch the moon from the darkened nursery window. Today, she had seen the very first crocus, but her mean sister Delilah wouldn't believe her, because the mean crocus had dis-appeared when they'd gone back to look. Delilah always got to see things first, because she was the oldest. But Daddy was com-ing home tonight, and this time Deborah was going to see him first. She was going to stay awake all night long, if she had to, and Delilah would be sorry. Maybe she would even cry. That would be nice. Her eyelids drooped, but she pinched herself awake.

Deborah counted the leftover patches of snow, which she hated. Actually, she hated them twice, once when they began to melt and again when they stopped before they were through. Leftover snow. Was that poor Mommy? Deborah squashed her nose against the pane and stared again. Yes, there she was run-ning across the side of the yard. She watched as her mother disappeared over a fence, moving in the direction of the church. Grandfather Penrod had given the church its church, she re-membered that because he'd told her so many times. But poor Mommy didn't go to church. Mommy?

Captain walked the last of his reeling troopers towards the door then followed them outside.

"It's a damn good thing we remember that night, and a damn good night that we . . ." Ephraim Barber's voice dwindled to a babble.

"It's become terribly embarrassing," Captain said loudly, hop-ing that they were sober enough to remember what he was about to say.

"Embarrassing?" William Treacher responded.

"Indeed. This proud community, which fought so bravely hardly deserves the humiliation of a name like Frog Level," Captain said, with a visible shudder.

"But, Captain, it is at the frog level . . . and not another one like it in all of New Jersey, so I've heard."

Treacher was seconded by Ephraim Barber. "Crazy place,"

he said cheerfully. "Walk through it any time of night will sober you up quicker than anything I know."

"It is a quaint name for a wilderness settlement," Francis persisted, "but we are proud citizens of a proud state in a proud nation, and I think we shout our primitive beginnings by our name. Many towns are now choosing new names that advertise their dignity and prosperity; often, the name of a locally prominent person becomes a convenient address for the town he has done so much for."

Will and Ephraim nodded doubtfully at the Captain, as they swayed to a common beat, responding to that secret melody heard only by those who are stupendously drunk.

Captain stared at them, furious. He heard no music.

Although the night was quiet, none of these men heard the bandits who moved out of the darkness to surround them. Marauders. Piney bandits. As the words flashed through his mind, Captain was certain.

"Are we too late for the party?" They could not see the man who spoke, but his voice was hard and mocking. Will and Ephraim stopped swaying.

Captain tried to count them—eight, perhaps ten. Far too many. "I do not know your name, sir, nor do I think I'd care to, but I am a very wealthy man and I can assure you a great reward for my safety. And that of my friends," he added belatedly. No one spoke. Feeling confused, Captain said, "Would you like my purse?"

"I decide what gets took. I decide who gets to live and who don't." The voice was cold and detached, not a hint of anger.

Suddenly, the man who had spoken stepped from the shadows and grabbed the Captain's gold pocketwatch, snapping its chain to hold it in the air. "This will do for starters." He smiled.

Captain stared in horror; he seemed not to even notice that his watch was gone. He could only gaze at the bandit's face, while his mouth hung open and he moved it helplessly, trying to make sounds—

"What's the matter, old man," the bandit said, but Captain simply stared and gasped, "Uhh— uhh—you—"

Joe shrugged. This man was boring. He fired one shot from point blank range, exactly as he'd promised. And Captain Francis Penrod died with his eyes still fixed on the bandit's face, convinced that he had just been shot by his son.

Joe Brewster kicked at the lifeless body and laughed. Then he turned to Will and Ephraim, who were shaking and sober and ready to scream for mercy. "Get on home," he roared, firing over their heads. Then he and his men mounted their horses; as Will and Ephraim fled, they galloped north into the dense pine forest.

Several minutes passed. Then Caroline Penrod stepped from behind the bushes, a flutter of misty white against the darkness. She walked slowly to her father-in-law's body, careful not to step in the spreading pool of blood. She had grown tired of waiting and was almost ready to give up when John Francis had ridden up with the men. There were no little girls with him, which pleased her. But then he shot his father and left so quickly that she hadn't even been able to tell him she was here. Now she would have to walk all the way home. She was glad that Father Penrod was dead, but she wished he hadn't bled so much. In spite of her precautions, her lovely white shoes were stained with blood.

Several hours later, John Francis finished his long walk home. The House of Penrod was completely quiet as he climbed the darkened stairs, but a thin crack of light beneath his bedroom door warned him that Caroline was still awake. In his exhaustion, the thought of having to cope with her made him feel dangerously edgy. He entered the room cautiously, then flung his traveling gear into one corner. Suddenly, Caroline wrapped her arms around him from behind, taking him by surprise.

"I saw you," she said in a joyous voice. "I saw everything. But why didn't you wait for me, John Francis? I wanted to go with you. I had to walk all the way home and my shoes got ruined. See?" She fluttered around to face him, and he noticed that her feet were bare. "Oh, hold me," she begged. "I'm so proud of you—no, don't kiss me."

He backed off, feeling confused. "Caroline, I'm very tired and I don't understand what you're saying. Please—"

"Of course, you must be tired. Come sit down in the chair, and hold me. Don't you want to touch me? You musn't kiss me remember. But everything will be wonderful now. I always hated him, and now he's dead. You killed him for me, didn't you? I *do* love you. We're going to be so happy."

Her words swam crazily, out of reach. He was focusing on her arms, which held him, on eyelashes that fluttered against his cheek, on long blonde hair that spilled onto his chest. Instinctively, he reached out to touch her breast. She pulled back immediately, but then seemed to change her mind and climbed into his lap. She settled so deeply into him that he could feel the double swells of her buttocks pressing through the thin fabric of her dress, pressing firmly against the bulk of his sex.

He could not remember when he'd last seen her so happy or excited. She bounced and wiggled on his lap, and he could feel his exhaustion fading. He reached for her breast, again. She slapped him. "*No*," she said. "I told you."

His anger was lessened by the fact that she was still rocking in his lap, apparently oblivious to the fact that his penis was slowly swelling, pressing into the cleft in her soft, squirming bottom. Suddenly, she rotated her hips, grinding against the base of his shaft. "She's doing this deliberately," he thought, wildly. "She means to torture me." He felt his control slipping and tried to focus on her words:

"I do love you, John Francis. Please, kill the rest of them—the little girls, too. I hate them all, I do. I'll help you—where is the pistol? If you give it to me, I'll kill them for us." Caroline leaped out of the chair, running to the corner where he had tossed his gear.

Good God! In a flash, he leaped after her—his erection had been wedged so tightly against her buttocks, that it nearly burst through his trousers, like a rebounding spring. Caroline was burrowing through the leather pouches, throwing aside the muddy boots and riding crop which he'd carried upstairs. "Where is it?" she demanded frantically, and John Francis felt a blinding sense of rage.

"Caroline, my pistol is downstairs, where it will stay. You're talking absolute nonsense and I won't listen. Now come here—" Lifting her from the floor, he kissed her roughly.

"No." She struggled furiously. "You're not going to touch me like that." Then a playful gleam came into her eyes. "If you do, I'm going to tell everyone that you're a murderer." She began to giggle, as her arms encircled his waist, driving his sex against her belly. She swayed against the pressure, leaning back her head to stare at him through half-closed eyes.

Where his mind had been was a raw, buzzing place from which he could no longer extract recognizable thought or feeling. Angry, frantic darkness. He spoke through it—"Liar. Bitch." As he moved to take her, she danced out of reach.

"I'm going to wake everyone up, right now, to tell them. Would you like that?"

As he moved towards the door, his only thought was to stop her. But as they struggled, she scratched him and without thinking, he slapped her, brutally. Caroline backed up, holding her cheek. "You hurt me," she said in a dazed voice. "Murderer." She whispered the word, and then spoke it louder. "Murderer. Murderer." Watching his face, she began to laugh. "Murderer!" she screamed.

He grabbed her, covering her mouth. She bit his hand. Scratching and clawing, she fought as he dragged her onto the bed. The buzzing sound in his mind became unbearable, and then suddenly he was at one with it: he was the buzzing. Power flowed through him, sweeter than life.

The riding crop lay near his hand. He reached out for it, watching remotely, as his hand closed like a claw upon the strap of springy leather. With one hand at her neck, he pushed her face against the sheets. Flinging her skirts high upon her back, he pulled down her lacy drawers, exposing her naked bottom. Her buttocks were small, but perfectly molded, like two creamy apples of flesh. As she kicked and struggled, they quivered helplessly, tremors rippling through the flesh.

He raised the crop, but even as he heard it whistle past his ears, descending, he could not believe he meant to strike her. The tidy crack! of leather against her flesh was more shocking than a pistol shot. She screamed. Then he watched, as a narrow, biting welt streaked across her right buttock—scarlet berries in the cream. Crack! Crack! Crack! The crop descended, as her buttocks leaped like waves before his eyes, turning and twisting as she tried to avoid the blows. Her bare bottom was glowing, ribboned with red. He watched the flesh grow more fiery; he felt it matched the red-hot pain that was stretching up his belly.

With a mindless, agonized cry, he threw the crop aside and pulled her up from the bed, turning her to face him.

To his surprise, Caroline came for him greedily, grabbing the back of his neck to force his tongue into her mouth. Her fingernails scratched at his back and he could hear the sound of fabric being ripped—her clothes and his. He knew that they were clawing towards each other's flesh like animals seeking their prey. Then fingernails were raking skin, streaks of pain, as he forced her down. They were sinking, sinking in a tangle of sheets and heat and scraped, driven flesh. Her legs were spreading wide and he drove into her: he took her screaming, down into the raw, buzzing darkness, to taste its special pleasure. Honey from a twisted comb—amber that flows sweetly, flecked with shards of pain.

A few hours later, there was frantic pounding upon the brass knocker on the House of Penrod's front door. Awakened, John Francis rose and hurriedly dressed, but then turned to watch Caroline in the first gray light of dawn. She slept without moving as her long blonde hair fell like rays upon the pillow. She was breathing so quietly that, for a moment, she seemed scarcely human. Lying in a mass of sheets and discarded clothes, she looked entangled, but innocent—like a fallen angel, he thought.

Downstairs, the pounding grew more frantic. John Francis raced down the stairs and opened the door to Ephraim Barber and William Treacher. They had finally collected their courage and had returned to The Penrod Inn, where they had collected the body of Captain Francis Penrod.

"Piney bandits shot him." William Treacher whispered. "Must have been fifty of them, at least. We didn't have a chance—"

"The truth is, we were drunk." Ephraim Barber's voice was filled with pain, and shame. "Will and me, we didn't even get a look at them, before we started running. I'm sorry, John Francis."

In morning light that suddenly seemed blinding, John Francis stared and listened and tried to make some sense of what he saw and heard: the jumbled, hoarse voices of the men, the long white bundle that they carried so gingerly over the threshold door. In distant corners of his mind, he could feel grief and horror forming . . . and a dim, whistling memory of Caroline's insane accusations. But these emotions were a faraway storm, that would surround him soon enough. At this first moment of impact, John Francis stared at the bundled body of Captain Francis Penrod with a single thought flashing through his mind. It had never occurred to him that his father could be stopped by a bullet.

Despite the death of Captain Francis Penrod, the future he had planned continued without a hitch. The local farmers who cultivated the Penrod lands as tenants had signed long-term leases so corn and wheat, beans, and potatoes continued to glorify the fields, and the Penrod purse continued to profit from each harvest (although the farmers had long ago spent the small sum of cash that Captain had traded for each lease). Jacob Hosey still ran The Penrod Inn as the proprietor had wished, with watered drinks and bribes to the stagecoach driver who brought in the most guests. Sand County continued to elect Captain's favorite senator and the community of Frog Level continued to stagnate in the prescribed Penrod fashion, with everything working perfectly . . . except for John Francis, himself.

He was completely lost in senate affairs in Trenton. Suddenly, there was legislation involving railroads and steamboats, canal and turnpikes, and free education—new ideas for which Captain had left no instructions. His fellow Federalists had all disappeared, but John Francis did not feel free to connect the Penrod name with Republicans or Whigs. And the problems he faced in Trenton were simple compared to those he faced at home.

In the months following his father's death, as John Francis recovered from his shock, he began to realize that Caroline had become dangerously unstable. She continued to taunt him with her account of the murder, deliberately provoking his anger. Waking in the middle of the night, he often found himself alone in the bed: Caroline would be drifting through the halls, muttering threats against the children. Sometimes she left the house, and he searched for hours, on the vast Penrod grounds, not knowing whether to fear her or be afraid for her. Patience and Hester assured him that Caroline never tried to hurt the girls when he was away from home, so John Francis spent most of his time in Trenton and tried to concentrate on his failing political career.

In 1830, he was accosted on the State House steps by a haggard woman whom he took to be a beggar. She said her name was Annie Lofts, that she had come to beg for the life of her lover, Joe Brewster, who was sentenced to be hanged on Gallow's Hill in Burlington. "He's your blood. Your brother," she insisted, incredibly. John Francis stared at the tattered woman who clutched his sleeve, and within five minutes he found out more about his life than he ever wanted to know: An outlaw, Daniel Brewster, had bragged of fathering the son born to Molly Penrod. A half-breed renegade, Brewster had taught his son to hate and his dying wish had been that Captain Francis Penrod should die by Joe Brewster's hand.

"You can save him," Annie pleaded. Too dazed to speak, he reached for his purse. Though she reached out automatically to take the coins, Annie looked at him with contempt. "I should have known. You look like twins, you and Joe. In spite of your fancy clothes and soft-like manners, you act like him, too." Turning to leave, she spat on the ground at his feet. "Maybe you'd like to go to Gallow's Hill to watch him hang?" It was more a taunt than a question, but Annie had struck home. Though he could not bring himself to attend, John Francis very much wanted to see this man who looked exactly like him die. Not, as Annie thought, for revenge. But he knew it was the closest he could come to witnessing his own death, which was the only thing he desired.

That evening he went to the home of India and Micah Honeyman and told them everything he had heard. While they watched, he wrote out his resignation from the New Jersey Senate. At dawn, they stood by his loaded carriage, as he prepared for his final trip home. "John Francis, remember that you need only send for us, and we will come to you." As she spoke, India's eyes gleamed with tears and behind her Micah nodded miserably. John Francis could not bring himself to speak; he drove quickly down the street, knowing that he could never invite his friends to the home he was returning to.

At home, he discovered more problems. As her daughters

179

grew up, Caroline's hatred for them increased, and they were too old, now, to be locked up in the nursery. In the spring of 1832, John Francis sent for a carpenter from Philadelphia, who was chosen for his discretion as well as his skill. At the senator's request, many improvements were made on the aging, deserted cabin by the cranberry basin. The carpenter reinforced the walls and put in a new roof. He cut a new window, placed high so that light could get in, but no one could see in or out. The new door was twice the usual thickness and was equipped with a heavy padlock. Inside there was a small white bed in one corner of the room, a washstand, and a simple wardrobe chest.

There was a long iron chain attached to one wall. This chain was carefully measured, so that its length stopped one foot short of the cabin door. The carpenter soldered to the chain a manacle of sterling silver made by a Boston jeweler at special request. The silver band was so beautiful that it might have been a bracelet, if it had not been so wide; if it had not been attached to an iron chain.

John Francis had only meant to threaten Caroline with the cabin or perhaps to isolate her when she became violent, in order to protect his daughters. Or so he told himself. But Caroline soon took up permanent residence there. In fact, she loved it. During her spells of wild misbehavior, John Francis punished her, and their love-making was violent, savage. He also took care of her in every way. He brought her meals and often fed her. He bathed her, brought her clean clothes, and every day he removed the manacle on her ankle, to rub the reddened flesh with ointment. She sat in his lap as he stroked her hair and rocked her before the fire. Then they would make love with absolute tenderness. He carried the key to her cabin on a leather thong around his neck. Every time the heavy metal pressed against his chest, his penis would begin to rise. In the sweetness of his domination, John Francis felt completely at the mercy of his prisoner.

The subject of Caroline was not discussed at the House of Penrod. John Francis attended to the family business in the mornings at The Penrod Inn. Every afternoon, he took tea with his daughters. He was excused from dinner, for it was understood that the master of the house had other things to do. Life in the front parlor proceeded quite elegantly, although there were no visitors. This splendid isolation continued until the summer of 1838. In late May of that year, Aunt Patience planted two columns of asters and one of marigold; Aunt Hester planted a discreet patch of lettuce, near the kitchen door. Delilah mastered an arrangement of "Lilla, Come Down to Me" (for keyboard and soprano) and performed it, repeatedly. Deborah painted lavender daisies onto blue velvet. And young Deirdre Penrod discovered Ethan Crouse, the minister's son.

———— *In 1844 and 1845, social reformer Dorothea Dix investigated New Jersey's treatment of the insane. She reported that keepers in Salem County beat inmates with blocks of wood and that everywhere the insane were chained in dark, foul rooms, thrown together with hardened criminals—one of the men she found in chains was a former county judge. Miss Dix issued a furious report to the New Jersey legislature and demanded $150,000 for the establishment of a state asylum. Eventually, her demands were granted, but the legislature's first response to her report was a resolution to vote $1000 "to carry Miss Dix across the Delaware, and get her out of the state."*

1838 _____

A Cabin for Caroline

IN 1838, the daughters of the House of Penrod were in full bloom. In fact, they were bursting on the vine—twenty-three-year-old Delilah and her sister Deborah, twenty-one, had flashing eyes, rosy cheeks, and high, full breasts. But still, no one plucked them. Even when fully ripe, corn does not fall from the stalk, nor fruit from the vine; these things must be taken. Alas, though Delilah and Deborah were fully ripe, they were dumb as corn. Once every week, they strolled together to Sunday service at the Cinders Church—the Penrod's only public outing. But they never noticed the hot greedy stares from local boys who, given the slightest encouragement, would gladly have stripped bare and devoured them (or proposed marriage, if that seemed wiser).

Deirdre was different. Although she was a firm-budded replica of her sisters' beauty, it clearly would not be necessary to drag her screaming from the vine. At seventeen, she quivered with hope; poised like a retriever in the field, she waited for the gun to sound, believing that her prize would fall from the sky. She was not sure what the prize would be, but she knew that she was ready. This was all she needed to know, on the last Sunday in May 1838, when she attended church with the rest of her family.

The Reverend Frederick Crouse had been presiding over the Cinders Church for the past ten years. He spoke so softly that it was impossible to make out more than a few dozen words from any one sermon. His congregation did not really regret these gaps in his orations, for filling them in had become an interesting way to pass time in church. But because they sincerely liked their minister, they made a point of showing rapt attention, leaning forward to hang upon any word he might choose to throw their way.

On this particular Sunday, Deirdre was leaning forward in just such a posture of raptness, with her lips slightly parted. Actually, she had just discovered that if she arched her back, her breasts pushed shocking bulges into the front of her dress. Flushed with this realization, her attention strayed, and suddenly she found herself staring into the wide green eyes of Ethan Crouse, the minister's son. Ethan was sixteen, but tall and broad as any man. His hair was the color of wheat. His smile was slow and devastating. His eyes—they demanded her, took her, devoured her. Across the sea of pious, listening faces, Deirdre and Ethan stared at each other with lusty recognition, like two pagan gods who have accidentally stumbled into the wrong ritual.

That afternoon, Ethan paid a call upon the House of Penrod. Though he was only received by Aunt Hester, he was not discouraged, for she had been delighted to hire him as gardener for the lavish vegetable garden that she dreamed of. The next day, Ethan showed up promptly after lunch, to work in the field behind the first stand of trees, close to the back of the house. His digging was fairly speculative, for he didn't know much about gardens, but he worked honestly as he watched the house, believing that someone inside was watching him, too.

Before a week had passed, his hopes were rewarded, as Deirdre strolled from the house to watch him work. She wore a simple cotton dress, but it was the color of ruby wine, which heightened the glow of dark eyes and bright cheeks; and it was at least one year outgrown, which heightened her bulges quite nicely. Deirdre barely spoke to Ethan—she simply stood there, dark and glowing, and he barely spoke to her but kept on working while his mouth went dry and blood churned through his veins. The next day, she returned and then every day that followed for a week. As the weather grew hot, Ethan stripped to the waist to work. She held his shirt while he washed the soil from his face and arms in the creek. Then, as though from long habit, they set out together on long, aimless journeys through the countryside.

They walked into summer, side by side. They did not hold hands. In fact, Deirdre and Ethan were not so much courting as biding their time. Their main attraction was not to each other —they were more like a pair of moths who collide, speeding on their way towards the same bright heat. And so they walked quietly, with senses racing, waiting for the madness, the blind compulsion that summer brings.

During these walks, their conversations were brief, encoded but always significant. Mostly they talked about the weather. In early June:

"Hot, isn't it," Ethan said, almost daily.

Deirdre sighed.

"Today's the hottest yet," he persisted. "Don't you think?"

"Aunt Patience says that it's not polite to say that. You should say, 'the weather is so very warm, today.' "

"What do *you* say?" he demanded.

"I say . . . it's hot." Her reply was followed by a long, satisfied silence.

Two weeks later, the topic had taken on new variations.

"The heat, it just can't go on like this," Ethan said. "I couldn't sleep at all last night, could you?"

Deirdre sighed.

"I just threw off the cover and lay there, couldn't scarcely breathe. Couldn't stand to have anything touching my skin so I lay there stark ravin'—"

"I looked out the window," Deirdre said quickly. "Last night, I couldn't sleep either."

Ethan thought about this. "Which direction did you look in?" he said finally.

"I guess I must have been looking over towards the Cinders," she replied.

Ethan stared. "You might have been looking towards me just when I was lying there naked as a—"

"Don't be silly," she said angrily. "I couldn't see you."

"But all the same . . ." his voice trailed off, into a long, thrilled silence.

By the last week in June, Ethan's body, from the waist up, was a gleaming brown. Against the tan, his eyes looked pale, impossibly clear. The sun bleached strands of cornsilk through his hair. Deirdre noticed all these changes in his body, these exotic alternations of light and dark. Within her own body, they produced a reaction as acute and intimate as a fever.

"Hot," she said irritably.

"Say, Deirdre, what do you suppose would happen if one day, you just got hotter and hotter until you couldn't stand it any more?"

"I don't know," she replied. "I suppose that I'd faint."

"Faint?" Ethan said, sounding disgusted. "I guess you'd explode up into the sky, like a hundred skycrackers." He looked at her with disdain. "You don't know much, do you?"

"Do *you?*" she said furious. Followed by a long, very complicated silence.

By the first of July, the heat and sun pressed so heavily against them that they took refuge in the cool damp shade along the banks of the cranberry basin. It was dark there—and so cool. Ethan made a bed from old sacks which he laid against the moist, curving earth of the banks. Summer was close by, but the world seemed far away.

"Sometimes I get worried," Ethan told her. "I feel like my life is starting to happen, in some other place, and if I don't get there, wherever it is, I'm going to miss it—my own life—and I won't be there. I'm not staying here, that's for sure," he said firmly. "As soon as I can figure out where I'm supposed to go, I'm going."

"I don't like to think about having a life," she said. "It makes me restless."

Ethan turned on her suddenly. "Did you count the stars last night?"

"There weren't any stars—too many clouds."

"Ha! You been staring out that window again. I caught you."

She laughed and then he leaned down quickly and kissed her. She held her breath, listening to the sound of his heart, and he kissed her again. Then he waited and she could tell he was holding his breath. There was just the sound of his heart until she reached up to stroke his hair. She could smell the sun there.

Suddenly she felt his hands, she felt him touch her. In the dark of summer shade, she closed her eyes, and then she touched him, too.

One day, when they had kissed until her lips felt hot and scratched, Ethan tucked his finger into her collar, pulling it wide enough to spill a handful of soil from the basin into it—it fell against her breasts, soft, heavy, violently sensual. She shrieked and blushed. Jerking upright, she twisted her body, making things worse, making it clear that she would have to open her blouse to get rid of the dirt. In the deep shade, she could not see her hands working at the buttons, or his hands upon her own. She could not even see the pale skin of her breasts, but she could feel him, touching her there. His fingers brushing, stroking, finding her there. The high whine of insects was starting up, very far away . . . a piercing, fluttering tremor, coming from beneath her skin.

It was midsummer at the House of Penrod. Aunt Patience watered her marigolds. Aunt Hester served cool summer salads and, fortunately, did not think to check on the progress of her garden. Delilah was struggling with the *arpeggios* in "The Fairies' Tryst," while Deborah painted pink daisies onto a piece of black velvet. None of them suspected Deirdre's long afternoon strolls, though she and Ethan no longer pretended to stroll anywhere. July was a constant, steamy itch that never left them, as their sessions at the cranberry basin grew longer and more frantic. Deirdre had been worried about taking Ethan so close to her mother's cabin, which was only hidden by a dense growth of cedar trees. To her relief, Ethan did not seem to know that it existed, and her mother was completely quiet.

Caroline Penrod was quiet because she was listening. Although she could not see out of the high window of her cabin, she could hear everything that went on at the cranberry basin —the giggles and the low, teasing murmurs; the long, complicated silences. She drew her own unique conclusions about these sounds. As she listened, she often reached down beneath the folds in her mattress to stroke the silver blade on the carving knife that she had stolen from her dinner tray. In the heat of midsummer, Caroline Penrod also began to bide her time.

Ethan brought fresh strawberries to the basin. He ate them

until Deirdre protested, demanding some for herself. "Just you wait," he said, smiling. He covered her mouth with his own, spreading the scent and taste of berries like a cool stain across her lips. He drove his tongue into her mouth—it was thickened, sweet with juice. She sucked at it, feeling the juice slide deep into her throat. Suddenly he released her, and handed her some berries. She took one into her mouth, pressing it with her tongue so that the juice ran out and small fragments of berry that they fought over, tongues twisting and darting against their teeth as their mouths were joined in a furious, driving battle. The taste of the berries was everywhere—sticky, clotted bits clung to their mouths, juice was running down their chins, and some dripped down onto her breasts. Ethan bent down to lick them. The liquid sounds of his tongue, the shivering smoothness within her, and the craving when his hands fumbled with her skirt. It was not horror she felt, but suspense—would it happen?

"Ethan, stop it," she mumbled.

"Oh Deirdre I just want to look at you, I just want to touch you once, I promise." He moved so close that she could smell the berries still on his breath and spoke the truth. "Deirdre, please let me put it in you. I just *got* to know what it feels like."

"Someone might see." It was the only protest she could think of.

"But it's dark here. No one can see."

"I can see out *there*. No."

"Meet me. Meet me here at night."

"No," she said, knowing that eventually she would.

By late July, they were running out of secrets. Deirdre was fascinated by the mysterious erection which bulged through his clothing. Sometimes it felt like a thick-tipped arrow, pushing through her, to her center. Sometimes it felt like a puppy wiggling in a sack. To see it would be unthinkable. But, one day. . . . "Oh Deirdre please just hold it; feel it please—"

"I don't want to look at it," she said. "Just let me touch it."

There was a moment of stunned silence, and then she felt her hand being guided to his, and something warm and unbelievably alive was placed in it.

Ethan moaned, as she searched for words to describe her wonder.

188

"It's so *soft*," she said tenderly.

"*Soft?* Deirdre for Chrissake." Ethan sounded hurt and the piece of flesh wilted in her hands. Sensing her power, Deirdre felt frightened.

"I'm sorry," she said, and reached out to touch it, to commiserate. He showed her how to stroke it, and quickly it bloomed in her hands—she felt an almost unbearable wave of tenderness for something which responded so eagerly to her attention. Suddenly, Ethan moaned again, and it nearly leaped from her grasp. It wilted again, and she felt something sticky and warm on her fingers. She sensed disaster. "I'm sorry," she said again.

"Oh no, it was wonderful. You were wonderful," Ethan said hoarsely. "You just don't know about it, do you?"

He did his best to help her find out. "Please, Deirdre. Meet me. Meet me tonight."

In early August, she said yes.

That evening, the air was dry and still; it seemed like darkness would never come. After dinner, Deirdre sat in the parlor with Aunt Patience and her sisters, staring out the window as she willed the light to fade. At last, she stood and announced that she was retiring. Then she escaped the House of Penrod through its basement kitchen and ran into the night.

As she neared the creek, Ethan's voice came from the shadows. "I didn't know if you'd come," he said, sounding almost awed. He moved towards her, as though he meant to embrace her. "I never saw you under the stars before," he said awkwardly.

Deirdre stepped back, suddenly aware of his strangeness. If he had told her at that moment that she was beautiful, she would have left him there, alone. But he did not, and he did not take her into his arms. Slowly, she relaxed. This was only Ethan, she reminded herself. Nothing was different tonight, except . . .

They walked to the cranberry basin tense and sleek as two animals on the prowl. They lay down upon the burlap sacks, spines pressing against the yielding, fragrant soil. There was a hollow in the earth, and they fitted into it. Above was the sky, a sparkled dome that curved downward to enclose, fitting them within the space of night. Side by side, they did not need to touch as they watched the sky, letting the force of summer drift through their senses. Summer was in the night—in fireflies, in

189

the soft sound of creaking. Heat was in the smell of the earth and the scorching clarity of stars. Heat was in the closeness of another body. It was the fever that sped the senses and flushed the skin after the sun was gone. Moths may fly towards the light of a flame, but animals are drawn by its heat.

"Ethan," she said. "It's all right."

She felt his lips upon her, cool and dry. The heat was in the way they moved against her skin. His hands were cool. The heat was in his touch and in his need to touch her, as he knelt to stroke her breasts. He pressed his body against her and she felt the heat there. She took heat from his mouth and hands and body, drew it into her, and began to find her own.

He raised her skirt. As it bunched around her waist, she felt him struggling with her underclothes and panicked. "Ethan, no—" but he pulled her to her knees and lifted her against him; on their knees they clung together, dizzy, damp with sweat. Pulling his shirt loose, she shoved her arms beneath, to feel him naked against her fingers. His erection seemed huge; he drove its hardness against her; and she pressed against it. The heat was in her mind now—it rearranged her thoughts, forcing her, forcing—suddenly she felt as though deep inside her, she was opening, as though some great, hidden rock had been rolled away, to reveal her fiery center.

She was opening, everywhere, heat was pouring through her. His hands fumbled with her clothes and this time she helped him. He pushed her back against the sacks, his face lowered towards her—a glimpse of shadow and bone, and then he entered her. The pain was quick and sharp. She cried out and hit him.

"Wait, Deirdre, please. I promise I won't move again unless you say so. Just let me be in you. Oh God it feels so good." He kissed her gently and brushed her cheek. "I feel so close to you," he whispered.

In the aftermath of pain, there was a heightened sense of clarity, and Deirdre felt him within her. The discomfort faded, as she considered the astonishment of it—his flesh filling a space so private, one that she could not fill herself. That humans could connect like this! His pulse beat deep in hers; she could not resist the rhythm of his heart anymore than she could stop the pounding of her own. She moved slightly, rising to his pulse, and the heat was returning, it spread slowly, ebbing and flowing, as she struggled to match his rhythm. He began to move more quickly, but she barely noticed the ache because she had found the tide; she was on a great rushing wave of heat, and now she knew where he would take her, towards that fiery center that stormed within her, hidden so long, the heat was coming higher, closer—she arched her back, driving him into her, higher—

Shuddering violently, Ethan collapsed against her. Inside her there was no rhythm; she moved anxiously, using her body to beg for it.

"Ethan?" she said. The heat made her voice foolish, she thought, like a child's.

"Oh Deirdre, oh gee, I guess I better get out of here, someone might see." He rolled off her abruptly, and with a peck at her cheek— "I'm, sorry"—he was gone.

She lay motionless on the sacking; heat was draining out of her body, through shameful gutters which, like the fiery center, she had known nothing about. He had said, "I'm sorry," taking the blame. But if he was right, wasn't she doubly shamed, because she hadn't even sensed the wrong?

The stars tilted drunkenly, as she touched the opening of her sex. It was wet with blood, and something sticky. For the first time, she thought of it as a wound, which frightened her, for she sensed that no healing tissue of scar would ever form there, to close this obscenity. With Ethan, she had felt scared but thrilled and somehow right; now, she felt alone and wrong. She wondered how she could live, deformed by this open wound. The heat was gone from her now; in the August breeze, she shivered uncontrollably, grateful for the warmth of tears upon her face.

Less than a hundred yards away, Caroline Penrod smiled sweetly at her husband, John Francis, who had just arrived with her dinner tray. Caroline had heard the activity at the cranberry basin and long ago, she had decided what she would do about it. "Oh Daddy, my ankle is so sore, today," she said, crying. "Can't you take off my bracelet, and rub it for me?"

He removed the manacle and carried her in his arms to the

bed, where he began to massage her ankle. Caroline leaned forward, until the entire upper half of her body was covered by her long blonde hair. As she leaned her head against his shoulder, her hand fumbled at the mattress, "I'm your little girl, aren't I, John Francis?" she whispered. "The only little girl you'll ever love?"

"Of course, my darling," he replied, without looking up.

She turned his face towards hers. "LIAR," she said coldly. Then she jabbed the knife into his chest.

John Francis felt a swift pain, then stared in shock as she backed away. He could feel warm blood spreading across his chest, but even as he stared at the stained knife in her hands, he could not believe that Caroline had actually stabbed him.

She stood white and drifting in the doorway, as the summer breeze fluttered her gown. "I'm going to kill your little girl. I'm going to kill all of them. I should have done it years ago." She disappeared into the night.

As John Francis pulled himself from the bed, he realized that it was more shock than injury which had kept him motionless. His chest was bleeding, but the wound did not seem deep, and though he was weak, he felt no pain as he staggered through the door. "CAROLINE," he screamed.

At the cranberry basin, Deirdre heard her father's shout; in her fright and shame, she believed that he had somehow discovered what she'd done. Barely aware of her actions, she scrambled upright and hurried towards her mother's cabin, where the voices were coming from. Her movements were stumbling but driven, as though she was sleepwalking. As she reached the clearing, Caroline burst through the trees, "I know everything," she screamed at her daughter. "I know what you've done. You deserve to die." As she floated across the sandy bank in her shimmering white dress, she looked to Deirdre like an avenging angel.

Deirdre watched helplessly, trying to focus on the scene. Something silver was flashing in her mother's hand—("Pretty Dee-Dee, pretty baby, come look out the window.")—there was a rustling in the bushes behind her but the silver was flashing —("Meet me, Deirdre, oh God sorry, sorry got to go.")— "Ethan?" she said—something silver was flashing at her eyes— "Mommy?"

"Caroline!" her father came screaming through the bushes, and Deirdre watched as he grabbed her mother, silver fluttered to the ground as her father's hand closed upon her mother's tiny wrist; there was a tiny snap—the breaking bone. Caroline turned on him, and they struggled at the water's edge. Deirdre could see the blood running down her father's chest as suddenly, with a terrible shout, he overpowered Caroline, pushing her into the creek; then he fell onto her, holding her down. There was a quick, ghastly splash. Bubbles collected in a froth. Water churned. Then it was still.

Dark water was so beautiful at night. It rushed through the summer, like time, Deirdre thought. Every moment had its broad rushing surface, and a current so deep that its direction was not even visible. The sound of rushing water grew louder and louder and seemed to fill her, washing, making her whole. She looked at the sky. The stars were bright. The night was creaking, all around. It was beautiful, and she was glad that she'd come—but she didn't know why she was standing here. She shivered and noticed that the buttons on her blouse were unfastened. She worked at them, wondering why her fingers seemed so clumsy. Then she turned for home.

By morning, the bodies of Caroline and John Francis Penrod had floated down the creek, to be discovered by the Reverend Frederick Crouse, who was up early looking for his son. Ethan had left a note: "Time to go. I love you. Goodbye." And then the Reverend Crouse was called upon to fish out of the water the bodies of Senator and Mrs. Penrod, who had left no note at all.

Deirdre might have explained what had happened to her parents; she might have explained the disappearance of Ethan Crouse. But Deirdre wasn't talking. Ethan's disappearance had not even struck her as newsworthy, for he had already deserted her in a way that she had never dreamt possible. Compared to this, geographical dislocation seemed a simple matter. On the subject of her parents' death, she kept a terrible silence which lasted through her sisters' easy tears and even through the graveside ceremony, with Reverend Crouse appearing even more hushed than usual, due to his own grief.

Deirdre would not mourn. Instead, she waited, dreaming of winter; she hungered for its walls of ice, for the heartless symmetry of snow. When December finally came, she sucked its ice into her, breathing pain in fumes like frost, until the numbness came. Deirdre Penrod believed that she would never know summer again.

When Micah and India Honeyman received news of the Penrod deaths, they immediately started for Frog Level. Near the end of their journey, just after nightfall, they traveled on a narrow dirt road. Suddenly Micah lifted his head, hearing a familiar, frightened whisper—"Micah? Noooooo Micah No!"

He put his hand over India's. "Did you say something?"

"No dear," she replied. "Are you all right?"

"I must be hearing ghosts again." He laughed but urged the horse to a faster pace.

"Micah I forbid you to visit those beavers while we're in Frog Level." In a more serious tone, she added, "Will it bother you to stay at the Inn?"

"No," he assured her. "No more ghosts, I promise you."

A sudden stirring of leaves startled the horse—an overpowering blast of wind rocked the carriage. An unearthly scream started high in the sky and then fell through it, sound descending—bone-splitting, unrelenting—and then a pair of huge claws ripped through the top of the carriage, flinging it upward. Screaming, the horse bolted, as spittle streamed from his bit. The carriage careened crazily down the road and before them, a dark shape split the sky, illumined in a dull, glowing red. India gasped, staring at a monstrous beast with the head of a horse, wings like a bat, and a huge, glowing—good God, *penis* —hanging from his belly. Before she could cry out, it struck again, just as Micah pulled her down to the floor, shielding her with his body. He turned upward, and she felt the force of the blow, as claws tore into his face and chest. The carriage overturned, spilling both of them into the dirt. India lay there stunned, as the beast seemed to dance in the sky above her, before it dipped its wings into the wind and disappeared. She crawled over to Micah and raised him in her arms. "Micah?" she whispered, but his eyes stared back at her, sightless. Slowly, she lowered him to the ground, and turned to face the empty sky. "Whatever sort of evil you may be, you have made a great mistake tonight," she raged. "You have let me live. I promise that I will spend the rest of my life tracking you down. And I intend to live for a very, very long time." She clenched her teeth, holding back tears. As she did so, she noticed a faint sweet sound that surrounded her, delicate as mist. Surely it was her imagination, she thought, because of grief or shock. But it seemed to her that the air was filled with the sound of soft sweet voices, weeping in the wind.

India buried her husband in the Cinders cemetery. In the first days after the accident, she offered a description of some beast too obscene to be considered anything other than a form of feminine hysteria; sensing the reaction, India stopped talking and began to make plans. In the depths of her grief, she was sure that Micah would understand.

At The Penrod Inn, she studied the local men who came to the taproom and was stunned by the weary passivity etched in their faces. She eavesdropped on their discussions, but heard no noisy, spirited debates; the men spoke quietly, and mostly they spoke about leaving. India wondered if her years in Trenton had made her ignorant about the misery of rural life, but excursions through the countryside strengthened her instinct that Frog Level was unusually impoverished for a rural community, despite the obvious displays of Penrod wealth. There was no general store here, no sawmill or gristmill operating along Sabbath Creek. In fact, there were no signs of progress or profit at all—except for those which had benefited the cause of Captain Francis Penrod.

Frog Level was dying. India believed that this was true. She thought about the excitement of Trenton—noisy politics and sooty factories, a huge wooden bridge which spanned the Delaware, and imported lemons for her morning tea. Then she remembered Micah and the beast that had killed him, and she thought about the daughters poor John Francis had left behind. She and Micah had never been able to have a child; India had accepted this fate, but she had never fully adjusted to it. Now it occurred to her that she might repay the kindness of her friend John Francis, who had always tried so hard not to hurt their friendship by declaring his love. Suddenly it seemed to her that Frog Level could be the busiest place in the world—for the first time since her husband's death, India smiled. She felt a bold and bossy spirit streaming through her, and knew that Micah would approve.

None of the Penrod daughters could remember exactly how India Honeyman came to live at the House of Penrod. Delilah thought that Deirdre and Deborah had asked her, and Deirdre thought the aunts had asked her, and Deborah thought that everybody had asked her, except Deborah. But India had not merely come there to live, she had come to change lives, and her swoop upon the Penrod nest reminded Aunt Patience uncomfortably of those words usually ascribed to Germanic tribes —swift and ravaging.

In the front parlor with its stuccoed ceiling decorated with gilt cherubs, India crammed her huge, noisy printing press, which continued to issue, on a weekly basis, the insidiously libertarian *New Jersey Post.* The press had arrived two weeks after India did.

"Are you sure that machine should be put into the parlor?" Patience had whispered, terrified. "Perhaps it wouldn't be, ah, comfortable in here."

"Since it is too large to fit into any of the other rooms, it is more likely to be comfortable here than anywhere, though how anyone could relax while being stared at by those vicious little pixies is something I'll never understand." India's voice sounded triumph. "Look here, Patience, what luck! We'll still have room for your pianoforte, if you don't mind its being pushed up against the wall like this."

Having arranged her enterprises, India turned her energies towards what she considered to be her mission: the Penrod daughters. At the dinner table, she tried to encourage them to speak on their areas of special expertise.

"In Greek mythology, Iris carried messages from the gods to man by traveling across a rainbow," Delilah offered.

"What is the seat of Sand County government?" India retorted, with eyes slitted.

"Captain did not want the girls to be confused by too many facts," Patience said hurriedly.

"As a result, they do not even know enough to be confused," India replied. "Well, I can see we have a great deal of learning to accomplish, if you are going to be of any use to me at all."

Since none of them had ever been of use to anybody, it was difficult to view such a declaration with anything but alarm. And if the Penrod daughters had known what kind of wild ideas this thin-lipped widow dreamed of, they surely would have sent her packing.

———— *Railroads were changing the face of New Jersey, but success did not happen overnight. An English-built locomotive, the* John Bull, *was reassembled in Bordentown by a handyman named Isaac Dripps, who improved British design by adding a whiskey barrel for water supply, hooking it to the boilers with a leather hose made by a local shoemaker. The* John Bull's *first commercial trip was not a triumph: returning from South Amboy, the engine collided with a wandering hog. The hog lost its head; many of the passengers did, too, as the train derailed, plunging into a ditch. Then Elizabethtown's little* Eagle *engine was challenged by a carriage and team of horses. The horses won by a full ten minutes. In spite of these setbacks, rural communities grew into villages alongside railroad tracks that led to Philadelphia and New York —primitive, tribal beginnings of what future generations would come to know as "commuter towns."*

1853 ————

Ivory Hall

FROG LEVEL had never seen anything like it—for the past ten years, the finest house in Sand County had been known as the Penrod Institute for Young Females—or more commonly, Ivory Hall, thanks to Captain's lucky choice of paint. Educated by India Honeyman, the Penrod females now struggled to teach eight young girls who tweaked tassels and rattled crystal door-knobs in the Penrod halls, running more often than they walked and laughing more often than they should. From Deirdre and Deborah, these students learned science and politics, English and math; from Delilah they learned art, and its contemplation. Aunt Patience had put up a noble stand against this invasion. "Girls, I do not believe that Captain ever intended for his home to be used for such a purpose."

"What a lovely surprise it must be for him then," India replied, and the deal was set. Since that day, the aunts had seldom ventured from their bedroom, and they certainly could not bear to read India's newspaper, which supported such ragtag issues as abolition, a ten-hour work day, and the unrestricted use of bloomers. Its editorial page also contained periodic warnings against some mythical beast India insisted upon referring to as the Jersey Devil, as well as intemperate reports from readers who claimed to be witnesses.

India was not on the faculty at Ivory Hall, but she did give lectures there from time to time. And though her views on politics were something to hear, her favorite topic went quite beyond the term "radical." In fact, it was sexual.

"Ladies. Instead of seeing yourselves as the weaker sex because of your emotions, believe in yourselves as ladies of strong passions. The difference lies in expectations. A lady of weak emotions expects little from life. A lady of strong passions expects a great deal and gets more than she's looking for, if she is lucky. I would like to speak to you on one aspect of passion, which you are more likely to find if you know how to look for it. Harriet, take your fingers out of your mouth and sit up straight. Now, does anyone here know about sexual matters?" India Honeyman did, and she had diagrams to supplement her talks. At Ivory Hall, not a pin was dropped as she gave expert testimony on a subject that wasn't on the curriculum. Her students were wise or grateful enough never to mention her talks at home, so no one ever discovered the breadth of education offered by Captain's descendants, although the school did get a reputation for producing New Jersey's finest wives.

Outside the classroom, India concentrated her lectures on the Penrod daughters. When she had arrived in Frog Level in 1838, India reluctantly concluded that Aunts Patience and Hester, who were both over seventy, were beyond help. But the sight of three young women with shining black curls, flashing eyes and glowing cheeks had been a delight—until she discovered their complete indifference to suitors. "It is time for some confusion," India decided as she gritted her teeth and struggled to bridge yet another educational gap (one which the Penrod aunts had particularly treasured).

She turned her attention first to the eldest Penrod daughter. Delilah was lavishly beautiful, although perhaps a bit overripe. But her lethargy was startling: she could sit for hours, apparently unaware that she was doing nothing. At first, India had found this admirable, since she assumed it was some sort of Oriental trance, but she soon discovered that Delilah's mind was as blank as her schedule. Delilah's singing voice was clear and light—it was the only part of her which arose on cue, or hurried anywhere. But after a few months under India's supervision, Delilah developed a springy trot, which worked wonders for her figure, and her dreamy gaze took on an attractive sheen of terror.

Delilah became the first daughter to succumb to India's views on passion. To run her printing press, India had imported her assistant, Hannibal Copper, from Trenton. Hannibal was tall and pale; he had a tangle of nest-brown hair, and the face of a baffled saint. He was the bashful, serious sort of person who is most comfortable when bustling activity is submerging his own (to him) eerie sense of quietness. In Frog Level, he felt exposed by the sparse population and was happiest around India's gregarious clatter. But Delilah's moist abundance had its own appeal, and she had a gift for mindless chatter, cultivated through years of parlor-sitting with her aunts.

Delilah deplored India's revelations about s-e-x-u-a-l-i-t-y, but she noticed Mr. Copper with an alertness that sent an anguished quiver through her virginal soprano. India noticed the noise, but could not pinpoint the source of Delilah's discomfort. Then the *New Jersey Post* twice missed its deadline. Apparently Delilah had been coming into the parlor to practice quite often, and Hannibal had encouraged her by turning off the presses. As a result, India's editorial condemning the New Jersey legislature (for attacking Dorothea Dix) went to press late, and her support for Dorothea Dix (for attacking the New Jersey legislature) never appeared at all. India raged, and Delilah wept.

"Do you think it would be too bold, if I asked him to turn my pages?" Delilah whimpered, confessing her love.

"Only the gods, who are immortal, can afford to be subtle," India told her. "The rest of us are working with a regrettably short lifetime, and you are putting a considerable dent in mine by this lack of resolution to your affairs. Do I make myself clear?"

"Indeed," said Delilah, swallowing hard. That night she sang her heart out. "Lilla, Come Down to Me" sounded like an Indian love call; "The Fairies' Tryst" sounded like the wail of a bitch in heat. Whether it was the sensuality of the delivery or the sheer volume of noise, India was never sure, but according to Delilah's breathless account, Hannibal had suddenly leaped onto the piano bench—"in the middle of the last trill, with the high C"—and throbbed her with bass notes until she quivered. Only the innocent stares of the ceiling cupids had prevented Delilah from total surrender; also, she reported that there wasn't an inch of floor space available in the parlor.

"A wise decision," India said, comforting. "You are not the athletic type, I think." Though India had doubts about the wisdom of this match, she made no objection, and Delilah became the first Penrod daughter to marry, in early 1845.

India turned her attention to Deborah, but she needn't have bothered—Deborah had taken to India immediately upon arrival. It was she who had first suggested the idea for the school —Deborah studied math and politics with the same passion she had once devoted to flowers painted upon velvet. In fact, she copied India's mannerisms and India's ideas so perfectly that she was soon driving Delilah to hysterics.

For several years, Deborah had been thinking about the kind of life she wanted, and how she could get it. One night in early 1850 she climbed out of her bedroom window; when she returned the next morning to pick up her belongings, she was driving a wagon with "California or Bust" painted on its sides. "I'm going west," she cried. "I'm going to search for gold—I mean, *we* are." Deborah pointed to the back of the wagon, where a local farmer named Simon Rutledge was dozing. "We'll get married as soon as we can," she told India.

"An excellent choice. Simon is the calmest man in this county." As Deborah watched her anxiously, she added, "It's just what I would do, my dear, if I were a few years younger."

"Thank you," Deborah whispered, leaning down to embrace her. "There just wasn't room here for both of us."

India waved goodbye, silently agreeing. She had found it unnerving to be constructed in precise detail by a younger model. "We are meant to live well," she thought, "but only once."

Classes at Ivory Hall continued undisturbed, because Deirdre was happy to take over Deborah's teaching duties. Deirdre lived for her work. She studied hard and never made trouble. But after fifteen years, she still refused to listen to India's arguments for passion.

"I will be a modern woman, like Dorothea Dix," she told India. "I will devote my life to education, and be perfectly happy. My father left me well provided for. You provide excellent company. I simply do not need a husband." When India persisted, Deirdre said angrily, "You are too romantic."

"Even my husband, who adored me, never accused me of

that," India replied. "Deirdre, whatever is at the bottom of all this?"

By fits and starts, Deirdre confessed her interlude with Ethan Crouse. "It was dreadful," she wept. "I should never have done it—I killed my parents."

"Deirdre, I can understand that you might feel guilty, but to accuse yourself of murder—"

"You don't understand," she broke in, and then explained what had happened the night Ethan left her, when Caroline attacked her at the creek.

"Surely you have never told anyone about this?" India said, trying to hide her shock.

"Nooo," she sobbed. "I should have. Then I could have gone to prison and written articles about the conditions there, like Margaret Fuller."

"Nonsense. The best way to help the unfortunate is by not becoming one of them." India leaned forward, speaking gently. "Now, listen carefully. You witnessed a tragedy, and because you loved the people involved, it is perfectly natural to believe that you caused it. But remember that I, too, witnessed a tragedy. If I had used my energy for guilt, I would never have found time for revenge." She smiled happily. "If revenge does not appeal to you, then there are other options."

India's advice did not have any noticeable effect, but she had other problems to worry about, in that summer of 1853: The Camden-Atlantic Railroad had laid tracks across South Jersey, but its route had bypassed Frog Level, stopping instead at a glassworks called Rowleytown, five miles to the west. India wrote violent letters to the railway officials, but they refused to alter their plans, pointing out that Frog Level had no product to offer the Philadelphia market.

After she received their letter, India paced her bedroom floor, long into the night. The next morning, she sent for a local farmer named Brand Johnson, who seemed perfect for her schemes.

Reading that note, Brand shook his head once. "Well," he said. A close friend might have recognized this gesture, for it was the closest he ever came to smiling. But no one in Frog Level knew Brand Johnson well. Seven years ago, he had lost his wife and two sons to a fever; for the past four years, he had lost his crop to nature. He was as poor as the played-out soil he tried to farm. His manner was sullen and hard. His neighbors kept their distance, which was just what he wanted.

Brand read the *New Jersey Post* every week, with a friendly sense of outrage—like most of his neighbors, he believed that its editor had gone a bit dotty with grief when her husband died, so he forgave her her opinions. Her attacks on the "Jersey Devil" were riveting, but although Brand had lost two of his best milking cows to some goddamn beast, it never occurred to him that the dotty old lady might be right. There had been too many other beasts in his life, for him to believe in a devil. But he was curious about India Honeyman, and the idea of talking to someone besides himself was actually pleasant. "Well," he said again, shaking his head. He hoped that his ancient, bony horse would survive the trip into town.

India surveyed her guest with satisfaction. Despite his faded shirt and ragged breeches, Brand Johnson made a formidable impression—powerfully built, and the grim set to his face did not hide the straight planes of his nose and chin or the beauty of brooding brown eyes. "Mr. Johnson, the railroad has passed us by, and it is time to fight back. I have asked you here to discuss a mutual enterprise," India told him as she passed the tea.

"I'm a farmer, not a businessman," he replied, staring unhappily at the cup she had placed in his hands.

"I'm aware of that. But surely you agree that the future of farming lies in specialization?"

He ignored her charming smile. "Didn't know you knew so much about it."

"I have made a study of many things," she replied sweetly. "For example, I know that the cranberry shrubs on this property used to provide the finest berries in the county, though they had been badly neglected. They are planted at a strange basin construction—I've never seen anything like it. If we could repair and duplicate this construction, I believe we could grow large quantities of berries—corner the market, so to speak."

"For cranberries, there ain't no market to corner."

"We'll worry about that later. Right now we need a specialized crop to attract the railroad, so that people in this area need not look to the west for a future."

Brand stared at her. "Here's the truth," he said. "Around here, the future gets further away with every sunrise."

"Then full speed ahead, Mr. Johnson," she replied. "We must catch up, and quickly."

He set down his cup, and shook his head. "Well," he said. "Well."

That afternoon, at India's request, Deirdre took Brand to inspect the cranberry basin. Within minutes she had decided that he was ignorant and rude; he suspected that she was a highfalutin' bitch. They walked in sullen silence until they reached the crumbling dams at the creek.

Brand studied the basin and tried to separate the branches. "Soils not dried out too bad," he said, "but these bushes have practically strangled each other. Didn't anyone think to cut them back?" He sounded furious, as though some heartless massacre had occurred.

"No one has been out this way in a long time," Deirdre replied. Since that summer, she was thinking. Since Ethan. Bushes strangle. People die.

"Hot, isn't it?"

"What?" she turned on him shocked. *Ha! Caught you peeking out that window again, Deirdre.* Ethan had been the color of toast. In the sun his arms had rippled with sweat.

"I'll need some tools and a place to put them," Brand said abruptly. "What's that shack over there?" He pointed to the cabin.

"It's nothing," she said quickly. "India—Mrs. Honeyman says that Aunt Cedar Brewster used to live there."

"It will make a fair tool shed," he said grudgingly. "I don't guarantee to spend regular time here—I got my own place to look after. Don't promise any miracles—these bushes are planted kind of strange. Kind of smart, too, maybe." He looked at them with distaste.

"Mrs. Honeyman will be delighted by your enthusiasm," Deirdre said icily.

"That woman's got some kind of strange ideas herself," he replied.

And one of them is you, Deirdre thought, furious; she could not imagine what India saw in this huge, surly beast.

They returned to the house in sullen silence, and Deirdre put the unpleasant encounter out of her mind—or tried to. But her visit to the cranberry basin seemed to have rekindled her interest in it—perfectly natural, she decided, that it stirred up her memories. Then it occurred to her that someone should keep track of that arrogant brute—"He might be stealing the tools. How would we know?" It did not seem strange to her that she began to take afternoon walks after her classes to watch Brand Johnson work at the cranberry basin. In the heat of summer, she felt too restless to study inside.

His callused hands were square, with large, scratched knuckles. Stopping to trim the bushes or kneeling in the dirt to repair the earthen dams, he moved with a crude animal grace that fascinated her—although he was ill-at-ease in the world, Brand seemed completely at home in his large angular body. She was pleased that he ignored her most of the time, that he did not send her away. She did not want to talk to this graceful oaf, but it was pleasant to watch him while he worked.

As the weeks passed, water flowed smoothly through the channels he had made; in the basin, the newly trimmed bushes began to thrive. Brand cursed the branches that scratched him. He cursed the dirt and the weather. But he did not curse the berries. He stroked their waxy surface, resting them in the cradle of his hands. When he looked at them his eyes turned soft and searching, like a lover's. He dug in the earth and shaped it; it darkened, turning moist as his hands caressed its life.

As Deirdre watched, it came to her that he was making love through the earth, to the berries. And she knew that she wanted to lie in the earth, she wanted to feel his hands upon her. She knew that she would burst into life beneath his soft, searching eyes. And there would be no branches to scratch him—just her arms softly twining to bring him down into the earth with her, so that she could make this deeply passionate man grow hard with life. The idea shocked and embarrassed her, but still, it began to possess her. At night, she would awake to discover that she was *not* in the dirt, in his arms—and then, she wept.

One day in early October, Deirdre came to the basin when

Brand wasn't working there. The cranberries were hard and already red. As she pulled a cluster from the branch, her hand trembled—believing his intimacy with the earth, it was as though Brand had forcibly seduced her through the changing season. His touch was in the ripening berries, in bright colors and frost. She put a berry into her mouth, feeling it cool, resilient under the pressure of her tongue.

Suddenly, she remembered the thick sweetness of strawberry, sliding deep into her throat. Without thinking, she bit down hard on the cranberry. An acid taste flooded her mouth. Kneeling, she spat the unripened berry into the dirt, but the taste of it was already flooding her senses. "Brand does not want me," she thought. "I would gladly force him into the dirt, but I cannot make him want me."

In fact, Brand Johnson did not want to love. He was purposely avoiding Deirdre Penrod's company at the cranberry basin, because he recognized susceptibility in himself, and he knew how to fight it. Last year, he had noticed that he was growing too attached to one of the stray cats that lived in his barn, so he'd gathered all of the cats into a sack, filled the sack with rocks and dropped it into the creek. He would not love again. He would not stand beneath a tree again, to bury love, in wooden boxes. He had loved, once. Never again would he risk such a horror.

By the first week in November, the cranberries were ripe, ready to be taken. Alone in his fields, Brand sensed this, could feel it in the crisp air that streamed against his face. Closing his eyes, he could see the ripened berries, waiting for his touch. He could not bear the thought that other hands would take them from the branch. Or worse, that they might not be taken at all —hadn't those silly females nearly destroyed the bushes through neglect? The thought made him furious. In a blind rage, he hitched the horse and headed for the basin.

She was kneeling in the dirt and did not hear him approach. Brand watched her, feeling his anger fade. Using one of the wooden scoops he had left in the shed, Deirdre was struggling to strip the berries from the branches. Bending awkwardly, with her long skirts tangled in the foliage, as the wind blew a curtain of long dark curls across her face. When she brushed the hair from her eyes, he could see that her face was smeared with dirt. In her dogged, stumbling movements, he could barely recognize Miss Deirdre Penrod, schoolmistress at Ivory Hall. But she was a perfect picture of the woman who'd been haunting his dreams.

Without speaking, he knelt in the dirt beside her. Covering her hand with his, he showed her how to move the scoop through the branches, to take the berries. Her motions became less awkward as she tried to match the deep, feathered rhythm in his swing. An hour passed. The afternoon grew bitter cold. He worked on, silently begging her to leave him, to quit, be gone. But she would not, despite the numbing wind, the aching muscles in her arms. She worked on, silently begging him to take her down, into the dirt, into his arms. But he did not. And so they worked on, separately, trembling side-by-side, like a pair of retrievers crouched in the field, who cannot fire the gun. Who can only think to tremble as they silently beg for the prize to fall from an indifferent sky.

The bushes were bare, now. The job was done. They gathered the buckets of cranberries and carried them into the shed. Inside, it was dark and dank as a tomb. Turning to watch the light fade from the doorway, Deirdre shuddered. The day was gone, her chance was gone, and she would be left forever in darkness—a cell that she had made, but could no longer endure. Brand turned, nearly bumping into her, and she realized that she was blocking the doorway.

She could not move. She could not let him go.

In the murky light, he strained to see her face, cursing the nearness of her. He knew that she would not move until he reached out to push her aside. And he knew that if he reached out, it would be to take her into his arms. He knew that he was shaking, as need for her stripped him of his pride and resolve. He felt himself naked of these layers and ashamed. But he would not touch her.

She put her hand on his crotch.

A sudden hiss of air—her breath, or his. Or perhaps the wheezing brake of time as, quite suddenly, it stood still.

She felt him—unmistakable, the curving mounds, that supple soft-ridged length of man. She felt him stirring—a velvet, bony mass that softly bulged his trousers. She pressed against it, feeling the rise, drawing the heat of his imprint into her hand.

His hand gripped hers, jerking it away. Her sense of loss was so great that she would have cried out, except that she was suddenly engulfed by a terrifying sense of shame. Turning, she tried to run, to outdistance the filthy crime, but her hand was trapped in his grasp. She fought him blindly, desperate to escape, but he pushed her against the doorway and held her roughly. Too ashamed to look at him, she turned her head against the door. She could feel him staring and knew the hatred and disgust that must be in his eyes. He lifted her obscene, ugly hand—the hand that had touched him—he raised it into the air, exposing her shame.

He raised it to his lips. As he stroked her clenched fists, her fingers opened, curling beneath his touch to reveal her palm. He kissed her there. Then she felt him touch her face, he was brushing her tangled hair back, feeling for the curve of her throat and then he was kissing her there and on the hair and eyes and lips. Beneath his touch she drifted with senses flowing as his callused, tender hands stroked her breasts, guiding ripples through her flesh—rippling deep within her, where frozen, buried things were stirring now, struggling to get free.

Ripples formed a rougher current as he pulled her against him. His hands made a current that streamed the length of her spine as he caressed her. Waves cresting onto the slope of her buttocks as he found their curves and fitted his hands over her there and lifted her to meet the force of his own desire. She felt an exquisite shock, and then her hips swayed, guided by his hands. She leaned against him, drifting as the current engulfed her.

She felt his hands beneath her skirts, and then he lifted her again. Her feet left the ground so effortlessly that she might have been a leaf flung into the sky. He held her waist tightly, folding her legs around him as he leaned her back against the door, so that she was resting in his embrace, high above the ground, held against the safety of his strong muscled thighs.

She clung to him, gripping his shoulders as desire swept through her. She kissed him hungrily, urgently on his face and neck and chest. Something deep inside her was opening, that

209

fiery, aching center. No! she was making a terrible mistake, but it was too late. She was opening, drenched in fire and ache—he pushed up into her, driving her against the door. His strength shocked her, and then his tenderness as she drifted, moving her arms and legs to hold him close, to feel his shape within her, to catch the sweet, hungry rhythm of his tide.

As she moved, searching and then meeting his desire, Ethan Crouse was the last thing on her mind. Her body knew only this moment, only this man who was taking her higher and higher, who was giving to her all that he possessed—heart and soul and mind were filling her, flooding her and yes, she took him, was taking him up, up, the aching fire was ripping through her body as passion caught the edge, suspended, and then exploded into sky. Sweet, spiraling brightness—as it swept her, she had one dim, happy thought: one hundred streaming *skycrackers*. About one thing, at least, Ethan Crouse had been right.

Deirdre and Brand Johnson were married on Christmas day 1853. In that same month, railway workers began to lay track for a spur line to Frog Level. Although no trains were scheduled to stop there, railway officials were sufficiently impressed with the cranberries India sent them (or exhausted by her endless appeals) to make this compromise. To connect with the train service at Rowleytown, India secured a railway flatcar that was hand operable, and she persuaded young ladies from Ivory Hall to operate it. India attached a large sheet to the top of the car to increase its speed. From a distance, it looked like a schooner sailing through the South Jersey Flatlands, but Frog Level's cranberries and its other produce made the train to the Philadelphia market.

That railroad spur kept the small community of Frog Level alive, as India Honeyman had known it would. In 1858, the ironworks at Audry blew out, creating a ghost town as the workers abandoned the New Jersey pines for the iron mills of Pennsylvania. India and Brand Johnson bought up acres of the turfed out bogland there and planted cranberry shrubs in the excavations. Soon they were producing more cranberries than Indian Jin had ever dreamed of.

Soon after Deirdre and Brand moved out to the Audry property, Delilah made it clear to India that the House of Penrod was a bit overcrowded. Enrollment at Ivory Hall had increased, even though Delilah, as its sole headmistress, had changed the curriculum to reflect her genteel tastes. No longer did India Honeyman give lectures on special topics, and her printing press was considered an annoyance. In 1859, India cheerfully moved her headquarters to the Penrod Inn and set up her presses in Mags Honeyman's former front parlor. The idea of spending her waning years in a public tavern appealed to her, although the Penrod Inn itself was waning—with the rise of the railroads, stagecoach traffic disappeared, and the large tavern was little more than a local taproom and meeting place. India made friends with Seth Hosey, who had taken over the tavern management from his father. Soon the noise from the presses of the *New Jersey Post* became part of the tavern atmosphere. After a few drinks, no one noticed.

India never gave up her search for the Jersey Devil. On bright, moonlit nights she could be seen floating across the fields on her railway flatcar, with her sail shimmering in the moonlight as volunteers from Ivory Hall pumped her along the tracks. Her trips through the countryside became widely acclaimed, particularly by those who were unfortunate enough to catch sight of her when they were drunk. She was considered hopelessly eccentric, and local residents became so used to laughing at her excursions that they never noticed the passengers who sometimes traveled with her. In this way, India Honeyman was able to help dozens of black slaves who were escaping north. Quakers from Salem and Cumberland counties, who organized the underground effort, knew that India's midnight rides were the quickest, safest way to transport slaves through the dangerous territory of New Jersey, which was the only northern state to support the Recovery of Slaves Act.

As the decade of the 1850s rolled to a close, local readers of India's *New Jersey Post* were informed that the "Know Nothing" party was a crime against immigrants, that nothing enslaved a people more than the act of slavery, that six-foot holes in the surface of Flying Horse Pike were more than she could tolerate, that the Jersey Devil was prowling and wouldn't Frog Levelers please cooperate? India also traveled to the exhibition of world

211

inventions at New York's Crystal Palace. She reported her trip in an article in which she refused to describe the details of a single invention; instead, she commanded others to make the trip.

Frog Level heard her out, somewhat wearily. Citizens were more interested in complaining about the price of a haircut in Rowleytown which had recently been raised to six cents. They wanted to hear about boom towns in the Rockies, about the silver strike at the Comstock lode. And many of them traveled clear to Camden on the day that the calliope came into town. But few of those who lived near the Frog Level could fully understand the forces which were pulling New Jersey towards another war. In northern New Jersey, Copperhead Democrats were a powerful voice, insisting that war with the South would bring industrial collapse; some political leaders openly counseled that New Jersey should secede from the Union and join the southern states. The citizens of Frog Level did not share India's Abolitionist fervor, but when President Lincoln declared war on April 12, 1861, and called for New Jersey men, sons named Treacher and Stread and Barber went off to war. Neither Brand Johnson nor Hannibal Copper volunteered, and they were not drafted. Brand was forty-two years old, and swore he was too old to fight with anyone but Deirdre. Hannibal was over fifty now, and he had always had painful arches.

It was not the years of war but peace that showed the change in Frog Level. This time, soldiers returned to farms which provided a future and to new jobs offered by Brand Johnson's cranberry bogs at Audry. On Sabbath Creek, a sawmill was operating and the general store at Rowleytown provided cloth from the bolt, cross-grained saws, and Emerson's Elixir; treasures from Philadelphia were now just five miles away.

By 1873, local farmers had begun to hold monthly meetings, forming the Frog Level Alliance to protect their common interests. Among their grievances were listed Wall Street speculation, Philadelphia wholesalers, New Jersey bankers, and the price of a haircut in Rowleytown, which had recently climbed to eight cents. They also officially protested India Honeyman's attendance at these meetings. India replied that she was ninety-nine years old but in excellent health and invited them to test her frailty by trying to throw her out. She had no takers.

At Ivory Hall, Delilah Penrod reigned secure. Crystal goblets were chiming once again, as twelve young ladies received an education in deportment, grace, and the arts. At least, that is what they learned from Delilah. But Hannibal, poor Hannibal . . . that tempting young flesh. Hannibal Copper dreamed of teaching a few lessons on his own.

———— *The influence of anti-war forces remained high throughout the war, but the New Jersey militia responded promptly to Lincoln's call for troops. Unfortunately, their arsenal of weapons consisted of two cannon captured at Yorktown, one taken at the Battle of Trenton in 1776, and about eleven thousand flintlock muskets, too rust-covered to serve as anything more than military mementoes. Even worse, they did not possess a single round of ammunition. In spite of this, three thousand officers and men sailed down the Delaware to war on May 3, 1861, while one Captain Charles Smith headed in the opposite direction, to New York City; there he managed to locate thirty-six thousand rounds of ammunition, which happened to be in the hands of a private dealer. Smith bought the entire supply and smuggled it out of the city, racing back to arm the militia as it steamed across the Chesapeake Bay.*

When the war was over, soldiers returned to a still-divided state. Throughout New Jersey, there was strong opposition to giving black citizens the right to vote. In 1867 and again in 1870, its legislature voted against ratification of the Fifteenth Amendment. In 1875, the state finally eliminated the word "white" from its voting qualifications prompting a New York editor to note that New Jersey was "back in the Union."

_The Copper Family

1873 ———————

Ceremony at the Stranger's Grave

AT AGE fifty-eight, Delilah Penrod Copper felt that she was clearly in her prime. She had never been an enthusiastic convert to India's philosophies; once she'd maneuvered that woman out of her home, she happily reverted to Aunt Patience's school of thought—or more precisely, the lack of it. Although most of Captain's estate had been spent during the establishment of Ivory Hall, there was still enough money to replace the parlor sofas when cherry-colored velvet lost its plush; and there was enough money to ease the burden of complete redecoration, from Chippendale desk to a ten-inch crystal parrot. (The desk had lost its key; the parrot simply lost its charm.)

Delilah took pride in the thought that although dear Captain was surely in heaven, *she* provided his eternal bliss, by ensuring that the Penrod tassels never grew haggard, that priceless silver always gleamed, proclaiming the most lavish life-style in Sand County, New Jersey. She also took pride in what she considered her prime role as headmistress—setting a gracious example for the students of Ivory Hall—and she took pride in being a wife. Beyond this pride, she took very little interest in the classroom or the bedroom.

She had always been indifferent to books, but her antipathy for sex had been a belated revelation. Typesetting was a dirty process, and in the early years of their marriage, Delilah had refused to allow Hannibal into her bed when he was still grimy from the presses. This initial refusal enabled her to understand that what she really objected to was letting him into her bed at all.

Passion was all right for those who had no access to hand-blown crystal, she decided; perhaps it even compensated for the lack of finer things. But finer things become soiled and disheveled when passion is not relegated to the masses. If sex were confined to the barnyard or pasture, she might have a go at it, once a year or so. She'd even had rather daring dreams about being taken by force, upon a sweating white stallion. Or perhaps it was *by* a sweating stallion—the dream was blessedly imprecise. But to be attacked in one's best lace gown, while reclining upon freshly scented sheets had no appeal. In a delicate world, passion appeared, well, indelicate.

Their marriage had been childless until sixteen years ago, when Delilah had suddenly given birth to their twin sons, David and Jonathan. Almost, as she had thought at the time, as though this unexpected birth was a sign that she and Hannibal needn't keep trying anymore. So Delilah had delicately informed her husband, "Please, dear, no," for so many nights in succession that he'd finally stopped asking. She had assumed that Hannibal, like her, was comfortably easing into his prime and no longer wanted the mess either.

That was her first mistake. For although clearly in his prime, Hannibal Copper not only wanted, he burned. But he no longer burned for his wife. He'd felt very much in love when they married, and he recognized that Delilah was still a beautiful woman. The silver streaks in her glossy black hair merely served to set off the sparkle in her eyes. Her complexion had not lost its exotic flush, and her figure retained its hourglass proportions (although it had grown to a scale which could easily hold enough sand to keep time for a week).

Unfortunately for Hannibal, the concept of Delilah had proved more intriguing than the reality. When not drenched in grace, and lace, she became panicky. She clutched at her femininity, the way a traveler in a foreign country will reassure himself by fondling the name tags he has sewn into his clothes. Hannibal found it increasingly difficult to search for the flesh and blood that were entombed by her incessant fragility. Finally, he stopped trying and left Delilah to her mysterious, oddly unenticing world of ruffles, doilies, and perfect high Cs.

Instead, he burned for the students of Ivory Hall. He could not keep his eyes from these young eager girls who skipped and ran, thrusting their impending womanhood forward, as though to hurry through its stages. In their springy gait and fresh awkward energy, he saw a beauty that had not been coddled and therefore appeared open and touchable. In their youth, he saw femininity that had not yet recoiled to seek refuge behind bars of lace. Virginity, purity, these were things to be revered, he believed. But couldn't a man celebrate, with his touch?

Hannibal had read a bit of mythology and the classics, and he knew that rites of worship had once been a bit more tantalizing than those offered by modern Christianity. There must be a way to pay homage to the turmoil that coursed through him when he stared at Miss Sadie Linnet, who was indisputably, the most nubile student that Ivory Hall had ever seen.

Hannibal had stolen one of her petticoats. He kept it under his pillow. Every night he drifted into sleep with that petticoat pulled over his head, as he inhaled the faint perfume from that part of the fabric which covered the most private part of Sadie's budding anatomy. He thought of it as her sacred site. That such adoration might be obscene never occurred to him. Hannibal was an innocent man. Like his wife Delilah, he had total faith in the innocence and purity of the youth residing at Ivory Hall.

That was the Coppers' greatest mistake. The female dormitory at Ivory Hall was a pubescent inferno. Cloistered together to wait out the years until they became marriageable, it was only natural that these girls began to anticipate the mysterious fate they would share. The unspoken bond of shared menstrual indignities made them blushingly intimate, and now that India's lectures on sex were forbidden, they were free to imagine the best, the worst, or the anatomically impossible.

Those who claimed any knowledge of men were listened to as though they were reading from a divine slab. News that a recent graduate was bethrothed always brought a flurry of whispers and screams. "If only she knew what she was in store for," an older girl would say, while the rest groaned. If only *they* knew!

The study of art, and its contemplation left plenty of time for sexual speculation; at Ivory Hall, the student body squirmed. Though drenched in grace, and lace, they steamed.

Miss Sadie Linnet led the whispers and screams. She was not aware of her effect on Hannibal, because she was not yet adept at sensing her power, but she knew that she had it. She did not know about men's eyes, but she did know how to look into a mirror. What she saw was large blue eyes with a fringe of thick, dark lashes; her skin was soft and fair, her nose was perfect. And best of all, despite her youth, she was indisputably *breasted*. When Sadie looped her bright blonde hair in pristine coils behind her ears, she looked at least eighteen, though not one bit pristine. Sadie knew that her incredible beauty compelled her to be a leader—how could she not know more about men than the other girls, when she had been so clearly designated an expert by nature?

Anabel Chess listened to Sadie's whispers with a mounting sense of doom. They had been best friends for three years, since their first day at Ivory Hall, when they had flung themselves across the same bed, sobbing for home. Anabel had loyally put up with Sadie's thoughtlessness, just as she knew that Sadie had indulged her own gawky shyness. But she was unprepared for the strains that beauty now imposed upon their friendship.

Until she watched her friend, it had never occurred to Anabel to look into a mirror. When she did, she saw bony cheeks, a furrowed brow, and a pair of large, thick spectacles. As for her hair, a more interesting shade of brown could be found in the bark of any tree. Anabel was embarrassed by her inadequacy—it was as though she was betraying their friendship by not growing beautiful as Sadie did. To Anabel, the mirror was charting limitations in a way that Sadie's thoughtlessnes and her own shyness had never been able to do. She hated the mirror, and she hated the whispers. Every night she wished that her name was Carlotta, so that she could become a nun. A famous nun.

The female dormitory at Ivory Hall was not the only source of adolescent steam. At sixteen, David and Jonathan Copper were accomplished voyeurs. They had started spying on the girls at such an early age, that when they had first been caught, they provoked not screams but howls of laughter. David had been enraged by this, and ever since he had led his brother in a series of pranks against the girls, which Delilah rarely caught.

Although they were both handsome dark-haired boys, David and Jonathan were seldom thought to look alike. David was taller and stronger, and his coloring was more vibrant than his brother's. In their lighted facial planes was the difference between the sun and the moon. David was born to get away with those very things that Jonathan was born to go along with, though David often saved his own skin by turning in his brother.

By the age of sixteen, David could describe the unclad body of every girl at Ivory Hall in graphic detail, and he did so every night as he lay in bed with his brother. "Sadie has titties already, and she just turned fifteen," he reported, ecstatically.

"I didn't see anything sticking up in her dresses," Jonathan replied.

"It ain't in her dress, silly. You got to look at where they're growing to see anything. All pointy and swollen, and I can tell she's really aching for it, the way she moves those hips. Her titties are a lot bigger than Anabel Chess's and Anabel is nearly sixteen. You can tell that girl ain't never going to amount to anything."

"I like Anabel Chess," Jonathan objected.

"You would," his brother replied. "You don't like titties much, do you? I know what you like."

Jonathan was afraid to speak, dreading what he knew must happen. It always happened when his brother's voice grew thick, when his brother's hand was rubbing at his thigh.

"Roll over, Jonathan."

"No." There would be silence, in which Jonathan could sense the danger. "Please, David. Let me do it with my hands. I promise, it will be good."

"Roll over. Do it."

Ever since their twelfth birthday, Jonathan had obeyed. He raised his knees, buried his face in his arms, and tried to ignore the pain. The shame of this nightly act seemed to coat him, like an unmistakable stench—Sadie's titties. Millie's hips. David's penis crammed between his buttocks. He felt no pleasure, and yet David would sometimes use his hands to make Jonathan's penis rise—shocking Jonathan with need and then laughing, turning away, leaving his brother to flail away until he came, for sheer relief.

It never occurred to either son of the House of Penrod-Copper that they were having sex. David and Jonathan were as ignorant and wistful as the girls they spied upon. And they might have remained so, if the smothered passions of Ivory Hall had not been accidentally ignited by the Presbyterian Church.

This was not a mistake. In fact, the church was trying to give the Reverend Elijah Brewster belated recognition, by honoring the Stranger's Grave. In 1769, a stranger had dropped dead at Dark of the Moon and settlers from the area had not bothered to attend his burial. This had led to one of Reverend Brewster's most famous sermons, about the sin of being a stranger. Afterwards, his repentant congregation had littered the grave with flowers, visiting there so regularly that Joshan Rane finally protested, claiming that the man would get no peace at all.

The grave rested in an unused part of the Cinders cemetery, where the foliage had grown high enough to create a secluded glade. When the church erected a large stone bench there, carved with Reverend Brewster's name, they meant to salute his faith and his oratorical skill. But the very first time Hannibal saw that high, broad slab, he had ancient sacred visions. Sadie Linnet's pristine flesh draped across an altar, as flimsily clad maidens danced around her. Like those of his wife, Hannibal's dreams were vague, but unlike Delilah (alas, there was not a white stallion to be had in the county), he had the means by which to flesh out his dreams. His means was the flesh of Ivory Hall.

Sadie Linnet was pleasantly surprised when Mr. Copper began to seek out her company. She had always been fascinated by his presence at the dinner table, where he rarely spoke, except to say "yes" to his wife. Beneath the tangled riot of his gray hair, he looked completely serene as he stooped over his plate, gazing at his food with such a joyful, sweet expression that Sadie wondered how he could bear to eat it.

Now she discovered that Mr. Copper could not only make conversation, but actually knew a great deal, for an old man. He knew a great deal about interesting things that she'd never heard of. For instance, he told enchanting stories about the days when a girl named Diana was actually worshiped for her beauty, or something like that, about rites so secret that no one knew them, about beauty anointed, and purity paid homage to.

From the sound of his voice, she could tell how glamorous and exciting it must have been for Diana, when man was still sensible enough to worship a woman. "Goddess"—it was such a lovely word. Actually, it sounded much nicer than "fiancée," or even "bride." Sadie did not dream about Hannibal Copper. But she began to share his dreams. And then, she began to persuade the other girls to share them too.

"Mr. Copper knows a great deal about these things," she told them. "He says that the moon must be right. The time must be right. And the goddess must be very, very beautiful."

"What's the ceremony about?" Anabel asked her.

"Secrets," she replied. "Mr. Copper says that in ancient times, every young maiden was anointed by the gods." There was a chorus of groans: to be "anointed," when the moon was right. It sounded terrifying. And absolutely thrilling.

Hannibal's petticoat-shrouded dreams were becoming more desperate. One night he suddenly bolted up in bed—"It shall be ten days hence," he cried. It seemed that the fumes from Sadie's sacred site had produced an oracular effect. Hannibal was not sure how he'd arrived at this date but he knew that "ten days hence" was the proper way to announce it. He was also sure about what the girls should wear: A single white petticoat, with the flimsiest chemise. With loosened, flowing hair and un-shod feet—and beneath her lacy costume, from waist to toes—each maiden must be purely, wholly bare.

When Hannibal confided the news to Sadie, she felt a dizzy rush. The gods had spoken. And in such flattering detail! Of course, preparations would take place in absolute secrecy. Of course, she would hide beneath the moon at midnight, ten days hence. The Chosen Maidens would await a signal from these gods, by the dark of the Stranger's Grave.

Sadie delivered this ultimatum to the girls, looking so radiantly beautiful that no one could doubt her divine selection, except her best friend. Anabel bashfully voiced her dissent, but the fact that no one agreed embarrassed her. "Maybe I am supposed to be shy, because when I speak out, I say disagreeable things." Believing this, her protests ceased, and finally she reluctantly promised Sadie that she would be a Chosen Maiden, too.

On the afternoon before this mystical event, the girls sewed long white ribbons onto their petticoats, with trembling fingers. Little Lettie Michaels wept uncontrollably from sheer excitement. As Sadie calmed her, she could barely hold back her own tears. Tonight, her life would change forever. She felt powerless to stop it. The forces had spoken, and she could only obey. "Please believe," she whispered to Anabel. "Please believe for me."

Anabel smiled and shook her head. But as she sewed, she noticed that her fingers trembled, too.

Hannibal was sewing, too, following a set of secret instructions from his gods. Delilah had not noticed his raid on the linen closet, nor the golden dessert spoons that he had carelessly scattered across the dining table, in order to steal the black velvet pouch which was meant to contain them. As she basked in her redecorated parlor, Delilah was the only member of the Copper family who was not trembling . . . because her sons were upstairs peeking from behind a closet door, as they watched the Chosen Maidens slip thin white petticoats over flesh that was purely, wholly bare.

The night seemed huge and strangely iridescent. Sadie and her maidens crept through its gleaming, shadowed surface—at midnight, beneath the moon, moving towards the dark of the Stranger's Grave. Crouching low, they passed the church and Reverend Crouse's cabin, traveling from tree to tree. By the time they reched the cemetery, they had frightened each other, thrilled themselves, and were more than half out of their wits. In these murky rows of crosses, friends looked like strangers, and each was a stranger to herself. Everything about this night was magical, and therefore did not happen. Even Anabel Chess felt the change and marveled to feel so free.

By the dark of the Stranger's Grave, he waited—a tall, white-robed figure whose hooded face was shadowed by the foliage. He held a long golden scepter.

"Enter." His voice was an abyss. One by one they crossed it, with Sadie moving first to pass through the foliage into the glade. As she did so, she could not resist raising her eyes, and gasped—the tall, mysterious figure had no face! Beneath the folds of his white hood, there was only darkness, though she could see a pair of gleaming eyes. An unknown god! Her heart beat faster as she whirled before his gaze.

He pointed at her, raising his scepter. "You will be first among them all."

Sadie nodded, nearly swooning. All along, she had known that it would turn out just like this.

Now he pointed to Anabel and Lettie Michaels, who stood anxiously nearby. "You two," he intoned. "You will prepare Sa —you will prepare the goddess for anointment." He turned to the maidens who trembled beyond his grasp. "The rest of you will dance around the altar."

As Sadie nodded encouragingly, the maidens began a slow awkward circle through the glade. "You must twirl!" the priest commanded, and they did so, as their petticoats rose in bells, revealing the purity of soft slippery thighs. Sadie had taken her place, reclining on the altar with her attendants at her head and feet as the white-robed figure moved behind, still watching the dancers.

"Oh, Diana!" he cried suddenly. "The moon is high. Comes the night." The dancing maidens stumbled to a halt, and stared uncertainly, "Oh, purity, grace and beauty divine—we worship you, Diana."

On her altar, Sadie fidgeted, feeling upstaged. But then the scepter hovered over her as the priest exclaimed, "See this young virgin before thee. In every way, she is thy equal." Sadie smiled, closing her eyes, as the priest turned to her attendants. "Prepare her sacred site," he told them.

Anabel and Lettie looked blank.

"Return to the others. I will prepare her myself." Sadie peeked one eye open, watching the priest lift the hem of her petticoat, and then closed it quickly, as she realized that he was raising her skirt, inch by inch. Cool air tickled her knees. Then a shocking breeze swept her thighs and ruffled the down on her stomach. She felt a tremor, and heard gasps and knew that this faceless god had exposed her from waist to toe.

He was murmuring, she could not make out his words. Waves of doubt and fear swept through her, as she waited helplessly, wondering what would happen next.

If the maidens had not been so intent on the action at the altar, they would have seen the bushes rustling, would have heard Jonathan as he whispered to his brother, "We've got to stop this, now."

David twisted his arm, pinning him to the ground. "Shut up," he said, then, "Look at that." His breath was coming hard.

Sadie felt a cold brass touch. She flinched, afraid to cry out. The god's scepter moved between her legs to the shivery spot that sometimes seemed to gently hum, the place she'd never touched. The tip of the scepter nudged her thighs apart; it was spreading her open, cold sliding into her, pushing gently, spreading mystical shivers of warmth. She sighed, relaxing to his gliding, hypnotic touch.

Suddenly, she felt the scepter leave her body. Surprised, she opened her eyes, watching the hooded figure as he bent over her, until the folds of his white hood brushed against her skin. She gasped as he made contact—the faceless god had lips! His lips had found that spot that hummed, they were brushing, kissing her there. Softness, warmth were rushing through her, tossed by waves of shock as dimly, she heard the Chosen Maidens gasp and shriek. Something was slipping into her, liquid and wiggly—a holy tongue was darting in and out, turning her soft inside, melting her with a mounting, blessed fire! "Yes, a goddess," she thought, in a blissful daze, "feeling goddess, goddess, goddess—" she arched her back, as the blessedness poured through her.

The other maidens stared in a disbelieving trance, as they tried to place the soft, slurping sounds that were coming from the altar. Then Lettie Michaels pointed, screaming: a wand of mystical flesh was growing, sticking up between the folds of the priest's robe. It lurched upward and then came to rest on the edge of the altar, tapping it like a fat restive finger. "It's magic," Lettie screamed, wondering if she should faint.

At her cry, the priest raised up slowly, as though in a dream. Then he clutched the folds of his robe and opened it wide, so that they all might see.

226

Lettie fainted, in a roar of maidenly screams. And then, India Honeyman burst through the hedges, storming the altar: "Outrage! Sacrilege! Hannibal, if that's all you've got to show these poor girls, then cover yourself, quickly. And remove that girl from that bench. Scandal!"

Cringing, Hannibal covered himself and crouched behind the altar, moaning "Diana," in such an unconvincing tone that no maiden would have believed him . . . except that none of them were left to witness his shame. Virgins were shrieking, petticoats careened in all directions, glowing in the darkness as they scattered, like beleagured fireflies.

"Hannibal." He heard India call his name, heard the contempt and anger, but something else was there, and so he looked up, to where she stood over him, at the altar. "Hannibal," she repeated slowly. Her right hand clutched at air, and then he watched her slump lifeless across the altar—an ancient woman whose breath came in rasps, lying where his blessed Sadie had been. He knelt to take India into his arms, knowing that she would be his chief accuser; she would never forgive him for what he'd done this night. And yet, when she stopped breathing, when he pressed his face against her withered breast and heard no heart, he cried. Hannibal was an innocent man, and he did not want her to die.

Hysterical maidens were streaming through the halls. Delilah did not hear them; in her tasseled, ruffled bedroom, she lay dreaming about a green disheveled pasture. She was galloping through that pasture on a stallion, lying nude upon its muscled back, with her face to the sun. She felt a presence near, someone brutal and exciting. She was terrified, but would submit. He was masterful and so strong—was it Brand? Was Brand near? He was coming, he was—screaming, diving out of the sky!! Then it was upon her, a beast, with wings like a bat, a horselike head that grinned, leering as he exposed a red-hot choking penis, six feet long. This obscene, monstrous thing was screaming, and her legs were stretched wide, she was begging for it—*Yes, do it, do it*—

—Delilah awoke, bolting upright as she burst into tears. This was that cursed India's fault! What unthinkable thoughts! And so, she promptly forgot them.

227

Other members of the Copper family still traveled through the iridescent night. Hannibal carried the body of India Honeyman to the Penrod Inn, still weeping over his luck, or lack of it. His son Jonathan was crawling through the bushes at the cemetery, trying to help a hysterical Anabel Chess find her spectacles, which she'd lost during her flight. In the darkness, her blind, frightened gaze seemed more naked than any flesh he'd seen.

And David Copper still rustled in the foliage, where he rammed into the goddess who squirmed in his embrace. Sadie's legs kicked at the sky as he plunged his mighty scepter. Her body rocked and trembled as she thrusted up to meet him, with her insides turning slippery from the hard, angry magic that was shooting through her body like a burning, blessed star.

By 1874, there were no longer students at Ivory Hall. Although Hannibal never confessed his crime, and his maidens kept their silence, Delilah was forced to close the school. She had been suffering periodic violent nightmares which left her hysterical and was reluctantly forced to conclude that her health had become as delicate as the rest of her. In spite of this, her spirits were high. India Honeyman had left her newspaper and her share of the cranberry bogs that Deirdre and Brand Johnson had developed near Audry to David and Jonathan Copper. At his wife's request, Hannibal retired from the dirty presses. She hired instead a meek young editor who could spell and set type but had no opinions. Delilah believed that journalism could be graceful, too.

Shortly after this windfall, the transformed newspaper began calling upon the town of Frog Level to change its name. The development of the cranberry bogs had helped the community grow, and citizens dreamed of becoming a township. But with a name like Frog Level, they could hardly boast at all. An editorial suggested that town fathers should meet to consider a change —perhaps the name of a locally famous family, who had done so much for the town . . .

Several months later, that meeting was held, in the taproom of the Penrod Inn. Deirdre and Brand Johnson had driven in from their farm near Audry to suggest that the name be changed to India. This idea received little support, and Hannibal's dutiful nomination of the name Penrod seemed headed for victory when the aged Reverend Crouse spoke up from a corner: "I've discovered that the name of the first family to settle here was Rane. Maybe we should do some digging into local history before we settle on something."

There was a delicate hush. Then Delilah stood, smiling. "Oh, let's not go to any bother. If some of you prefer the name of Rane, well, I'm sure that my own family's contributions to this area need no advertisement."

Hannibal stared at her dumbly, knowing that his wife had plotted for months to install the Penrod name. What he didn't know was that on that very morning, Delilah had discovered a collection of dusty manuscripts in the Penrod attic. These were stories that Micah Honeyman had written, recounting the early history of Frog Level. Delilah had entertained herself for nearly an hour, reading about panicky soldiers and filthy half-breed savages. Then she'd carefully collected every page of Micah's manuscript and fed it into the fire. She had no intention of encouraging more research into the town's history, although she comforted herself by deciding that Micah Honeyman had been as demented as his wife.

Thus Frog Level and the frogs within it became part of Ranewood (Ranewood Township), New Jersey, on August 9, 1875. The newspaper India had founded took a new name, *The Ranewood Star;* it was published as a weekly local with no apparent editorial content, but ample space for local ads and even a society column, of sorts. It provided a faithful mirror for the town, although newspaper offices still remained in the sagging Penrod Inn while Ranewood grew to the north and the east. The center of human activity was slowly moving away from the frog level. Ranewood's general store was nearly one mile to the east, and fewer people showed up for services at the Cinders after the Methodists built a church closer to the new center of town.

The total population of Sand County's newest township was nearly two thousand people; to most of them, the Copper family's vast estate was the showplace of rural Ranewood. Whether blacksmith or tenant farmer or errand boy, they ran to fulfill requests. The people of Ranewood joked that even a stranger passing through would respond to a Copper summons, as the frog level took on the luster of a fashionable neighborhood. To the misfortune of Reverend Crouse who remained at the Cinders presbytery cabin, the lure of the land was no longer religion but social aspiration. Although fewer people in Ranewood Township came to his services, nearly everyone coveted his address.

In 1882, the House of Penrod-Copper passed to a new generation. Delilah and Hannibal had lived out their graceful prime, leaving behind a considerable estate. In addition to 499 and ¾ acres of land surrounding the frog level, Jonathan and David Copper also acquired the remaining interest in the cranberry farms at Audry. (They inherited the estate from Deirdre and Brand Johnson, who had no children.)

Jonathan Copper had married Anabel Chess in 1880. They built a small frame house at Sabbath Creek near the cranberry basin. It was that small plot of land which Indian Jin had chosen for her hut. Cedar and Rane had built a cabin there before them, which John Francis Penrod had renovated for his wife. Jonathan took over full supervision of the cranberry farming operation at Audry, because his brother despised the job.

David reigned over the remaining Copper holdings—the Penrod Inn, which he repaired at an enormous cost, cherishing the obsolete building like an antique family pet. He also controlled the news that *The Ranewood Star* saw fit to print, and he strode across all 499 and ¾ acres of his vast estate from time to time. Most important, he and his wife (the former Miss Sadie Linnet) controlled the lordly, tasseled manor house and continued its lavish traditions. Mrs. David Copper was a brilliant hostess. With their beautiful home and their dazzling style, this couple would have made the social grade in any American city. In the rural community of Ranewood, they were considered deities.

In the year 1893, children in the schoolhouse next to the general store were struggling to memorize the verses of Henry Wadsworth Longfellow's "Evangeline," while their teacher listened, wondering if she should really shorten her skirts, as the *Ladies Home Journal* had suggested. David Copper invested in the stock market, while Jonathan discovered that Queen Victoria's passion for cranberries had an international effect: at last, the world was clamoring for more berries than Ranewood could produce. Sadie Copper had discovered the *Tales of Uncle Remus,* which were appearing in the *Atlanta Constitution,* and she read them aloud to her friends. There were no telephones in Ranewood, although New York and Boston had already developed a long-distance line; there was no electricity. But two of the Copper homes now had indoor plumbing. A third house had no plumbing—but then none of the Coppers knew that it existed, except for David himself. At the northernmost corner of the estate, he had built a plain wooden shack that stood at the end of a narrow dirt lane. The land was so densely forested here that the house was submerged in shadows, even at noon.

Gentlemen from Philadelphia rode down this shadowed lane. They came to find a private world, where a public man could pursue his honest tastes. Where a family man could sport with gentlemen of his own kind. The liquor consisted of excellent brands, kept in abundant supply. The cards were unmarked. And the women were clean. David took care of all of these things. He had built the house, and he took his pleasure there. The problem was, he could not take his wife . . .

———— *The simple pleasures of New Jersey society were not always so simple, or so pleasant. Throughout most of the nineteenth century, public executions were occasions for celebration, with booths for liquor and gambling set up among the gathered crowds. The condemned man always arrived in style, in a carriage with military escort, and a minister stood by his side to read his confession aloud to the spellbound audience. Horse-racing was a common sport among young men, at county tracks or down crowded village streets. Bull-baiting was also popular, especially in Jersey City and Paterson, where hundreds of spectators thrilled to the sight of dogs tearing apart a bull and an occasional buffalo. The fans were loyalists; one night Paterson officials tried to break up the contest, and the participants simply turned both the dogs and the bull onto the police.*

1893 ―――――
The Shadowed Lane

THE FORMER Miss Sadie Linnet now ruled at the house of Penrod-Copper. She was envied throughout the county for her wealth and beauty, and for her tremendous breasts, which still bounced round as baby melons through her dresses, despite her thirty-six years. But Sadie was indifferent to her thumping breasts, to her full, sliding smile that seemed to beg a man to drop his pants. If she had still looked into a mirror to judge her worth, she might have laughed more often; she might have cried, from happiness. Instead, she looked at herself in her husband's eyes, and measured her lack in his gaze. Although she dressed in elegant gowns and gave the family crystal its fabled transparent *ting!*, she felt that she was a failure and lived in the sweetness of her dreams.

To be a goddess—Sadie still remembered the trembling, the bliss. It did not seem to matter that Hannibal Copper had been a fool, that she had fooled herself; what she longed for from that night was anticipation—not dread or speculation, but the *certainty* that joy was sure to come. Now that she knew her husband well enough to predict his every move, what she longed for was uncertainty. But she was sure that David despised her —it was in his eyes, his lips, and touch.

He came to her bed regularly, once or twice a month. But since the first days of their marriage, his assault upon her had been so formal and perfunctory that she could hardly call it desire. "A wife's duty," her mother had told her, not knowing that her newly betrothed daughter had already sampled the task. But Sadie had believed that David would never "do his duty," that he would ravage—her bones would split and he would leave her streaming, from the force of his desire.

Instead, as the years had passed, she marveled at the crushing force of her despair. The truth had been all the harder to bear, since she had seen the adoration she craved in the eyes of her brother-in-law Jonathan as he looked at his wife. That Anabel Chess should turn out to be the goddess!

Sadie devoured the signs of their passion and nearly choked on bile. At social gatherings, it was always awkwardly clear that they wanted to be together. Sadie never missed the way in which Jonathan reached out to brush the inside of Anabel's wrist, or how she automatically tilted her head towards the sound of his voice. Every time Jonathan looked at her, Anabel blushed—and they had been married for nearly nineteen years! It was foolishness and yet absolutely heartbreaking, for Sadie could not remember when she and David had ever looked at each other that way, even though they had so much more to look at than the Jonathan Coppers.

On three occasions, Sadie had heard her husband's passionate groans—he was sleeping beside her, and she awoke to find him tossing in his dreams. She heard his hunger, remembered it, but she could not arouse him. After eighteen years, she was used to the fact that when she entered a room she attracted the attention of everyone there but David Copper. She was envied by all of her friends, admired for her beauty and charm, but such adoration meant little to a wistful goddess, who had always believed that the marital bed would become her shrine.

Anabel Chess Copper no longer remembered that she had once longed to be Carlotta, the famous nun. She had not been in love with her husband when they married, although she was so touched by his kindness that she mistook it for romance. On that awful night in the cemetery, Jonathan had somehow found her; in her blindness and terror, he had helped her so tenderly that from that time on, she could not look at him without feeling a warm, grateful flush.

When her term had ended at Ivory Hall, Anabel returned home and soon became miserable, for now she was expected to talk and flirt with young men who knew, as she did, that she was not pretty. Jonathan had begun to visit her there, and her joy in his kindness increased; she had happily accepted his proposal, though now she knew that he had only offered it because he could not stand to see her pain.

The discovery that they had married without love was embarrassing, but they were forced to admit it soon after their first anniversary, when they discovered that they were falling in love. Their passion bloomed slowly—a huge drifting flower with petals that fluttered their senses. They took its nectar in darting, astonished sips like a pair of giddy bees.

The small clapboard house at the cranberry basin seemed an unlikely setting for such a grand passion, but Jonathan loved its tiny cluttered parlor where distinct aspects of Anabel seemed to coalesce like a visible perfume. He sensed her everywhere—in her delicate animal sketches, which lined the walls, in the piles of musty books and the slightly frenzied color scheme, caused by her nearsighted devotion to chintz.

Anabel loved the dining room with its strange and homely oaken table which Jonathan had insisted he knew how to build. It did not matter that the meals placed there tended to slide southward, that the gravy bowl poured itself if not carefully watched: their table was rarely set for more than two places. Sadie deplored this quiet reclusive existence. "Honestly, Anabel, you might as well live on a farm," she told her friend. Anabel smiled, too shy to admit that she felt as though she lived in the curling heart of a flower.

David Copper lived his dreams in a crude wooden shack that he'd built on a shadowed lane. He managed it for ten fine gentlemen from Philadelphia who liked liquor, cards, and fast, hard rides—on blooded mares, or women. David admired these hard-drinking men; their company excited him, and he believed he was their friend. He stocked the house—with food and drink and whores. In return, he took his pleasure, for although the gentlemen had never invited him to become a member of their club, they had all agreed that he could use the women.

Here, David was free to act out the dreams which had tortured him since marriage, things he could never ask of his beau-

235

tiful Sadie. He told a whore, "Roll over. Bend over." He said, "Do it." Squeezing apart the cheeks of her buttocks, he drove his fiery aching penis into her, dreaming of titties and hips until he finally exploded in passion, calling his brother's name. Among these women, David felt no shame. They were like animals, he thought, born to serve man's pleasure.

His favorite was his most recent acquisition, a black girl named Kadar who was only sixteen. When he'd first laid eyes on her on a street in Trenton, the high rounded buttocks that strutted beneath her skirt had immediately excited him, and he'd leaped down from his carriage to proposition her on the spot. At the club, some of the men objected because Kadar was dark-skinned instead of tawny. David defended his choice "You won't find a finer ass on any 'poon. And I swear to you, gentlemen, she's still a virgin."

He heard condescending laughter. "You surely are a country boy," one remarked. "There's no such thing as a nigger girl virgin."

David cursed himself silently. He never seemed able to strike the right note with these men in spite of his efforts. He stalked into the kitchen, feeling a familiar excitement, disgust and anger mingled with lust. Kadar was there, chopping vegetables by the stove. Wordlessly, he grabbed her and tilted her across the back of a high wooden chair, pressing her face against the table by holding her neck as he lifted her skirts and entered her.

Thrusting deeply, he was barely aware of his surroundings when he heard an excited voice. "Go to it, David boy—hey, what hole you poking into? *Goddamn!*"

David crouched over Kadar, burning with shame as the man who had laughed at him earlier called to the others, "Come in here, quickly! You've got to see this." Then he turned to David. "Do it," he said, and suddenly David could hear the excitement in his voice.

"Do it, David." The men were gathering around him, feeding his excitement as he ripped into Kadar, pounding her buttocks helplessly. When he came, there was a chorus of cheers. Then several of the men decided to try it "David's way," and it was David's turn to watch. The experiment was considered a great success, and Kadar's black skin became a minor inconvenience, compared to the pleasures of her ass.

236

When the men grew bored with cards and the white women, they would seat David in a high chair with Kadar lying face downward across his lap. Pushing her skirt over her neck, David would spread the cheeks of her buttocks and hold her there, while each man took his turn in her narrow quivering hollow, and the others watched. David rubbed his swelling penis against the softness of her belly—the scene filled him with pulsing, joyful lust that he'd never experienced before, even in his dreams.

Kadar had no favorites among the men—she hated them all. She had accepted David's offer because he frightened her, jumping down from his carriage with his horse rearing and plunging so close to her face, and because she knew that in Trenton, she was slowly starving to death. Things were bad here, even worse than she'd imagined, but it was not worse than hunger. Now she had food, and the other whores were kind. When the men were away, she cooked and sewed; she had planted a small garden behind the house, and the women teased her, because nothing would grow in such deeply shadowed soil. Kadar didn't care. She spent hours working in the garden, while the sound of women's laughter drifted from the house. She stored up these memories until the men were there, and her skirts fell across her neck. As pain ripped through her, she made a list of her dreams: celery, cabbage, some tansy root, for tea . . .

Kadar had lived at the pleasure house for several months when she met Amos Wade. Working in her garden on a day when no men were visiting, she suddenly became aware that someone was watching her. "Come out, fool," she said harshly, feeling terrified.

A ridiculously tall black man stepped from behind the trees —skin like a cocoa bean, she thought reflexively, despite her fear.

"What do you want?"

"I heard there was a house out this way," the man replied in a quiet, gentle tone. "Just came to look, on my way home."

"Now you've seen. So get out." Kadar stood, ready to run.

"You remind me of a starry night," he said softly, without moving.

"What's that supposed to mean?"

"I guess it means that I like to look at you."

She looked at him with distaste. "I'm a whore, mister. You pay to look at me, and right now I'm paid for. The men that are paying don't want me to be looked at by a nigger."

She raced through the back door, and Amos heard her turn its lock. The rasping metal brought him to his senses in a way that her warning had not, and so he turned back up the sandy, shadowed lane, walking to his wagon. When he'd first heard the rumors, his instinct had told him to stay as far away as possible; if there were women here, they were not for the likes of Amos Wade. But curiosity, an emotion in which he seldom allowed himself to indulge, had overtaken him—or perhaps it was anger, against the blinders which the people in this area expected him to wear.

Amos was Ranewood's first barber, and their first black citizen. When he had set up his shop in one side of the general store, it suited the town just fine, because he was an excellent barber; it also suited that he lived far north of the town in the Pines, just close enough to make the early morning trip to open his shop on time. The white men who came into his shop had heard vague rumors about the existence of this house, and suddenly, Amos had needed to know more than they did about something.

As a result, he had seen the most beautiful woman he ever laid eyes on. On his way home, Amos tried to convince himself for his own safety that he had made her up. "But if that is true," he told himself in the days that followed, "then the mind must surely cling to its own inventions. For I cannot get her out of my thoughts." He found himself returning to the shadowed lane. He hid among the trees to watch the house. Although he never tried to talk to Kadar again, one day when she was digging in her garden, she found a note:

My name is Amos Wade. If you ever need me, my cabin is two miles north, in the Pines.

She dug her fists into the barren soil where her celery should be growing. "If you want to help, you got to pay. Nigger man with cocoa skin, you might as well be on the moon, as two miles north." But she did not throw the note away.

At the pleasure house, Amos Wade had seen a dream, and David Copper had made his come true. Now Kadar's dreams were growing in spite of shadows. But Sadie's dream still festered, although she had begun to sense the existence of David's house in the smell of his clothing and breath. His absences grew more frequent; he no longer moaned in the night. He had not touched her as a lover in nearly six months.

On a Friday afternoon, she watched him drive off; that Saturday she dined alone, surrounded by her crystal; on Sunday, she throbbed to the stroking beat of the costly grandfather clock.

It was too much. Sadie questioned the servants, who whispered the rumors to ward off her rage. Her mind was racing as she dressed to ride in a habit of mulberry wool. The flared skirt clung perfectly to her rounded hips, and the amethyst pin she used to secure the creamy silk folds of her blouse made her eyes turn the color of violets. But she looked in the mirror and did not see her eyes or hips or her coils of golden hair. All she saw was the veil on the brim of her black bowler hat: it was hanging awkwardly. Sadie tugged it straight and ran from the house.

After saddling her mare, she galloped through the woods, searching for her husband. Soon she found the shadowed lane, and at its end she found a house. Several dust-covered buggies were drawn up outside. For a moment, she tried to believe that this part of their property was rented to people whom her husband had forgotten to tell her about. Then there was the sound of women's laughter and a loud male voice: "Take that slut where you can do her some good, Samuel." Sadie gasped, as her dreams were burst. For that voice belonged to her husband.

She entered the shack quickly, before she could change her mind. She stood just outside the doorway of a large smoky room that smelled of liquor and sweat. Six men were seated around a table; they looked dangerously drunk. One of them, a tall, powerfully built man with thick blond hair was pounding the table and calling out for a woman.

With a shock, Sadie realized that her feet were moving; when they stopped, she found herself standing in the middle of the room. She heard her voice—a sluttish laugh that could not be her own. The men looked up. "Here I am," she said. Something wild was coursing through her as she watched them stare with open greed.

The blond man stood up, stumbling slightly. "You must be new. David didn't tell us about you."

"He didn't tell me about you," she replied, and the men roared with laughter. Sadie joined in, feeling slightly hysterical.

"He sure fixed you up with fancy clothes." The blond man approached, still laughing. "What do you look like without them?"

She stared at him, and a flush of heat swept through her. "I look real good," she said in her coarse, sluttish voice—the new voice, that she loved. "I look real good, mister."

He awkwardly pulled at the front of her blouse, but she quickly backed off. "Let me show you," she said. Tossing aside her riding jacket, she began to unfasten her blouse. Working slowly, she swayed her hips and laughed, as the other men left their cards to gather around her. She peeled back her blouse, savoring the knowledge that her breasts were beautiful. As she watched their faces, the hunger there rocked her, with waves of bliss. "Well?" she said, arching her back as she turned slowly before them. "Am I beautiful?"

"David never brought us anything this nice before." The blond reached out to fondle her breasts, but Sadie pulled away again.

"You think I am more beautiful than his other women?" she demanded, almost pleading.

"Hell, yes," he replied looking a little confused.

"SADIE!" She turned, to see David staring from the doorway, as though he could not believe his eyes. "What are you doing?" he said, hurrying towards them.

Sadie laughed. "Darling, these men want what you won't take. Isn't that right, gentlemen?" she demanded as they backed off, uncertainly. "You do want me, don't you?" They nodded, mesmerized as she caressed her breasts. David tried to cover her, but she jerked away. "No!" she said, then turning to the men, she told them, "Hold him!"

They drunkenly obeyed, as Sadie said, "You can have me—each one of you. I promise you that I'll be worth your time."

240

She smiled. "There's only one condition," she said, pointing to her husband. "I want him to watch."

David struggled uselessly, calling her name, but Sadie knew that the men were too drunk and too excited to listen to him. Looking towards the door, she caught sight of a frightened-looking cluster of women. "I have no quarrel with you," she said. "But I want you to leave now. *Get out*," she repeated, and they scattered, like a gusted heap of limp, ragged leaves.

Sadie quickly turned back to the men, too excited to despise those women and this dirty, smelly room. *She* was the woman now, and the rank male sweat clinging to bodies hungry for her seemed like coarse perfume. She inhaled deeply, shaking her hair loose. "Let me show you what you're going to get," she told them.

There was only the ragged sound of breathing, and her husband's muffled cries as Sadie slowly removed her clothing, down to her lacy underclothes. Then she looked up, drinking in the stares. "I believe that you are betting men. Why don't you decide by chance who gets to take these things from me and be the first?"

The blonde-haired man grabbed a deck of cards and began to deal one to each taker. The first man showed a six of clubs. "Don't worry," she consoled him. "There will be plenty left for you." The next man, so drunk he could barely stand, groaned when he was dealt an eight. The cards were passed to trembling hands, and then a quiet, dark-haired man turned up an ace. "Come to me," Sadie said, impatiently, excited by his looks. She took his hands in hers and placed them onto her breasts. "Are they beautiful?" she asked. "Do you think that I am beautiful?"

"You are beautiful," he said hoarsely. As he began to fondle her, she caught his wrists, guiding his fingers across the tips of her breasts.

She heard groans. "My god, Sam, get on with it," said one of the men. The dark-haired man was fumbling with her chemise, and Sadie helped him. Then her lacy drawers were sliding to the floor, and she stepped out of them, completely naked. She spread her legs, turning towards her husband. "Do you like it?" she asked him. When he struggled to get free, the men holding him twisted his arms cruelly and smothered his shouts.

Sadie laughed. She gloried in the sound of it, the crude,

naked sounds coming from her throat were beautiful; she knew it. She could not stop laughing as she faced the men. "Take me," she said. "Do it."

The blond moved forward, but she shook her head. "This man is first," she said, as the dark-haired man moved to embrace her. She arched into his arms, shocked by the hardness that pressed against her. She felt herself being lifted, he was carrying her in his arms, to a couch she hadn't noticed, in the corner of the room. The other men crowded around, but Sadie shook her head, pointing to the foot of the couch. "Bring my husband there," she ordered. "I want to watch his face."

David was shoved directly into her sight, although Sadie barely recognized his blotched, contorted face. He struggled uselessly, unable to speak.

Sadie turned to the dark-haired man. "You may kiss me now," she said. The scent of brandy invaded her, borne by his tongue; she breathed it, turning dizzy from the force of his kiss. His hands were moving over her, rough and demanding as the voices that surrounded her, urging him on. He moved onto her, and she felt his urgent, driving need as he sucked her tingling breasts. All of his fury seemed to invade her, and she pulled him against her, hungrily, aching beneath his rough caress. Her legs were being parted—he penetreated her abruptly, a swift, fiery shock that made her gasp.

Then she caught sight of her husband's face. She laughed as a harsh, driving rhythm forced her hips against the couch; a coarse, joyous power was surging through her as she raised up, still laughing, to match the harshness, the hunger that throbbed between her legs. She felt herself slipping, out of control, her senses were gathering, to scream—arching her neck, she climaxed violently, calling out David's name.

Each man took his turn with Sadie Copper as she had promised. She loved them all and took them hungrily, moaning beneath the rough caresses, flinging her head back as she thrust against their power. But she never closed her eyes. She loved to feel the men inside her and loved their desperate cries. But she did not watch their faces—it was the look in David's eyes that split her bones, and left her streaming with desire.

By the time the last man had taken his turn, the members of

the pleasure house had sobered up enough to realize what they had done. David Copper still struggled weakly. Almost tenderly, they knocked him out with a single punch and scrambled for their buggies. In less than three hours' time, Sadie had managed to clear the house of its pleasure and break up the club.

After they left, she lay quietly on the couch. She could barely make out the outline of her husband's body, lying near her on the floor. From time to time he stirred, so she knew that he was alive. It occurred to her that she should go to him—thinking that, she wanted to laugh but her throat had forgotten how to make those lovely, sluttish sounds. Suddenly, she felt afraid. She had given herself to a roomful of men—because of David. Was that love? she wondered idly, thoughts skimming at the edge of her exhaustion and pain. She knew that her clothing was ripped and stained; there would be bruises on her body. Was love a bruise—some dark stain on her heart?

Sharp darts of pain flashed through her as she struggled to her feet; she stumbled, dizzy, and forced herself to crawl to the place where David had fallen. Lying down beside her husband, Sadie put her arms around him, rocking him gently as she cried. And darkness spilled in layers from the windows, submerging their huddled forms in shadow; submerging their dark shadows in the night.

The whores who fled from Sadie Copper did not travel far. Kadar led them two miles north to the house of Amos Wade. Two of the women eventually returned to Philadelphia, but the others stayed in the Pine Barrens, drifting off to live with other men. Amos cared for the women, but he would not sleep with them, and he refused to touch Kadar until she consented to be his wife. On February 9, 1894, they were married by a preacher in the Pines. On the wedding night, the groom discovered that his wife was still a virgin. Although he said nothing to Kadar, Amos was forced to certain conclusions about the virility of white men. Patrons of his Ranewood barbershop noticed an improvement in this black man's attitude, which had been a shade too arrogant. Now he lathered white faces with solicitous care; in fact, he felt downright sorry for them.

David Copper often came into the barbershop; he sometimes

bought the medicines which Kadar made from the herbs in her garden, but Amos was careful never to mention his wife's name. David and his wife continued their lavish entertainments; as a hostess, Sadie was still admired for her beauty, charm, and breasts. But now she was envied by women guests, who could not help but notice that her husband hovered by her side, that her fingers curled so tightly in his grasp. That such passion could exist, after so many years of marriage! the women told their husbands, somewhat bitterly. No one guessed that it was not desire, but everlasting horror which inspired this tenderness.

By the beginning of the twentieth century, Ranewood's population had stabilized at about five hundred people. As new stores were built—drygoods, boot and harness maker, dispensary, and a pottery shop—the center of town continued to shift towards the northwest, as though its citizens could sense Philadelphia in the wind. There were nearly fifteen hundred people in the total area of Ranewood Township, most of them farmers whose cranberries, potatoes, tomatoes, and corn now reached Philadelphia by rail from the Rowleytown junction in less than four hours.

All ten thousand residents of Sand County were officially proud of Ranewood's cranberry farms. Other counties adopted their method of bog cultivation, but most of the one and a half million people living in New Jersey paid little attention to Sand County or Ranewood and none at all to the frog level—with the exception of the David Copper family, whose members were highly regarded in society. People living in northern industrial counties had little to do with southern New Jersey, except for an occasional trip to the newly erected boardwalk at the resort of Atlantic City. In the city of Newark, factories run by electrical power were mass-producing textiles and leather goods and more machines. There were street lights and moving picture shows, phrenologists, and dentists.

By comparison, the town of Ranewood might have been living in another time, or state. But citizens of Ranewood preferred to compare themselves with some of their neighbors in Sand County, who seemed to live in another world altogether. Residents of the sparsely populated Pine Barrens were known as

"Pineys"; they rarely came into town. The wealthy in Newark might own a Ford roadster, but thirty citizens of Ranewood owned bicycles. The Pineys had none. Pineys did not take a day train to Philadelphia and then transfer to an all-steel Pullman car for a trip into New York's Pennsylvania Station. Pineys did not have a policeman or a fire hose pumped by steam. Their women had no access to Philadelphia fashion—fishnet stockings and Merry Widow hats. Pineys lived in shacks. They were filthy, lazy, bred too much, and were possibly lunatics. Believing the worst about the Pineys was a Ranewood civic duty; it enabled them to believe the best about themselves.

In 1903, the Penrod Inn stood empty when the offices of *The Ranewood Star* finally moved into town, and the heavy oaken bar finally fell through the taproom floor. In that same year, the Cinders Church was abandoned when Presbyterians erected a new church next to the conveniently located Methodists. Despite all rules of architecture and logic, the ancient wooden building refused to fall down; the regional Presbyterian council was finally forced to hire carpenters to dismantle it. The bones of original Frog Levelers were carted off to a cemetery at the new church in town, along with Reverend Brewster's memorial bench. A stone plaque was laid to mark the spot where the Cinders had stood, but officials needn't have bothered. After several years, grass still refused to grow within the lines of the path that Seneca Rane had made. Now a wide stripe of barren earth divided the rise above the frog level—the path to nowhere, local residents joked. Or so it had become.

In spite of the changes, the land surrounding the frog level had become essential to the civic pride of Ranewood—even those citizens who had never been invited to the House of Penrod-Copper became enraptured by the new activities at Sabbath Creek. One small point of pride was the cranberry basin which Anabel and Jonathan Copper still operated there; Ranewood proudly proclaimed the site as "origin of the bog cranberry industry in New Jersey" and proudly displayed it to out of town visitors as "Aunt Cedar's Cranberry Basin."

More important were the human Beavers who now labored by Sabbath Creek—Ranewood had a baseball team, with pin-striped shirts and snug black caps and games scheduled on al-

245

ternate Sundays. These twelve young men battled the youth of Rowleytown and contenders from Salem and Ocean counties. Although the rise above the frog level had not been so barren since 1691, when Seneca Rane had built his cabin there, it was more popular than ever as baseball attracted larger crowds than the Cinders had ever done. The entire town turned out for the games and walked up Seneca's path to a perfect natural grandstand. Visiting players sat on the left side of the stripe on the rise, and Ranewood sat on the right. The fans exhausted themselves in screams (except for the official mascots who continued to slap mud onto their dams in the creek).

In 1913, a special July Fourth celebration was planned: the Beavers were scheduled to play against their archrivals, the boys from the Pines. These Pineys didn't have uniforms or a name; they didn't even have a team, exactly. According to Ranewood gossip, they simply fell into a wagon and headed for the Beavers's field, hollering like the drunken hooligans, which in fact they were. The result was a vicious rivalry that thrilled everyone. Ranewood believed that its dashing, handsome youth was going up against not just the enemy but a barbaric horde. The Pineys enhanced this image by helping themselves to fistfights and as much free beer as they could find.

On the morning of the Fourth, everyone in Ranewood was preparing for the holiday. The women put on white lawn skirts or dotted Swiss and fried up all the chicken in town; the men rolled up their sleeves, took off their stiff white collars, and put together tables for the crowd. In their house by the cranberry basin, Anabel and Jonathan Copper were helped by their daughter Susannah who was seventeen and hated baseball. Deep within the Pines, the Pineys's team wagon was already on its way, along with fair-haired Caddy Lofts (who rode down with the athletes at their request). Amos and Kadar Wade were on the road early, bringing their only son. And at the House of Penrod-Copper, Sadie and David tiptoed through their extensive toilettes, careful not to disturb Ranewood's genuine hero: the dashing, handsome Jeffry Copper was still sleeping. All of these people were heading towards a holiday they wouldn't soon forget.

———— *The reputation of New Jersey residents living within the Pine Barrens was unfairly damaged by a report entitled "The Pineys" published by social worker Elizabeth Kite in 1913. Miss Kite had visited cabins in the Pines for two years, compiling accounts of incest and intermarriage, of children who shared their bedroom with pigs, of a young mother who was not sure if her child had been sired by her husband, brother, or father. New Jersey newspapers printed excerpts from the report, to the astonishment of many residents in the northern counties who had not known that the Pine Barrens existed. Throughout the state, residents were traumatized by Miss Kite's revelations, and Governor James T. Fielder found it politically expedient to suggest to the legislature that the Pine Barrens be somehow segregated from the rest of the state. "These people are a serious menace . . . they have inbred and led lawless and scandalous lives, til they have become a race of imbeciles, criminals and defectives." The effects of this distorted impression lingered for many years, as many in New Jersey sincerely feared the taint of "Piney blood."*

Baseball and the Beavers

IN A vaulted room turned golden by streams of summer dawn, Jeffry Copper threw back the sheets to gaze in rapture as his glowing, spectacular penis rose to greet the morn. He didn't know at eighteen, that he looked exactly like his great-grandfather John Francis Penrod. In fact, it would have surprised him to discover that his gorgeous face and body weren't tailor-made, as he assumed, but a medley of hand-me-downs. But he did know that the females of Ranewood tossed in the night, whispering his name into their pillows. Jeffry slept like a log. But waking in the morning was to him even sweeter than a dream, for although he was invariably aroused by the sight of a pretty girl and by even the thought of her thighs, he had a special fondness for the erection which nudged him awake at dawn. It was as though the most sensitive part of him had suddenly noticed the rest and was rising to salute its incredible luck, in being part of Jeffry Copper's flesh.

In the glowing dawn, he watched it grow, looking flushed and juicy, as a drop of moisture formed at the tip—blooming like a dangerous fruit, he told himself. He smiled as he pictured an unsuspecting female's hand reaching into foliage to seize it and then hesitate, as her fingers traced the strange shape—not a peach? But it would feel warm and strangely tempting and her fingers would curl around it, then squeeze impatiently, not wanting to bruise it but wanting to see and taste . . . He reached down automatically to stroke the aching fruit, but jerked his hand back, midair—today was the Fourth, and he was pitching in the most important game of his life! Compared to what lay ahead, his magnificent erection seemed like no more than a bawdy trinket.

He could wait until the town had gathered by the picnic tables at the frog level, and then he would stride among them as pitcher and star of this day—*his* day. As each hour passed, warm shivers of pride and excitement would be coursing through him, the admiring crowds would be a caress, their screams would stroke him to a frenzy, and he would beat against the glory until he and lust were one—one gorgeous, six-foot aching penis, equipped with a dazzling smile. The rest would happen, easily. For him, it always did. As he jumped out of bed to douse himself with cold water, the day seemed to arc before him in the air, like a shimmering, rainbow-hued wet dream.

The sun rose higher in the sky as the wagon drove the visiting team, along with Caddie Lofts, out of the Pines, towards the celebration at the frog level. Swinging her legs above the sugar sand road, Caddie languidly batted at the Piney hands which swarmed at her breasts, as though she were swatting at flies. She prided herself on noticing that the air was cool, the sun was hot, and the sky looked bright as paint. She was a sensitive girl, she reminded herself, not like most of these Pineys who wouldn't have been able to tell sunrise from sunset, if one didn't make the lights go out.

Caddie knew that the boys who surrounded her couldn't see that a girl's eyes and smile were as pretty as her bosoms or that she might have delicate hands. But as a sensitive person, she could only pity their lack of the finer things. As she squinted happily into the bright paint sky, Caddie reminded herself that she had reason to feel sorry for them—because on this glorious holiday she knew, long before they did, that none of these Piney boys was going to be slipping into her privates.

Just behind the team, Cassaday Wade rode in a wagon with his parents, Amos and Kadar. In spite of the fact that he was black and never took a drink, the Pineys regarded him with pride, for Cassaday could pitch fast or slow, curve or slider, and his spit ball was the driest in the county. Each player's bat was his invitation to risk, to go wild in the cramped, careful universe which he had inherited. Sometimes he got smacked nearly out of the field—not often, but it happened. This only seemed to add to his excitement; he was not invulnerable. Standing alone on the mound, he would watch the white faces, one after another, as their bats fanned the air and they slunk away defeated. *Out! Out!*

Baseball wasn't Cassaday's life—it was better than his life. It did not bother him now that his family rode in a separate wagon or that they had brought their own lunch. He was going to pitch today, so it did not matter that the Wades would be standing alone. After all, the best had always stood apart.

The wagons turned a final corner, and the spectacle at the frog level seemed to engulf him—a human pitch made from color, movement, and sound that was too beautiful to be called noise. More than four hundred people were gathered there, laughing and talking. Cool white lawn dresses mingled in a sea of summer brights, while children raced through the crowd, making pastel streaks. Watching as his teammates tumbled out of the wagon in front of him, Cassaday allowed himself a smile. Most of these Pineys worked as hard and drank no more than their Ranewood neighbors. But they enjoyed their barbaric reputation and so they hit the ground staggering and hooting, like the drunken hooligans which the home crowd knew that they were.

As she helped her mother heap fried chicken onto an already overloaded platter, Susannah Copper flinched at the noise coming from the Piney wagons. Susannah had been admiring all that was classic and therefore beautiful about this day. True, it was only Ranewood, but there was grace as well as excitement in the crowd, which gathered to celebrate its athletes and its democratic ideals. She watched as her father, Jonathan, approached the table and tried to help her mother. "Women's work!" Anabel cried, but he grabbed the chicken from her hands as the other women giggled. Susannah blushed—now that was classic love! Aunt Sadie and Uncle David were moving through a crowd of admirers; even though she knew that they were old, nearly fifty-seven, Susannah admitted that they took her breath away—now that was classic beauty!

Then she caught sight of Jeffry and flinched again. She hated her cousin, perhaps because she'd always known that he'd inherited the family beauty. But he had something more—*hubris* the ancient Greeks had called it, foretelling woe, but here in Ranewood it appeared to be an asset. A sculptor could have told her that she was beautiful, but even though at seventeen Susannah searched for ancient beauty, she could not see the classic lines that formed the angles of her own face and body. Lacking hubris, she saw only the angles, and so she turned away from her cousin's beauty, feeling suddenly ashamed. That was when she first caught a glimpse of Cassaday Wade. *Oh my!* thinking "panther" and "lord" and "poet" in the space of a second, she dropped a piece of chicken, forgetting to blush as she stared. Was that classic?

Cassaday was too busy helping his mother lay out their lunch, in a secluded spot near Sabbath Creek, to notice the pale young woman who was spreading the tables for the Ranewood feast. And Jeffry Copper was too busy basking in the excitement of fans to notice Caddie Lofts, although she was quick to notice him. That was what being sensitive was all about, she told herself, brushing away the fingers that were poking at her privates. She'd heard tell of Jeffry Copper and now was seeing him in the flesh, so to speak. And the sight of his flesh was flashing through her bones something fierce. But Caddie was noticing other things, too; for instance, she'd never seen so many fancy pink dresses or so much cole slaw ever gathered together in one place before. Right now she heard that a bird was singing, right up in that tree above the beer kegs that were chilling in the creek. It was a gift, noticing that bird and those beer kegs, just like the gift of Jeffry Copper, who she couldn't help taking another peek at. Ah, she thought, catching the flash of him in her bones, it was nice to be a sensitive girl. The sort that noticed a gentleman.

"PLAY BALL!" The shout was like a cannon shot, as the fans deserted their lunches to head up the narrow dirt path on the rise; Pineys settled on the left, with the hometown on the right, and both sides had an excellent view as Cassaday Wade stalked to the pitcher's mound. Standing apart from the crowd, Amos and Kadar watched this elegant, handsome creature and wondered where on earth he had come from. So did Susannah

Copper, as in quick succession, he struck out Ranewood's first three batters. As the Beavers took the field, a hush fell on the crowd. Then Jeffry Copper stood on the mound, lean and magnificent, as he took out Pineys, one-two-three. Both sides of the bleachers erupted in cheers—this was not going to be a rout but a savage fight to the finish.

As the teams changed sides, Caddie Lofts joined in the cheering. She had sampled a bit of the beer, seeing as how that bird had practically been singing on top of it, and although she hadn't really liked the taste, she'd taken a few sips to make sure, and then a few sips more to celebrate the idea that she was trying it at all. Now the singing of birds seemed to catch in her throat, making her giggle. And that Jeffry Copper was singing in her bones, making her wonder what might happen, if a sensitive girl had a bit more beer.

By the sixth inning, the score had seesawed back and forth so many times that fans from both sides had become slightly numbed by their screams. An exhausted quiet spread through the crowd. Susannah Copper watched Cassaday come to bat against her cousin. The black man seemed so solemn, she thought, not returning Jeffry's sneer but instead nodding slightly as though to acknowledge a challenge. Wasn't that Greek? Or maybe Nubian, in this case, although certainly not a slave. The movements of his body were noble with a faintly liquid grace. With difficulty, Susannah returned her gaze to her cousin, preparing to cheer for him; but even though her lips had never tasted beer, a different name was singing through her flesh.

Jeffry Copper had pitched two strikes before he noticed Caddie Lofts, who was laughing like a drunken jaybird in the front row of Piney fans, with blonde curls falling into her face and her skirt pressed into her by the breeze. Godalmighty, he could see the line of her thighs, all the way up—WHACK! That goddamn Cassaday slammed into his fast ball, and now the nigger was running those bases like he was making off with a watermelon. As Cassaday slid home, Jeffry felt his fury rise—now *he* would have to hit at least one home run, maybe two. There would be only one hero today. Forcing the blonde from his mind, he struck out the next two batters, pitching with savage intensity, and retired the side.

The war was on, and the crowd grew tense as the score continued tied. On the rise above the frog level, there was a sucking of breath, as Jeffry Copper came to bat in the top of the ninth. The first pitch was low and outside—BALL! screamed the umpire (the editor of *The Ranewood Star*) who was feeling a little tense. The Ranewood fans screamed with joy; Cassaday merely frowned and nodded his head, as though to acknowledge his mistake. The next pitch left his hand almost immediately—*Strike!* The umpire whimpered. He should have refused to do this. His wife had warned him. As Jeffry glared at him, the referee began to pray that the next pitch would be a ball. Then he remembered the merciless Pineys and simply prayed that he would not be hurt too badly in the fight that was sure to follow the game.

Cassaday's third pitch was a curve ball, slightly wide; he cursed as he released it, feeling his mistake before Jeffry slammed into it. The proximity of the beer kegs had debilitated the Piney outfield, which was still struggling to corner the ball as Jeffry galloped across home plate. The Beavers's fans went wild. Cassaday recovered, striking out the next two batters, but it didn't improve his spirits. Thanks to Jeffry Copper, the Pineys were three strikeouts away from defeat.

Jeffry pitched three perfect strikes and bowed low to acknowledge the cheers. Then a burly Piney hit a short fly ball and took second base by knocking the baseman out. The next batter was so beer-glazed that he could barely focus his eyes; he never saw the pitches that set him down. Two outs, and Cassaday Wade was up to bat. He let the first pitch pass: STRIKE! the umpire screamed above the noise of the crowd. He took the second: WHACK! The crowd looked up, shading their eyes, as the ball kept going—beyond right field, above a stand of cedar trees, still impossibly going, going, as Cassaday rounded first base with a puzzled look on his face, as though he, too, could not believe it could travel so far—SPLASH! It landed by the dam in Sabbath Creek, scattering the beavers. No one had seen a baseball hit so far before.

Cassaday crossed home plate, scoring the winning run. He was mobbed by his teammates, one of whom cheerfully upended the umpire, and then Jeffry Copper waded in with several Beavers: suddenly, the fight was on. Cassaday saw the hatred on Jeffry's face as he punched his way through the mob, heading for the Pineys's star. Just as Cassaday raised his fists in welcome, he felt a hand touch his shoulder. "Son," his father said, pulling him back from the fight. "This is not for you." Cassaday heard Jeffry's laugh, as he reluctantly retreated towards the hill where his mother was waiting. His triumph in the game seemed pointless, compared to his shame, for he realized that his father was right. Neither Ranewood nor his Piney teammates would welcome him on the field right now. No man wants to be hit by a black man's fist. And no man wants to be protected by one either.

Susannah Copper watched Cassaday leave, believing that he was too noble to take part in the crude violence of a brawl. Caddie Lofts was too busy to notice anything but the muscles aleaping in Jeffry's arms as he split through Pineys like they was so much kindling. She was disappointed when the fight was broken up, especially when Jeffry was escorted off the field by two stuck-up looking females, one of them wearing the very pink dress that she'd yearned for all day. Sometimes sensitivity could be a burden, she decided, comforting herself with a large golden swallow of beer. Her thoughts were diverted by the sight of a Ranewood family, going over to socialize with the Wades —some of those fancy Coppers, no less, though not Jeffry's parents. It was the funny looking ones, with that tall, skinny daughter who at least had sense enough not to wear a pink dress, 'cause all the money in the world couldn't buy her the faintest sign of a bosom.

Jonathan Copper stammered and stared at his feet, wondering why he'd ever thought that his family's visit might put the Wades at ease. Beside him, Anabel smiled at Kadar. "I've been using your tansy remedy for years, for my headaches, and I'm pleased to have this opportunity to thank you for it. Is it true you grow all your own herbs?"

"I keep a garden," Kadar replied, trying to smile as she wondered how much this charming lady knew. The awkward silence grew, as Susannah turned suddenly to Cassaday.

"You were beautiful today," she said, then turned bright red. "I mean, you played beautifully today," she muttered, as she joined her father in staring at the ground.

Cassaday just looked at her. He felt like he was drowning and dimly wondered why there wasn't any water. He knew that his parents were waiting for him to speak, but the words forming in his mind had nothing to do with what a good black boy should be saying to a lady like Susannah Copper. "I hope I didn't harm any of those beavers, hitting that ball into the creek," he said finally.

Susannah looked up, and smiled. "I thought of that, too, so I checked on them afterwards," she said. "They seemed to be just fine."

Cassaday smiled back, and then they both stared at the ground.

"I hear that there will be a fireworks celebration tonight," Jonathan said desperately, in the silence.

"Yes sir," Amos said, looking relieved. "The town of Ranewood surely does know how to celebrate the Fourth."

"It surely does," said Mary, and Kadar smiled. In a comfortable silence, they stood together, as sunset drenched the crowded field below, fusing its color, movement, and sound with one shade of amber light.

In the trees surrounding the picnic tables, lanterns were being lit. It was just like a fairy tale, thought Caddie Lofts, as she burped, ever so gently. Who would have thought that a man like Jeffry Copper would have singled her out for a chat. They had walked for a bit, with him teasing her to try some beer so she'd sipped a bit while he showed her the grounds. "Our frog level," he'd called it, thrilling her to the bones. What could fancy pink dresses mean to a man who owned his own frogs? Now he was filling up a plate for her and carrying it through the crowd so everybody could see that she was too much a lady to dish up her own slaw. As he seated himself beside her, she served him a dazzling smile. "It's a crime, letting Cassaday play for the Pineys," she told him. "You know, those folks put nigger curses on the ball, that's why he wins."

"Really?" Jeffry said, feeling his spirits lift. This was a new interpretation of the day's events, and one that he was eager to consider. He noticed that Caddie ate with a hearty appetite which he hopefully identified as depraved, since most of the ladies he had known could scarcely be persuaded to nibble on a crust. "More beer?" he said. She shook her head, and beamed when he refilled his cup. If he had gone up against some god-damn magic then that put a different face on things, he decided. But still, the day had not been his, not quite. Caddie's breasts heaved slightly as she gobbled down her chicken, and he began to smile. After all, what could a day of glory mean to a man who claimed the night?

He whispered into her ear. She giggled and blushed. "No," she said. Several minutes passed, and then he was heating up the same ear with his whispers. She giggled and giggled, making him coax a bit. It was nice to be coaxed by a gentleman. There was a bit more chicken and a lot more beer, and her ear was nearly smoking from the words it heard. And then, when she was warm and breathless just from the thought that she might say yes, she did.

"Stay here when the rest of the crowd goes down to the creek for the fireworks," he told her.

"I don't want to miss them," she said, looking uncertain.

"You won't," he assured her, whispering in her ear.

She giggled, blushed, and stayed. A sensitive girl could hardly resist sensation when it was flashing through her. Still, it was a shock when he lifted up the edge of the picnic tablecloth, urging her beneath it. Smack dab in the middle of things, where any-body might discover them! She'd never heard of such a thing. But being a gentleman, at least he'd picked high ground. Think-ing that, she scooted in and he crawled after, pulling the cloth down behind them.

The table was so high that she could sit straight up without bumping her head, but being so tall, he had a bit more trouble, so it was fine with her when he eased her back against the ground, resting her in his arms while he leaned over her. He kissed her, and her nervousness dissolved in the cool, soft pres-sure of his lips. How elegant he was, stroking her here and there so gentle that she might have been a baby, except for the things she was thinking. Being touched by a gentleman surely made a difference—none of that grab and stab stuff, and his fingers weren't greasy in spite of the chicken. His kisses were making little quivers in her skin, making her hurry to help him unbutton her blouse. His lips were trailing down her throat—

oh glory, he was kissing the base of her neck, where the life beat hardest. She raised up, lifting her breasts to his touch, as dizziness swept through her. She'd never been kissed on the neck before, in fact, she was lucky to have got a kiss at all, but here he was making a pattern of quivers and flashes that was taking over her senses—true enough—she'd never felt this way before, even with cousin Billy.

He was kissing her hard now, the way she liked, but not fast, so a girl had time to think about what was happening. He was dipping under her skirt to stroke at her legs, turning her toes to jelly. Licking at the tips of her breasts, he reminded her of a puppy, but she had to admit that his tongue was whipping her up like crazy, making her wiggle down below. She felt her legs parting and wondered how it had happened, but his hands had claimed her now, he had the right to slide her drawers down, kissing her into slickness like he had, and God knows she wanted it, would beg him for it if he wasn't already lifting her bottom, with her ankles hanging by his ears, as he filled her up, feeling strong and sweet, all at the same time. He moved so slow and gentle, making her want more, but she didn't want to seem too eager, then she sort of wriggled, and he seemed to read her mind, driving deeper and bigger, letting her swallow him up, with the hardness pounding, streaming through her more golden than beer. She knew that time was passing, somewhere, that the world was right outside, waiting to find them, but time meant nothing compared to the cries and the rhythm, and people who could find you . . . find you pounding, and crying out, meant nothing, nothing at all. She knew that she was climbing and felt confused, almost wanted him to stop 'cause he couldn't leave her here, without a world but him—and then she was flying, as though she'd been flung from a slingshot that had known where to aim her, all along.

"*Aaaaaaah!*" The crowd along the banks of Sabbath Creek expelled a single breath as the sky was lit with scarlets and a fire of molten blue. Roman candles spiraled, as rockets formed a galaxy that made the stars seem paltry for their lack of human might. Watching the fireworks, Susannah Copper trembled from the pent-up flow of classic forces which spiraled through her, almost unpleasantly. Suddenly she burst into tears, clinging to her father's arm. Anabel Copper reassured her husband with a look. Susannah was sensitive, and the excitement of the day had simply proved too much for her.

The final volley of rockets lit the sky, and two hundred faces lifted in unison to take in the glory as streamers of orange and red transfigured the night—the single breath, inhaled to "*Aaaah,*" began "EEEEEEEK"! BEAST! Suspended in the sky and lit by fire, a grinning horse's head appeared—a ghastly monster with wings like a bat, and something huge was dangling from his belly! Eyes bright as embers were staring down as he twisted his head from side to side, raking in the crowd with his gaze. He thrust his belly forward and gracefully danced as his giant dangling penis began to glow like a heated coal—began to sway like a flaming snake in the starless sky—

Howls of diabolical laughter rolled like thunder through the crowd, drowning out their screams. The editor of *The Ranewood Star* kept shouting, "India Honeyman was right!" but nobody listened. They were all too busy running for their lives. A human riot of color, movement, and sound headed towards the picnic tables near the hill, where Jeffry Copper was caught up in the glory of scoring twice. Drenched in sweat, in a tangle of clothes and limbs, he heard the shouts, but couldn't stop—his feet were jerking beyond the tablecloth, where everyone could see, and they were coming, coming—screams and frenzy, he could tell that the world had found him, watching as the mighty stud was ripping into the mare, making them go crazy. The screaming crowd, and he was coming, ripping into the screaming filly—coming, coming, he was coming, with a high-pitched stallion's scream.

No one was injured in the riot which ended the frog level's glorious Fourth, but the celebration did have an impact on local traditions. On July 5, 1913, a resolution banning the use of fireworks at any future celebrations was passed by the township council. Also, the Ranewood Beavers lost their mascots: on that same morning, it was discovered that the beavers had abandoned their dams at Rane's Creek at some time during the night. After 223 years of living in the same neighborhood, it appeared that they had finally seen enough.

Arguments about the existence of the Jersey Devil flourished for several months but soon gave way to more serious news about the growing war in Europe.

Propaganda stories from both sides spoke of atrocities which often turned out to be imaginary, and *The Ranewood Star* was filled with the latest European rumors; the most widely believed was a report that a large Russian army was traveling through Scotland and England to join Allied forces on the front. Although the story was completely fictitious, it was corroborated by eyewitness accounts of bearded Russian soldiers in Glasgow and London.

By 1916, the causes of woman's suffrage and Prohibition were gaining support. *Birth of a Nation* was playing in Philadelphia, but the sinking of the *Lusitania* overshadowed more peaceful news, and when President Woodrow Wilson asked Congress to declare war on April 6, 1917, the citizens of Ranewood shared the fervent joy which swept through the country. On the first day of the draft, over 300,000 men from New Jersey registered for duty. Jeffry Copper marched off to Hoboken, New Jersey, where he boarded a ship bound for France, along with many of the Ranewood Beavers. Cassaday Wade managed to get himself shipped off a few weeks later with a black regiment, and then Susannah Copper defied her parents and shocked the town by sailing for Europe, too, to serve as a volunteer nurse.

Sadie Copper organized the local war effort, working with a desperate frenzy. On the day her son left for Europe she sewed bandages for seven hours until her fingers bled. She collected peach stones for gas masks and planted the huge back garden entirely with potatoes for the land army, farming the crop herself. Every night she fell into bed exhausted but she could not sleep, as premonition echoed through her mind, like a curse. It was not enough. Long before that day in August 1916 when Jeffry Copper heard the whistling descent of the artillery that exploded in his trench, Sadie knew that he was dead. On the day he sailed for Europe, she had heard that whistling rocket and had seen his shattered arm flung into the air, then come to rest across his face where the top of his head had been. This vision had returned to her again and again, and though she had fought it with every type of magic she could think of, she knew —had always known—that it was not enough.

Six months after Jeffry's death, Sadie was still working her magic—she could not stop it. Fewer women attended her bandage-rolling sessions now, and the neighbors' doors were often closed in her face when she appeared once more to beg for peach stones or to sift through ashes for bits of coal. Whenever a local boy was killed, she collected masses of white flowers, making them into a huge wreath to hang upon the grieving mother's door. In the spring of 1918, she sent such a wreath to Kadar Wade, although her husband begged her not to; Cassaday had died on duty in the mess hall, when a grease fire exploded in his face.

When the war ended on November 8, 1918, many of Ranewood's returning sons faced a tragic reunion. In September and October of that year, nearly ten percent of the town's population had perished from influenza, as an epidemic swept the state. Anabel and Jonathan Copper were among the victims, as well as Sadie's husband. As she grieved, she no longer doubted David's love—"like swamp brier and vine," she decided, "we clung together, living in a terrible place." Now Sadie had no one to cling to, no son to live for, and no war to relieve her uncontrollable frenzy.

When her niece Susannah wrote to her from France in the spring of 1919, Sadie felt that it was a miracle. According to the letter, Susannah had married an American lieutenant overseas; he had later been killed in the war. Now she was stranded in Paris with their two-year-old son, Damon, and she asked if Sadie could send her the money to come home. Anabel and Jonathan Copper's house by the cranberry basin had been badly damaged in a storm after their death, and Sadie had not ordered it repaired. This gave her the perfect excuse to beg Susannah and her child to come live with her in the House of Penrod-Copper.

Susannah and Damon arrived at the huge columned porch on September 2, 1919. She wondered briefly, at her aunt's appearance—Sadie's hair was white now and tied in clumps with orange and yellow ribbons, and the woman who had always dressed in such elegant fashions was wearing white kid gloves, a narrow skirt of mauve chiffon, and David Copper's smoking jacket. Sadie wondered briefly why Susannah's eyes were ringed with shadows, why her fragile beauty had taken on the lifeless perfection of a Dresden figurine. But as Damon claimed their attention, this curiosity waned.

Sadie Copper and Susannah and Damon Thomas lived together at their fabled, ancestral home through the decade of the 20s. Women got the right to vote in 1922, and knee-length skirts became the rage; Sadie and Susannah didn't care. To them, 1922 was the year in which Damon lost his first tooth. In 1925, neighbors in Ranewood were talking about the arrest of John Scopes for teaching the theory of evolution; they were listening to songs on their gramaphones—"Tea for Two" and "Yes, Sir, That's My Baby." For Susannah and Sadie, 1925 was the famous year in which Damon got his first haircut. In 1929, Mickey Mouse became an overnight sensation; the next year, the stock market began its fatal decline; by 1932, Ranewood knew all of the verses to "Buddy, Can You Spare a Dime?"

Sadie could hardly be bothered by these events. She was completely wrapped up in her family. She had always liked Susannah and had even dreamed of a match with Jeffry, despite the fact they were cousins. Now that Susannah was living with her, it seemed more and more like this marriage had occurred, and that Damon was her grandson. The boy was a Copper, she told herself; the family had an heir. And now Damon was growing into a handsome youth, so much like Jeffry that perhaps he *was* Jeffry—certainly he was that dashing, handsome kind of lad which would set female heads to spinning.

———— *New Jersey managed to openly defy Prohibition laws throughout most of the 1920s, but no amount of rebellion could have warded off the catastrophic effects of the stock market crash. There were thirteen million Americans out of work in 1932; in New Jersey, the average person's income was $479 a year—little more than half of their earnings in 1929. Thousands of families simply had no money at all and no hopes of earning any. Government programs offered weekly food allowances of one dollar per person with a maximum of eight dollars per family, and several counties started public works programs. But there were too few jobs and too many families who faced the possibility of starvation for the first time in their lives. Many Americans chose to escape their fears by flocking to the movie houses in greater numbers than ever before, to see Mack Sennett comedies and glittering melodramas like* Grand Hotel. *Others, mostly men, began to travel in search of jobs, traveling in railroad boxcars or on foot as they drifted from county to county, state to state, looking for whatever work they could find.*

The House of Penrod-Copper: Reunion

IN THE huge, pale house that Captain Francis Penrod built, Damon Thomas grew up—the apple of his mother's eye, a solitary harvest that redeemed the dying Copper tree. On the night of their arrival, Sadie Copper had taken one look at the child which howled in Susannah's arms and her heart had leaped as she recognized her beloved son Jeffry—dark as a gypsy and full of spirit. She would gladly have piled peach stones to heaven in order to please him. Instead, she baked thousands of cookies and built marvelous toys from sticks and ribbon and spoons, which he loved almost as much as she did. When Damon ran into her arms, smiling up at her, Sadie felt a rush of pure joy, and the murmurings in her mind grew still. Neither she nor Damon seemed to mind that she called him Jeffry.

Susannah did not try to prevent Sadie from spoiling him, because she lived for her son's smiles, too. Hadn't she sensed Damon's strength and beauty even before he was born when, carrying him high in her womb, she'd marched through the streets of Paris so proudly that he might have been a banner? Afterwards, of course, it had been different; she'd been alone in a foreign country whose language she barely spoke, with an illegitimate child, and the man she would have borne all of this for was dead. In her son's handsome, smiling face, Susannah saw the image of his father, Cassaday Wade. Neither she nor

Damon seemed to mind that he spent so many hours in her arms, as she stroked him and whispered words that he could not understand.

Susannah had used her final store of strength to bring Damon home to Ranewood, to the house which had always been the pride of the Copper family. At first it had worried her, bringing her son so close to those who might recognize the exquisite beauty in his face. But then Sadie had greeted them so lovingly, and the high, familiar walls of her childhood had seemed to surround her, like an embrace. She found that she was able to sleep, for the first time since Cassaday's death. It seemed to her that the house was lulling her to sleep with beautiful dreams—just the sensation of floating within the rhythm of his breath, completely at peace. It was as though Damon was contained within her or she within him—or perhaps they were floating together in a gentle, constant sea.

As the years of Damon's childhood passed, the alabaster walls of the House of Penrod-Copper took on a transparent sheen, like an eggshell held too close to light. The boy's isolation was complete; Susannah supervised his education, reading to him from the large library of classical literature which Hannibal Copper had acquired. His aunt entertained him; Sadie was one of those rare adults who made good sense to a child. Master Thomas was a happy boy, and every year he grew up to look more and more like—Damon. Huge dark eyes dominated his face, but the angled planes there belonged neither to Jeffry Copper nor Cassaday Wade; they belonged to his mother. His skin was paler than either man's had been—like a rose of the palest brown. Of course, he did not look like Lieutenant Thomas; there was no such man. He simply looked like Damon: radiant smile, angled bones, and a faintly liquid grace.

By 1933, the House of Penrod-Copper was crumbling inward like a hollow shell that slowly yields to an unseen, unendurable pressure. The Depression had finally settled over the frog level, like a spell of morbid weather. When headlines from the cities had first proclaimed its coming, news was that people had no money—Ranewood farmers shook their heads. Never having had enough themselves, they knew how inconvenient that could be. But by the time that berries and potatoes were ready to go to market, they understood that this time, the *wrong* people had no money, and things were going to get worse.

The Coppers were one of those families that had no money now. What remained from their estate was land, but no one had the money to buy it. When he was ten, Damon laughed as Sadie pitched live snakes onto the columned porch to chase away those fools from the Ranewood Bank; he loved to run through the halls with his aunt as she chopped at rats with her hoe. The Depression seemed like another of his aunt's games, and he didn't notice that the crystal and silver gradually disappeared from the dining table, to buy meat and sugar for the cookies that he loved.

Susannah didn't notice the change, either—she was barely interested in food, let alone how it was served, and she enjoyed wearing the same pale sacque dresses that she had worn fifteen years before; she had been happy then, and her gowns were a bouquet of misty memories—pink rose voile and crepe of lilac blue. Her dreams had become more consuming now, for there were images—of her lover Cassaday as a boy, smiling as he held up a bunch of wildflowers; of Cassaday bathing in Sabbath Creek, waving to her and then wading towards shallow water to rise from it naked and gleaming like a god. The problem was that she hadn't known Cassaday when he was a boy. The sound of her son's breath still suffused her dreams, but it no longer sounded quite so soothing.

In 1933, Damon was fifteen, old enough to understand that the Copper family home was collapsing around them. There were now gaps in the sagging roof, floorboards that could no longer be trusted, and the velvet draperies disintegrated in his hands, like maroon-colored dust. Although he did not care for himself, each sign of decay that he found made him panicky, because he felt helpless to protect the two women whom he loved.

His mother's touch was exquisite to him. As a child, he remembered being held by her for hours and the lace that she always wore at her throat smelling of musty violets. She leaned down to whisper, and her head curved like a blossom as she told him how brave and handsome and loving his father had been. Resting his cheek against the scented lace, Damon could feel his father's presence surround him like a beautiful shadow. And he adored Sadie—his brave, foolish playmate who seemed as beguilingly innocent as the strands of bright ribbon that she wove through her hair in order to trap the voices that hid within it. Watching Sadie and his mother live in this decaying world seemed to him a form of mutilation; it was as though a pair of beautiful valentines were being scraped of color and lace. Damon knew nothing about how to fix things and sensed that the job was too big for him, but his desire to protect them grew, like the mold that spread across the cupids on the frescoed parlor ceiling.

Susannah had always told Damon that his father had appeared to her suddenly like a hero summoned to the quest, like a lightning bolt from the gods. It seemed to him that Billy Lofts appeared in exactly that same way in the spring of 1933. Damon discovered the man standing in the unturned soil of Sadie's garden behind the house.

"You ain't planted enough," Billy said, as though his presence were perfectly natural.

"We don't need much," Damon replied, embarrassed to admit that the house and grounds were too much for him, that he did not know how to fix things or to make them grow.

"Maybe you don't need so much for the three of you," Billy said. "After all, one of you is likely to be standing in the wrong place when that roof falls in."

Damon felt helpless before this man's knowledge of them; his statement had the ring of prophecy. "I don't know what to do," he admitted.

"I know that, too," said Billy, and he calmly walked to the back door of the house and then through it, as though he knew everything, including the fact that he belonged at the House of Penrod-Copper.

Billy Lofts knew about the Coppers because he had been at this house before; Miss Sadie had made use of his services in the past to pawn her jewels and silver trinkets, because Billy was always able to find a buyer and never troubled her creditors at the bank with news of the transaction. Since Sadie never questioned the sum of money he returned to her, Billy was able to grant the sweet old lady this favor at a considerable rate of profit.

Now he had drifted down from the Pines, looking for money and a place to hide for a spell. Billy attributed his money problems to the fact that he claimed too many of his children; as for needing a place to lay up, well that was a chronic problem, too, brought on by irate husbands and fathers with miserly instincts. Babies and men were the cause of his problems, nothing more. Who could fault him then for spending as much of his life as he could with the ladies?

Sadie Copper had chattered away to him, about the other occupants of this house, but that still hadn't prepared Billy for his first impression of Mrs. Susannah Thomas. He heard her first, a voice like rustling leaves that teased his senses, making him pause just inside the back door with Damon by his side.

"Damon, who is our guest?" Her large gray eyes had a stillness that made them look transparent, like a pool of unshed tears. She was painfully thin, and yet her figure had a tensile grace, suggesting that a woman might taste sweeter, taken from a slender jar. "I'm looking for work, ma'am," he heard himself say. "Couldn't help but notice that you could use some fixing up here."

Susannah stared at him, looking bewildered, but then she looked at Damon, who was pleading with his eyes; Billy watched, as she seemed to reconsider. "We cannot pay you," she said, finally.

"I'd gladly settle for room and board," he told her.

"There is a bedroom in the basement, beyond the kitchen," she replied. Then she looked at her son, and Billy hungered after the softness that crept into her gaze. As he followed Damon downstairs, he reminded himself that he'd only come here to lay up for a spell and to leave with as much of the Copper's crystal and finery as his wagon would hold. Mrs. Susannah Thomas was simply not in his plans.

Billy Lofts made his home in the basement bedroom; working together, he and Damon began to plant the back garden. In the afternoons, they tried to repair the largest holes in the roof of the house. Billy found a scythe in the tool shed; he showed Damon how to use it, in order to cut the tall grass which threatened to engulf the house. He showed the boy how to prop up a sagging beam, to use a hammer and saw and chisel. Although he had noticed that Damon had inherited his mother's stillness, and suspected that the boy might be frail, Billy had to admit that he'd never seen anyone work harder. In no time at all, Billy had eased comfortably into the role of supervisor; he even began to enjoy Damon's company, because the boy asked him questions about everything and admired anything that he did.

Although not a modest man, Billy might have been startled by the depth of Damon's admiration, if he had guessed it. To the sixteen-year-old boy this huge, capable man was sheer dazzle compared to the distant, gallant shadow of a father he had never known. He loved to watch the curt, sure moves of Billy's arms as he worked the scythe; he loved the careless strength that coursed through Billy's muscled shoulders and through his booming laugh. Damon began to believe that some strange sort of vitality radiated through Billy's skin and passed to him, connecting them together with a feeling that was like an excitement.

Billy knew everything. For instance, he told Damon that this was a man's world, and ladies were here to provide a bit of heaven on earth. This idea seemed thrilling and exactly right —that a world for men existed beyond the magic of the women whom he loved. As he worked beside Billy in the garden, Damon found himself daydreaming that he and Billy stood side by side, rescuing his mother from some peril. They clasped arms to lift her high upon their shoulders, and she laughed as he had never heard her laugh before. In his dream, Billy loved Susannah, just as Damon did, because she was so beautiful. Sometimes Sadie came running through this dream, chopping up imaginary rats with her hoe and then everybody laughed. His mother served tea, while he and Billy stood together beneath a dazzling sun with their arms about each other's shoulders, and the scent of musty violets mingled with the tang of Billy's sweat.

Working alongside Damon, Billy had his daydreams, too. He dreamed that Mrs. Susannah Thomas lay spread-eagled before him, with fear showing in her beautiful gray eyes as he ripped apart her dress. But then he stroked her, rubbing his hands across her fragile, incredibly soft flesh as he watched the tension leave her face—her head dropped back, and when she opened her eyes again, he saw the naked, hungry look that he'd seen before, when she looked at Damon.

Susannah came out of the house every day, to watch the men

work, and she noticed the relationship that was growing between them; she hated Billy Lofts for it, because she believed
that he was usurping the devotion that should have been Cassaday's; that is how she perceived the love which she clearly saw
on her son's face. Her fury only increased the nightmares that
were plaguing her. Every night, the sound of her son's breath
engulfed her, the soothing tide and her joy within it—but then
the rhythm came hard and urgent as the darkness took on
shape—corded muscles, gleaming flesh, and Susannah knew
that he lay beside her—*Cassaday oh please* she reached out, biting
hungrily at his flesh and the sound of breath was rasping; it
mingled with the feel of mouths and bodies touching, mingled
with the ragged sobbing of her breath.

Bolting awake in the airless, shabby bedroom, Susannah
would open her window and stare into the sky, but there was
nothing in the heavens for her. What she wanted was in this
house. She wanted the taste, the smell, the feel of him inside
her—Cassaday, in her son's flesh. The dream sickened her, but
she could not rid herself of it. Even during the day, she found
herself flowing as she watched her son, and she knew that the
storm inside her had nothing to do with a quiet, constant sea.

Sadie had dreams, too, and she shared them with everyone:

"Sadie was a goddess. Did you know?" she announced to
them, as they drank lemonade in the afternoon sun.

Billy was closest to her. "Ma'am," he said, bowing low. "If I
may say so, you still are a goddess." As Sadie bestowed a girlish
kiss, Billy watched Susannah's face, hoping—yes, she smiled,
really smiled at him.

"Sadie was a whore. Did you know?" she asked Susannah, at
breakfast, while she munched her toast.

Susannah leaped up to embrace her. "No, Sadie, no," she
whispered. "That must have been a dream," she said, weeping
as she remembered her own.

Sadie said, "Don't worry, Jeffry. I'll never let them hurt you."
Damon held her hand and stared through the window at Billy,
wondering what could hurt him in a world where this man was.

Sadie stared at Billy Lofts. "Fire!" she said. "Go away!" No
one else was near, and Billy tweaked the ribbons in her rumpled
white hair and laughed.

Spring blended into summer, and the hollow shell of the

House of Penrod slowly mended, beneath the brightening sun. There were no tassels, no carvings to mimic filigree, but the roof no longer leaked except in unimportant places, and the third and twelfth steps of the huge hall stairway no longer gave way. Susannah continued to dream as she watched Damon, who was lost in his view of Billy, who saw all of Susannah in his dreams. Sadie watched everything, as voices and colors formed a pleasant twirl through her mind.

On the first day of unendurable heat, Susannah made sandwiches and lemonade to take to the men in the garden. When she carried the tray from the house, she found no one working there; then she heard splashes from the creek and realized that Billy and Damon were cooling off in the water. Putting down their lunch, she started to return to the house, but suddenly she found herself running, skirting behind trees so that she would not be seen until she reached the creek; she crouched behind foliage so close to the men that she could see the faint pattern of her son's breath in the rise and fall of his chest.

As Damon turned towards Billy, she noticed his back and the newly formed muscles that broadened his shoulders and rippled with the movement of his arms. They began to wrestle, playfully, and she was stunned by Damon's strength and the deep bass notes in his laughter—he was a man now, with a muscled back that would feel like velvet beneath a woman's hands, with strong arms that could hold and lift her—No! They were heading towards her, wading slowly out of the water. Susannah caught her breath, but she could not force herself to turn away. Billy stepped onto the bank first, and she felt almost impatient, even as the power of his sexuality stunned her, like an unexpected blow. But Billy was blocking her view—why wouldn't he move?—*oh please* Cassaday, Cassaday—suddenly just as in her dreams, he was rising from the water like a god. The simple fact of his naked beauty penetrated her, leaving her breathless; she stared at him, divorced of all other feeling, as the scene before her seemed washed in light too brilliant to be real. Her body tensed, yet felt strangely ethereal as desire was flowing through her, as she crouched like an animal poised to spring at him—Damon! This was her son! Nausea choked her and the sense of horror was overwhelming. Susannah was shaking, and she felt as though her body might fly apart like a clock too tightly wound; she tried to run, but her legs would not support her, and so she crawled into the foliage, crouching there until long after the men had gone.

Hours later, Susannah stumbled back into the house and hurried into her bedroom, where she bolted the door, as though she might protect her son by locking herself away from him. The force of her desire was killing—like a weapon within her, sharp as the blade of a knife. She felt herself mutilated by the cutting, she was ripping apart as her feelings spilled like blood. She felt weakness spreading through her along with the pain; almost gratefully, she huddled on the bed and slipped into fevered dreams.

Suddenly, there was noise—Damon was knocking at her door, calling out in a puzzled voice; she knew that he wouldn't leave until she bid him goodnight. Working the lock on the door, her fingers shook, and she tried to control her thoughts. She must keep the blade inside her; she must not let it slash him, this deadly knife.

The corridor was dimly lit; she could barely see his face as he leaned over her, whispering words of concern. She heard herself mumble some reply—nonsensical, the sort of words used when one is forcing back a scream—GET OUT! she wanted to say, or HOLD ME!—but the knife was twisting, she would die before she let him taste the bleeding. He leaned down to kiss her. His lips tasted wonderfully clean, and for an instant she swayed against him, feeling dizzy.

As she did so, she felt the force of his erection. Shock sent her out of control, and she pressed against him, hungrily. Immediately, he stiffened, and then she pulled herself free, pushing him violently from the door as she slammed it against him.

Susannah heard his footsteps, hurrying down the hall, and she collapsed against the door, as the room seemed to fill with harsh, tangled sounds of breathing. The knife was slashing through her, out of control, and there was no stopping the violence; her body was a liquid stream that demanded more than memories. This room would destroy her; Susannah ran from it, but the sound of breathing seemed to follow her down the hall, and she knew that this time, she would not wake up from her dreams. With one last desperate act of strength, she turned away from her son's bedroom door and fled down the stairs towards the basement room of Billy Lofts.

Moonlight was filtering through vines that covered the casement window there; it filled the narrow room with a faintly greenish light. As she walked to the bed where Billy slept, Susannah felt as though she were traveling underwater—no more soothing tide, no storms, she thought. She would sink beneath their power, beyond the cutting of the knife. She stared at the man who sprawled naked and snoring on the bed with a half-empty bottle of bootlegged whiskey still clasped in his hand.

For an instant, the memory of Cassaday drifted through her like an intoxicating smoke. Then she remembered her son's body—rigid with shock against her and then he was running, ashamed.

She took the bottle from Billy's hand and tilted it to her mouth, gasping at the taste. As she loosened her robe, letting it fall to the floor, he began to stir, but his eyes didn't open until she moved over him to slide her hands through the curling hairs on his chest. He started awake, looking at her in disbelief; she stared at him without speaking but continued to rub his chest.

The look in his eyes disgusted her; she licked her lips, desperate to taste the liquor on her breath. When he reached out to touch her, she flinched, but then his hands were on her breasts and suddenly she understood, because the knife was slipping through her—his touch was coarse and greedy, and she wanted it, *any* hand on her breasts. *Any* mouth would do, pressing tightly against her lips, as long as it slid a path of slickness, teeth and tongue along her neck. The knife was turning, feelings spilled for any man who forced her down, as her fingers tangled in his hair. She felt the play of muscles in his back, the strength of him as he gripped her buttocks and lifted her, like any man he drove into her with a searing shock, a fullness inside her, incredibly sweet.

Not Damon! The thought flashed through her—it was not her son she needed, to feel Cassaday inside her. In this man's crude, driving rhythm, as her body flowed and twisted up to meet him, in the heated stain of his breath upon her cheek, she found the long, slow rhythms, the cool, maddening feel of Cassaday moving inside her, hard and sweet like bark and honey as she begged him *Cassaday oh please.* She felt him, rocking faster and faster; Cassaday had never been like this, violent and selfish, but she felt them both, the difference was slashing through her, loosening a double rhythm of liquid and fire. She arched back, no longer caring which man was in her now.

Standing by the basement door, Damon watched as Billy drove his mother's body against the sagging mattress, and he heard Susannah's cries. Damon had been too upset to sleep—still embarrassed by his gross display before his mother, who clearly had been repelled by the touch of his uncontrollable erection. Ever since he and Billy had swum in the creek, Damon had been in a state of excitement, and so he had finally decided to wake up his friend in order to beg him for some advice. And so he discovered them together—his exquisite Susannah and Billy Lofts. Their naked bodies were twisting and their flesh made a sound of slapping as they heaved in the greenish light which seemed to coat them, like a stain of slime.

Minutes passed in silence as he watched them, hidden by the door. He studied the spectacle carefully, as though to convince himself that it was true. And then he began to run—leaving silently, up the stairs and out of the house and into the world which his best friend Billy had told him all about.

Susannah and Billy did not hear Damon leave; Sadie Copper did, but she did not try to stop him. At dawn, while Susannah and Billy were still lying together in the basement of the house, Sadie moved quietly along the corridors upstairs, from frazzled draperies to tassel-less brocades. "Fire," she whispered. "Get out, now." The torch that she held in her hand burned brightly as she carefully kindled the blaze, and soon the burning rooms lit the house; and then, the flaming House of Penrod-Copper lit the dawn. Sadie stayed inside, because the flames were brightest there. "Fire," she said. "I knew it, all along."

By midmorning of July 17, 1933, fire had destroyed the house that Captain Francis Penrod built and everyone within it. His great-great-great-grandson Damon Thomas did not learn about the fire for many years, however. Damon kept on running, and because he did not stop, eventually, he reached Hollywood, California. There he was "discovered" by a talent scout behind the refreshment counter at Grauman's Chinese Theater.

Dark and handsome, with angled bones and a faintly liquid grace, Damon captured the hearts of American women, cast as the strong-but-sensitive soldier, the forceful-but-tender lover, and the tough cowboy loner with a tragic past who rides through the West with a kitten. In this third movie, he falls in love with a Quaker schoolmarm and goes to a gunfight unarmed, at her request; riddled by bullets, he falls to the ground and dies in his sweetheart's arms, holding his kitten who is miraculously unharmed. This closing scene caused a nationwide outbreak of weeping and turned him into the nation's number one all-American hero: Enriko Ponce, the debonair bachelor whose press bio explained that his father had been a Russian prince and his mother, a Polynesian heiress (who still lived on her vast pineapple estate which covered several islands).

Enriko Ponce never returned to the land by the frog level, and he never married, which apparently ended the line of Penrod-Copper. But his ancestors made it to the silver screen—in his eyes and mouth and dashing, handsome flesh: the English nobleman Josiah Ross and Indian Jin; Cedar Honeyman and Daniel Brewster, who died on a barroom floor; Amos Wade and the nigger whore Kadar; and most important, perhaps, Captain Francis Penrod. Nearly 170 years after his glorious future, Captain finally became at least one part of a star.

Enriko Ponce did not claim the 499 and ¾ lands of his estate at the frog level, so his inheritance passed into the hands of the state of New Jersey. The rubble of the House of Penrod-Copper was soon overgrown by grass and weeds, until there was no sign of human habitation left upon the five hundred acres of land; only the odd strip of dirt that Seneca Rane had made on the empty rise above the frog level still remained. Farmers no longer leased the fields for cultivation—their contracts with cranberry and vegetable cooperatives provided a more profitable way of life. The beavers no longer worked on the creek, but the frogs still sang, and the scarlet oak still reached out with its branches. Cranberries grew at what now was known as Aunt Cedar's Cranberry Basin. The years passed, and the land collected its dust.

The frog level lay just east of the town of Ranewood, but Ranewood seemed to have turned its back. Residents there slowly eased out of the Depression by the late 1930s. Although prices for farm produce were still low, life was more comfortable than ever. The town had its own movie theater now, and admission was twenty-five cents. The tiny Ranewood Hotel offered a four-course Sunday dinner for fifty cents, and most families could even afford a car, which could be bought new for eight hundred dollars. In addition to the public library, people now could subscribe to Book-of-the-Month Club, which delivered John Steinbeck and Sinclair Lewis right to the doorsteps of Sand County, even to Piney shacks. Radios tuned to Philadelphia delivered strains of "South of the Border," or Arturo Toscanini, as he conducted the NBC Symphony Orchestra.

Those radios also brought a stream of reports about another European war and this time pro-war sentiment was nearly unanimous. When their radios blared out the words "Pearl Harbor" on December 7, 1941, Ranewood was ready to fight. As *The Ranewood Star* exhorted them to "JOLT THE JAPS!" nearly eight hundred young men (from a town of seventy-five hundred people) volunteered for duty. As sons went off to the Kasserine Pass, Bataan, and the Bismarck Sea, New Jersey became the staging and storage area for the largest invasion force which the world had ever seen.

World War II drove through the town of Ranewood in jeeps. It landed a force of soldiers on leave from huge military bases in the Pine Barrens. The dining room at the Ranewood Hotel was overrun, and new restaurants quickly sprang up. In canteens, bars and USO dance halls, Ranewood learned to do the jitterbug. Business was thriving; wages were high and the growing town overtook the old railroad junction at Rowleytown, where the glassmaking works had dwindled and finally died during the Depression. India Honeyman would have said it was just revenge.

Ranewood celebrated the final surrender of Japan in a state of euphoria. By that time, nearly two thirds of the town was involved in some sort of "war work"; seventy of those men who had gone off to fight did not return. The town's contribution to the war had been tremendous, and the war had contributed to the town. It had even changed the land at the frog level. At the site of Daniel Honeyman's old tavern (which had been transformed into the Penrod Inn), a cinder block building of marginal charm had been erected in 1942. This building housed a restaurant which had attracted crowds of soldiers during the war. It was called Aunt Cedar's Cranberry Inn, although it was owned by a Ranewood lawyer named Joe Capezi. Behind the main building, there were seven small sheds which were painted white and known as cottages, although each was barely large enough for the double bed within it. Those double beds had far more to do with the popularity of the inn than cranberries, which never appeared on the menu.

One of those Ranewood families which had risen to prominence during the war years was that of Theodore and Margaret Huggsey. Theodore owned a small cannery on the southern edge of town, and it had become one of the state's leading suppliers for GI mess kits. The Huggsey family had gone all out for the war, and they were the kind of family that a small town always takes pride in. Teddy and Margaret were a hardworking, adorable couple. They had two sets of adorable twins, who were full of adventures. They had an adorable dog. And their newest addition to the family—a daughter—had been born on V-J Day. Adorable.

Ranewood's world had changed so quickly that the idea of peace seemed a little bewildering. In the year 1949, some of its citizens were still making adjustments. They learned the words to new songs, like "All I Want for Christmas Is My Two Front Teeth." They learned the meaning of new words, like Cold War. And some, like Theodore Huggsey, struggled to find a peaceful destiny. In pursuit of his dream, Teddy would travel to the wilderness at the frog level.

——— *New Jersey made an heroic effort for the war. It ranked fifth in the nation in war contracts, for ships, airplane motors, explosives, radar, uniforms, radios, food. One thing that New Jersey supplied was "parts"—components for larger, more important things that were put together in other states. For this contribution, it was awarded still another title, "The Component State." Most of these factories were in the industrial counties of northern New Jersey, but the southern part of the state did its share, too, producing uniforms, radios, food, and plenty of hospitality for soldiers from across the nation who had been sent to the Pine Barrens to await embarkation. The military base at Fort Dix processed over one million draftees and to the north, Camp Kilmer (which had been open pasture land in 1942) sent more than one hundred thousand soldiers per month off to overseas duty. Small towns suddenly found themselves playing host to crowds of young strangers who bounced to the jive and blazed a message through the pines: "Kilroy Was Here."*

The World Comes to Ranewood

1949 ————

Adventure at Aunt Cedar's Cranberry Inn

ON THE first Saturday in August 1949, Theodore Huggsey woke up feeling cross; this filled him with horror, because until just recently, Teddy had never felt cross in his life. He had never had an unkind thought, or spoken a harsh word to his dear wife Margaret, their precious children and loyal pets, or their black retainer, 'Mimah. His employees at Huggsey Cannery considered him the ideal boss; if there were a litmus test for temperament, Teddy would have proved himself pure alkaline. But within the past few months, vile thoughts had begun to churn through him like the acidic outpourings of an alien, tumescent gland.

The worst of these thoughts centered around dear Margaret Huggsey, who was his perfect wife and a model mother. Then why did he so often wish that a horde of vicious midgets would carry her deep into a snowy forest to rip apart her dear, sweet flesh with their teeny-tiny pliers? Six weeks ago, on her fiftieth birthday, Teddy had dreamt of bending over Margaret's pale sweet body as she slept to light the tiny wicks he saw peeking from the tips of her breasts. Two tiny flames sprang to life; he sang to her, quite tenderly, as flames melted down her breasts, spreading to the rest of her body. Then he gave his birthday horn a little toot and dear Margaret exploded, drenching him in a burst of angel food-ish flesh.

Remembering these dreams, Teddy pulled the sheet over his head, desperately recalling the days of their courtship when Margaret had seemed everything desirable in woman, the essence of femininity—mysterious and slightly edible, like those delicacies which ladies cook from secret recipes and serve only to each other at ladies' luncheons atop a bed of greens or rice. His experience with the opposite sex had not been extensive, but Margaret was certainly the only woman he'd ever known whose breasts were actually fluffy.

And throughout the years of their marriage, he reminded himself, she had never denied him; he had nibbled those fluffy riches in every season, at any time of day. Margaret's sexuality was acquiescent and vaguely solicitous, as though lust were a mild infection that should be promptly treated, in order to keep it from spreading. He had no reason to complain. Why, then, this insidious crossness towards his precious wife and family, and those vile, unthinkable thoughts about his secretary, Miss Lana Lilly?

Remembering Lana, Teddy pulled back the sheets, and glanced at the clock—it was past noon! Why had Margaret . . . ? Of course. Bearkins needed his rest. Feeling her tenderness wash over him like an oily, boiling tide, Teddy lurched into the bathroom. If he could have wrapped a Huggsey can around the feelings sloshing inside him, he was sure that the contents would eat away rust.

He shaved quickly, staring at his reflection. Perhaps his dreams were just a sign of age, he thought—both he and Margaret were fifty now—or perhaps a belated reaction to the war. Gosh, everything had seemed so exciting then, with the entire Huggsey family working for Uncle Sam—none of them too close to the fighting, thank goodness. As Teddy had often pointed out to his wife, that would have spoiled everything. Margaret had organized canteens at the military bases in the Pines, while he'd put in eighteen-hour days at the cannery, turning out beans and peaches that stormed the beaches at Anzio, Normandy, and Guadalcanal. The oldest twins, Dick and Babs, had been in uniform—Dick had joined the navy with his chums, and dear, sweet Babs had shredded paper for Army Intelligence. The younger twins had pitched in, too, and when their youngest daughter, Popo, was born on V-J Day, the Huggsey victory had seemed complete.

Now the great fight was over, and it was time for the family to reap the peace. Their oldest son Dick was still on carrier duty, with those crazy cut-ups he'd brought home during his last leave; but daughter Babs was back from Washington; she'd be married soon and settled down right here in Ranewood. Teddy was almost embarrassed by the profits his cannery had made on those GI peaches and beans; at last, he and Margaret would be able to build the house of their dreams. Everything was wonderful, wasn't it? Life was clearly extending to the Huggseys a most cordial, hearty handshake.

Teddy dabbed his face with a towel and stared at the sullen, restless gaze reflected in the mirror—his own unfamiliar eyes. "Forget the handshake," he thought with bitterness. "What I really want is a goose in the balls."

Those sullen eyes showed shock, then turned away. At the Huggsey home, the only "balls" were round and red and thrown to Barky; as for a goose, the family shared just one each year, stuffed with 'Mimah's chestnut dressing.

Teddy hurried downstairs, feeling evil thoughts surge through him as he caught sight of the younger Huggsey twins, Howdy and Holly. At fifteen, they seemed to be growing into short, fat, and foolish versions of their mother.

The twins were pasting photos into the family album, oblivious to the malevolence that he breathed into the living room. A Phillies baseball game was blaring softly from the radio.

Teddy struggled back his demons. "Hello there, my darlings," he managed, in a rasping voice. "What's the score?"

Holly answered him with a helpless shake of her curls. "I don't know, Daddy. It keeps changing."

Guttural sounds were forming in Teddy's throat. He forced a cheery wave and fled, as bright, vile images cartwheeled through his brain. Barky was sleeping on the mat by the front door. Daddy Huggsey aimed a kick—Barky squealed, flew through the air—then he was running to his car.

Driving through the streets of Ranewood, Teddy took slow deep breaths, and the demons slowly receded. Surely he could not have really felt that urge to slam the photo album on Holly's chubby fingers, pounding it with his fists until she screamed? He was a devoted father, and a happily married man, he reminded himself. Margaret's gentle, fluffy heart was the soufflé around which he'd happily sworn to tiptoe for the rest of his life. He was not the sort of man who broke a family's heart with dreams of Lana Lilly—he was simply having another man's dreams. Some sort of psychic accident. To prove this, he would drive down to the cannery to catch up on some paperwork. Teddy began to whistle; a devoted family man provides for them, even on Saturday, he reminded himself. Where the demons had been howling within him there were only Munchkin giggles.

As he drove into the parking lot at the cannery, his heart gave a shiver and lodged in his throat—that peppy blue Rover could only be *her* car. Lana was here! Impossible, he told himself. She probably just forgot to drive it home on Friday. Miss Lilly was not compulsively meticulous as demonstrated by the condition of her files. But as Teddy hurried through the entrance to Huggsey Cannery, the music from Lana's typewriter rattled through him, evocative and thrilling, like a metallic overture. An overture to what? he thought desperately.

There she was with her blonde head bobbing, eyes bright and avid, like a canary pecking over a cuttlebone. "Miss Lilly?" he said, feeling awed. There was no response. "Lana!" he cried.

She looked up and burst into smiles. "Oh hi, Mr. Huggsey. I just couldn't get this done on Friday, so I decided to hop in and finish today, quick as a bunny." She pointed to the mass of papers on her desk and giggled, somehow managing to wrinkle her nose in the process.

"That's swell," he told her. Then, with a burst of courage, "But I'm sure that a popular gal like you has better things to do on a Saturday."

The nose wrinkled again. "To tell you the truth, I don't have any plans." The bright eyes turned misty. "I think I'm feeling a little bit blue." She turned away quickly and began to type.

Teddy rushed into his office and shut the door. What a break —no, what a disaster! Think about Margaret, the kids, and Barky. But the only thoughts he could manage were the images of Lana he'd seen in his dreams—peeking over her shoulder at him, while she posed in a nifty red bathing suit; looking helpless and sexy as a breeze blew up into her skirts, lifting them above her downy thighs; Lana fresh from a bubble bath, wrapped in a huge terry towel which was slowly unwrapping—her round blue eyes, that perky nose, her great big, cashmere-covered— go on, *say* it—"Bosoms. Knockers. *Tits*," he howled.

He stopped short, terrified, but Lana's typewriter clattered on, without missing a beat. "I can't go on like this," he realized. As he paced his office, it suddenly occurred to him that Lana might be the cure, not a symptom of his malevolent disease. She could be the goose, the one adventure that Daddy Huggsey needed. In fact, Lana might be able to prevent the murder of his wife. From deep within him, helpful Munchkin voices cried, "Do it, do it for Margaret and the kiddies."

"By gosh, I will," he thought, but where? There was only one place that he'd heard of in the area which had a reputation for encouraging this sort of thing. Aunt Cedar's Cranberry Inn supplemented its business with a handful of tourist cabins, which were generally known to be available for you-know-what. His heart was thumping like a Sousa march as he dialed the telephone.

"Aunt Cedar's Cranberry Inn."

"I'd like to reserve two dinners and a cabin," he hissed. "Six-ish. Name of John Doe."

"Right," said the voice. "Key will be under your plate. Don't steal the sheets."

Teddy hung up and stared at his shaking hands in disbelief. Could it be this easy? After thirty years, to slam the oven door on Margaret's fluffy heart? Suddenly, he remembered the matter of Mrs. Doe—she would turn him down, he knew it. Opening his office door, he leaned through at what he hoped was a rakish angle. "Lana," he told her, "I've got a swell idea. Why don't you let me take you out for a steak. To tell the truth, I'm feeling a bit blue, too."

"Oh, Mr. Huggsey." Her smile was dazzling. "You're the *best*."

Her knockers, boobies, tits were bouncing as she squirmed in happiness. "Don't thank me, dear," he said warmly. "It's the least I can do."

Lana smiled up at Mr. Huggsey as he tucked her chair beneath the table reserved for the Jonathan Does at the Cranberry Inn. She decided that Teddy was a nice man, who was going to feed her some steak. This was the extent of her thinking about the evening ahead; she wasn't wracked by anxieties, like her boss. At an early age, Lana had discovered that she preferred humming to thinking; humming produced a pleasant sensation, and you could snap your fingers to it if your fingernail polish was dry. No one ever kept time to thinking. When she'd graduated from high school, she'd been forced to think about the future; it was then that she discovered the virtues in humming silently. True, she could no longer feel that comforting buzz in her throat, but now she could hum anywhere and nobody noticed.

For the past seven years, she had punched in promptly at Huggsey Cannery to hum silently through her day. She typed, filed, and smiled to her own secret music and was paid quite nicely for it too. Until recently, she had been content; she was young, pretty, and had the freedom to choose what songs she would hum. During the war, she'd had a lot of sweethearts from Camp Roud, but the war was over now and what was worse, she was twenty-four; lately she'd been humming the blues. Lana figured she had one good year left, but then what? She might have to give up her musical career, in order to think. But not yet, she reminded herself, as the waitress set a pink, fizzy drink in front of her. Lana sipped it quietly and noticed that the two couples seated at the next table were producing a catchy sound. She drifted to their voices and soon her foot was tapping to the beat.

"How's that chicken, Fred?" a woman said, presumably to Fred.

"My chicken's fine, Helen. How is yours?" said Fred.

"Mine's fine. Mary, is your chicken good?"

The other woman smiled. "It tastes fine. How's yours, George?"

Pause. Then Helen and Fred together: "George got the steak."

"Oh." Another pause. "How's your steak?"

"The steak is fine." Then George looked up. "Say, how's that chicken?"

—Goshdarnalmighty! Teddy clenched his napkin, fighting back a scream. How's a fellow supposed to work up a romantic mood in the face of that stuff. Worst of all, Lana was bobbing her head in time to their voices and appeared to be falling into some kind of trance.

"DRINK UP," he shouted, shaking her arm.

Her head snapped towards him. "HHHmmmmmm?"

"Your drink."

"Oh," she said, and drained it.

Teddy felt his spirits rise. He beckoned to the waitress. "Two steaks, please," he announced. "The little lady will have a medium and I'll take mine bloody. And one more of those little pink drinks, with a double Scotch for me."

The waitress smiled as she moved away, and Teddy fought back the sudden fear that she'd gone to call his wife. That was ridiculous; no one here knew him, and besides Margaret would never suspect. At fifty years of age, she still believed that falling raindrops were the angels' tears. Throughout the meal, he wondered how to break the ice, how to woo Lana, how to coax and win her. Nervously he kept reordering drinks, planning how to broach the subject of the key to the cabin door. As it turned out, that wasn't necessary. After four double Scotches, the keychain slithered from his sweaty palm and coiled on the napkin, like a metallic serpent.

"Ohhhhh," Lana fizzed, bobbing above her drink. "Are we going to be naughty, Mr. Huggsey?"

Ice definitely broken. "Why don't we try this out on a few doors, and see?" he replied. An oven door was slamming, but he barely noticed the sound above the pounding of his heart.

The key fit into the lock of cabin number two. Teddy held the door for Lana and followed her in, watching her hips swivel beneath her snug green skirt and wondering how to get them out of it, in the kindest, quickest way.

He didn't have to worry. Quick as a bunny, Lana had shucked her clothes and stood before him in lacy underwear, tugging at the zip on his pants. "The light—" he said feebly, but his boxers were already hitting the floor. He felt a little overdressed, from the waist up, and decided to loosen his tie.

Lana didn't seem to notice. She was doing wonderful things

to him down below, and there was a peculiar, scratchy sensation. Lifting his shirttails, he looked down to see a narrow ring of tightly braided fibers. Working carefully, Lana was guiding the ring—oh no! Onto his *manhood*, making it prickly and tight, making it feel like a big throbbing monster of a downright, say it say, "Cock." He murmured, feeling terrified.

She smiled up at him. "My sweetheart from the Marines gave me this ring—he said on the island of Sumi every young bride designs one for her hope chest."

A war souvenir—well that was all right, but, "Don't you think it's a bit snug, my dear?"

"Just wait." She giggled. "You know, my sweetheart was a very famous Marine. He was really at Guadalcanal and won four medals."

I hope he didn't give those to her too, Teddy thought. The thought of pins wasn't pleasant. But the sensations aroused by the ring were actually fine—a slight, steady pressure that seemed to call for blood and muscle, for all the grit that a man possessed to get down to his *cock* . . . goddammit hot and hard and let's show them, men . . . let's get the job done, storm the beach and leave 'em senseless, screaming, screaming. "FUCK," he shouted. "FUCK."

"Not yet," she said, tickling him and giggling. "Guess what else I've got."

He wasn't up to guessing. He was barely up to waiting, while she rummaged in her purse.

The something else turned out to be two pairs of handcuffs from another sweetheart, a generous MP. "He had a very distinguished career," she told him, snagging each wrist as she chained his arms to the sides of the cot. "He put down the Hersey Bar riot at the Camp Roud PX quite personally."

Teddy's arms were dangling high; his cock was standing on end. Immobilized and throbbing, he watched as from the bottom of her purse, she produced a length of rope.

"Another gift?" he croaked.

"This one's from me." She giggled, and then tethered his ankles in no time at all.

Spread-eagled and lying completely naked beneath the glare of the overhead bulb, Teddy began to worry about the condition of his flanks. For one thing, his Sumi ring was bursting. "Are there any more surprises?" he asked, feeling like he could bear it, if there were.

"Just one," Lana shrieked. She backed to the opposite side of the room and took a flying leap to land upon him—a tit, tit, twat landing, she informed him, courtesy of her sweetheart in the Screaming Eagles.

All three points connected, and Teddy was seeing stars. Slowly, air returned to his lungs; breathe in, breathe out, he reminded himself. Don't get caught on the ground. Oh gosh the hairs on his calf were lighting up as she licked her way up his leg. Staring down, he caught a glimpse of his incredible braided cock—standing straight as a flagpole. Oh, glory.

Nibbling on his thigh, Lana paused to giggle. "Mr. Huggsey, you're being infiltrated."

Do it baby take the hill—he heard a shout, it was his own, his cock was on her side—"Oh, yes!"

She raised up and planted herself upon him, streaming on his pole. Together they took off, racing to storm the bunker, take the hill, they were bouncing, screaming, they flew through flak, and then he was shooting into sky. "Incoming mail," he screamed. "Banzai," she screamed, and grabbed his neck.

In the tender hush that followed, Teddy slowly became aware of the fact that he was ready to go again. In fact, part of him was still gunning for action. He wriggled in his chains, unable to believe it.

"It's the Sumi ring," Lana whispered.

Indeed, the Sumi forces were clearly calling in their reserves, swarming for an attack. Teddy searched his memory, for the list of friendly nations—surely the Sumi had been Allies? Then WOW the earth exploded, and five more times that night Theodore Huggsey went the distance. He sweated, groaned, and trembled, but he never stopped coming, as Lana drove him on and on, driving deeper, with the growling purr of a hungry Sherman tank. He'd never felt anything like it, but there was simply no stopping, and victory, victory! Goshdarn, it was all so red, white, and blue.

Near dawn Teddy lay limp in his chains, dozing and exhausted. Startled by a prickly sensation, he jolted awake with the panicked, dismal feeling that his cock was gone. Lana stood before him fully clothed as she tucked the Sumi ring into her purse. He searched for words to fit the occasion and considered quoting a general, but all he could think of was *Nuts*. "Lana," he murmured, "you were—"

She cut him off, throwing a snappy salute. "Soldiers never say goodbye," she said, in a brave voice. She looked at him. "I miss the war," she said.

"So do I." Teddy tried to smile, but he simply felt too blue.

And then she was gone, running from the cabin. He would have held out his hand to bring her back, but he couldn't move it.

He couldn't move it because it was still chained to the cot, along with his other hand. "Lana?" he called softly. "LANA!!!!!"

But the pullback was complete. And so, at 7:10 A.M. in cot two, Theodore Huggsey waited helplessly to surrender; far from his home and loved ones, he prepared to submit to the mercy of the chambermaid.

While he waited, the demons inside him turned flame throwers onto the Munchkins; they bombed and strafed and turned the survivors into lightbulbs. The Munchkins died with a whisper. "Don't worry, Teddy," was their sigh, as voltage sizzled through them. "Barky was on our side."

The divorce of Mr. and Mrs. Theodore Huggsey shocked Ranewood, for they were known to be a devoted couple with a model family. The details of Daddy Huggsey's adventure were vividly recounted by Miss Louella Hosey, who wormed her way onto the Ranewood Ladies Bowling Team through her role as the chambermaid in the scandal at the Cranberry Inn. Margaret Huggsey and their younger children moved into that dream house in Ranewood; Teddy and his new bride, Lana *née* Lilly moved to Seattle, looking for new fish to can.

While the Huggsey children grew up in Ranewood, Teddy gradually discovered his desire to murder his second wife. In 1952, Lana caught her toe in the toaster. In 1954, she accidentally wrapped her pet canaries in aluminum foil and stored them in the freezer. Six months later, she served them to his boss for dinner. In the following year, in her haste to paper the den, she glued to death their only child. She set the house on fire in '53, '55, and twice in '56, trying to heat up TV dinners. Addled beyond belief, Teddy retired early, became a Democrat and considered growing facial hair.

The town of Ranewood retained roughly the same population (7500) throughout the fifties, but the statistics were misleading. Although the number of people who lived there did not change much, the character of their community did. During the decade of the 40s, Ranewood had grown into a booming rural community—its economy had thrived during the war. During the 50s, however, a blue-collar work force came into the area, drawn by new factories for food-processing and chemicals that were established in nearby southern counties.

The settlement of Cooper's Ferry where Jupiter Laud had operated his ferry service was now the city of Camden. Less than thirty-five miles from the frog level were the factories belonging to the Campbell Soup Company. The settlement of Raccoon where Seneca Rane had traveled nearly seventeen miles to buy supplies was now the town of Swedesboro, home of the eastern division of the Del Monte Corporation. In Cumberland County, where the citizens of Greenwich had once held New Jersey's own tea-burning party, Seabrook Farms was now fast-freezing one million dollars worth of vegetables. Although small local operations like Theodore Huggsey's cannery had been swallowed up by corporations, Ranewood businesses reaped the benefits of union-negotiated paychecks.

Ranewood felt the effects of immigration, somewhat belatedly, as Italians, eastern Europeans, and blacks moved into town, drawn by the nearby factories. A new high school was built, and by the steps of the township council house, members of the Sand County DAR erected a small granite slab that related the glorious story of the Battle of Frog Level; Captain Francis Penrod's name was mentioned twice. And all along Main Street, the changing face of business marked the progress of the 50s.

By 1953, Americans were worried about inflation and communists—in Korea and in Hollywood. Women were sporting "Italian" haircuts and the Metro Theatre in Ranewood began to offer films with stereophonic sound. The town also got its very own branch of J. C. Penney's, a Toonville record store, and a business called the Wash-O-Mat, where machines operated for a nickel. Two people reported to *The Ranewood Star* that they'd seen the Jersey Devil, but no one paid much attention; they were much more interested in searching for the flying saucers which were rumored to have already landed in the Pines.

By 1957, parents were suffering through coonskin caps and hula hoops and "Hound Dog." Nearly every home now had a television set, on which they watched President Eisenhower win re-election by a landslide. A new word was "segregation" but it seemed to be a southern problem; citizens in Ranewood were more worried about Sputnik, and the drive-in theater which had been built on the edge of town. Two new clothing stores for women opened, but the Bon-Ton soon went out of business because its owner had thought that Ranewood was ready to discard its shirtwaists for "the sack." In the summer of 1957, parents watched *Sayonara* in the newly air-conditioned Metro Theatre; at the Pixley Drive-In, their children necked and watched *The Fly*.

By 1963, Ranewood had two foreign restaurants: Tony's Pizza, and the Hallelujah Chinese Restaurant, where everyone ordered chop suey. The new words were beatnik and missile gap, and both of them seemed very far away from Main Street, although air raid drills were still held in the public schools: *What to Do in Case of Nuclear Attack*. The students of Ranewood High gave a hootenanny and memorized the thoughts of President John F. Kennedy. City fathers erected "Walk" lights and wondered if the Midas II would close that damn gap.

A few signs of the times began to emerge: Popo Huggsey opened a head shop next door to the palatial home of Mrs. Babs Huggsey Munk, but Englebert Humperdinck still had more fans than Bob Dylan. At Ranewood High, there were strobe lights at the prom, but the closest most students came to a hallucinogenic experience was at the Beavers football games, when the majorettes twirled their fire batons. For most of Ranewood, the sixties was only twenty-one inches high, as it appeared on their television sets. Protest would have seemed more real if it had taken the form of a telethon. By 1968, the words had changed to "riot," "Tet," and "Yippee," and Ranewood had seen enough; the times were definitely changing, but at least they could be turned off. Babs Huggsey Munk unplugged her set and even sister Popo, as she hitched a ride from Woodstock, wondered why the dawning of Aquarius seemed so much like a sunset.

The five-hundred-acre tract of land at the frog level remained largely neglected, except that it developed popularity as a lovers' lane; the passionate youth of Ranewood could hardly resist its wooded isolation or its frogs. But in 1965, one hundred acres of land which had belonged to Seneca Rane was bought by a Sand County developer who erected a two-story apartment building—twenty shoebox units with built-in beige carpeting, known as the Ranewood Vieux. Too far out, said the citizens of Ranewood, but the apartments were rented, just the same. Some of the people who lived there, like Popo Huggsey, had no place else to go. Others, like Jenny Kovach, didn't exactly know where they belonged. The decade of the '60s was a confusing time in which to be young, especially in southern New Jersey and in a town like Ranewood, where many people would swear that the sixties never happened at all.

———— *In 1950, New Jersey's population was nearly five million. For the next decade, the state mirrored the tastes and growth of the nation so perfectly that it earned another one of its invaluable nicknames, "The Typical State." In 1952, the state voted for Dwight D. Eisenhower for president. Joining in the national mania for surveys, New Jersey discovered that its favorite meal consisted of fruit cup, vegetable soup, steak and potatoes, peas, rolls and butter, and pie a la mode. The state also proved a valuable testing ground for new varieties of Campbell's soup, and its "typical" faces provided the means by which the nation judged Crest toothpaste and Clearasil.*

In 1962, New Jersey's nickname as "The Corridor State" took on new meaning. The lower deck of the George Washington Bridge was opened, opening another link to New York at a cost of twenty-two billion dollars. Then a satellite called Telstar that Bell Laboratories in New Jersey had been developing was launched into the sky; in that same year an astronaut born in Oradell, New Jersey, also orbited the earth. His name was Walter Schirra. With these three events, New Jersey finally offered proof to the nation that from within its boundaries, one could go (a) nowhere (b) anywhere or (c) simply out of it all.

1969 ——————
The Sparkling Field—
and Grass

JENNY KOVACH lived in Apartment 3B at Ranewood Vieux; if she leaned out over the balcony of her terrace, twisted her body to the west, and squinted, she could see the wildflower field which had defied Seneca Rane. Jenny loved the flowers. She had never married, and as assistant librarian at Ranewood High, she had never held a job that meant more than a steady paycheck. At the age of twenty-eight, she was a lifetime victim of unrequited passion—Jenny Kovach was in love with motors. This affair had begun in her mother's laundry where she had played for hours as a child, pressing her small, arched body against the shimmering warmth of the clothes dryer door as she watched the tumbling colors inside. The vibrating comfort that filled her was exquisite, even nicer than being rocked in her mother's arms, and the rumbling motor became a signal for excitement and tenderness.

Jenny's years at Ranewood High had been thrilling, not because she'd discovered boys, but because she discovered their cars. The parking lot behind the gym throbbed with passion— the sturdy purr of a Corvair Monza, the buzzing Vespa scooters, Fairlanes, Falcons, the incredible jazz of a souped-up Chevvy. The boys who had driven them seemed a legitimate extension of their machines, and after a long, fast ride through the Pines had made her heart pound with excitement, Jenny was perfectly willing to park. She loved to make out, and sometimes could even be coaxed into the backseat of the car. But the sole of one of her tasseled Weejuns always stayed on the floor; she never went all the way.

Ten years later, the situation was unchanged. She had dated and dated—leaning against the hood of an idling car, she could almost believe that she was in love with its driver. But when the engine switched off, part of her did, too. Motors turned her on; it was that simple. She loved summertime: waking up to the whine of a power mower, listening to speedboats on the lake—on clear summer nights she could even be lulled to sleep by the faraway whine of stockcars that roared in giant loops at the Speedway in the Pines. Winters were long and hard: the sound of wood crackling in the fireplace did nothing for her, and you could stuff the hush of a snowstorm. Dead batteries and whining tires. Every spring, Jenny looked forward to the blooming of the wildflower field. The flowers made her feel excited and hopeful. As she leaned out over the balcony, twisted her body, and squinted, Jenny Kovach waited to happen.

In Apartment 5C at Ranewood Vieux, there was no balcony, but there was a lovely view of the wildflower field if you braced your legs against the bathroom window frame and hung out backwards. In this apartment lived Popo Huggsey, age twenty-four. Since the age of fifteen, Popo had been happening, and none of the Huggseys knew how to stop her. When her mother Margaret had remarried and moved to Canada, it was agreed that Popo could stay on in Ranewood with her friends to finish high school. Almost immediately, she became Ranewood's first hippie, although that was not the word which local citizens used to describe her; most often, they said she was a mess. By 1965, Popo was regularly commuting to Greenwich Village; she brought back such exotic terms as "Anti-Establishment," which most of Ranewood still associated, somewhat shakily, with game shows and spelling bees.

Popo's favorite word was "fuck." Although her use of the term was all-encompassing, she also used it to describe her favorite activity, which she claimed to have indulged in 1,715 times by the spring of '69. She claimed a wide and varied sex life that none of her contemporaries could match, even Popo.

But most of her listeners believed Popo's tales about picking up hitchhikers who were invariably eight-inchers, about underwater orgies and Greyhound quickies, about being fucked in the rear by a nun.

Jenny Kovach didn't always believe her. "A nun? Are you *sure*, Popo?"

"Well there seemed to be a lot of white cloth flapping around, but it was pretty dark," Popo admitted. "I guess that it could have been a giant swan."

Jenny was Popo's friend; she defended her to older sister Babs, who at forty-three was nearly driven craaaaaazy, by her own account, by Popo. Since Popo liked to keep her family up to date on her activities, Babs often found notes tucked into her Woman's Club agenda: "Dear Babs: Do you remember Barky? He was the first—boy could that dog fuck. I came five times. Love and Peace, Popo." One night Babs got a ship-to-shore call from her brother Dick, aboard his carrier. "Say, Babs," he said, "what's this about old Barky? Little Popo dropped me a line, and—"

"Don't mention it," wailed Babs. "Don't *mention* it."

For Jenny, Popo wrote poetry. "Coming is the sneeze that spreads the germ of love. So do it, fuck and fuck and do it, fuck and fuck and fuck. Peace and love, Popo."

Jenny wore Villager shirtwaists with a strand of pearls; she had cardigans for every season, and her Weejuns always had tassels. Popo wore jeans and sandals, tie-dyed skirts and undershirts, and 2,137 (by her count) beads, which she never took off. Jenny had never been all the way; Popo had written an *Epithalamion*, in the mode of Spenser, dedicated to thirty-seven different ways of coming. In the barely Aquarian Age of Ranewood, they were good friends. On an icy January night in 1969, they split a pizza at Jenny's apartment. (Popo, who swore she was Class 1, Macrobiotic, had carefully sprinkled brown rice on her half, and given away the anchovies.)

"I know you feel out of it, Jenny," she told her friend, "but really, would you like to be part of the scene that your high school friends are in. I mean Wow, Jenny, their idea of sex is strictly mink farm stuff."

"Mink farm?" Jenny repeated, gobbling anchovies.

"You know—lots of it, in conservative positions, with off-spring. That's not your scene." There was a pause while Popo, murmuring shit and fuck, scraped brown rice from her pizza. "What is your scene, Jenny?" she asked finally.

Jenny looked at her. "I like the sound of motors," she said finally.

Popo smiled. "Wow, don't be embarrassed. You know, in your own square way you're very bizarre."

Soon after this conversation, Popo presented Jenny with a gift.

"What is it," Jenny asked as she pulled away the wrapping.

"Don't think too much about that. Just turn it on."

Jenny plugged the oddly cylindrical device into the wall. Instantly, it began to rumble and hum. "Nice," Jenny said, feeling its warmth surge through her hand. "But what does it do?"

"It soothes away tension in a variety of areas and—oh fuck, Jenny, haven't you ever heard of a vibrator?"

The device leaped out of her hand onto the carpet, where it writhed and hummed. "I *couldn't*," Jenny said. "Oh, Popo."

Popo stared at her. "Would it help if I swore to you that I know for a fact, Eleanor Roosevelt used one of these on a regular basis? See I was fucking this guy in the FBI, and—"

"Popo, stop LYING," Jenny said, feeling hysterical.

Tears formed in Popo's eyes. "You're my friend. I want you to feel good. Is that a crime?" She rushed out of the apartment with a rattle of beads, before Jenny could stop her.

Feeling good? Is that such a crime? Jenny wondered. She picked up the grisly device and locked it into its case, but Popo's words haunted her. Is using a vibrator considered the same as going all the way? she wondered. Who cares? I'm almost thirty.

Jenny packed the box into the top of her closet and climbed into bed. The air was cold, and comfortless, and in the darkness, she felt as though she could hear that tiny motor roaring through its box. Impossible, she thought, but the impression of sound persisted; to banish it, Jenny got out of bed and rummaged through the closet, and quickly opened the box. The vibrator inside was silent, but she noticed that its switch was turned slightly towards the on position. Maybe it's broken, she thought. She plugged it in, and the buzz of love filled the room.

Jenny's mouth went dry, and she could feel her heartbeat accelerate. Just try it once, she thought. For Popo.

Oooooooh. Ooooooooooooooooh. It was better than an idling Chevvy.

Well, maybe once more, for Eleanor.

Oh yes oh god oh oh oh uh. It was better than even the clothes dryer.

Once more, for me.

OhhhhhhhhhNO oh god oh oh oh *WOW*. Oh, Popo. My dear friend. This is better than *anything* has ever been before.

In the next weeks, Jenny considered her fate. At least, she knew now that she wasn't frigid. Sneezing had become a way of life. But Popo's poem had intimated something more, hadn't it? Jenny wondered. Do I really want to have the boundaries of passion defined by the length of my extension cord?

Now that she knew what she was missing, she searched for possibilities. Mr. Haldern in A3 was charming but at eighty-two years of age, he might not be up to seducing an aging virgin— and if I killed him, she thought, I'd never forgive myself. Dora and Milo Cally lived in A7. She took out the garbage wearing nothing but a see-through aqua negligee; unfortunately, so did he. Scratch the Calleys, she thought. Not my scene.

Champ Santini lived in C4. He was the right age, the right size, and a former Ranewood football star who taught shop and auto repair—maybe we have lots in common, Jenny thought. She invited him to dinner, drinking the wine the week before so that she could melt candles into the empty bottles. Champ arrived promptly; he didn't kiss her or bring flowers, but he did pinch her at the door and he became drunk so rapidly that she finally realized he was supplementing her wine with a flask he'd taped to his thigh. He crouched above the table while her lasagna turned to putty, demanding that she relive every Ranewood touchdown he'd ever scored. When he'd tried to center her cat, she'd screamed. He left before dessert, complaining of a pulled hamstring.

Scratch Santini. Not my scene. But who was?

In the spring of '69, as though it knew of Jenny's problem, the wildwood field bloomed more gloriously than anyone could remember. Daisies, violets, clover, daffodils formed a riot throughout, and a tiny glistening white flower known in the area as "sparkle" bloomed in mats at the edges of rocks and trees, forming iridescent strips that shone through the night; best of all, the scent of fresh wild mint was everywhere.

It rinsed the night, including the terrace air of apartment B3, where in early May Popo had joined Jenny for a Burger Fry. Actually, Popo had brought her own dinner—a steaming bowl of brown rice, which she was now topping off with Jenny's sugar, cream, and bananas.

"Organic food is great for you," Popo declared. "Do you have any more cream? Half and Half will do."

The scent of mint washed over the terrace. Jenny sighed.

"Far out," said Popo. "Makes me feel like fucking."

"What doesn't?" Jenny asked, turning her hamburgers on the grill.

"Art Linkletter. Throwing up. That's about it," she replied.

Jenny was silent. "Popo," she said finally. "I feel like doing it too."

Popo did not ask doing what, but remained completely silent, and minutes passed as the hamburgers spit and charred and turned to ash. Jenny watched, unable to stop their destruction.

"Some very close friends of mine are coming down from the Village, tonight," Popo said finally. Her voice sounded oddly subdued. "I really think that you should meet them."

"I don't like blind dates," Jenny said.

"Who said anything about dates?" This exasperation sounded more familiar. "Honest, Jenny, this is *beyond* people. It's freedom, peace, and love."

"Where is all of this going to happen?" Jenny sounded old and mean, especially to herself.

"In the wildflower field," Popo replied. "We're just going to fucking happen."

"You're meeting your friends in a *field*?"

Popo stared. "It beats hanging out at the Dairy Queen."

By the time they left the terrace of Ranewood Vieux, it was nearly midnight. At Popo's insistence, Jenny had worn jeans, although she'd retained a snappy pin-striped Brooks Brothers shirt.

"Unbutton a bit," said Popo. "And your feet. TAKE THEM OFF!"

Jenny looked down at her tasseled Weejuns. "My feet will get dirty," she cried.

"Dirt is organic," Popo informed her. "Weejuns *definitely* are not."

Jenny slipped off her shoes. She had to admit that it felt good as they walked across the grassy night, with the things in it tickling her feet.

Suddenly, the wildwood field loomed before her; there was a collection of shapes, too large and expectant to be flowers. Jenny felt panicky and silly. "Why didn't I stick with Champ Santini?" she thought. "At least he would have let me keep my shoes on."

"Peace," cried Popo.

"Peace and love," voices replied, as a tangled, hairy collection of youngish people—maybe six?—emerged.

"This is my friend," said Popo, pointing to Jenny.

There were smiles, and a rattle of beads. "Aren't you going to introduce me?" Jenny whispered.

"We're not into labels," said a bearded man, kindly.

"Names are not organic," Popo said firmly.

"Great Field. Great Flowers," the bearded man said to Popo.

"Wow," said a girl with long blonde hair.

There was a pause. The bearded man included Jenny in his smile. "Why don't we sit down and just relate to each other for a while."

That sounded friendly enough, almost cozy. Jenny plopped down beside him and said, "Are you a student in New York?"

"I'm a teacher, baby."

So is Champ. Ah well, "What do you teach?"

"Life. Reality. Where It's At. And a little organic chemistry, to pay the rent."

Organic chemistry—he must be smart! And he looks great, but then, in this light, who wouldn't? In this light, even I must look great, she thought, and smiled, really smiled at him.

"Pretty," he told her, but he was busy, lighting up a cigarette. Funny, how he puffed it. Funny, how he passed it around—OH NO!!!! Jenny's heart was pounding. This was a reefer—marijuana, narcotics, dope fiends—poor Popo must be terrified—"Popo?"

Seated opposite her, Popo took in a long drag and sucked air with a flourish. "Good shit, Jenny," she said. "You'll never know until you try."

Feeling good. Is that a crime. What's your scene. You'll never know, never know, never know—Jenny inhaled, feeling breathless and already dizzy. Leaning back, she choked on smoke. "I don't feel anything," she announced.

"Relax, baby, let it happen."

But it's *not* happening, she wanted to scream, as the joint was passed again. She'd heard that marijuana had no effect on some people, well she was one, poor Jenny Kovach, no sex, no fun to take a drag, and nothing—

RIGHT ON RED. She'd seen the sign of course, but the drivers in front of her had stopped for a game of jacks. THIS LANE ENDS ELEVEN FEET. Eleven? Barely enough time to shift her wings and w-h-oooooops. Hello trees, hello stars and people and flowers and toes, I feel every one of you hello and I feel me. I think I'm stoned. I'd better tell them. Move, mouth. Open, mouth. Tell them . . . . "Wow I mean it was really incredible and it was like I could see these other drivers on the highway and they'd stopped to take their tire jacks out of their trunks and they were playing this ENORMOUS game of jacks and this huge red ball come bouncing onto the road and it was—"

They were laughing. She was laughing. Hhhhhellooooooooo, people.

"I think you're stoned," said her bearded friend. He was so witty. Why hadn't she noticed that before?

Popo was laughing. Beautiful Popo. "I love Popo," said Jenny. "I love trees and stars and gra-a-a-a-a-aaaaasssssss."

Everyone got hysterical, which was nice. I'm witty, too, Jenny thought. Why didn't I ever notice that before? And I must be beautiful, because I'm being kissed by this witty man whose beard is so tickle-y. Warm, tickling mouth and hair—

Wait a minute. When did my beautiful witty friends take off their clothes???????

"WAIT A MINUTE," she said, not stoned at all.

The bearded man touched her. "Don't be afraid," he said. "You can watch, if you'd like." Now that was sweet. Euphoria returned, in a rush. This was so much better than being chased by a man who wanted you to do the 32-30-reverse with him. Now she wasn't being chased at all, and wasn't it perfectly natural, with her wings in glorious high gear, to watch her beautiful, witty friends cavort among the flowers? The smell of mint was *un-be-lieve-able*. The smell of mint was *amaaaaaaazing*. And in this darkness, how much of these naked, roiling people could she see?

Actually quite a bit. The girl with long blonde hair was using it to tickle the bearded man's stomach, while one of her hands stroked at the chest of the redheaded guy who was frenching her with his tongue, both hands at her breasts while her (blonde female) hand was fondling a penis—whose? Jenny wondered idly—suddenly they seemed to be sticking up everywhere. Oh yes, the one poking out of the bearded man's belly. A plump brunette had wrapped her legs around another guy and his head had disappeared between her thighs, but a skinny girl was licking the balls of his feet and bouncing up and down on the fingers of a disembodied hand that seemed to come from nowhere. Where was Popo? Should she scream? There was a body at the bottom of that pile. Surely that could not be little Popo, at the very center of all that kissing and touching, being subjected to all of those fingers, and that stroking—all that loving—thought Jenny. Not my scene? Not my scene?

The bearded man extricated his hand from the skinny girl in order to wave at Jenny. "Come share the feeling."

"Well," she said, meaning "no."

Seven figures emerged from the grass and walked towards her. They unbuttoned her blouse, ever so gently. There was the *ziiiip* of her jeans and down they slid, also gently, plenty of time to scream, if she wanted to. She didn't, but she said, "That's enough for now," and they left her in bra and panties as they lifted her high, so high above their heads.

"Trust us. Love us," they said, and she was flying in their arms. The smell of mint was amaaaazing, and she could feel the smiles of her friends, she would die for them, trust them, love them, fuck names, it was really quite amaaaaaazing. Loving. Her own smile warmed her body. "Love," she told the stars. "Love," her friends repeated as they set her down in the middle of the iridescent flowers.

Soft hands upon her, spreading love. Peace, the whisper that was sliding into her throat, stroking her thighs and the smell of mint was *amaaaaaaaaaaaaazing*. Soft mouths for smiles and kissing. More kissing, please. My dear sweet naked friends, I have been a fool *yes touch me there* I have been a square *ohgod you are drivingmecrazy* and so all of your touching is just enough, I can feel the breaking inside me. "There's just one thing," she said, amazed to hear her voice. Fourteen hands stopped stroking. Seven pairs of eyes looked worried, nervous, dazed.

"Would you mind," she said, "I know it's silly, but the sound of motors drives me wild."

"Hey baby, we don't have one," said the bearded man.

"Of course you do," Jenny said firmly. "Anyone can do the sound of a V-8, right?" In the middle of the field, she stood and ripped off her brassière. "I want to hear a Monza," she screamed.

"RRRRRRRRrrrrrrrrrrr," said the bearded man.

"MMMMMMMMMRRRRrrrrrrrrrr."

"Wow," said a girl with long blonde hair.

"You do it," Jenny told her. "I want to hear a Fairlane."

"RRRRum, rrrruuum, ppptttRRRRRRRRRRR," growled the blonde. The redheaded guy leaned his head onto her stomach. "Man, that is *extreme*," he cried.

In the middle of the flowers, they formed a colossal traffic jam. "RRRRR m, ruuum, ruuuuuuuum," said Popo, diving for a cock. The redhead screamed. "I was shifting gears," she cried.

"Easy," the bearded man told them. "This is very organic."

And so they managed to rumble in low gear, playing with toggle switches and various buttons and building themselves into the process to one giant, aching PRRRRRRRRRRRRRRRRRRR—

"We're off!" screamed the bearded one, and everyone was panting, twisting down the tracks, and their senses were flying as Jenny led the pack. Oh god, she was speeding and sense of motor was all around her, toes were humming and fingers, and she was humming, humming with the feeling, the loving inside her, she was taking off—

"Slow down," whispered the bearded man, "you're getting ahead." His tongue moved into her mouth, silent, liquid, soothing her yet revving her up, saying slow but burning her up with his touch.

"Tell me, make me," she told him and someone's hands were driving her, fingers slipping in her to shift her higher, higher, tearing her apart, she could hear the whine of flesh—

"Stop," she said, frightened. "It's too fast."

"Noooo. It's terrific," the other drivers told her.

"Grrrrrrrrppppooowwwwww," said the redhead, pumping into Popo. "Do you get it? I'm a fucking Rambler!"

"Oh wow oh wow oh wow you're a fuckin fascist Porsche," Popo told him. "With wire spoke wheels and a lot of leather. *Wow!*"

The bearded man leaned over Jenny. "Are you ready," he said softly.

Oh, yes. For about the last ten years or so.

"What do you want from me?" he said, tenderly.

"Can you do a clothes dryer?" she asked.

He laughed. (He was so witty and she was so beautiful . . .)

MHHHHHHHHHMMMNNNNNN," he roared, pushing into her.

"MMMMMMMMnnnnnnnnnn," she said, meaning it. And then he stopped and kissed her all over, the way that no dryer had ever done. He rumbled and roared, and the sound of motors was all around them as he pressed into her gently, then harder but slowly, slowly until she moved her hips to meet him, taking his vibrations—she arched up, pressing against his spine as the feel of him was in her mouth and deep inside her, she could feel it, driving tongue and cock. She ground herself against him, and he groaned but kept on rumbling. He was panting. She was panting. She twisted against the pressure. She wanted to feel it, loved it, the pulsing, humming. "Oh yes please," she said softly. "Just tell me what you want me to be."

His whisper touched her ear. "Just be yourself, baby."

Oh god, why hadn't she thought of that? Oh god why hadn't she, oh, thought of that . . . he was . . . she was, oh, oh, the most beautiful. Oh yes just throw your head back, baby, throw it back and scream . . .

The air was filled with the scent of mint and sweat. Seven

bodies play dripping, exhausted, panting, among the trampled flowers. Only Popo was still gunning her engine.

"Peace, Popo," begged the redhead.

"Forget it, Popo," said the blonde. "His batteries are dead."

The bearded man looked into Jenny's face, to make sure that she was smiling. When he saw that she was, he stroked her hair. "You're a very special lady," he said. "You made it happen, tonight."

"I did?" Jenny said. The grass had begun to wear off, but she still seemed to be flying, gently, near the earth now, she would soon touch down but not quite yet . . .

"You are far out," he said.

That was so beautiful. Far out. "I'd always thought that I was simply weird."

He kissed her. He smiled, and then he left her, when the others left; they disappeared across the field. Only Popo was left beneath the stars, sniffing at the mint.

"Thank you, Popo," Jenny said.

Popo studied the sky. "People don't say that to me very often," she said, sounding almost frightened. Then she spoke quickly in a more familiar tone, "I feel a great need for some organic hot fudge sauce. Bananas. Whipped cream. Peanut butter. Mozzarella and jelly beans. Your basic sundae. Unless you have tofu or some whole-grain ice cream?"

"Would you settle for vanilla? Actually, I was just craving the same thing."

"You must always listen to your body," Popo told her solemnly. "Especially when it is stoned. That's when it sings."

After eating only two organic hot fudge sundaes and some frozen pizza, Jenny went to bed. She slept until noon and woke up happy. One year later, she was married to the new Civics teacher at Ranewood High, Tommy Ryan. He had never heard of motors as a turn-on; at thirty-four, he thought that civilization had peaked with the early albums of The Lettermen. He didn't smoke marijuana, and Jenny never did again, either. He was so straight that he didn't even like fresh mint in his iced tea. None of this mattered to Jenny. She roared with him, through the night, and he was better, unbelievably better than anything had been before. Because Jenny Kovach, who knew how to be herself, had finally fallen in love. Thank you Popo. Thank you bearded stranger and the amaaaaazing smell of mint. Thank you peace and love.

In the year 1970, air waves above the five-hundred-acre tract of land on the outskirts of Ranewood were crackling with the sweep of events, but humans scarcely made a dent. At the Rane-wood Vieux, life was transient, with short-term leases and no pets. Passion came and went. If Micah Honeyman was right about ghosts, then perhaps the spirit of Seneca Rane lingered to gaze at nearby farms, where the harvest produced a higher yield than he ever dreamed possible. But with all the benefit of machine and fertilizer, this modern corn raised up from the earth no differently than his had done, and he must have won-dered if it tasted any sweeter. The chains of Captain Francis might be clanking in the wind as he mourned the decor at Ranewood Vieux—beanbag chairs and Parsons tables, stainless steel and white-on-white. And not a single tassel nor a hand-blown crystal goblet, not a single cupid cavorted, fully-clothed.

But of all of those who had lived upon the land, it was the spirit of India Honeyman which inadvertently wreaked its de-struction. For many years, the suburbs of Philadelphia had sprawled southward into New Jersey, along the path of existing railroad tracks. By the early 1970s, Philadelphia executives found it desirable to escape not only the city but also the sub-urbs, and the railroad spur at the frog level created a uniquely valuable piece of wilderness real estate. In 1974, a development company purchased all five hundred acres and immediately began construction of a self-proclaimed "Paradise for Condo-miniums," which they called East Rane.

Construction crews cut down the great scarlet oak tree; they rechanneled the path of Sabbath Creek. A hydraulic crane cleared the giant rock from the riotous wildflower field so that bulldozers could tear up its flowers. Bogs were drained, and woods were razed, and the frog level was completely demol-ished. Forty condominium units were erected, and Seneca Rane's path disappeared along with his rise, which had blocked the view from the clubhouse terrace. East Rane offered only the best—in tennis courts, drainage, and neighbors. There were a few drawbacks: on the magnificent eighteen-hole golf course, golfers complained that the water hazards on the fifteenth and seventeenth holes were populated by the noisiest frogs they ever heard. But the condo community was a spectacular success.

The 70s had come to Ranewood. In addition to their television sets, the town could now spy on the nearby paradise of East Rane, as the decade came to pass. Streaking, freaking, EST and I AM ME, East Rane related to everything. Its inhabitants had primal screams and pasta machines, they snorted, jogged, had their consciousness raised, and charted biorhythms, while passion flourished upon the land, in every conceivable position; with every implement devised by man. Every taste got its own space, in the age of aerobic narcissism.

Few residents of nearby Ranewood followed the lead of Popo Huggsey, who sold out her head shop and moved into condo number 12, where she became a freelance therapist. Most of the town struggled to adapt to stores which now catered to the wealthy commuter set, where the purchase of cheese was no longer a comfortable choice between American and Swiss, and Oreos could hardly be found amidst the mountains of imported English biscuits. The children of East Rane flooded into their schools, taking over the uniforms of Beavers and even those spectacular fire batons. Ranewood reeled, and by the end of the decade even Popo Huggsey wondered if a lifetime devoted to fulfilling her needs was really all that fulfilling.

The condos of East Rane did not survive the changes wrought by the 1980s. The celibacy craze banked its passion, and the Persian Gulf War forced another change in its real estate. By the early 1990s southern New Jersey had become the cosmopolitan center for the western world. In the region once known as the Pine Barrens, where shacks had scattered through a nearly deserted forest, a giant city and supersonic jetport had been constructed. It was the largest terminal on earth, with lights that on a clear night could be seen from as far away as New York City. Completed in 1991, it was proudly proclaimed the Walter Cronkite International Airport. A city of one quarter million people served the facility; they kept the sidewalks clean and directed the awesome traffic—over one thousand trans-Atlantic flights per day, and an hourly shuttle to the cities of Beirut,

Berlin, and London. (A slightly smaller facility in California served the cities of Tokyo, Peking, and Sydney. Carved from the wilderness of a redwood forest, it was known as the Reagan-Redwood Memorial.)

By the mid-1990s the entire state of New Jersey was five per cent grass—which is to say that it was ninety-five per cent concrete, steel, and glass. The Northeast Corridor of the United States had become nearly one continuous city, as New York, Philadelphia, and Washington formed an urban mass. To protect the Northeast Corridor (transportation and communication center for all Petro Allies), missile installations had been set around the perimeter of the massive airport. East Rane disappeared, replaced by a base camp for five thousand men, barbed wire, and underground silos. Five hundred acres of concrete (five percent grass) were off-limits to those residents living in the nearby high-density Ranewood Zone, most of whom earned a living from the solar trains that shuttled between the buildings at Walter Cronkite International.

On an early spring day in the year 2000, in spite of these military restrictions, one resident of the nearby town—a woman of fifty-five years—was trespassing on base property. She hiked down a narrow beltway, waving to supply trucks as they passed. Her feet were bare, and she was picking strands of grass. Ordinarily such behavior would have attracted attention, but the guards on duty recognized Ms. Popo Huggsey, who had always been a little bit strange.

Within the stony enclave of the CESTAT-CIMPAC missile site, another local resident—Corporal Dwayne Perkins—was on duty at his computer. Corporal Perkins was not barefoot, and he was not considered particularly strange by those who knew him. Actually he and Popo Huggsey had nothing in common, except for the fact that on this April day in the year 2000, these two ordinary American citizens would be caught in a strange and terrifying place, known in New Jersey as the Ranewood Zone.

2000 ─────

The Frog Level: Revelations

ON APRIL 21, 2000, Corporal Dwayne Perkins was on duty at Control Base Ranewood, seated at the modular panel of the computer CESTAT-CIMPAC, which was guardian for the sixty STX Dog-Jupiter missiles lodged in bunkers around the base perimeter. Perkins was feeling restless. He'd just lost another six dollars in the Coke machine upstairs and that made ninety for the week—petty cash, but still it added up. Besides, he was lost in dreams of Wanda Canelli. She was the most beautiful girl he'd ever seen in his life, although so far he'd only gotten a couple of close-ups on the Video screen. The Pentagon dating service that the post provided allowed servicemen to be mated with females from a surrounding area of three hundred miles and according to all cable affiliates, Wanda was the girl of his dreams. In her female-modified sportswear, she had looked goddamn well-modified, and she had dimples, too. The Corporal sighed, remembering. On his next leave from this shit-turd base, he was scheduled to meet her in Philadelphia—that swinging city known as Sodom of the Military Effete, where a twenty-four-hour nightlife catered to the tastes of off-duty personnel from Northeast Corridor Defenses.

Perkins was temporarily the only man in the control room of CESTAT-CIMPAC, which put him automatically in charge of missile coordination for the entire eastern United States. Frankly, he didn't give a shit. He cared about Wanda and his lunch—his favorite GI-issue Cracklin' Chicken. Since the strike in 1993, it was mandatory that each serviceman receive one fast-food meal (or its facsimile) twice each week from the base cafeteria. Shit on a shingle, shit in a box, Perkins thought happily as he dismantled the elaborate cardboard and paper wrappings which the Pentagon had been ordered to supply along with the chicken.

He bit into a thigh—warm, tender meat. Ah Wanda, he thought. If I could get out of this shitfuckawful place and just sample your thighs. Your hair is the color of honey. I'm gonna call you honey, Wanda. I'm gonna buy you a teddy bear and eat you out twice a day, I promise.

They had exchanged VidiTrans Codes. Who's fucking you now, honey? Perkins wondered. Who's buying you teddies and feeling you up and eating you out—I bet it's a fucking Marine. His teeth grated on bone.

On the modular panel of Computer CESTAT-CIMPAC, a row of lights suddenly burst into life, blooming simultaneously in yellow.

Perkins removed a piece of cardboard from the remaining chicken breast and chewed: I'll come into you with forks, honey. I'll slice you out with knives, and you'll be begging for your Teddy, and I'll slap you, cunt you, oh Wanda, oh my baby, did I hurt you? Pretty mouth on my cock, don't cry honey.

As Perkins demolished the breast, lights that had bloomed in yellow (CESTAT-CIMPAC) began to flash in red: Sucking sweet meat, honey. I should have ordered the Cracklin' Crispy extra spicy for you. I can tell you've got a temper.

From CESTAT-CIMPAC, there was a harsh, chronic buzzing.

Perkins looked up and noticed the lights. "Fuckfuckfuck, fucking system's fucked again," he thought, then he groaned at the sound of running footsteps behind him.

"What's the trouble, Corporal?" Colonel Hardesty's voice was booming in his ear.

"Fucking system's fucked again, sir," he replied.

CESTAT-CIMPAC bloomed in both yellow and red, as a rhythmic buzz-beep-buzzing filled the room.

"I want CESTAT-CENTRAL," said the Colonel, pointing to the communicators. "Contact CIMPAC headquarters at the Pentagon, and I want the White House too. Get every one of those bastards on the line—goddammit, this is the third false alarm in six weeks. Or maybe those crazy Russky missiles are goddamm females—always screaming, 'I'm coming, I'm coming.' "

"An interesting theory, sir," said Perkins, mindful of his leave.

Beyond the concrete walls of Control Base Ranewood, where neither man could see, sixty STX Dog-Jupiter missiles equipped with nuclear warheads began to thrum within their silos. Programmed in the mid-70s, they came to life without a hitch, assuming class ten readiness. The earth quivered. Stirring in their electronic nests every Dog-Jupiter checked A-OK and felt a throb or two. Go-check ten. *Unh, unh, now I feel it coming to me, I got the Mew-zick! and don cha know that we can do it (cause I got the size and I'm on the rise).*

RED. RED said the light of CIMPAC-CESTAT, as Perkins swallowed the rest of his breast, without chewing.

"Have those calls gone through?" the Colonel shouted.

"Sir, you only gave me the Centrex numbers and the listing for the White House switchboard—"

"Goddammit, that's all you're classified to know."

"But Sir, I need the area codes."

Go-check seven. *Here comes heaven, oo-ee bay-bee! Gonna trench the French, gonna spay Milan, gonna blow a toot for Uncle Sam—yeah, bring a spasm, leave a chasm—Here comes the Mew-zick! Cause I got the force and I'm right on course.*

"Fuckit, fuckit, Sir, I've got Cincinnati on the line—the ASPCA. They say that fourteen puppies will be destroyed, unless they are immediately adopted!"

"Hang up, Corporal! Keep trying."

Go-check Three, got the chemistry oo raise a blister on your brother, melt your sister into Mother, yeah, shake my booties, fry your cooties, cause I got the stuff and this ain't no bluff.

At Control Base Ranewood, Perkins screamed. "Sir, I've got California!"

"California?" The Colonel shook his head. "Don't be absurd. Hang up, Corporal. Just hang it up."

They peeked out of the ground in a scattered circle which surrounded a place which had once heard the thunder of frogs —sixty steely-hard, throbbing, silver-tipped pricks that were on the rise. Courtesy of the Ranewood Zone, Dog-Jupiters were

maximized. *Unh the beat and the heat got the tide for the ride Waaaaaaaaahhhhh! Because I love you! Now's the Big O Barbeque, feel so high then toodle-oo—here's the flow, time to go—*
CAN'T STOP THE MEW-ZICK!

The Jersey sky screeched into white.

Suspended in a rosy, glistening bubble which hovered high above the earth's surface, Popo Huggsey watched it happen. The end of the world, that's what it reminded her of. She whirled to stare at the slender, silver-haired man who worked feverishly alongside her. As she watched him adjust patterns within a globed panel of colored lights, she wondered—for the dozenth time in the past hour—why she wasn't screaming.

"What's going on down there?" She pointed towards the earth, where the lights had disappeared, along with the surface of the planet! All that Popo could see was a strange, whirling mist that completely encircled whatever remained; it looked like a huge cloud of dust.

"Don't be concerned, Popo," the man told her. "Everything will be all right, but it will be several minutes before you can see anything."

He smiled at her—quick and devastating, and she struggled not to adore him. His large green eyes were extraordinary—oddly dimensional and so brilliant with lights that they seemed faceted, like jewels. She gazed into them, trying to resist the mood of blissful contentment which had been growing since her arrival in this shimmering bubble. This isn't a dream, she told herself. You've been kidnapped—get mad, Popo. She tried to frown. "You're not from around here, are you?" Gazing into the sparkling abyss which surrounded the bubble, she realized that this was possibly the dumbest question she'd ever asked.

"Once upon a time I lived in New Jersey," he replied. "But that was many years ago—over 250 by your count."

She looked at him uneasily. "Are you . . . real?" This seemed more polite than "Are you dead?"

The stranger smiled, an iridescent flow of emerald, ivory and silver. "Certainly I'm real. My name is Desire Laud. I am the Galactic Shepherd (T Class) assigned to this solar system." As he spoke, his fingers brushed the silver webbing of his uniform chest, where a broad labyrinthine *T* was etched with golden thread against an ivory background. "Everything about me is real," he told her. "But then 'reality' is just a tradition, isn't it? An act of faith, like any other?"

"What?" Popo felt a languid haze. Turning to avoid the sight of the billowing dust ball which had been earth, she stared instead at the strange golden insignia—its glittering threads traced a swirling, expansive pattern which seemed to enhance the euphoria she was struggling against. She looked away and found herself staring once more into Shepherd Laud's eyes. "I don't understand," she insisted. As she lifted a hand to point to his insignia, her fingers moved automatically to caress the shimmering threads. "What does it mean?"

He looked startled and suddenly bashful. "T Class stands for *tender*," he replied.

When she laughed, he smiled again, and his eyes turned so radiant that Popo could almost feel the touch of emerald light upon her face. She leaned towards the shining, and when he reached out his arms to her, his body seemed purely an extension of the extraordinary radiance in his gaze. She floated happily into his embrace, without thinking of further questions. It was enough to stand quietly in his arms, gazing through the pliant, shimmering surface of the bubble, which was faintly swirled with color. I'm fifty-five years old, she reminded herself —too old for any of this to be happening. But do feelings ever grow up? Her ascension into the bubble now seemed part of a distant past and scarcely worth troubling about. True, she had been standing beside the barbed wire barricades at the Ranewood base when a dazzling light had engulfed her, sweeping her upward as though its beam was a funnel of warm air. Then she had landed inside some sort of bubble with this remarkably foreign man who seemed to have made the earth disappear. But was any of this really important?

The walls of the bubble shimmered gently, making patterns in the misty colors of its surface. The changing lights looked soft and moist, like the shades of a rainbow. As she watched, Popo felt the soft, shimmering color glide through her—a faintly drifting sensation, as though her tired, fifty-five-year-old body was no longer a labored connection of muscles and fat but a vibrant pool in which her bones were basking. Flesh turned liquid, luxuriant, and her senses submerged within it, darting like tiny fish to mark the changes in his touch. His arms tight-

314

ened, pulling her closer against him and she closed her eyes, resting her cheek upon the cool, slippery threads of the golden labyrinth.

The minutes collected, like pearls upon an invisible strand, and still she lingered there, gathering the pleasure from his caresses. Slowly she became aware that the iridescent surface of the bubble was giving off a slight vibration—not movement, exactly, but an internal, pulsating glow that translated its brilliant colors, so that they were shimmering inside her. She felt his lips brush the top of her head—quick, stunning contact that turned her mind to a vaulted place that was bare and filled with light. She lifted her face to meet his, and the shape of their kiss was palpable—a shining mass that nearly drowned her in its mist. His body curved against her, an annihilating force that raised an arc through her shimmering body, deepening the colors that raced through her flesh. Coral and gold, the palest blues streamed through her, turning her flesh to mystery, turning her mind into rainbowed flesh. The luminous pulse which compelled her seemed the very opposite of passion, and yet she had never felt such desire. She was no longer aware of her breasts, could not have found her flesh if her life depended upon it; she could not even make out the shape of his body against her, as her senses leaped to meet him in a tumbled, aching mass of color and light.

Unmistakable, the radiant flash of intersection—a convergence of rainbows as her senses leaped once more to absorb the shock of transcendence, and then she swallowed the shining, his shining was in her as they poured separate radiance, then dissolved into one pulsating stream of light. The force of it was dazzling, a quivering curve that crossed through time and mist; she swam the stages slowly, rising through a thickened, radiant surface to linger near the crest, as she strained to glimpse the utmost rim of the arc, where the rainbow foamed to a dazzling white fire. "Beyond flesh," she whispered. "Flesh is just the means to an end. This is the end." The flash was unpredicted: colors blasted into white. Then pitch descended, and eternity passed, giving the molten mass the time to gradually perceive itself as flesh.

"My name is Popo." Thought seemed extravagant, but she nourished the impulse as though forcing herself awake. "I'm in love with a shepherd who lives in a bubble. That's nice." Then she remembered the rest of it, reaching out by reflex, because she was sure that she felt the warmth of his embrace. But only the bubble held her close. Shepherd Laud was fidgeting with the controls, as they slowly descended towards the earth.

Popo leaped up, disbelieving—there it was! A familiar blue and swirling mass, with continents and oceans zooming into such brilliant relief that she might have been staring at a globe. In a moment of shocking joy, she searched for words to describe its beauty and rightness within the abyss. "It looks so—alive." She cried out, excited. "Everything is just as it was before."

"Not quite." He adjusted more color into the rainbowed panel, and the rippling movement in the bubble decreased as it floated through a cover of cloud. Popo recognized the Atlantic coastline of the eastern United States and the nipped-in waist-line of New Jersey as it leaped into view. Now they shimmered slowly towards the west, until they hovered just above a vast expanse of green, dense forestland. It was mostly flat and a little bit boggy.

"Fantastic scenery," she said. "Is this a national park?" As they idled near the treetops, she noticed a small clearing, where mallow, violets, and clover were blooming in riotous profusion. Suddenly the atmosphere within the bubble was permeated with the faint, unmistakable aroma of wild mint.

"That's *my* field!" She strained against the iridescent surface, trying to get a closer look. "But that can't be. That field was destroyed in 1974, when East Rane was built." She looked up, suddenly wary. "Where are we?"

"We are directly over the Ranewood Zone." Desire gave a coaxing smile. "Isn't it beautiful?"

She shook her head. "That's not possible—" then glimpsed movement in one corner of the clearing below. A group of human figures scattered through the field, running for the op-posite woods. Their uniforms were unmistakable. "Those are men from the missile base. But where is the base?" She felt a flash of terror. "You did this." When he nodded, she was not surprised. "But what have you done?" She murmured so softly that she might have been speaking to herself.

"Popo, you must believe that I had no choice." When she didn't respond, he turned away, staring unhappily at his shimmering control panel. "Those flashing lights you saw were caused by missile intercept, the first strike in an accidental nuclear war—some sort of bizarre form of computer override," he added, sounding bemused. "What do you know about 'disco'?"

"Disco lives," she repeated dully.

"Not any more." A certain pride, almost smugness, crept into his tone. "You must see that it was necessary to intervene. We actually did very little." He came close, guiding his arm around her so that they rested against the bubble's marbled glow. Popo didn't resist—he had said "we," which surely meant that she along with everyone else she knew as "we" had been conquered. There seemed nothing more to be frightened of.

"You see, given the passage of time and specific environmental conditions, land has the power to regenerate itself, correct?"

"Correct," she repeated, barely listening. The bubble had begun to shift to the west, and she could see the winding path of Sabbath Creek, which she remembered from her childhood. As they floated past an oddly angled stand of pine trees, there was a clamorous croaking. "That's the frog level." She smiled, in spite of her mood. "It was the lovers' lane for Ranewood High—I spent hours there, I mean—"

"Please try to concentrate." He squeezed her gently. "That cloud of dust you saw today was caused by the technological assistance which we provided. Nothing fancy, merely a considerable compression of time and those specific conditions I mentioned. As a result, earth's seasons changed with rather drastic speed. We protected human life, although I imagine they found the change of scenery a bit traumatic. And now," he said happily, tapping the bubble wall, "what you see below is the Ranewood Zone, as the land existed before civilization began.

Popo stared disbelieving at the forest. "No," she said slowly. "If what you say is true, there should be a strip of barren earth leading up that small hill. Nothing would ever grow there—it was a natural phenomenon. Everybody said so."

"Are you sure about that?"

In the field below, tiny khaki-coated figures formed into a line, and began to march through the flowers. "I'm not sure about anything, anymore." She strained to see into the horizon. "What about Walter Cronkite International—did you destroy that, too?"

"It's a beautiful pine forest, nearly impenetrable. As for the rest of it, the city of Rome is now a series of small, rolling hills, Moscow could be planted in potatoes, and London will make a lovely playing field, once it's cleared of trees."

"The *'rest of it'*?" You mean that there's nothing left in the entire *world*?"

"All that is left is the world itself and the people."

She stared at him, too shocked to feel anger or grief. "But what will happen to the people?" she whispered. "What have you done to *us*?"

"We have done very little," he told her. "They will do the rest. In time, a few of them will begin to understand that on this day, one of mankind's oldest fantasies came to pass—a second chance. These few will spread the word to others, and if enough of them believe, perhaps it will become true."

"This second chance, will it turn out differently?" She counted the marching figures below—twenty-five, thirty—not enough to fill one car on the shuttle express to Walter Cronkite.

"Why shouldn't it be better? Humans have shed some innocence, retained their values and technology, and regained the full potential of their planet. You must believe in them, Popo." His smile was tender, artlessly radiant, and she felt her doubts dissolve beneath the beguiling power in his gaze.

"I do believe," she told him. "But I don't understand. None of this seems real to me."

"Reality has been a very popular concept down there, hasn't it?" He spoke indulgently, as though pointing out a weakness for sweets. "But consider this. You watched me make those technological adjustments which saved your planet from destruction. On earth humans will perceive the result as a miracle, but does that make their survival any less 'real'?"

Popo looked at the glowing rainbowed panel, at the shimmering bubble, and Desire's radiant, dimensional eyes. "It's easier to believe in miracles," she told him. "And now I'll be a part of one, down there."

His smile disappeared. "I'm sorry, Popo. My calculations were complete when you wandered into that restricted zone. I couldn't risk letting you stay there, and now you can't go back. Those are the rules."

"Oh." There was a long silence, and she realized that, viewed in perspective of the day's events, her own fate was a relatively small piece of news. "Not quite real," she muttered trying to smile.

He shook his head. "Popo, reality is just a room with a door that locks from within. It's time you unlocked that door—you haven't even been out of the house." He smiled, and then she felt her own smile—tender, artlessly radiant—and she knew that she had surrendered.

There was a sudden flash of light. The bubble leaped, and Popo stared down as a monstrous BEAST appeared below, diving for the flowers. The ghastly creature had wings like a bat and a horse's head with lips pulled back to form a leering grin. It howled, and the humans dove for cover.

"The Jersey Devil," she cried. "He's *real!*" Then she paused. "Or is he?"

"Of course that beast is real. But why is he real—because those people down there have created him? Or perhaps you think he believes in himself?"

Popo shook her head, unable to follow the thoughts of this man who was, after all, extremely foreign.

Within the luminous bubble shell, the colors began to swirl, deepening to vibrance. Popo felt the accelerating shimmer, as they began to soar. The Jersey Devil turned to a howling, strutting gnat, and still they rose until the earth dropped, blue and shining, from her sight. She blew a kiss and closed her eyes, absorbing the force of flight.

A glistening, rainbowed bubble was climbing through yesterday's stars towards a distant, sparkling field. There it drifted, gathering light and awaiting the impulse of travel. Humans watching from the earth fixed the time and charted its place, proclaiming a beautiful star. Then the bubble burst. Soon after, Shepherd Desire Laud and Ms. Popo Huggsey (formerly of the Ranewood Zone) reached wilderness, entering a world that lies beyond the stretch of mortal bone, but abides in its infinite marrow.

Tucked within Desire's silvered arms, Popo dreamed and smiled. It was going to be beautiful.

ABOUT THE AUTHOR

REBECCA SINGLETON was born in Morgantown, West Virginia, and also lived in Atlanta, Georgia, where she graduated from Georgia State University in 1972. Formerly an editor with a New York publishing house, she traveled southern New Jersey from Tom's River to Cape May while gathering materials for this book. She currently lives in New York with two cats who are working on her new novel.